BLOOD NEVER DIES

Bill Slider and his team face a mystery when an unidentifiable man appears to have committed suicide but all signs point to murder

A boiling-hot August day and a handsome young man is found dead in his bath, exsanguinated. Bill Slider's colleague takes one look at the body and is convinced something isn't quite right. As Bill investigates, he reluctantly has to agree. But as Slider and his team try to identify the man – whose personal papers are missing, along with his wallet and keys – it seems that the more they find out about him, the less they really know...

Recent Titles by Cynthia Harrod-Eagles from Severn House

THE COLONEL'S DAUGHTER
A CORNISH AFFAIR
COUNTRY PLOT
DANGEROUS LOVE
DIVIDED LOVE
EVEN CHANCE
HARTE'S DESIRE
THE HORSEMASTERS
JULIA
LAST RUN
THE LONGEST DANCE
NOBODY'S FOOL
ON WINGS OF LOVE
PLAY FOR LOVE
A RAINBOW SUMMER
REAL LIFE (*Short Stories*)

The Bill Slider Mysteries

GAME OVER
FELL PURPOSE
BODY LINE
KILL MY DARLING
BLOOD NEVER DIES

BLOOD NEVER DIES

A Bill Slider Mystery

Cynthia Harrod-Eagles

Severn House Large Print
London & New York

This first large print edition published 2013
in Great Britain and the USA by
SEVERN HOUSE PUBLISHERS LTD of
19 Cedar Road, Sutton, Surrey, England, SM2 5DA.
First world regular print edition published 2012 by
Severn House Publishers Ltd., London and New York.

British Library Cataloguing in Publication Data

Harrod-Eagles, Cynthia. author.
  Blood never dies. -- Large print edition. -- (The Bill
  Slider mysteries ; 15)
  1. Slider, Bill (Fictitious character)--Fiction.
  2. Police--England--London--Fiction. 3. Detective and
  mystery stories. 4. Large type books.
  I. Title II. Series
  823.9'2-dc23

  ISBN-13: 9780727896391

Severn House Publishers support the Forest Stewardship Council™
[FSC™], the leading international forest certification organisation. All
our titles that are printed on FSC certified paper carry the FSC logo.

FSC
www.fsc.org
MIX
Paper from
responsible sources
FSC® C013056

Printed and bound in Great Britain by
T J International, Padstow, Cornwall.

For Edwin – thanks for keeping faith

Blood, though it sleeps a time, yet never dies;
The gods on murd'rers fix revengeful eyes.
George Chapman: *The Widow's Tears*

ONE

Bloody Sundae

Exsanguination was the word Slider found wandering around his mind. The skin of the body in the bath was so pale it was almost translucent. It didn't look real. A wax effigy marinading in low-grade tomato soup. Whack a tank round it, he thought, and you'd got yourself a Damien Hirst.

It was stifling up here in the attic flat, with the sun beating down on the roof only inches above his head, like trying to breathe through a blanket. For once August was doing what it was supposed to, and it was baking hot; though the sky was veiled in high, thin grey, so it was heat rather than light that was bouncing off the pavements outside. Probably this old house had no insulation at all between the ceiling and the slates, on which you could have fried an egg had you been so wanton as to try. A pigeon's egg, maybe. He could hear them pattering about on the flat roof of the dormer and offering each other lifelong devotion. In here, the rusty, dirty smell of blood was sickening. He'd far rather think about pigeons; but it was his job, and, breathing shallowly through his mouth, he

9

dragged his mind back to the matter in hand.

The dead man seemed to be in his late twenties or early thirties, and tall, nearly six feet to judge by the way he'd had to bend his knees up to fit in the bath. His features were pleasingly regular: nobody looks their best dead, but exsanguination had left the victim with a sculpted, alabaster appearance, like the bust of a Greek god. His hair was thick, brown with rather obvious blonde highlights, and fashionably, if not expensively, styled. He was lean, and his skin was smooth and healthy. The words 'fit' and 'buff', in the way his teenage daughter would use them, wandered into his mind and then out again.

A suicide is a detective sergeant's business. The uniformed officer, PC Renker, who had attended the 'unexpected death' shout, had taken one look and radioed back to the factory for a DS; but Hollis, whose turn it was, had not liked what he had seen. He had been there only a few minutes before calling it in as suspicious, and Slider, who had been sitting down at his desk all day, trying to light the fire of his brain with paperwork, had been almost glad to respond.

'It don't look right to me, guv,' said Hollis, the Mancunian lamp-post, 'but I can't quite put me finger on it.'

Physical beauty is a matter of millimetres either way. Move a nose a fraction sideways, add a whisper more curve to a mouth or chin, and perfection is made or marred. But scrawny frog-eyed Hollis, with his despairing hair and feather-duster moustache, was in a different class altogether. He made Peter Lorre look like a model

10

from a knitwear catalogue. And yet he had a tremendous, mysterious charm which made members of the public trust him. He was a damn good policeman, which was all that counted with Slider – though not, of course, with the media-obsessed top bods in the Job, who would never promote Colin Hollis to any position that might get him on camera.

'Soon as I got here,' Hollis said, scratching the undernourished tundra of his pate, 'I thought, it dun't look like a suicide to me. Eric felt the same, soon as he walked in.' Eric Renker was in the next room, talking to – or rather, being talked at by – the landlord. 'It's too – tidy,' Hollis concluded, with the awareness in his voice that tidy wasn't really the word he wanted.

The flat *was* tidy, and that in itself was a surprise. 'Flat' was an over-generous description: it was really just a single attic room at the top of a tall Victorian terraced house of the sort that abounded between the Uxbridge Road and Goldhawk Road. They had each once housed a single family, but they were so perfectly calculated for splitting up into sublets, the architect in Slider wondered if the Victorians hadn't really had a time machine after all, and had seen how things would turn out.

This room under the roof had been elevated from bedsit to flat by partitioning off a slice to make the tiny bathroom. In the main room was a sofa bed, a single wardrobe and chest of drawers, a small kitchen table with two chairs, and along one wall a kitchen counter containing a sink and gas hob, with a refrigerator underneath

11

and a microwave on top, and a geyser on the wall for hot water. On the end of the counter was a small portable television facing the sofa, and on the table a large portable radio/CD player of the sort that used to be known as a Brixton Brief-case.

The whole house was a typical developer's job of magnolia walls and industrial beige carpet, plasterboard partitions and awkward corners, cheap ugly doors and the sort of furniture made of wood-effect veneer over chipboard that would age disastrously quickly. As he trod up the stairs, Slider had noted the marks on the walls and the stains on the carpets, and had imagined with a shudder what he would find at the top.

But in the attic flat the carpet had evidently been cleaned of all but a few intractable stains, and the walls repainted so recently there was still a faint smell of emulsion on the air. And most of all, it was tidy, every surface clear and clean. A single man, living alone in this sort of bottom-end rental, with inadequate cupboard space and no supervision, would normally have turned it into an assault course of discarded clothes and unwashed crockery, papers and possessions, and the dominant smell should have been of feet, sweat and a hint of spoiling food.

And then there was the bathroom, also tidy and clean. There was a bath (because of the slope of the roof there wasn't the height for a shower), a WC, and a washbasin with a small mirrored wall cupboard above it. Everything was so tight that a splashy bather would have constantly wet the toilet roll. On the other hand, the loo with the lid down made a useful place to stand your drink while you were in the bath. Bending his head sideways and squinting, Slider could see from a faint ring-mark that that was exactly what someone had done in the recent past.

He stared again at the body: there was something about it that suggested prosperity above the level of its surroundings. Something about the healthy skin and hair, the good teeth just revealed by the drop of the jaw, the buffness in general, made him think that however down on his luck the deceased must have been to come and live here, it must have happened recently. Someone like him ought to have had friends or relations who surely could have given him a spare room until he got back on his feet.

If it was suicide, perhaps he had embraced degradation as part of his self-loathing? But then, the flat was so clean and tidy, and the victim himself was clean, shaved and shampooed, which did not speak of terminal despair. No, he could see why Hollis had called it in. It was odd.

And the oddest thing of all was the wound that had let out the life: a single cut through the left external jugular, after which his essence had simply drained away into the bath. The left forearm rested across the abdomen, the right arm was hanging down outside the bath, and on the floor below the hand was a Stanley knife with blood on the blade. He appeared to have died quietly, without struggle: there had been no splashing. The tiny bathroom was still immaculate. It was the most efficient suicide Slider had seen.

He heard Hollis behind him; his breath tickled the back of Slider's neck as he looked over his shoulder at the corpse, willing it to give up its secrets. 'There's summat wrong with it,' he said. 'I dunno – what do you think, guv?'

'It's an unusual method, that's true,' Slider said, ever cautious. 'Men don't generally cut.'

Women slashed their wrists – often as a cry for help, not intending to die – or took pills. Men threw themselves out of windows, hanged themselves, or put a hose from the exhaust through the car window, but they didn't usually cut.

'And who cuts like that?' Hollis said. 'How did he find the right spot wi'out a mirror?'

'He could have looked it up, I suppose,' Slider said. 'Or maybe he had medical expertise. He could have been a doctor.' There were many ways for a doctor to disgrace himself, which might lead a man to suicide. But then doctors could get pills, couldn't they? Wouldn't that be an easier way out?

'He ent got doctor's hair,' Hollis said. That was true. The cut was too assertive, the blonde highlights too theatrical. 'But there's summat else. I can't put me finger on it.'

'I know,' Slider said. 'As you say, the whole thing's too tidy.' If you were driven so far into despair you decided to end your life, would you really tidy up the flat so completely? What man wouldn't need a drink before he did the deed? But in the other room there was not even a used glass in view. There were no clothes lying about—

'There are no clothes lying about,' Slider said

14

aloud in a eureka tone. 'Whatever he was wearing before he got into the bath, he put them away.'

Hollis snapped his fingers. 'That's what it was,' he said. 'I knew there were summat. You might want to die in a nice warm bath, but put y' clothes away all tidy first?'

'It's perfectly possible,' Slider said. Tidy habits were learned early, and early habits tended to stick. 'But it's not likely. I agree with you. It doesn't look like suicide to me. I'm going to call in the circus.'

Big, Nordic-blonde Eric Renker, who could have starred on a poster for Strength Through Joy, was out on the landing at the head of the stairs, still listening to the landlord. Both of them turned eagerly to Slider as he came back from the bathroom, Renker hoping for relief and the landlord recognizing a more important audience for his troubles.

Renker introduced him. 'This is Mr Milan Botev, guv. He owns the building.'

Botev was short and swarthy, his head emerging from his shoulders without the bother of a neck: a large, round head with thick, bushy black hair. He had the kind of heavy beard-growth that would necessitate shaving several times a day, and as his face was a contour map of old acne scars, there were little dark outcrops down in the ravines that the razor couldn't reach. His shoulders were bulked with muscle, and Slider would have bet they were as furry as a bear's, too; and his hands were like planks. But his feet were small and rubbery, and as he moved on the spot in his annoyance, Slider thought he would probably be swift and silent when it was called for. You wouldn't hear him coming, until he got you.

'It was him found the body,' Renker continued.

'How did you happen to do that?' Slider asked.

Botev scowled – though that may have been habitual – and clenched his fists as he spoke. His voice was harsh and his accent was thick. 'I have telephone call from tenant – she live in flat below this one. She complain that music is too loud – very loud – going on and on. She say she bang on the door and no one comes. So I must come and do something. Ha! I say, nothing to do with me. What am I, your father? But she insist, make fuss, and I must come. So I come, and what do I find? Pah! Bad, bad! I do not like bad things happen in my houses.'

He glared up at Slider as though it were all his fault. Slider guessed that it had been all Renker's fault for the past fifteen minutes and was sorry for him.

'So what did you do when you got here?' Slider asked.

'I hear the music, yes, very loud. Like party, only no sound of people. So I also knock, knock, and when no one come, I go in and turn it off.'

'How did you get in?'

'I have keys,' Botev said, as though *that* was obvious. He held up and shook a bunch of Yales, each with a different coloured plastic half-moon over the top, and stretched out the luggage label attached to the large ring so that Slider could read the address written on it. 'This keys this

16

house. I have other house also. Keys all my places.'

'What time did you enter the flat?'

'I already tell *him–*' the spherical property mogul gestured towards towering Renker with what was almost but not quite contempt – 'it was a little after half past nine. I do not know exactly.'

'Go on. What did you see?'

'I see at once the room empty, just like now. No one there. I went over, turn off music. He left it on, maybe, I think, and went out, forgetting. But one time I had tenant who die of heart attack in lavatory, so I think I must go see. I go to bathroom door and there he is, in bath. Bad, bad! So I use mobile and call nine-nine-nine.'

'Did you go in to the bathroom?'

'No need. I see from the door he is extremely dead.'

Extremely – yet, that was the right adjective. 'Was the bathroom exactly as it is now? Did you touch anything or remove anything?'

Botev grew angry again. 'Nothing, nothing! Do you think I am idiot? Do you think I do not know nothing must be touched at crime scene?'

'Suicide is not a crime,' Slider said mildly, wanting his reaction. Though it had not looked quite like a suicide to him or Hollis, it could still be one; and if not, it was obviously *supposed* to look like one.

But Botev said, 'Sure it is. Kill yourself *big* crime to God, to church. Bad, very bad sin. Make God very angry.' He shook his massive head in stern condemnation. 'And besides, it

17

make it hard for me to let flat again, when people know. Give me much trouble, maybe, cost me money.'

Thus morality met commerce with a screech of tyres.

The tenant who had made the complaint was in her own flat below, being interviewed by Rita Connolly, the Dublin DC. Lauren Green had the bright eyes and pale, dry skin of someone who has been up all night, but the events upstairs had banished any trace of sleepiness.

'Well, I work nights,' she explained, sitting on her bed so that Connolly could have the single chair, a Victorian-style plush-covered boudoir chair from which she first had to remove a heap of clothes and stuffed toys. The room was smaller than the attic room above, and had a shower-room instead of a bathroom, so compact it could almost have fitted into a wardrobe, and more or less did; and the kitchen consisted of a sink and double gas ring, disguised by a bamboo folding screen. But unlike its upstairs rival it was filled to suffocation point with the owner's possessions, clothes, ornaments, magazines, and a multitude of cuddly toys. Every inch of wall was covered in pictures, cut out of magazines and home framed, the frames decorated with seashells, sequins, little cut-out hearts and flowers, beads, feathers. Silk scarves were draped from corner to corner of the ceiling in rainbow stripes, the central lampshade was crimson silk with long fringes and sported a plume of feathers the Prince of Wales must have been missing, and

18

there were so many ferns and trailing plants suspended in front of the window, the room lurked in adumbrous obscurity like a cave at the bottom of the sea.

'I like things nice,' Ms Green had said in response to Connolly's first recoiling stare. There was a burnt herbal smell, too, that made Connolly suspicious; but after a moment she decided on probabilities that it was joss sticks, not ganja. She would have betted that Lauren Green was a bath-with-scented-candles type, too, had she but possessed a bath.

'What do you do, so?' Connolly asked, opening her notebook. The morning light filtering through plants and coloured scarves made everything appear to move gently like seaweed. She would have to make notes by feel.

'I work at Sarges in Poland Street – you know, in Soho?'

Lauren Green was youngish, in her twenties, Connolly guessed, and though plain in the face had a reasonable body. 'Stripper?' she enquired automatically.

'I'm a waitress,' Lauren replied, with faint affront. 'Just because it's in Soho ... The pay's better than round here.'

'Sorry. I didn't mean anything,' Connolly said. 'I just thought you'd a grand figure.'

She was instantly placated. 'Oh. Well, dashing around serving keeps you fit.'

'Tell me about this morning. What time'd you get home?'

'Well, after we closed and cleared up, I stopped off for breakfast with one of the others – Jez, he's bar staff as well – he's gay, he's my best mate. He's a real laugh. We often have breakfast together. Well, I don't like to cook here, because the smells get into everything, and I like things nice. So it must have been about half seven when I got home. And coming up the stairs I could hear the music. But in here it was the worst because it must have been right above me.'

'Had you had that trouble before?'

'No, never. Not with this bloke. The one before, Surash, he used to play loud music a lot, but not generally in the morning, and we were mates, so he was good about turning it down if I was trying to sleep. But this new one, well, I don't really know him. But I've never heard a peep from him, only footsteps going across the floor sometimes, you can't help that in a flat, and now and then a sort of murmur like it might be a telly, but not on loud. Nothing I couldn't sleep through. I didn't even know he had any music till this morning, and it was ridiculous, thump thump thump right through the ceiling. So I went up and knocked to ask him to turn it down, but there was no answer. I reckoned he couldn't hear me through the noise, or he'd fallen asleep, God knows how. I knocked a lot, then I came back here and banged on the ceiling, but nothing. I was at my wits' end, so I rang the landlord. Well, I didn't know what else to do.'

'Mr Botev?' She nodded. 'You rang him direct? Isn't there a letting agent?'

'Nah, he wouldn't pay an agent. Sooner keep the money himself. Not that he likes being disturbed, he lets you know that all right, but he

20

gives you his number when you first come, in case of trouble. Like I had water through my ceiling once when Surash left the bath running and went out. Well, he come and turned the taps off, but it was months before I could get him to fix the ceiling. I had this big bald patch and all brown round the edges. I was ringing him every day in the end, so he got a decorator in just to keep me quiet, I reckon. Anyway – what was I saying?'

Connolly could see she was becoming dazed with fatigue. 'You rang him about the music upstairs.'

'Oh, yeah. Well, he didn't want to come – didn't think it was an emergency. It was an emergency to me all right. I had to sleep. So I said if he didn't come I'd call the police. That got him out. I heard him coming up the stairs and went to the door, and he give me a filthy look as he went past, and told me what he thought of me, but I can take that. Anyway, he lets himself in and I hear the music go off, so I goes in and shuts me door to get ready for bed. And that's all I know till the police come and all this starts off. So he topped himself, did he?'

'It looks that way,' Connolly said. 'You say you didn't know him very well?'

'Not at all, really. Though Mish downstairs said he was well fit. He's only been here a few months. I think I've only seen him once, when he was coming in the same time as I got home. He held the door for me – the street door – and I followed him up the stairs, and I thought "nice bum". He didn't say anything to me, though. I

21

didn't even know his name.'

'Apparently it was Robin Williams. Does that mean anything to you?'

'No–o. Or – wait! Oh, no, I'm thinking of – there's a film star called Robin Williams, in't there?'

'It isn't him,' Connolly said drily. 'Did he ever have visitors, that you know of?'

'No, but I work most evenings. I never heard anyone up there, or saw anyone. Like I said, I've only ever seen him the once.'

And she said it with regret. A well fit, single man living upstairs from you was a resource not to be wasted. Connolly felt she could follow Lauren's thought processes perfectly, and was proved right when after a pause, she went on, 'He was probably gay, though. The really buff ones always are.'

Freddie Cameron, the forensic pathologist, for whom the word dapper might have been coined, looked just a trifle less so than usual, though Slider could not immediately put his finger on the area of neglect. In deference to the weather, he was wearing a suit of biscuit-coloured linen, but not even a heatwave could make him neglect the jacket or fall short in the bow-tie area. But there was something slightly frazzled about him, all the same.

'Everything all right, Freddie?' Slider asked, cutting to the chase.

Cameron made a *moue*. 'We've got the grand-children,' he said, in the sort of way a person might say they had termites. 'They've just got old enough to be dumped on us while Stephen and Louisa go on holiday.'

'Well – that's nice, isn't it?' Slider said hesitantly.

Cameron rolled his eyes slightly. 'Of course, we adore little Clemmie and Jasper. It's not their fault they haven't been brought up properly. I don't understand it,' he added plaintively. 'We were always quite strict with our two – table manners, please and thank you, don't interrupt, don't touch without asking, that sort of thing. So why didn't they pass it on to their own?'

'Reaction,' Slider said. 'The pendulum will swing back one day.'

'Not soon enough to save us,' Freddie mourned. He smoothed back his hair, then felt for his bow tie, something Slider had never seen him do before. Hitherto Freddie had always *known* he was perfectly turned out, even on a Monday morning. 'I must say I didn't cover myself with glory this morning,' he confessed. 'In the middle of chaos in the kitchen, Martha had a fit of the nobles and said "You get off to work, I can manage." And I'm ashamed to say I embraced my inner coward and made a run for the door.'

'I once made a run for a rabbit,' Slider reflected. 'When the kids were small.'

'You'll get yours, buster,' Cameron said, narrowing his eyes. 'The time will come...'

'Not too soon, I hope,' Slider said. 'Mine aren't old enough to mate yet.'

'Don't bank on it. Anyway, who have we got here?'

'The landlord says his name is Robin Williams.'

'Ah,' said Freddie. He put on his glasses and advanced to the bathside and studied the body. 'Who would have thought the old man to have had so much blood in him? Unusual method.'

'That's what we thought. Which was partly why we thought it might be murder.'

'On the other hand, it has its advantages, if you get it right. Rather a peaceful death.'

'Yes, we noticed there was no splashing. Suggested he didn't struggle, which was a point for suicide and against murder.'

'Also it was a vein, not an artery, which takes time – time enough for him to fight back or struggle out of the bath if it was murder,' Freddie said. He leaned over and felt the face. 'Rigor just beginning here. Of course, he's been lying in cold water, which will have delayed the onset.'

'So when does that put it?' Slider asked.

'Oh, say, six to twelve hours, very roughly. Can't be exact, as you know, but probably you're looking at an evening bath rather than a morning one.' He rolled back the eyelids. 'Ah, now, you see – pupils much dilated. I think our friend here took some kind of narcotic before jumping in. That might explain the lack of struggle, if it were murder – send him to sleep and then dispatch him. Very efficient.'

'Unfortunately, that also fits in with suicide,' Slider said. 'Suicides are notorious for the belt-and-braces approach. Will you be able to tell what he took, given that most of his blood is now mingled with twenty gallons of bath water?'

24

'Oh, we'll work something out,' Cameron said airily. 'Based on the total volume, calculations can be made. There may be traces in the tissue or residue in the stomach, depending on how quickly he died. The pathology will be clear, anyway. If it was a large dose, there would be oedema in the brain cells, the heart sac, congestion in the lungs. Leave it to the experts, old thing, and don't worry your little head about it.'

'Right. I'll go away and worry about something else.'

The forensic team – what Slider's firm called the circus – were in, like vengeful ghosts in white coveralls, masks, mob caps and slippers, and the photographer with both still and video cameras. Bob Bailey, the Crime Scene Manager, tutting over Botev's unfettered presence before the shout, had already taken the fingerprints and a buccal swab from the indignant owner before he was hauled off to the station to make his statement. 'God knows what he's touched,' Bailey grumbled.

The first thing they discovered was that the tidiness was not just skin deep. In the main room the wardrobe contained some jeans and chinos, a pair of leather trousers, a couple of jackets, the drawers a few T-shirts and underwear. There was some food in the fridge: cheese, bread, a vacuum pack of four apples, half a lemon, several cans of beer, some bottles of mineral water, a bottle of vodka, and some small cans of tonic. Otherwise, there were no signs of life at all. The cutlery and crockery had all been washed and put away. The kitchen surfaces were clean, and the bin under the sink was empty, with a clean bin-liner in it.

What was even more suspicious was that there were no personal papers anywhere, and nothing by which to identify the occupant: no wallet, no credit cards or driving licence, and no mobile phone. Yet there was a watch in one of the drawers in the small two-drawer cabinet at the end of the sofa that presumably served as bed-side cabinet. It was quite a nice watch – not super-expensive, but a Tissot Chronograph probably worth about two-fifty, which suggested that the absence of the wallet was not simple robbery. It suggested, *au contraire*, that the murderer – if it was murder – had gone to some trouble to remove all traces of who the victim was; which further suggested that they would have taken care to leave no trace of themselves.

Bob Bailey, dancing on Slider's heart, said cheerfully, 'Maybe it was suicide after all. Just a very neat and tidy bloke.'

'But why would he want to conceal his identity?'

'To protect the people he's leaving behind.'

'Thanks. You're a great help. '

'I only said "maybe".'

When one of Cameron's assistants appeared just then to say the doc had the body out of the bath and would he like to come, Slider was glad of the distraction.

Lying on the plastic sheet, dripping raspberry syrup like a melting ice-cream treat, the pale body looked even more unnatural. In reality, the corpse was no more a human being than a plastic mannequin in an M&S window was. But unlike the mannequin it once had been. Death was so mysterious, Slider thought, not for the first time. The difference between a human being and a dead body was so profound, it always amazed him that the thing that made the difference, the vital spark, could disappear so instantaneously and completely. You'd think it would at least leave an afterglow of some sort that would fade gradually like the sunset from the sky. But it didn't. Tick – alive; tock – dead. That was all there was to it. And no going back.

Robin Williams had been young, healthy, with all his life before him. Now he just didn't exist any more. This object that was left was merely rubbish, something to be disposed of, no good for anything at all; but while it had held that animating spark it had been a thing of beauty, purpose and almost limitless potential. Slider looked at the fit and nicely-muscled frame over which Freddie Cameron was poised, and felt unhappily moved by the awful waste.

Did he kill himself, driven by some huge reversal in his life to come to this meagre flat and end it? And if so, why had he gone to such lengths to conceal his identity? Why should it matter to him after he was dead? But then young suicides, perversely, often did not really believe in their own deaths. They planned them like a piece of theatre with the inchoate idea in the back of the mind that they would be there to see the results, the effect it would have on people.

27

Suicide was the ultimate narcissism. Those driven to it by fear or despair could be just as efficient, even ruthless in carrying out the execution, but it was seldom stylish, and rarely involved concealing their identity – they just didn't care any longer.

But an accumulation of factors was telling him this was not suicide. And that was an even bigger waste. 'You've got something for me?' he asked hopefully. 'I keep veering between suicide and murder like a compass needle in a magnet shop.'

Cameron looked up at Slider over the top of his half glasses. 'As it happens, I think I *may* have. If you look at the musculature of his arms, you'll see they're slightly different from each other. It doesn't show up on women much, or on bods who work out, but for ordinary folk like thee and me, who have to use brute force occasionally in the course of an average life, the dominant arm develops slightly larger muscles.'

'Handedness,' Slider said, in a light-bulb moment.

'Just so. Of course, you used to be able to tell from the hand itself, in the dear dead days of writing with pens, but no one these days has a writer's bump on the middle finger. But chappie here's not very muscular – more your aesthetic type. And I can see he has slightly better biceps on his left arm than on his right. But the cut was to the left jugular, which would not be natural to a left-hander.'

'But the way he was lying in the bath, with his left side to the wall, would make it a natural cut for a right-handed murderer leaning over him.'

'Just so. If you can prove that he *was* left-handed, you're away.'

Slider was already looking in the bathroom cabinet. He emerged triumphantly holding – but carefully with a gloved finger on the head and the tail – an electric razor, a black Phillips Phillishave. 'Treasure trove,' he said. 'I was hoping for shaving tackle but an electric is even better. It'll give a whole set of prints, thumb at the side of the head, forefinger in the middle at the back, and three fingers and a palm round the grip. If they're left-hand prints rather than right-hand...'

'You'll have your proof,' said Cameron.

Slider stuck his head out of the bathroom door and yelled for Bob Bailey and the portable fingerprinting kit.

TWO

Good Morning Vat Man

The house had three storeys plus a semi-basement, and there were two flats to each of the middle floors. Botev had given the names of his other occupants, and Slider discovered why the address had seemed familiar when he was called out: he knew the basement tenants. Mish and Tash – for some reason their names always made him think of an Edwardian music hall conjurer's act – were prostitutes and had come to police attention on a couple of occasions, though they were generally no trouble. Slider believed in getting working girls on the police side – they could be very useful sources of information – so he had a good relationship with Mish. Tash was a recent addition and he didn't know her well.

He decided to interview them himself before returning to the station, and found them awake and agog – Michelle perhaps a little more gog than Natasha, but then she was the brighter of the two, and she knew Slider. Tash was still rather wary, and lurked behind her friend's shoulder like something waiting to be tripped over.

Mish greeted him eagerly – not, he supposed,

for his personal charms but for what he might tell them about what was going on – and got the coffee on.

'I know you don't like instant,' she said kindly, 'but I got some o' them sashits of the real stuff. I'll do them.'

They were both bed-haired and smudge-eyed, wearing large towelling bathrobes, one embroidered 'Sheraton Heathrow' and the other 'Crowne Plaza Paris'.

'It's this businessman, one of my regulars,' Tash explained sheepishly. 'Stays in all the best places. He always brings us something, dun't he, Mish?'

'We haven't had to buy shampoo or conditioner for years,' Mish agreed.

'That's where we got the coffee,' Tash said. 'But he eats the chocklit mints,' she added sadly.

'So what's going on upstairs?' Mish asked. 'We see Milan go in like a madman this morning, and Nicky from upstairs comes out and says he's giving Lauren what-for on the stairs, and the next thing you lot start arriving. Then it's the forensics, and someone said it was him on the top floor. Well, we couldn't sleep now if we tried, could we Tash?'

'I could, I'm dead on me feet,' Tash said. 'Has something happened to him, then, the top floor?'

It was a pretty sharp deduction, Slider had to give her.

'It looks as though he's committed suicide,' Slider said.

Mish, bringing over his mug of coffee, looked at him sharply. 'Only looks like?' she said. 'Sit

31

down, make yourself comfy. So, what – you think it's somethink else?'

'I can't say at the moment,' Slider said.

The girls kept their home nice, or as nice as you could with a basement. There was a penetrating smell of damp, which was almost but not quite subdued by the stink of synthetic peaches from the wittily-named 'room freshener' plugged in to the wall. There were patches of plaster coming off in some corners and a stain the shape of Australia on the kitchen ceiling. Botev was not the sort of landlord to concern himself about such things. But everything was clean and tidy and with modern furniture from IKEA; it had a bright and homely look. There were two bedrooms, a bathroom and a good-sized kitchen, and since the bedrooms were their places of work, they did all their socializing round the kitchen table, which was where Slider now placed himself, with the girls either side of him, and a plate of biscuits in the middle.

'What can you tell me about him?'

'Well,' said Mish, glancing at her friend, 'not much. He's not been here that long. What is it...?'

'Coupla mumfs?' Tash hazarded.

'When was it? We see him move in, dint we, Tash?'

'He come one afternoon. We was just going down the shops and we see him from the window.'

'So we went out,' Mish concluded. 'We thought, "Hello," we thought, "things are looking up."'

'He had on these really tight black jeans and this leather jacket...'

'He was *well* fit,' Mish confirmed. 'Couldn't think what he was coming to a dump like this for.'

'How did you know he was moving in and not visiting?'

'Well, Milan'd said he'd let the top floor. We knew it was empty 'cos ol' Surash, what lived there before, he was a mate, and we knew he'd gone. Moved on to better things. Which is not difficult, let's face it, after this place. Anyway, Milan was there to give the new bloke the key. We see him waiting on the steps. He come in a taxi, the new bloke. Didn't have much with him—'

'Just a suitcase,' Tash put in. 'And a sports bag—'

'And this little telly.'

'And a carrier with, like, food. And a laptop.'

'He couldn't carry 'em all. He asked the taxi driver to help, but *he* wouldn't, a course.' She made a sound of disgust.

'Wouldn't Mr Botev carry something for him?' Slider asked, taking a custard cream. Anything to disguise the taste of the coffee.

'Milan, help? He wouldn't spit on you if you was on fire. No, he'd gone up ahead, so we went up to help. I said, "Hello, we're Mish and Tash, we live in the basement. Can we carry something for you?" And he kinds of looks at us a bit startled, and he goes no, no, it's all right. But I goes, "You can't leave this stuff lying on the pavement, not if you don't want it nicked," so I

33

grabs the telly and takes it up the steps.'

'And he's got the suitcase and the laptop so I grabs the carrier and the sports bag.'

'But when we're in through the front door into the hall, he gets all determined. He says thanks but he won't trouble us to climb up all those stairs,' Mish concluded, 'and I could see he meant it. So I can see he's not going to be the friendly type.'

'I mean, we wasn't exactly looking our best, was we, Michelle? We was only going down the shops.'

'But he didn't want anything to do with us, you could see that. Didn't even tell us his name. So I thought, "Your loss mate," and we leave it.'

Slider pondered this and the naff hairstyle versus the good skin and teeth, and came to no conclusion. 'I wonder what he was doing here,' he mused aloud.

Mish nodded. 'You got us. We asked old Botev, but he just said he didn't know. Didn't care, more like. You can't ever get an answer out of him. He wouldn't tell you the time if you asked him.'

'Did you see much of him after that?'

They looked at each other again. 'No, I think we only saw him once or twice after that,' Mish said, 'and that wasn't to speak to. He was going out one evening just as we were coming home, and we kind of crossed on the pavement. I said hello, but he kind of turned his head away and hurried off. You know,' she added thoughtfully, 'I can't help feeling I'd seen him somewhere before, but I can't put me finger on it.'

'It was only because he was fit,' Tash said.

'No, it wasn't that,' Mish said more surely. 'I just felt I'd seen his face somewhere. Maybe he was famous for something.' She looked up. 'I don't even know his name,' she said in a moment of realization.

'Didn't Mr Botev tell you?'

'Didn't think to ask him. What was it, anyway?'

'Botev said it was Robin Williams.'

'Robbie Williams? You're 'aving a giraffe!' Tash exclaimed. 'He dunt look nothing like Robbie Williams.'

'*Robin*, not Robbie,' Slider said distinctly. Interestingly, that name did not register with them.

'No,' Mish said slowly, 'that doesn't mean anything. Maybe I was just imagining it.'

'Or maybe that wasn't his real name,' Slider suggested tentatively. 'There was nothing in the flat to identify him.'

They didn't seem to find that unusual. 'Lot of people in this house don't want anyone to know who they are. They come and go. Last year there was this Middle Eastern bloke, we thought he was a terrorist, covered his face with a scarf when he went in or out so's you wouldn't see it. And before Surash on the top floor there was about six I don't know what, Turkeys or Russians or something. We never did sort them out, did we, Tash?'

'We couldn't tell 'em apart. Coming and going. But they didn't want to be seen either.'

'Tell me about the other residents here now,'

Slider said, taking another biscuit. He'd got most of the coffee down.

'Well, there's Lauren underneath Mr Robbie Williams I Don't Think,' Mish began. 'She's a waitress up the west end. Bit of a dipstick – into all that alternative therapy bollocks, all spiritualism and reincarnation. She's been here about – what? – a year, just over? Opposite her there's poor old Ronnie Brown. He works up Heathrow, maint'nance. His wife chucked him out for another bloke, she's got the house and he has to pay her and the kids alimony. He's been here nearly a year. Don't get caught by him or he'll tell you his life story and start crying.'

'Oh, he's all right,' Tash defended him. 'It's a bit sad, really. He loves them kids.'

'Then above us there's Nicky and Graham.'

'They're gay. Nicky's a barman down Notting Hill. I dunno what Gray does.'

'I don't think he does work,' Mish said. 'He's a lot older than Nicky. I don't think he's *very well*.' She gave Slider a significant look. 'They been here, what, eight, nine months. And opposite them there's the two Pakistani boys, been here a few weeks.' Another look. 'I don't know what they do. I wouldn't ask.'

'You could ask Milan,' Natasha said, 'but he wouldn't tell you.'

'He may have to tell us things,' Slider said. 'I doubt very much that he's up to date with his tax and VAT.'

'VAT!' Michelle said derisively.

'And there's the matter of fire regs,' Slider went on smoothly. 'I didn't see one single fire

36

door in the whole house.'

Now they looked alarmed. ''Ere, you're not going to make trouble and get us chucked out, are you?' Mish cried. 'After I made you the good coffee and everything. I thought you was our friend.'

'It won't come to that,' Slider said. 'The threat will be enough.'

'Depends,' Mish said thoughtfully. 'I mean, he's owned this house – what? – two years, and he's been down here for a drink and a chat a few times, but *I* don't know what he's mixed up in. I don't reckon much of it's stuff he'd want to talk about.'

'Well, I don't want to either. That's not what I'm interested in. I want to know about Robin Williams.'

Mish narrowed her eyes. 'Which means you don't think it was suicide, or you'd—' She stopped as though her switch had been thrown, staring at the wall. 'I saw somebody,' she said at last, starting up again. 'I was seeing one of my customers out – must've been, oh, two o'clock this morning, round about then. Sunday's a big night – lot o' blokes like poor old Ronnie upstairs get very lonely of a Sunday. Anyway, I was knackered, and this was my last. I came out to the door with him, and he went up our steps, you know, up out the area, and when he'd gone I just stood there a bit, gettin' a bit of fresh, and I see someone come down the steps from the street door and cross the pavement to a car parked there.' She scanned Slider's face for reaction, and asked, 'Could that be something?'

'Why didn't you mention it right away?' he asked.

'Well, I never really thought about it. I mean, you don't, do you? People are coming and going all the time. But whoever it was, they were carrying a black plastic sack full of something.'

'Did you get a look at them? Was it a man or a woman?'

She frowned in thought. 'Hard to say. I *thought* it was a man – well, I thought it was one of the Paki boys, to be honest, cause it was about their size – like, slim and not very tall – but I s'pose it could have been a woman.'

'It wasn't Botev, then?'

'No, I'd know *his* shape anywhere. This person was wearing kind of dark pants and top, and a beanie so I couldn't see any hair, so it could have been a woman. But I just sort of thought it was a man. He opened the back door of the car and threw the sack in, and that's all I saw, because I went back inside then. But I suppose he must have driven away, because the car's not there now.'

'I suppose you didn't see the reg number?' Slider asked without hope.

'I wasn't really looking,' Mish said apologetically.

'Bloody hell, Michelle,' Tash exploded, 'you seen all that and you didn't say. Why didn't you call me out to have a look?'

'Because you were busy, and I didn't know it was important,' Mish said exasperatedly. 'Haven't you been listening? I said, I wasn't really taking any notice.'

38

'Can you say what sort of car it was?' Slider cut across the budding argument.

'I dunno. I think it was black. And it had four doors.' She shrugged. 'I don't know the different makes.'

'What about the black plastic sack? You said it was full. Could you tell how heavy it was?'

She stared again. 'Not very,' she said at last. 'I mean he was carrying it all right, not staggering along. And he swung it into the car. I'd say it was bulky more than heavy – like maybe it was full of clothes.'

And perhaps it was, Slider thought – along with personal papers and wallet and mobile – and a laptop. Unless it *had* been one of the other tenants, or a guest of theirs. Or customer. There was going to have to be a lot of careful questioning, and a lot of time-consuming cross-checking, which was a nuisance. Because although the sack, its contents, and the murder might not be connected, there was a chance they were, and the beanie-clad figure and the sack were well away from here by now.

'Did I see a murderer?' Michelle asked in a small, impressed voice.

Natasha looked at her with mouth ajar. 'I thought it was suicide?' she said.

'We don't know for sure that it wasn't,' Slider said, a form of words which confirmed each of the girls in her separate view.

Renker had gone with the body and the coroner's officer to the morgue: as there was doubt as to the identity, continuity had to be ensured, and he was the first officer to have seen the body. Hollis had brought Mr Botev back to the station. When Slider arrived, he fetched Mackay from the CID room and went in to question him, and let Mackay do the asking while he listened and studied the man. Botev was clearly unhappy about his surroundings, and was glaring about and sweating heavily. He complained vociferously about having been brought to the station. 'I done nothing wrong! What is this, police state?'

He had little to tell them about the deceased. He had given his name as Robin Williams, but Botev had not asked for any form of identification. 'Why should I? Name mean nothing to me. Long as he pay rent and make no trouble, call himself what he like.'

'And *did* he pay his rent?'

'Sure he did. Wouldn't be there otherwise.'

'How did he pay? Cash, cheque?'

'Cash,' said Botev. Of course, thought Slider.

'Did he give you his previous address? Any references?' No in both cases. 'So you really knew nothing about him.'

'What I need to know? ' Botev said simply. 'He want room, I got room. He pay me, I leave him alone.'

It was a nice choice of words, Slider thought, looking at the meaty hands resting on the table. On the shady side of the street, might is right. Some landlords had to pay and retain a couple of shaven-headed suit-bulgers with hams for hands to put their point of view across, but Botev was like a boulder in human clothes. What he lacked

40

in height he made up for with a usefully low centre of gravity.

Mackay pursued the barren path doggedly. 'How did he find out that you had a place vacant? Was it through an agency?'

Botev gave the suggestion a contemptuous snort. 'Advert. I put cards in shops. Many cards, many shops.'

No trail there, then, not after three months. Slider came in for the first time. 'There must be something you can tell me about this man,' he suggested. 'There he is, dead, in your house—'

'Kill himself!' Botev interrupted indignantly. 'I not control this. If I know, I throw him out, do it someplace else. Not my fault!'

Slider went on as if he had not spoken. 'I'm sure there are many things about that house you would rather we didn't know about. Illegal immigrants, drug dealers, not to mention over-occupancy, fire-regulation breaches, probably planning breaches too. And then there's the question of tax and VAT. If you think having the police on your back is bad, you should try Revenue and Customs. I promise you they make us look like little fluffy kittens by comparison.'

Botev licked his lips, and his eyes looked angry and trapped. 'What you want from me?' he cried. 'I know nothing.'

'I want to be sure you're on our side, so that if you find out anything, or hear anything, or re-member anything about this man, you'll tell us.'

Under Slider's unwavering stare, Botev open-ed and shut his mouth, his eyes roving for escape. Then, like a torture victim blurting

41

something, anything, that might get him off, he said, 'He painted room – painted walls. And cleaned carpet. He ask when he see room, can he do it before move in. I say yes. Why I care? But it crazy, I think. Why he do that?'

Why indeed? Slider thought.

Slider's boss, Detective Superintendent Fred 'The Syrup' Porson, was a walking example of reasons not to get promoted. He disliked meetings, hated politics and was practically allergic to golf. He hadn't got the first notion of schmoozing, avoided senior pressmen, and believed the role of politicians should be to come up with the money and leave the police to do the job their own way. In fact he was an old-fashioned copper who was roundly despised by his well-groomed, corporate-friendly, jargon-squirting superiors, who viewed his bumpy bald head, shaggy eyebrows, elderly wardrobe and non-PC impatience with the cult of victimhood as a betrayal of everything the last decade had stood for.

He had kept his job through all this evolution thanks to a couple of high-profile successes for which, with the best will in the world, those above him had not been able to claim all the credit. But they would see to it he never went any further. He didn't look right. He just wouldn't fit in. They would never want to have a brainstorming breakfast or a working lunch with him. They probably secretly suspected that he ate with his mouth open.

Porson got back from headquarters at Hammersmith, where the latest 'initiative' had been explained to him, in a less than rosy frame of mind, to receive the news of the Conningham Road case.

'Case?' he growled at Slider. 'A case of walking your chickens before they can run, if you ask me.' Another reason the high-ups didn't care for Porson was that he used language like a man flailing at wasps – usually effective, but never a pretty sight. 'I go out for a couple of hours and you mobilize the entire eighth army.'

'The fingerprint evidence shows he was left-handed,' Slider said sturdily, and explained about the electric razor.

'And the cut was a right-handed one?'

Slider demonstrated. 'Even if he'd tried to cut himself on the left side with his left hand, his elbow would have been banging the wall. Very awkward. And why would he? He'd naturally tilt his head over and cut on the right side. But a right-handed murderer...' He demonstrated again.

Porson was reluctantly mollified. 'All right. Sounds as though you've got *something* to investigate. What else?'

Slider explained about the lack of ID, the clothes, and the black-sack man.

'What about this Botev? He sounds a bit tasty. Could it have been him?'

'It's possible he might have been involved. He couldn't have been black-sack man – he's got a very distinctive figure, and the girl was sure it wasn't him. And I don't think he would have been the murderer. If he had been going to kill

43

Williams, he wouldn't have wanted it done on his own premises.'

'Safest place,' Porson countered. 'Somewhere you can control things. But that bath stuff, nancying about – half-arsed attempt to make it look like suicide – no. That doesn't sound like a straightforward gang-bashing, punishment hit or whatever. If that's what you're suggesting.'

'I'm only suggesting Botev might have some interesting friends and contacts. I just feel there's something odd about Williams being in that flat in the first place. A shabby, furnished room, where they don't even clean between lettings? If he didn't care about such things, why did he clean and paint it himself? If he did care, why go there?'

'Cheap,' said Porson. 'Lick o' paint and a carpet shampoo don't cost much, but rent goes on and on. If he was strapped for cash...'

Slider frowned. Williams had nice clothes, and he just didn't *look* poor. But poverty can come on quickly, especially these days. 'As to the suicide thing,' he added in fairness, 'if we hadn't discovered he was left-handed, it would have looked quite good.'

'Good enough for an amateur to think it would pass mustard, I suppose,' Porson grunted. 'So what are you going to do? Lean on Botev?'

'Yes, sir. Interview the rest of the tenants. Ask the neighbours if they saw black-sack man and the car. And meanwhile, we've got deceased's fingerprints. We'll run them, and the name, through records and see if anything comes up.'

'And if nothing does?'

'There's Mispers. And we'll circulate a mug-shot to the usual places. After that, I'm afraid we'll have to go public to try and find his next of kin.'

Porson met his eyes. Going public when all you had was a mugshot of a corpse was not nice. 'Let's hope it won't come to that,' he said shortly.

'No, sir.'

'Well, get on with it. I don't like the sound of this, and I hope it turns out to be a suicide after all, or some simple mistake, or something. Maybe he was ampidistrous? But I suppose you've got to go through the motions, do it by the numbers. Let me know if anything comes up. Otherwise, I'm not here.'

Porson waved him away and bent his blood-shot eyes on the heap of 'reading matter' that every meeting these days seemed to generate, in the way that lily beetle grubs generated those slimy lumps of – well, if you were a gardener, you knew. And since his dear wife had died, Porson had had to take over her garden. Disrespectful to let it all die, he had thought, but he wasn't sure he had the aptitude and he was preparing himself for disasters and guilt. Meanwhile ... He opened the first file with a sigh like a gale through a pine forest.

THREE

Tattoo Parlous

Ronnie Brown was tracked down at work at Heathrow, where he did minor maintenance, mostly replacing lights and unblocking lavatories. He was a poor, meagre sort of person, faded and cowed by life. The only exciting thing that had ever happened to him was his wife throwing him out, which was why he longed to talk about it, to everyone he met, even to a policeman investigating a suspicious death. Kept to the point, he could offer no information about the man upstairs, having never spoken to him, though he had seen him once, getting out of a taxi outside the house as Ronnie Brown was walking towards it on his way home one evening from Hammersmith tube station. He hadn't heard anything upstairs on Sunday night. He confessed to being a heavy sleeper. He'd been woken by the sound of Botev rowing with Lauren on the landing outside, and had then become aware of the music coming from the flat above. It hadn't been going when he went to sleep, about half ten, quarter to eleven. He hadn't heard loud music up there any other time. Upstairs was usually a very quiet tenant.

46

Nicky and Graham were more voluble – or at least, Nicky was. Graham, lying on the sofa with a rug over his legs, despite the summer heat, was clearly undergoing some extreme treatment, for he was grey and skeletal and had a cotton scarf tied round his head, pirate-style, to conceal his hair loss. Both were determinedly cheerful, however, and expressed deep concern over the fate of the man upstairs.

'Robin Williams? Isn't it terrible, we never even knew his name,' Nicky said. 'Poor soul, horrible to think of him killing himself all alone up there.'

But Graham looked at Swilley, who was doing the interview, and said, 'I don't think he did kill himself, otherwise this very glamorous lady detective wouldn't be here, looking so stern. You think it was something else, don't you?'

'We don't know,' Swilley said shortly. 'We're trying to find out something about him, because there's nothing in the flat, and we don't know who his next of kin was.'

'Well, it's no use looking at us,' Nicky cried gaily. 'We did try to make friends when he first arrived – we always do, don't we, Gray? – but he wasn't having any. Very grim and *ne me touchez pas*. I thought he was just a bit of a *phobe*, you know? But Gray thought he was nursing a tragedy, didn't you, Gray? Takes one to know one, all that sort of thing.'

'Tragedy?' Swilley queried.

'Why else would he be here? *We* wouldn't, if we could afford anything better,' Nicky said. 'But the things you can't get on the NHS are

47

expensive, and—'

'No need to tell everyone our private biz,' Graham interrupted him firmly. He looked at Swilley. 'I thought he had that look about him – you get to recognize it. As if he'd been bereaved. A kind of tightness round the eyes, and a blank-ness underneath – like the lights are on, but nobody's home.'

'We'd gone up there with a bottle of wine to welcome him to the house,' Nicky took up the story. 'He was perfectly polite, but he made it plain he didn't want anything to do with us. Said thanks, but he had a lot of work to do, maybe another time, blah blah blah. Classic brush-off.'

'Obviously there wasn't going to be another time, so we shrugged and left it,' Graham finish-ed.

'Have you ever seen anyone calling on him, any visitors?' Swilley asked.

'No, and I'll tell you something else,' Nicky said, 'he never has any mail. It comes through the letterbox downstairs and whoever gets there first puts it on the shelf just inside. Which is usually me, because we have the most so I pop down early and sort through it. And nothing for Mr Top Floor – that's why I didn't even know his name. No mail, no friends, no visitors – poor boy! I wish we could have befriended him.'

Graham was looking thoughtful. 'Last night,' he said.

Nicky stopped and stared at him. 'What? What about last night?'

'You were asleep, you wouldn't have heard. I don't sleep very well,' he added to Swilley. 'I

48

often lie awake most of the night. Anyway, someone came up the stairs. Couldn't have been Lauren, because she was at work, and Ronnie was already home by then – it must have been after midnight. And it couldn't have been Malik or Rafi because the footsteps went on upwards. Besides, they don't bother to walk quietly or talk in whispers. Clatter and bang with them, no matter what hour they come in! So it must have been this – what was his name? – Robin Williams, with someone.'

'You heard him talking to someone?' Swilley asked.

'I heard the footsteps coming upstairs, and then a man's voice – I don't know what he said – and then someone said "Shh!" and the footsteps went on up the next flight and there was some whispering.'

'You never told me all this!' Nicky cried like one bereaved.

'Didn't know it mattered, did I?' Graham said. 'I don't bother to report every time I hear someone in the house move.'

Nicky clapped his hand to his cheek and said, 'That must have been the murderer with him! You heard a murderer!'

'Going "Shh!"? How exciting,' said Graham with deep irony.

'Well, but was it?' Nicky appealed to Swilley. 'Did the murderer walk right past our door?'

'They'd have had to, to get up there, wouldn't they?' Graham said with exasperated patience.

Swilley caught a hint of appeal in his eyes and said, 'We don't know it was murder. It looks like

49

suicide. All we want is to find out something about the man so we can find his next of kin.'

'Well, I'm afraid we've failed you,' Graham said sadly. 'We knew nothing about him. And that means we've failed him, too.'

'But we *tried*, Gray,' Nicky said urgently, taking hold of his hand and pressing it. 'You can't say we didn't *try*.'

'Maybe not hard enough,' said Graham.

Malik and Rafi turned out to be students at a very bogus-sounding language school in Clerkenwell – and given that Clerkenwell was at the opposite end of the city, Slider would have bet neither of them had ever been anywhere near the address on the letterhead. Judging by the state of their room, cleanliness did not rank anywhere near godliness with them; nor did the number of their heads match the number of mattresses and heaps of cushions and blankets marking out sleeping places on the floor. And judging by the smell in the room and their extreme nervousness, they were in the habit of wiling away the time with recreational tobacco.

But they seemed to know nothing about the upstairs tenants, and given how much trouble they were already in without getting mixed up in murder, Slider was inclined to believe them. They claimed to have been at a party on Sunday night until the early hours. They had not noticed the music upstairs when they came in, but loud music was probably not something they would take notice of anyway. It was annoying, but he would have to check their alibi before he shrugged them off, which was a waste of manpower and time. He looked forward to passing the whole mess of their dubiously legal presence on to the specialist squad and wishing them well of it.

Most of Slider's firm were back and writing up their reports when Detective Sergeant Atherton, Slider's bagman and friend, strolled in. He had been to an awareness top-up seminar, and returned ready for some plain talking, short words, and if possible an entire absence of concepts.

Atherton never managed to look quite like a policeman, with his fastidiousness and his beautiful clothes and the fact that he spent more on a haircut than any of the others spent on a shirt. When he had been in uniform there had been something almost surreal about the sight of him in *that* tunic and *that* helmet. He had looked like a very handsome actor playing a policeman in a comedy sketch. He had been so obviously out of place that many of his colleagues simply assumed he must be gay, despite his multiple sexual conquests, because they couldn't account for him any other way.

One of the early reasons for Atherton's devotion to Slider had been that Slider had never, from the first meeting, looked at him askance. Slider had his countryman father's view that God had made all creatures different for His own purposes. A horse was not a cat and a cat was not a dog, and only a fool would want them to be. Slider had taken Atherton for what he was and worked him that way. And Atherton, who was

51

not any kind of a fool, had not taken long to work out that, in his own way, Slider was just as much of a misfit in the Job: it was just that he didn't *look* different.

The first thing Atherton saw as he reached the CID room door was DC McLaren, working his keyboard with one hand and mournfully eating cottage cheese with the other. His new girlfriend was running him ragged: putting him on a diet, making him have his hair 'styled' instead of cut, making him buy new clothes. She had even given him a manicure, and khazi gossip had it she was threatening him with a facial. McLaren, newly lean, fragrant and polished, and bewildered by a variety of unfamiliar sensations and unsatisfied hungers, bore with it all because after years of living alone in divorced slobbery, he was hopelessly, grotesquely in *lurve*. But to his colleagues he seemed a shadow of his former self. Atherton almost felt a twinge of sympathy.

He looked up as Atherton came in. 'What was it like, then? Was it good?'

'The usual. Policing of the Future. It seems we've been doing it all wrong so far,' Atherton said with delicate irony.

'Not that,' McLaren said. 'I meant – there's a DS I know at Kensington went last week. He said they had these amazing kind of cakes at the coffee break.'

Atherton toyed for a moment with telling him there had been boxes of mixed Krispy Kremes, but decided in the end it was cruelty to animals. 'There was nothing like that. Just plain biscuits.'

'Oh,' said McLaren, losing interest.

'So what's been happening while I've been away?' Atherton asked, looking round at the general busyness. 'Something come in?'

'Suspicious death,' McLaren answered. 'Looked like a suicide, Renker radioed for Hollis, but now the guv reckons it's a murder.'

'I leave you alone for two minutes and look what happens,' Atherton said, and headed for Slider's office.

'Robin Williams! It's a joke, isn't it?' Atherton was perched on Slider's windowsill. He had a feline ability to look good in positions that would have been awkward for anyone else.

'Not necessarily,' Slider said. 'It's a common enough name. Fathom's putting it through records.'

'Hmm. But I'm thinking that there would have been no need to remove anything that showed his ID if he'd already given his real name to the landlord.'

'Point.'

'*If* that's what happened. Maybe he didn't have any ID in the flat to begin with.'

'Why wouldn't he?'

'Lots of reasons. Maybe he wasn't really living there – it was just a base for something, and he had his real home somewhere else.'

'I've thought of that,' Slider said. 'But that raises as many questions as it answers.'

'Oh, more,' Atherton assured him easily. 'Far more.'

'Fat comfort you are,' said Slider.

'I'm not here to comfort. I'm here to keep you

all on the intellectual straight and narrow. You seem to have got steamed up about very little. Why shouldn't it be suicide? Just because there were left-hand fingermarks on the razor? Maybe he was ambidextrous.'

'That's what Mr Porson said.'

'Listen to that man. Or he may have switched the razor from his right to his left hand to get at an awkward bit.'

'Yes, but you don't, do you? You just turn your head or stretch.'

You don't, but someone else might. Look, the way I see it, here's a man down on his luck, lost his job probably, forced to go and live in a cheap furnished let.'

'Which he paints and carpet-cleans before he moves in.'

'Why not? He's still got a bit of self-respect at that point. And a tin of magnolia and a bottle of detergent doesn't cost much. But after a couple of months of hopelessly hunting for work, he's so depressed, can't see any future for himself, so he gets in the bath and ends it all.'

'No papers, no wallet, no phone, no credit card,' Slider pointed out.

'Papers – got rid of them all when he lost his previous home. You say he looked middle-class-ish? Suppose he'd had a good job, nice home, big mortgage, living it large, then with the down-turn he gets sacked, suddenly it all crumbles to dust. He runs up debt, can't pay the mortgage, home gets repossessed, has to sell all his worldly goods. Burns all the bank statements, letters, bills and what-have-you. Ends up on the street

54

with just what he can carry in a suitcase.'

'Graham upstairs said he looked as though he'd had a tragedy,' Slider admitted.

'There you are. As to no wallet, credit card, mobile etc – I refer you to my previous answer.'

'He had a nice watch.'

'A man has to tell the time.'

'But why didn't he sell it and buy a cheap one? And Ronnie Brown said he saw him come home in a taxi one day. Can't have been all that broke.'

'Maybe he'd been pounding the streets looking for a job all day and was so fed up and footsore he thought, soddit, I'm taking a taxi, to hell with the cost.'

'And what about black-sack man?'

'Something to do with the naughty boys, probably. Unless it was a figment of an overheated imagination.'

'You'd explain anything away,' Slider said sourly.

'I don't see why you're bothered about it, guv,' Atherton said. 'No reason at all why it shouldn't have been a suicide.'

'You didn't see him,' Slider said.

'Can't get emotional over it,' Atherton warned.

'Wait,' Slider said, remembering. 'Here's one – as well as no wallet, et cetera, there were no keys.'

'Ah,' said Atherton. 'Well that's trickier. He'd have had to let himself in with something.' He paused and added reluctantly, 'So it does look as if there was someone else there.'

'And they gathered up all his personal gubbins and took it away—'

'In a black plastic sack. But I wonder why?' Atherton said thoughtfully.

'Didn't know what might be incriminating so grabbed everything meaning to sort it out later,' Slider suggested.

'Which supposes there was something incriminating amongst said gubbins,' Atherton concluded.

Slider sighed and stretched. 'Well, either way, we have to investigate at least until we find out who he was.'

'Probably when we know the who, we'll know the why, and it will all become obvious.'

'Thank you, Pollyanna. Give a yell for someone to get me some tea, will you.'

Fathom appeared at the door. 'Guv, got the PNC results.'

'I'll come.'

It was not good news. The name Robin Williams was not uncommon, and because it was sometimes an abbreviation they had extended the search to Robert Williams as well. There were two local, and eighteen national subjects of those names with criminal records, and none of them, quite evidently from their photographs, was their victim.

The fingerprints had come up with no match.

'Which means we know the corpse had no criminal record,' Atherton summed up, 'but we still don't know if that was the corpse's real name. Worst of all possible outcomes.'

'Start circulating the photograph to the usual agencies,' Slider said. 'Check the name and the mugshot with Mispers.'

'Right, guv.'

'And there's overtime for anyone who wants it this evening, canvassing the neighbours who were out at work today. I'd like to get a lead before we're reduced to going public with a photo of a stiff.'

The city evening had a used feeling, body-warm and slightly smelly; the carbuncular sunset was lurid with oranges, pinks and purples that only God would have thought of putting together. Slider arrived home with gritty eyes and a sinus headache, and the feeling he always had at the beginning of a case, that there was just too much to do and too many things to find out – a depressing apprehension of too many balls in the air for it to end well. He was a man who had always sought out responsibility, but that didn't mean he actually had to *like* it. He was a harness-galled horse that backs itself between the shafts out of sheer habit.

There were no lights on in the house when he pulled up before it – glad, as always, that the front garden had been replaced with hardstanding, so the old days of cruising the neighbourhood looking for a parking space were over. Joanna's Mazda was there facing outwards. She always backed in – said it made her nervous not to be able to make a quick getaway. There were ways in which she had retained the boyishness of her bachelor days, despite marriage and baby George. It was the orchestra, of course, that kept her that way: musicians egged each other on to behave like lads. It was like the Job in that

57

respect. Coppers and musicians, they were all Peter Pans.

The house was quiet, smelled of clean dust and old wood. There were worse things to smell of, he thought. They had a lot to do to it still, but money was tight and time was tighter. He stood in the hall listening to it breathe, then went in search of his wife. He found her sitting on the concrete patch – you couldn't in all justice call it a patio, still less a terrace – just outside the French windows from the drawing room. She was quite still, staring down the dark garden at the last of the heat, swelling and redness just sinking below the trees at the end. The remaining member of the diagnostic quartet, the *dolor*, seemed present in the set of her shoulders.

'Everything all right?' he said quietly, not to startle her.

She jerked anyway, coming back from a long way away, half-turned her head to him, then stood up to kiss him hello. 'George was restless. Couldn't get to sleep for the heat, poor lamb. I got him off eventually – he's quiet now.'

It struck him that the answer, like the embrace, was an evasion. Freeing herself from him she moved past him into the house. 'Hard day? Shall I get you a drink? Beer? Gin and tonic?'

'I'll have a cold beer, thanks,' he said, making to follow her.

She heard the movement without seeing it and said, her back still to him, 'No, no, you sit down and watch the sunset. I'll bring it out to you.'

She seemed gone rather a long time. He sat, pulled off his tie and undid his top button, and still had time to remove his shoes and socks before she came back. His feet wriggled gratefully in the open air like puppies shown affection at last. The concrete felt delightfully cold to his soles after a day shut inside. The air was just beginning to cool off and the night was pleasingly quiet with so many families away and the traffic at summer neaps.

'Here we are,' she said, appearing with a tray. 'Supper's cold, so we can take our time.' She had brought a small bowl of cashew nuts as well, cold beer for him, a glass of wine for her. She put everything on the small table in front of him, and sat beside him – a seamless performance, except that she hadn't once met his eyes since he got home.

He took a long drink from his glass first, then put it down and said, 'What's the matter?'

'Matter?' she said vaguely.

'You seem out of sorts.'

'I told you, I had trouble with George. It's tiring when you can't do anything for them. How was your day?'

Oh well, he thought. If she doesn't want to say ... So he told her about the case.

'And you think it's murder?' she said when he'd finished.

'I'm sure of it. Just instinct, really.'

'Instinct can be the reaction to a lot of little clues collected subliminally,' she said.

'Is that you comforting me?' he said, amused.

'Just telling you I trust your instinct more than Jim's,' she said with the first smile of the evening. 'So what do you think happened?'

'God, I don't know! But it has a nasty look about it. Too tidy and organized. People aren't generally that good at murder.' He finished the beer. 'Not that I'm advocating the frenzied attack, you understand. That's nasty, too.'

'But a bit more human?' she suggested.

He looked at her. 'Animals just follow instinct. It's only humans who perform calculated acts of vileness.'

There was nothing to say to that, and he realized he had cut conversation off at the pass. And yet he could feel his twanging nerves begin to settle just at being here, and with her. He had a moment of intense sympathy for all the policemen (some in his own team) who couldn't go home after a beast of a day and relax with the one they loved. The Job took a lot out of you, and if you couldn't refill the tanks in your off time ... Well, they all knew burnt-out cops.

They sat on a while in silence, but he could feel her easing, too. He ate the last cashew and stood up. 'Shall we have something to eat?'

They sat opposite each other at the kitchen table and ate the chicken, bacon and avocado salad, and finished the wine she had opened, and though they talked, it was about humdrum, household things. He had hoped she would open up but she didn't; and, loving her, he let her alone. She would tell him in her own time, he supposed; though he hated to think of her having a troubled mind. But probably she felt the same about him, and there was nothing she could do to help him with his.

* * *

Freddie Cameron rang Slider in the morning, sounding fresh and restored. 'The couple next door have taken the children out for the day with their own. Peace on earth, goodwill towards neighbours. So I came in early and got on with your post, and Martha's taken the phone off the hook and she's going to garden all day. So all's well with the world.'

'Hey nonny no?' Slider suggested.

'At least. And possibly even a derry derry down. Now your corpus, best beloved: a fine specimen altogether. Shocking waste! No sign of any drug abuse. No needle marks. Well nourished. Looks admirably healthy – all the internal organs in the pink. As it were.'

'Is that it?'

'No, there were a couple of interesting features. Firstly, the tattoos.'

'I didn't see any tattoos.'

'You wouldn't from where you were standing, at the bathroom door. They were on the side away from you. Left thigh and left ankle. They're rather interesting and nicely done. I've sent over photographs for you. The important point is that I think they're fairly recent. Tattooing affects the body like second-degree burns, and healing follows certain stages. I think they were done within the past few months.'

'Maybe he was a footballer,' Slider said, thinking of David Beckham. 'He's got the highlights for it.'

'Hasn't got big enough thighs,' Cameron replied smartly.

'Anyway, what am I thinking? They make a

fortune. He wouldn't be living in a flat like that. Second point?'

'Second point, when I opened the stomach I found food residue – pizza, to be specific – which he must have eaten within three hours of death – I would say between one and two hours.'

'Ah,' said Slider. 'That gives us something to work on.'

'Also some spiritous liquid – I would guess vodka,' Cameron went on. 'But no capsule cases. The pathological evidence that he had taken a narcotic was clear. You see the significance?'

Slider did. 'Because how did he take it, if not by capsule? He might empty the contents out of the capsules, but why would he bother if he was committing suicide? On the other hand—'

'On the other hand,' Cameron finished for him, 'if it was murder, you can't say to your intended victim, "Would you mind just knocking back these little red and black jobs, old horse?" You'd have to empty them into something on the sly.'

Slider nodded, then realized Cameron couldn't see him and said, 'Yes. The thing that puzzles me, though, is that if it was a murder that was meant to look like suicide, why not cut the wrists? That would have looked more natural.'

'Squeamishness?' Freddie suggested. 'Also messiness. The murderer doesn't want to get blood all over himself. Slippery customers, wrists, especially when they're wet and bloody. This left no mess to clear up. The killer cut a vein, not an artery, so there would be no spurting. Just nice, slow, tidy bleeding. I imagine the

62

victim got into the bath under his own steam – as it were – and the murderer waited until he dozed off to do the deed.'

'Which means we're looking for a murderer who can persuade a man to take a bath while they're in the house.'

'Taken with the pizza and the vodka, it does suggest a degree of intimacy,' Freddie agreed. 'The TV repair man doesn't say, "I'll run you a nice warm bath, dear." Mine doesn't, anyway,' he added regretfully. 'So, some food for thought?'

'A four-course dinner,' Slider said. 'Thanks, Freddie.'

In the first mail was a preliminary report from Bob Bailey to the effect that all the main surfaces in the flat had been wiped. The only fingermarks they had found that weren't the victim's were Botev's – on the flat's entrance door, the on-off button of the CD-player, and the bathroom door jamb.

'Which bears out Botev's story. And makes it almost definitely murder,' Slider said to the troops.

'Almost?' Swilley queried.

'It's physically possible that the victim wiped things down himself, but why would he – especially as he left marks in other places – on the razor, the lid of the loo and the flush handle, for instance. I think for all practical purposes we can count that out and assume it was murder.'

'Well, that's a relief,' Connolly said.

'Yes, too many caveats spoil the broth,' Atherton said. 'So, what now?'

'The pizza's good, guv,' said Hollis. 'I mean, that's almost bound to be local. Nobody buys a pizza a long way from home.'

'It might have been delivered,' Atherton said.

'Either way,' said Hollis. 'You don't want it cold.'

'We've got an approximate time, too,' Slider said. 'If it wasn't delivered, if he called in on his way home from somewhere, he may have had the murderer with him, and we might get a sight of them on someone's security tapes. If it *was* delivered, the delivery person may have seen something.'

'And in either case someone might have known him,' said Swilley. 'Guys living alone eat a lot of takeaway pizza.'

'He must have eaten it out, at a restaurant,' Atherton said. 'You seem to be forgetting there was no empty pizza box in the flat.'

'Black-sack man took it away with the rest of the stuff,' Swilley said witheringly. She was tall, leggy and *Baywatch* gorgeous, and often faintly antagonistic to Atherton, whom she had viewed in times past, in his woman-hunting days, as a philandering, sexist pig. Even though he had calmed down, not to mention settled down, you generally could have chipped bits off the way she looked at him and dropped them in your gin and tonic. 'The pizza, the vodka, the bath – it's all part of a seduction scene. There was someone there with him.'

'Well, we *know* that,' Atherton said, withering back.

'A woman, I mean,' Swilley said.

'Needn't be a woman,' Connolly put in. 'He might a been light on his feet, for all we know.'

'Either way, it probably means the pizza was delivered,' Swilley said.

'Job for somebody,' Slider intervened. 'Asking round all the local pizza places.' Everyone looked at McLaren and then away again.

'I'll do it if you want,' he said meekly.

'I wouldn't put temptation in your way,' said Slider. 'Mackay, it's yours.'

'What about these tattoos, boss?' Connolly asked.

She was examining the photos. The tattoos were rather fine work: on the victim's left thigh a leaping tiger, very fierce and muscular, and on the left ankle a dragon winding round, the forked tail on the inside and the fire-breathing head on the outside. 'Leaping tiger, hidden dragon,' she said. 'Sure this is a grand piece o' work altogether. You'd be looking for a real artist.'

'What do you know about tattoos?' Slider asked, amused.

'I haven't got one meself,' she said, 'but me sister back home got this little bluebird on her shoulder. Only about the size of me thumbnail, but me Da went mental, said she might as well go out and rent herself a lamp post. But he's a dinosaur, me Da. Everyone's got 'em these days. It's body art.'

'It's utter stupidity,' Atherton countered.

'Don't sugar-coat it, Jim,' Swilley murmured. 'Say what you really mean.'

'Anyway,' Atherton went on, 'you're hopelessly out of date. All the big stars are getting them removed now. Johnny Depp, Angelina Jolie, Charlie Sheen...'

'Sure, how would you know?' Connolly asked, trying not to be impressed.

'I read the papers,' he said. 'Little trick you pick up as you go through life. Point is, if they were recent, it means he'd managed to get through the rest of his life so far without them, so why suddenly do it now, just when it's going out of fashion?'

'I'd bet it was a new girlfriend,' said Connolly, 'and she dared him to do it. Me friend back home dared her boyfriend get one on his lad. He got her name, Wendy.'

'He had "Wendy" tattooed on his penis?' Atherton asked with the greatest scepticism.

'T'was fierce romantic,' said Connolly. ''Course, it only said "Wendy" some of the time. When he got excited it said, "Welcome to Dublin, have a nice day."'

FOUR

Unnatural Smoothness

The source of all wisdom about tattoos at Shepherd's Bush nick was PC Kevin Organ, whose unfortunate name was so far beyond satire he was probably the least teased man in the Job. In a youthful attempt to out-cool his disadvantage, he had had his arms so extensively tattooed they looked like two rolls of *toile de jouy* wallpaper, and he could never take advantage of short-sleeve order when it came in in the summer.

He was rumoured to have other artistic gems too, in other, hidden places, but Slider preferred not to know about that. He was not as vocal on the subject as Atherton but in his mind tattoos were a social marker, like piercings, and they didn't belong on policemen, who ought to fade into the background of their uniform to be really effective, not make fashion statements at any level.

Fortunately, Organ's organic furbishment was not Slider's problem. Also fortunately, Organ was on duty that day, and at Slider's summons came climbing up from the trolls' dungeon behind the front shop where the woodentops lived, to the airy cloud-borne fastnesses of the CID room, to be consulted.

There were, Organ told them, four tattoo parlours in the immediate area, plus a couple of mobiles, who advertised on the Internet and came and inked you in the comfort of your own home. The four with premises were Punktures, The Fill Inn, Inkerman's, and Blues 'n' Tattoos – it seemed that imaginative names were all part of the culture.

The mobiles were Krazy Kris and Needlepix. 'But you can forget them,' Organ said as he examined the photographs of Robin Williams's decorations. 'These are nice inks – classy stuff. Krazy Kris, and Mona from Needlepix, couldn't do anything as elaborate as this. Apart from anything else, you need a steady hand, and Mona drinks, and Kris, well, he's getting on now. Must be nearly seventy. Whatever you asked him for, you'd end up with a snowstorm.' He admired the photographs again, taking his time, pleased to be the centre of good attention for once. 'I'd say they almost certainly came from Blues 'n' Tattoos, in Hammersmith Road,' he pronounced gravely. 'If not them, then Inkerman's, but I'd try Blues first. Honest John's the bloke's name, he's the owner, and he's a real artist.'

'Is it a pukka emporium?' Atherton asked. 'Or is his sobriquet ironic?

Organ didn't get forty per cent of the words in that, but he followed the force of the enquiry. 'Oh, he's right as rain,' he said. 'Never been in any trouble. Pays his taxes and everything.'

'Ah. His price is above rubies.'

'Well, you got to pay for quality work,' Organ said defensively, then frowned. 'Who's Ruby? She another mobile?'

'Just for that,' Slider said sternly to Atherton, 'you can go and do the enquiry.'

'Me? No! What do I know about tattoos?'

'You'll know more when you've done it. The acquisition of knowledge is the cornerstone of civilization.'

Organ stumped away back home to the nether regions, reflecting that it was true what he'd heard, they were all bonkers in CID. Totally tonto.

Blues 'n' Tattoos was half way along Hammersmith Road, in a small parade of shops which were a reminder of how nice Shepherd's Bush must have looked when it was first built. The two-storey Victorian buildings were identical to the yellow-brick, slate-roofed terraced cottages in the adjacent roads, except that the ground floor had a shop window instead of the residential bay; so they blended in perfectly, and gave a gentler, more humane face to commerce. The entire parade was still made up of small businesses, too – the square footage was too small to attract chains. There was a newsagent, a café, a dry-cleaner (SPECIAL SUMMER OFFER ON DUVET'S, BLANKET'S, CURTAIN'S! it announced possessively), a pet shop, a baker's of the sort that specializes in white loaves and the sort of cakes that look home-made without being in any way tempting, and next door to that, Blues 'n' Tattoos.

The man in the tattoo parlour looked just the way you'd expect someone called Honest John to look, if you lived in an ideal world that had never known the cold breath of irony. He was tallish, solid, middle-aged, with a pleasantly unremarkable face, kind eyes and thick, healthy hair beginning to go grey. The main room of his shop was plain but clean, with lino on the floor, chairs around the wall, and a rack of magazines. It could have been a dentist's waiting room except that the posters featured not the horrors of tooth neglect but the several thousand designs you could choose to have permanently pounded into your pink and cringing flesh.

There was a desk at the end opposite the door, and a doorway behind and to its right, leading, Atherton supposed, to the torture chamber beyond. It was curtained with those multicoloured plastic strips. Wouldn't a decent, solid, soundproofed door have been better, he wondered, to deaden the cries of the afflicted?

The man behind the desk stood up when Atherton came in and surveyed him with a friendly and professional eye. 'Hello! What can I do for you?'

'Are you Honest John?' Atherton asked.

'That's what they call me. You've come at a good time – very quiet today. Don't look so worried! I've been doing this twenty-five years and I haven't lost a customer yet.'

'Oh, I haven't come for a tattoo,' Atherton said, unable to disguise a shudder – largely because he wasn't trying.

Honest John gave the sort of reassuring smile

that could have brought dead puppies to life. 'What's up? Afraid of needles?'

'You use *needles*? I thought they were kissed on by soft-eyed Tahitian maidens.'

'You're a card, you are,' said Honest John. 'What *can* I do for you, then?'

Atherton produced his brief and introduced himself. Honest John's smile faded slightly, but he gave the impression of a man with no shadows on his conscience. 'I hope nobody's complained,' he said. 'I'm very careful about hygiene and I don't do minors, faces, or anything obscene.'

'It's nothing like that,' Atherton said. 'Someone suggested you might be able to identify this tattoo – that it might be your work, or if not, that you might know whose it was.'

Honest John took the photograph of the tiger and looked at it for a long time without speaking, his face unreadable.

'Do you recognize it?' Atherton prompted.

'It's one of my designs, all right,' he answered neutrally.

'And this one?' He passed over the dragon. 'We have reason to believe they were done fairly recently.'

'Both done on the same person?'

'Yes.'

'Well, they're definitely mine.' He looked at Atherton with an anxious probing stare, trying to fillet out the nature of the trouble heading his way.

'Do you remember doing them?'

'Funny enough, I do, though it was a while

71

ago. Coupla months, at least. Let me think. Was it – just after Easter, maybe? No, just before Easter, because we were quiet. Get a lot of kids in during the school holidays.'

Three months ago, then, Atherton thought. 'Tell me about it,' he said, pulling up one of the waiting-room chairs to the desk and sitting down expectantly. Honest John sat resignedly on the other side and placed his hands on the desk top, the gesture of a man prepared to tell the truth, the whole truth and nothing but the truth. Atherton had seen the same gesture many times in the interview room back at the station, but on this occasion he suspected it was genuine.

'It was quiet, like today,' said Honest John, whose real name, he told Atherton, was John Johnson. 'Beginning part of the week's always quiet. I've thought about closing Monday and Tuesday, but I haven't got anything else to do, really, so I sit in here and do my paperwork, and work out new designs, so if anyone does come in, I'm not turning away trade. Anyway, it was a Monday or a Tuesday morning this man comes in.'

'Alone?'

'Eh? Oh yes. He walked in off the street and I took one look at his clothes and thought, hello, he's come to the wrong shop. Like you, y'see, he didn't look the type. Cords and a jacket, he had on, and very nice shoes – most people round here are in jeans and trainers, and a lot of them through my door are covered in piercings. But he was a tall, good-looking bloke. Money coming out of every pore, that's the way he looked

72

to me. Kind you'd expect to see in Berkshire driving a Range Rover towing a horse trailer, you get my drift?'

'Yes,' said Atherton. 'Very graphic.'

He seemed pleased. 'I notice things,' he said. 'You have to in this trade. You get all sorts – junkies looking to rob you, kids on a dare their mums and dads don't know about, girls egging each other on, dating couples. You have to give them advice as well as the work. Practically an agony aunt, me.'

'Go on,' Atherton prompted.

'Anyway, he wasn't the usual sort of person that comes in, that's what I'm saying, which is why I remember him.'

'How did he seem? What was his mood like?'

Johnson considered. 'Kind of grim but determined, is how I'd put it. He didn't smile at all, and he seemed kind of – preoccupied, if you like. Following his own thoughts. Not the sort of mood you get a tattoo in, and I half thought he'd back out when it came to it, but he knew his own mind all right. Quite confident. So I show him the books and he picked out the tiger right away. Then he asked for a snake round his ankle. I said everyone had snakes and wouldn't he like something a bit different. I showed him the dragon and explained how it could wind round, and he liked that idea, and went for it.'

He ran a finger absently over the design – he had a workman's hands, not an artist's: strong, blunt, steady. Hands you'd trust.

'Well, when we get in the back room, he takes off his jacket, and he's got a short-sleeve shirt

73

on, and I see he's got no other tattoos – not visible ones, anyway – so I reckon he's an ink virgin. That's what we call 'em. Well, it's a longish job, and you don't sit there in silence, do you? So I try to get him chatting. He wasn't big on answers, just yes and no, not volunteering anything. I ask if he's had a tattoo before and he says no, and gives a sort of look, like as if he wishes he wasn't doing it now. So I ask what he wants 'em for. And he says, "Oh, just an idea I had," and then he changes the subject and starts asking me about the trade. He had a lot of very intelligent questions, not the usual daft stuff people generally ask, and I tell you, he got me talking like it was a chat show. It wasn't until afterwards I thought, he was just stopping me asking him questions. But it was skilfully done.'

Atherton nodded thoughtfully. 'Did he tell you his name?'

'No, it never came up.'

'Don't you take names and addresses of your customers?'

'Not generally. There's no need.'

'How did he pay?'

'Cash. That's the usual thing. I gave him my little talk about aftercare and gave him a leaflet, sold him a tub of tattoo goo, took the cash and away he went.'

Atherton got out the mugshot and handed it to him. 'Is that the man?'

'Yes, that's him – but I think his hair was different. Maybe darker. And cut a different way.' He looked up anxiously. 'This photo – is he—?'

'Yes, I'm afraid he was found dead. It looks

74

like suicide.'

'Oh dear me.' Johnson seemed genuinely upset. 'Oh deary me. That nice lad? What a dreadful thing. But why would he do it? He seemed all right. A bit dour, maybe, but not nervous or depressed. The opposite, really – like a man with stuff to do. Who would have thought ... Did he leave a note saying why?'

'He didn't leave anything. We don't even know for sure who he is. All we have to go on is the tattoos – hence my visit, hoping for a name.'

'Oh dear. Well, I'm very sorry I can't help. But in my line of business people just come in off the street and usually pay cash. You don't take names and addresses any more than a sandwich bar does.'

'I understand,' said Atherton. 'It's a pity, though. Can you remember anything else about him that might help us?'

'Like what?' Johnson screwed up his face in thought. 'I don't know, I've told you what I remember, his nice clothes and—' Something occurred to him. 'Wait, yes, there was one thing. I don't know if it means anything. He'd had his legs waxed.'

'Waxed?'

'To take the hair off,' Johnson expanded. 'Like women do.'

'Yes, I know what it means.'

'I noticed because of course it made my job easier.'

'Maybe that's why he did it.'

'Maybe. It's unusual though. They were smooth as glass. It looked really unnatural.'

Unnatural smoothness, Atherton thought. And when something was unnaturally smooth, you couldn't get a grip on it. Like this case. 'Well, if you think of anything else, here's my card. Give me a ring. Anything, however trivial. You never know what may help.'

'Oh, I will,' said Honest John. He looked at the photograph again with a sort of reluctant fascination. 'Can I keep this? I could ask around. I get all sorts of people coming in, and someone may've seen him somewhere.'

'Yes, by all means,' Atherton said. 'Any help always gratefully received.'

'Waxed legs?' Slider said. 'What does that tell us? Why would a man wax his legs?'

'Swimmers and cyclists do it to cut down on resistance. Athletes of all sorts do it,' Atherton said, 'because they have a lot of massages, and it can hurt if you're hairy.'

'He wasn't muscled enough to be an athlete.'

'Surgeons sometimes wax their arms because it makes scrubbing up easier.'

'But it wasn't his arms.'

'Well, some men just like the look of smooth skin,' Atherton tried.

'But he wasn't still waxed, so it can't have been that he liked the look.'

'So what do *you* think?'

'It could have been something he just tried out and didn't like. Or there was some reason we haven't twigged. I don't know. It just adds to his peculiarity.'

Atherton was thinking. 'Is there a pattern

here?' he asked. 'False name—'

'Probably.'

'—county cords to visit Honest John, tight jeans and trainers to move into Conningham Road. He's acting a part.'

Slider sighed. 'I thought from the moment I saw him he didn't fit in at that flat. The tattoos are just a little touch of insanity to add to the mix. If he was your high-flier suddenly gone bust and reduced to a furnished let, why would he get himself tattooed? It's just too frivolous.'

'I'm losing enthusiasm for that theory,' Atherton admitted. 'And the missing keys suggest black-sack man was something to do with it, and did take stuff away.'

'It's not only the keys,' Slider said. 'Freddie Cameron says Williams took some kind of narcotic, but if it was suicide, what did he bring it home in? No suitable bottle or packet in the place. He could have had a pocketful of loose capsules, but where are the capsule cases? And if it was just a powder, he couldn't have brought it back in his cupped hands, could he?'

'The murderer brought it in and removed the evidence,' said Atherton. 'I'm a willing convert to your side. So where do we go from here?'

'We've got the pizza to follow up. Still some neighbours to canvass. McLaren's on car movements in the area at two a.m. Selective circulation of the mugshot – and I think we'll circulate the tattoos as well. Nothing from Mispers?'

'Not yet.'

'Then we just plug on, and hope something comes up before we have to go public.'

'I must say it's rather peaceful not having the press hanging round and tripping us up every step.'

'Yes, not terribly eye-catching news, nameless man found dead in cheap rental flat,' Slider said. Over the years he had attended all too many human endings like that, but generally the deceased were either old, obviously poor, or drug addicts. This man wasn't any of those; but the longer he could keep the press out of it the better.

'It's going to be a long one,' he concluded.

The taxi driver looked exactly like a London cabby out of a movie. He was a spare man of about five foot six, probably in his sixties, with the deeply lined face of a smoker and a smoker's voice with a Shepherd's Bush accent. He had a thick, shapeless nose, a chin like a nub of pumice stone, brown-framed glasses and wiry silver hair sprouting from under an old-fashioned flat cap, which he whipped off courteously as he was shown into Slider's room.

He gave his name as Harold Barnes.

'It's about this photograph – sir,' he added at the last minute, having subjected Slider to a quick analysis.

'Please sit down,' Slider said, charmed with the novelty. Not many people called him sir these days. 'Can I get you a cup of tea?'

'Very lovely of you, sir, but I won't trouble you. I fill up too much I gotta keep stopping, if you get my meaning. And time's money in our line o' business.'

In that case, Slider thought, he ought to get

businesslike. 'You recognize the man in the photo?' Taxi drivers were one of the usual places mugshots were sent, along with hospitals, social workers and the other police forces.

'Yes, sir, I do. I picked him up in Kensington High Street one morning.'

'Do you live in Kensington?'

'No, I live in the Bush, but I often cruise down that way. Ken High Street's a good place to pick up fares. It's a rubbish tube from there, and there's lots of the sort of people live there that don't like going in buses.'

Slider nodded. Behind Ken High Street there were blocks and blocks of Edwardian and between-wars luxury flats, inhabited by wealthy elderly and middle-aged ladies, who had probably never been on a bus in their lives and didn't mean to start now.

'So you picked him up—?'

'He flagged me down, just about the end of Allen Street – down that end of the south side.'

'And when was this?'

'Oh, a good while ago. Coupla months, anyway.'

'Then why do you remember him?' Slider asked. 'One fare among so many?'

''Cos of where I took him.' The cabbie gave Slider a cocked and sly look, like a parrot spotting a peanut. 'He give me the address, and I thought, "Hello," I thought, "I know your game." He asked me to take him to Ransom House, Luxemburg Gardens.'

'Luxemburg Gardens – that's Brook Green, isn't it? But what's Ransom House?'

79

'You not come across it? That's where they make all them blue films.'

'Porn films?' Slider said. Something rang a bell in Slider's mind.

'Not the real rough stuff, I don't mean. The semi-respectable stuff you can get in the back rooms o' video shops.'

'How do you know this?' Slider asked. He didn't look like the sort of man who watched blue movies.

As if he'd heard the thought, Barnes said, 'I don't go in for that sort of thing meself. Watched a bit of one once, years ago, and it was just embarrassing. Didn't know where to look. But Ransom House has bin there, ooh, must be twenty years, and I've took plenty o' fares there in my time, so I know what they do.'

Slider nodded. 'So you thought he was going there to *act* in a porn film?'

'Well, he looked about right for it – tall, nice looking. He seemed a bit nervous, too, kind of sitting forward, tense. So I says, to jolly him along, like, "This your first time?" And he looks a bit startled and says, "First time what?" and I says, "Going for an audition, are you?" And he stares a minute like he might be going to say he didn't know what I was talking about. Then he sort of relaxes and laughs, rueful like, and says, "Yeah, I don't know whether to hope I get the job or not." So I says, "They pay good money, from what I hear." And he says yes, but a bit distracted like, as if he's thinking o' something else. Well, that's all the conversation we has till I drop him off. He pays me, and while I'm

80

putting the money away I see him go in out the corner of my eye, and that's all I know about it, sir,' he concluded with something like satisfaction, sitting square and upright on his seat with his cap on his lap and his faded blue eyes looking expectantly at Slider through the lenses of his specs.

There didn't seem to be anything else to ask, except, 'Can you remember any more exactly when this was?'

'Like I said, a while ago.'

'Was it before Easter or after?'

He thought a moment. 'Got to be after. When did we have that bit o' nice weather? Beginning of May, wasn't it? Might have been then, because it was a warm day, I remember that. He was wearing jeans and a T-shirt, no jacket. And when I see he was nervous, he was sweating on his upper lip, and I wondered meself if it was the heat or the nerves, you get me?'

'Yes, I follow. Well, you've certainly given us something to follow up. Thank you very much for coming in.'

'Just doing me jooty,' Barnes said, pleased.

'Ransom Publications,' Atherton read from the printout, 'is the publisher of soft-core porn films, their most famous titles being the *Office Orgy* series, which now number thirteen and have acquired cult status. Not with me, they haven't,' he interpolated.

'I've heard of 'em,' Connolly said. 'Me sister Sheila's boyfriend and his mates were into that stuff. There was another series before that called

College Orgy. That got up to *College Orgy Ten.*'

'It mentions that here,' said Atherton. 'And *Hospital Orgy* and – what's this? Can it be? Yes, *Shopping Mall Orgy.*'

'Great titles!' said Connolly. 'I'm guessing here, but would you say imagination's not their mighty strength?'

'You don't need imagination,' Mackay said. 'It's all there on the screen.'

'Yeah,' McLaren growled, and they exchanged a glance. It hardly surprised Slider to learn that tying one on and then watching a blue movie was the way some of his firm relaxed off duty from time to time.

'There was this one, *Office Orgy Three* I think it was – classic!' said Mackay. 'This bloke comes in to mend the photocopier and there's this couple having it off on top of it, and he says, "You could damage the paper feed like that". I mean, brilliant or what!'

'Hurr,' McLaren agreed, with as much machismo as could be expected from a man who has had all the bacon sandwiches in his bloodstream exchanged for yogurt.

'If I may continue?' Atherton said patiently. 'Ransom Publications is a branch of the Marylebone Group. And the Marylebone is a property development and management group, with its registered address conveniently in Cyprus.'

'Conveniently?' Slider queried. It meant they couldn't make enquiries about it at Companies House.

'Convenient for them, not for us,' said Atherton. 'So three months ago our victim waxes his

82

legs – and who knows what else besides – gets himself two tattoos, and about two weeks after that—'

'He'd have to wait for 'em to heal,' Connolly said. 'First they bleed, then they weep, then they scab and peel—'

'Thank you,' Atherton interrupted hastily. 'Two weeks or so later he goes for an audition at a porn-film firm. That's nearly a tongue twister.'

'I wonder what they have to do in an audition,' Fathom mused.

'Don't,' said Swilley sharply. 'Boss, we don't know he was going for an audition. You don't put your hand on your heart and swear truth to a cabbie.'

'No,' said Slider, 'but he went there, and he seemed nervous, and why else the wax and ink?' That was what had stirred in his mind while talking to Barnes. 'Anyway, we haven't got a whole lot of other leads to follow. And I don't have to remind you, detecting is like an electric kettle – you have to cover the elements.'

'At least they might be able to confirm his name,' Atherton said. 'That would be a step for-ward.'

'See what else you can find out about Ransom Publications,' Slider said to Swilley.

'Yes, boss,' she said.

'And the Marylebone Group.'

Brook Green was a subsection of Hammersmith, between it and Kensington, taking its name from the open area of grass and trees also called Brook Green. There once had been a brook, too, but as London had spread westwards in the nineteenth century it had been put into a pipe, where it still ran under the Brook Green Hotel. The area was home to an elite independent girls' school, St Paul's, where Monica Dickens had once been a pupil. In an earlier age, Gustav Holst had been its music master, and wrote *The Planets* during his tenure there.

Slider wondered what the school authorities thought about having Ransom House as a neighbour, but when he and Atherton arrived he concluded that it was discreet enough for them not to know about it. It was a small nineteen-thirties office block, half the ground floor of which had been rented off to a printing firm. Beside the main door a brass plaque simply had RANSOM HOUSE engraved on it, with no indication as to the nature of the business. A check with Paxman, the uniform sergeant on duty downstairs, had told him there had never been any trouble there.

The heat was less oppressive than yesterday, and there was a pleasantly verdant smell on the air from the grass and trees. The late sun was filtering through the leaves of the plane trees in a flickering, gold-green, Hollywood sort of way, and there ought to have been swelling string music in the background signifying a romantic encounter was about to unfold. But there was only the muted roar of traffic from Hammersmith Road, and two police detectives with hot feet, and suits they'd had on all day, ringing the bell of an extremely closed-looking office door.

There was an intercom grille in the wall, and a

woman's voice answered simply 'Yes?'

'Detective Inspector Slider of Shepherd's Bush. I would like to speak to somebody in charge, please.'

There was a pause, and then a buzz. They pushed in, to find themselves in a small, anonymous hall, with stairs visible straight ahead through a half-frosted door, and to the left, an open door into an office. The office was also anonymous, containing nothing that might give a clue to the nature of the business conducted here. The Crittall windows were frosted, the carpet was green, the walls cream-painted. There were two desks, filing cabinets, cupboards, computers and telephones, everything you would expect; and it was very tidy. But the one occupant – a middle-aged woman, smartly dressed and still handsome – seemed to have settled herself in comfortably, with a fleet of framed photographs on her desk, a row of plants along the windowsill and a reproduction of Monet's 'Poppies at Argenteuil' on the wall. Slider got the feeling she had been there a long time.

She looked up at them with a motherly smile. 'May I see your identification, please?' Having inspected their briefs thoroughly, she said, still smiling, 'Well, what can I do for you? I hope we're not in trouble? Not a complaint? We like to get on well with our neighbours and everything upstairs is soundproofed.'

'No trouble, no complaint,' Slider said. 'We're trying to find out something about a man who came here one day a couple of months ago. We think he might have worked for you.' He offered her the photograph, and she took it, looked, frowned unhappily as she realized what it was, and handed it back.

'Yes, I think he did work for us for a time. Look, I think you'd better speak to Paul. Paul Barrow. He's the boss. Let me buzz up to him for you.' She had a brief conversation, muted, turned away from them so they couldn't hear, on the telephone, and then said, 'You can go up to the studio. Through there, turn left through the door and up the stairs.'

On the way up, Atherton said, 'I've never seen the inside of a porn studio. I'm not sure I'm ready for this.'

'Steady, boy,' Slider said. 'Don't expose yourself.'

At the top of the stairs was a vestibule with swing doors, which they pushed open into the studio. It was the width of the building and ran most of the length, making a room about twenty feet wide and thirty feet long. The windows, which were on the left, on the street side, had blackout blinds over them, and the opposite wall was windowless and painted off-white with a floor to ceiling grey backdrop curve in the middle of it. There were diffusers, reflectors, light stands and lamps, and an electric fan on a tall stand. On one side of the room was a jumble of props – a large bed, cheval mirrors, plastic plants in pots, tables and chairs. On the other side was an IKEA-type metal storage frame with shelves covered in technical equipment and smaller props, a wheeled rack of costumes, and a table covered in empty polystyrene cups, plates with screwed-up paper napkins on them, and over-loaded ashtrays.

On a high stool in the middle of the curve sat a young woman in red high heels, white stockings and a suspender belt, being photographed by a man all in black, while a pixie-like girl in leggings and enormous boots clutched a clipboard and looked on. As they came in the model put her arms unhurriedly over her more important naked parts, and the man made a sound of exasperation and turned to see who had interrupted them.

'Who the hell are you?' he demanded, scowling. He had a strong Neil Oliver Scottish accent. 'You can't just come waltzing in here. It's not a friggin' tourist destination.'

He was slim, not very tall, in tight black jeans and a body-hugging black T-shirt. He had a rather pale, peaky face, spiky black hair that looked dyed, and a little bit of black beard from the middle of his bottom lip over his chin, like John Travolta in *Swordfish* – or perhaps, given his thinness and pallor, like an absent-minded Hitler.

Slider introduced them again, and he came forward, still scowling, while in the background the pixie tossed a robe to the model, and they went and huddled out of the way, conversing in whispers and watching nervously.

'We're trying to find out something about this man,' Slider forestalled what was obviously going to be a tirade about police persecution. 'We think he worked here at one time.'

He handed over the photo, and the young man

87

looked, and then looked troubled. 'This picture ... he's ... is he?'

'Yes, I'm afraid he's dead. You *do* know him, then?'

'Yeah, it's Mike. Mike Horden. But what—?'

'He seems to have committed suicide. When did you last see him?'

'It must be – oh – a couple a months ago. He's not worked here for a while. God, the poor guy! I wonder what got into him?'

'What first brought him here?' Slider asked. 'I don't suppose you advertise vacancies in the *Guardian*.'

'Tommy brought him in. Tommy Flynn.' He was still staring at the photograph, as if mesmerized. 'He—'

'You looking for me?' They were interrupted at that moment by a powerful, sixty-a-day voice, and looked round to see a man who had come through one of the doors at the far end. He was in his late fifties, with thick, longish grey hair, a fleshy, powerful face and glasses. He had the bulky body of a sportsman gone to seed, clad in grey flannel pants, navy deck shoes and a plain white shirt, open at the neck and with the sleeves rolled up. His strong hands were decorated with several gold rings and a gold wristwatch, and in one he carried a polystyrene cup and in the other an unlit short cigar. He walked towards them, his eyes sharp, suspicious, analysing.

'Paul, these guys are—' the man in black began.

'Yeah, all right, Ewan, I can deal with it,' he stopped him contemptuously. He stared at Slider.

'I'm Paul Barrow, producer. What can I do for you, gents?' It was asked in a tight, get-out-of-my-hair way, while guiding them gently but firmly towards the exit. Despite its fleshiness, his face was as hard as his eyes, and not built for expressiveness in the same way a brick wall isn't. You couldn't imagine any circumstance in which you'd appeal to his better nature. They were out in the vestibule before he stopped. Slider had got his spiel out again and Barrow, having looked briefly at the photograph, said, 'What d'you want to know about him?'

Slider manoeuvred himself subtly so he didn't have his back to the stairs, and said, 'He came here one day a couple of months ago. We think he came for an audition in one of your films.'

Barrow gave a snort of derision. 'Audition! That'll be the day. Yes, he came here looking for work.'

'Did he tell you anything about himself?

'He said he'd done some film extra work. He certainly talked the talk – had all the vocab, knew what to do. Knew a bit about cameras too. He didn't seem like the usual type we get – too posh – but he said he needed the money, so I said we'd give him a try. He stripped well and he was nice looking so I tried him out, but he couldn't act. You might think there wasn't much call for acting in our trade but you'd be surprised. Makes all the difference between dross and cult, and my movies are cult. This guy couldn't act his way out of a paper bag. We need wood, but not that sort. I used him as background furniture in a few scenes but I can't afford to carry people.

He'd have been better suited to working the other side of the cameras – he knew his stuff all right – but I didn't need another cameraman. So I let him go.'

'You sacked him?'

'Told him I didn't need him any more. The bodies are all freelance. I only employ the tech staff and Alice downstairs.'

'Was he upset?'

'I don't think he was surprised. He must have known it was muck in or sling your hook. If you ask me,' he added, staring at them like a large dog wondering which bit to bite first, 'he was hoping to get into directing from the beginning. Between takes he was always hanging around, nattering about the cameras and asking questions. Trying to look keen. Instead of having a coffee and a smoke like the rest of them. Anyway, he went, and I haven't seen him since. Is that it?' he concluded impatiently. 'I've got a lot to do.'

'Just an address. I presume he gave you one?' Slider said.

'You'll have to ask Alice downstairs. She deals with all that sort of thing.'

'Thank you, I will,' Slider said. 'We'll leave you in peace now, Mr Barrow, and thanks for your help.'

He started down the stairs, his neck hairs bristling as if they expected that at any moment he would be shot in the back. At the bottom he glanced back and Barrow was still standing there, watching them, to make sure they were going. The look he was giving them was so searing it could have removed warts.

When they had pushed through the door at the bottom, Atherton muttered to him, 'Robin Williams, Michael Hordern? Who was he kidding?'

'I don't suppose anyone would have believed Clark Gable or Alec Guinness,' Slider said. 'At least it suggests that Robin Williams *was* a false name. Better a known unknown than an unknown unknown.'

Through the door they could see Alice Downstairs clattering away on her keyboard, her eyes on some document to the side. 'Toss you for her,' Atherton muttered.

'You can have first go. Use the famous charm.'

Atherton went in first, Slider effacing himself behind. Alice looked up and smiled. 'All right?' she asked.

'Yes, except that I talked to the photographer for some time thinking he was Mr Barrow.'

'Oh, that's Ewan Delamitri. He's the director. He's very artistic.'

'Yes, he seemed like the artistic type.' Atherton smiled. 'Anyway, we spoke to Mr Barrow and he referred us back to you for Mike Horden's address and so on.'

'Oh, right,' she said. 'I'll have a look. I expect we've still got it.' She stood up and went to one of the filing cabinets.

'So, do you remember when Mike Horden came in the first time? Looking for work?'

'Yes, I do, as it happens. He wasn't our usual type, so he did rather stick out like a sore thumb, poor lamb.'

'What is your usual type?'

91

'Oh, you know,' she said vaguely. 'Leery young people. Mad for it. Hyped up.'

'Coked up?'

She turned and looked at him carefully. 'I've never seen anything taken here. But you know how young people are, especially in any branch of show business – booze, pills, lines. They don't see anything wrong with it. But he didn't seem like that. He seemed to be stone-cold straight – and very nervous. Sweat on his upper lip. Ingratiating smile. I suppose he needed the job badly. I hoped he'd make it, but he didn't last long.'

'I understand Tommy Flynn introduced him?'

'That's what he said – that Tommy had recommended him to come along. Tommy's been working here a long time. One of our regulars. A good boy – very reliable. Don't ask me where he met Mike Horden.'

'No, I'll ask Tommy, if you can give me his contact details while you're at it.'

'Oh. All right,' she said. She turned a moment later shoving the drawer in with her shoulder, and wrote rapidly on a sheet of paper. 'Look,' she said, withholding it a moment, 'Tommy's not in trouble, is he?'

'Absolutely not,' Atherton said, injecting sincerity into every line of his face. 'We just want to find out something about Mike's background. He's a bit of a mystery so far. Can't find his next of kin or anything.'

She seemed to relax at the words 'next of kin'. So explicable, so unthreatening. 'Poor boy,' she said. 'But someone must be missing him. He didn't seem like the sort who went through life without attachments.'

'What did you think of him? In general?' Atherton asked, still waiting for the sheet of paper.

She frowned. 'Rather sweet,' she said. 'Out of his place – he really didn't belong here. And terribly sad.'

'Sad?'

She nodded. 'That's what came across to me. In great waves. Not that he said anything, you understand, but I could feel it underneath. I supposed he'd got into financial trouble and was hoping this was the way out. But – that photo you showed me ... it looks ... is he...?'

'I'm afraid he seems to have killed himself,' Atherton said gently.

'Oh no. Oh dear. The poor young man.' She sighed. 'One always wishes one could do more. If only he'd said, I might have been able to send him on to someone else, get him help. But I haven't seen him in – it must be two months.'

'It's not your fault,' Atherton said.

'But to kill yourself over money ... I'm sure something could have been done. I wish he'd told me, poor lamb.'

She had absently passed over the paper, and Atherton pocketed it quickly before she could change her mind. 'Talking of money,' he said, 'do you have his bank details at all?' She looked blank. 'For his salary or wages or whatever you'd call it?'

'Oh, no,' she said. 'He was paid cash. The really casual ones often are. They're all freelance, you know,' she added, with a change of tone and expression. There was a wariness about her now. Paying cash wasn't illegal but it looked a bit less than completely respectable, and she perhaps expected some awkward questions about book keeping.

But Atherton kept on smiling, and Slider was also smiling as he intervened to ask, 'Can you tell us the date he first came here, looking for work?'

She thought for a moment and said, 'Yes, it was the first day after the May bank holiday. That would be Tuesday – let me see – the third of May. Yes, because I'd been away that week-end at my sister's and she'd given me a new photo of the children. I was putting it in a frame – here it is – when he came in. He mentioned it – said how pretty the children were, and I thought what nice manners he had. Most of the youngsters who come in – well, they're a different animal altogether. As I said, he was really out of place here.'

Slider digested this a moment, then asked, 'What happens to the films after the shooting's finished? They're not processed here, are they?'

'Oh, no. Paul does the initial editing with Ewan – he has an editing suite upstairs. Then it goes to the works in Solihull – it's on a business estate – where it's finished off and the discs are made and packaged. Then they go to the ware-house in Staines where they're stored and distributed.' She seemed pleased with the new direction of question, as if it was lighter going, and volunteered, 'I expect you'd like those addresses as well?'

'Yes, thank you. That would be very helpful,' Slider said. She copied them down for him on a fresh sheet and handed it over. He thanked her again and they departed, leaving her looking thoughtful, unhappy and perhaps a little apprehensive.

Outside, Slider said, 'I wonder what she's worried about? A bit of unofficial cash accounting, or a lot of illegal drug taking?'

'Like she says,' Atherton shrugged, 'there's a lot of it about.'

'Which?'

'Both.'

'I liked the look of that Paul Barrow,' Slider said, as they made their way back to the car. 'There's a man ripe for taking down if ever I saw one.'

'Well, it's given us a few more things to check,' Atherton said. 'And a mobile phone number for Horden-stroke-Williams. I wonder what name we'll find him under next? Charlie Chaplin? Hedy Lamarr?'

'You don't know who Hedy Lamarr is,' Slider said with some certainty. 'I'm wondering, now,' he added, 'whether he didn't just make someone suspicious, given the fact that everyone seems to think he was out of his place. It would be tragic if he was killed for making a crim nervous when all he wanted was money to pay off his bank loans.'

'What, more tragic than being killed for any other reason?' Atherton asked.

'Point,' Slider conceded.

FIVE

Barrow, In Fairness

The address Michael Horden had given – 26 Abbots Close, Abbots Road, W12, which sounded beautifully plausible – was in fact a false one. There was no Abbots Road closer than East Ham, or Abbotts Road closer than Southall, and there wasn't an Abbots Close in either of them.

'So it's bullion to bollocks the name's false as well, guv,' said Hollis.

'Maybe,' said Slider with a sigh. 'You're putting the name through records?'

'Yes, guv. Fathom's on it.'

'What about the mobile number?' Slider asked.

'Pay as you go. I'm getting the call list.'

'Let's hope that will lead somewhere,' Slider said, from the depths of a man for whom all rivulets run into the sand. So far there was nothing on the pizza. None of the delivery places had been to the address, and no one had recognized the mugshot.

'But there are still more places to ask,' said Mackay. 'I started with the chains, but a lot of small Italian restaurants do pizzas, either eat in or take away – or both. Depends how big an area you want me to take, guv.'

'If he ate in a restaurant, it could be as far away as Notting Hill, and I wouldn't like to guess how many Italian restaurants there are in W11,' Slider said. 'I can't have you endlessly trawling the eateries of old London. Do the Bush as far as Hammersmith Broadway and leave it at that. Anyone else we'll have to hope to catch with a public appeal – because I can see it coming to that.'

Mackay departed, and Atherton, perched on the radiator, said, 'Neil Desperado, as Mr Porson says. The pizza was always a long shot. Did you know the Dalai Lama is very fond of pizza?'

Slider looked up suspiciously. 'Oh, really?'

'He always has the same topping. He rings up Domino's and says, "Make me one with everything."'

'I knew I shouldn't have asked,' said Slider.

'At least Tommy Flynn's wasn't a false address,' Atherton comforted him. 'And then there's Ransom Publications, Unit Three, Commercial Way, Brunel Industrial Estate, Staines Road, Hillingdon. That's almost aggressively real. Close to Heathrow cargo terminal and the M4 – handily placed, indeed, for almost anything.'

'Why should you think Horden-Williams had anything to do with them? There was no suggestion he'd ever worked there.'

'I don't know,' said Atherton. 'It's just that Paul Barrow was so very tasty, he's left me with an unscratched itch.'

'Well, scratch away. Go and see what you can

find out about him. But get someone to bring me a cup of tea, will you?'

Connolly was on the trail of Tommy Flynn, and first tried his address in Palliser Road. It was a turning off the Talgarth Road, the dual carriageway that became the A4 – one of the two main routes out of London to the west, engorged with traffic and roaring like a waterfall day and night – and the air was piquant with exhaust fumes. Perhaps because of that the houses had not been gentrified as they otherwise might: tiny little Victorian terraced cottages, two storeys of yellow brick and slate roof, most of them divided into flats, their miniature front gardens paved to hold the wheelie bins, and the peeling paint and grubby curtains giving evidence they were rented, not owned.

There were two bells by the front door, neither with a label, so she pressed both good and long. Finally a very cross-looking, panda-eyed woman opened the door, revealing a flight of uncarpeted stairs straight ahead and an open door to the left into her flat, from which emerged a smell of old, cold frying fat, dirty carpets and cigarette smoke.

'What do you want?' she demanded, scowling. 'I hear you ringing upstairs as well. What are you, selling something?'

'I'm looking for Tommy Flynn,' Connolly said.

The woman scratched slowly at her unwashed hair, hauled into the inevitable pony tail. She had a tight stretchy mauve top straining over such

98

considerable bosoms she looked as though she was minding someone's bottom for them, and baggy sweat pants below. She could have been any age from twenty to forty. In the background, the television blithered its daytime brain-rot. Life, Connolly thought. Hate it or ignore it, you can't love it.

'He's upstairs,' the woman pronounced resentfully. 'What you ring my bell for?'

'There's no labels on 'em, I didn't know which was him,' Connolly said. 'D'you know if he's in?'

'How should I know? I'm not his bloody mother. Who are you, anyway? If you was a friend of his, you'd know where he lived.'

Connolly found this a remarkable piece of deduction from a woman whose brains cells were almost visibly leaking out of her ears. 'Give us a break, wouldya?' she said with a friendly smile. 'All I had was the address. It didn't say upstairs or downstairs.'

'Yeah, well, he's upstairs, and I could do without him, with his stupid bloody music and his friends coming round all hours and his drugs. I got two kids down here, you know? I don't want them getting into that stuff.'

'I don't blame you. You've a mother's feelings, so you have. Anyway, it seems he's not in. D'y'know where I can find him?'

'He's prob'ly down the Three Kings, playing pool,' she said grumpily, unwilling to be charmed. 'You shoulda tried there first – he prac'ly lives there. Is that it? Only I'm missing *Doctors*.'

'Thanks. You've been a real help,' Connolly said, and turned away.

The woman contemplated that for a moment before she decided it had been ironic. 'Yeah, an' up yours, an' all,' she shouted at her back, before slamming the door.

The Three Kings had once been a glamorous Edwardian hotel, and now was a basic boozer, five minutes walk away down the Talgarth Road. It was empty and barnlike, dim and comfortless, and kept itself going with sports shown on several large TV screens. Connolly was from the old school and thought a television in a pub was an abomination, the denial of everything a pub ought to be – which was a place that felt as nearly as possible like your own front room, where you went to meet people and talk to them.

The screens were variously showing athletics, golf and motor-racing, and there was a surprising number of men there (no women) considering it was a work day. They stood or perched on stools, with glasses in their hands, staring at the screens with the same sort of blankness as she imagined was on the face of the woman watching *Doctors*. Jesus, Mary and Joseph, they looked like they'd had their brains sucked out through a straw, she thought. Civilization had taken two millennia to deliver the flat-screen TV. It was the height of hilarity.

She went up to the bar and the barman drifted down to her all the time watching the screen opposite him, which was showing motor racing – marginally less fun than watching stalagmites grow. Unable to get him to look at her, she leaned across the bar and shouted against the roar, 'Is Tommy Flynn here?'

'Is who?' the barman asked. Well, yes, she was forgetting – this wasn't Dublin. Bar staff didn't know the names of their customers.

'Have yez got a pool room?' she tried.

'Upstairs,' he said, jerking his head towards the far corner without taking his eyes from the action. One identical car inched minutely ahead of another and fell back again. Breathtaking!

She headed for the corner, passing the door to a separate bar where an even bigger television was showing tennis – a handwritten notice was fixed to the door frame, RUGBY WORLD CUP SATURDAY ENGLAND V SAMOA – and found the stairs. Half way up she could hear the click of balls, and followed the soft sound into a high-ceilinged room with long windows on to the roaring road, which must have once been an elegant reception room, and now had a bare wooden floor, three pool tables and not much else.

One young man was sitting on a high stool between two of the windows, cigarette in one hand and cue in the other, watching as another man shaped up to strike the cue ball. On a table up against the wall were two pint glasses of thin yellowish liquid – they looked like particularly large urine samples, but Connolly guessed they were lager – and a tin lid on which rested another smouldering cigarette in blatant contravention of the smoking laws.

Connolly paused until he had taken his shot, and then said, 'Tommy?'

101

They both looked at her, and the player, who had straightened up, said, 'Yeah? What?'

He was young, slim, and almost as good looking as he probably thought he was, with tanned skin, designer stubble, and tousled curly brown hair. He was wearing painfully tight jeans and a slightly grubby white sleeveless T-shirt, which showed off his muscled arms and some rather complicated tattoos over his biceps. Connolly could imagine him at the gym, watching himself in the mirror as he worked the weights and admiring the way they wriggled as he flexed.

On the downside, his eyes were bloodshot, and that he was wired was obvious from his rapidly shifting focus and the way various bits of him jiggled at rest. Another helpful clue was the dusting of white powder round the rims of his nostrils.

He subjected Connolly to a rapid once-over, and then grinned like a monkey and said, ''Ello, darlin'. Nice tits.'

'Yeah, nice bum yourself,' Connolly replied, injecting a bit of grimth into it. 'Settle down, I want to talk to you.'

Undeterred, Tommy put his cue on the table and stepped round the end of it, to lean against the long side and look her up and down again. 'What's a nice girl like you doin' in a place like this?'

'Oh, that's original,' said Connolly.

'Come looking for The Flynn, eh? An' I don't blame you, darlin'. Lots o' girls have travelled the old Silk Route before. As in Silk Root, geddit?' He gave an explanatory thrust of his

102

pelvis. 'J'wanna come back to my shag-pit for a little bit of that old Tommy magic? Let me light your fire, baby, y'know what I'm sayin'? I got some sweet blow, some tabs of E, and I ain't got to work till tonight. We can rock the Kasbah a-a-all afternoon.'

Jeez, what an eejit, Connolly thought. 'Would y'ever listen to yourself?' she said. 'Janey Mack, you're in Barons Court, not Orange County.'

Out of the corner of her eye she had been watching the friend, who had got down off his stool and had been quietly working his way towards the exit, evidently a bit more on the ball than The Flynn. When Tommy mentioned the blow, he abandoned subtlety and did a legger out of the door and down the stairs.

Tommy turned his head towards the movement, registered what had happened, frowned and said, 'What's up with him?'

'He's twigged that I am not just a babe, Tommy darlin', I'm a policeman babe. A copper. The plod. A Gard. Are you with me?'

'Where's your uniform, then?'

'Jesus, Mary and Joseph. I'm a detective constable, ya gom,' Connolly spelled it out. Unlike his friend, Tommy was evidently too amped to worry about it. Besides, people who took a lot of drugs socially often forgot, or refused to believe, that they were illegal. He only grinned the wider. 'Woah! I've never got it on with the filth before. New experience or what! It's getting me going. C'mon, darlin', you are hot. Let's go and r–i–ide to the stars on Tommy's love rocket.' He made a taking off gesture with one hand so extravagant he had to grab the table with the other for balance. 'I'm gonna bang you till your ears rattle, babe.'

'Will you cool the head, for feck's sake,' Connolly said with sobering weariness. 'I want to talk to you about Michael Horden.'

'Mike? What you want with Mike?' He was still grinning and jiggling, but she could see now he was listening. 'Jeez, that's a downer. I mean, Mike's OK, but he is not Tommy. No way.'

'Never mind. I want to know about him. You worked with him, didn't you, Tommy?'

'I ain't seen Mike in weeks,' he said, the grin fading into sullenness. 'You are really puttin' me off now, you know that? I was ready to give you the full benefit of the Flynn Big Bang, and we could have had us a nice time, you bein' what I would normally call one shaggable babe. But now you're goin' to have to do some fast talkin' to get me back in the mood, know what I'm sayin'?'

'Mike Horden,' Connolly said implacably. 'Tell me everything you know about him and I won't pat you down and nick you for your stash. All right? I'm not interested in your drugs or your scrawny little bod, Tommy me darlin', just information about Michael Horden. You got him the job at Ransom's, didn't you?'

Tommy shrugged. 'He asked me if they were taking people on. I told him they were always interested in new people, if they looked right.'

'And did he look right?'

'Yeah. He was a top-looking bloke. I told him he ought to sign on wiv a nude butler agency. I

104

do that, some nights. You can make top dollar, 'specially if you talk posh.'

'Did he talk posh?'

'He was tryna talk street wiv me, but he was posh underneath. You could hear it. But he said he wanted to get into movies.'

'Wait a minute, he came to you specifically to ask you about getting into skin movies, is that right? He approached you, not the other way round.'

'Yeah, like I'm tellin' you.'

'How did he know you were in the biz?'

He shrugged. 'Everybody knows The Flynn.'

'So how did you know him?'

'I didn't. He come up to me at this club I go to, the Forty-Niners?'

'Yeah, I know it.' It was in Kensington Park Road – Notting Hill. 'Had you seen him before?'

'Yeah, I reckon. Not to talk to, but I'd seen him in there. He was tall, fit – sort of bloke that stands out. I mean, I ain't gay,' he said sternly, to scotch any misunderstanding, 'but in the business, you get to notice the way people look.'

'So he comes up to you, never having spoken to you before—'

'No, wait, he had,' Tommy said, frowning in thought. 'Coupla nights before that, he comes up and asks me if I could sell him any charlie. Well, I didn't know who he was. Anyway, I don't deal, only to me friends. I told him I only had enough for meself. So he asks me if I know where he can get some.' He grinned suddenly at the memory. 'Man, in that place? There's more snow than Siberia. I told him to go and hang around the

105

bogs and ask the first bloke that comes in and doesn't have a slash!' He laughed uproariously at his own joke.

'But apart from that, you didn't know him? So how did he know you were in the porn-flick business?'

Tommy shrugged. 'Someone musta told him. Like I said, everybody knows me. He asked can you make good money at it, and I says yeah, look at me.' He made a gesture with his hands out to his sides. 'I was wearing me good threads,' he explained. 'Then he says can I get him on. I tells him to go along and ask, and say I sent him. Well, he musta been serious because the next time I go in, there he is. He did good, too. He looked great, and he could act, an' all.'

'Act?' Connolly queried.

Tommy looked hurt. 'Yeah, you outsiders think there's nothing in it, just get some wood on and bang away and that's that. But I can tell you, real porn fans can tell the difference in a minute between a good skin flick and a bad one. I mean, we wouldn't have got to *Office Orgy Thirteen* if it had just been a load of boring shagging. They're real movies, with a plot, lines and everything. People love 'em. They're classics. They're witty.'

'Yeah, I heard that,' Connolly said. 'You been doing this a long time, then?'

'I'm a star, didn't you know that?' He grinned, full of himself again. 'Want my autograph? I got an interesting way of writing it – you won't believe how I do it. Can't show you here, though.'

'Love a God, would y' calm down. Am'n't I

106

telling you, it's Mike Horden I'm interested in. So you say he was good at the job?'

'Yeah, he was top at it. He was a top geezer, too. We hung out together. We had a laugh, know what I mean? He useter come up my place and we'd have a few drinks and roll a doobie and mellow out. Listen to some sounds. He knew a hell of a lot about music – introduced me to some bands I'd never even heard of, but they were brilliant. This one—'

Connolly was not interested in his musical taste. 'He took drugs with you?'

He looked hurt. 'Weed ain't drugs, man. Like vodka ain't alcohol.'

'Did he use charlie? E? Speed? Anything apart from marijuana?'

'Not wiv me. But he asked me where he could buy charlie, didn't he, so he must have.'

Connolly nodded. 'So this great guy, your pal Mike – you haven't seen him lately?'

'Not for weeks,' Tommy said, sniffing and wiping his nose on his forearm. 'Man, you are really pulling me down with your questions. Seventy quid's worth of best Bolivian marching powder up my schnoz and you're bringing me right back down to earth.'

'Never mind, Tommy darlin'. Nearly finished now, then you can go and snort till your ears meet. You know it'll make your face cave in at the end? By the time you're forty you'll be breathin' through a straw stickin' out your neck.'

'Christ, I hope I'm dead before I'm forty!' Tommy said. 'What else d'you want to know about Mike? Quick, get it over with.'

107

'Did he tell you anything about his background? Family? What he did before?'

'Nah, we never talked about that stuff. Just the job, sounds, movies, birds, that sort of thing.'

'Did he have a girlfriend?'

'He never told me about one. Never saw him with anyone.'

'Didn't you think that was odd? Good-looking geezer like him?'

'Nah. It's separate, innit, blokes' time? You don't wanna mix 'em. I mean, he didn't come round and watch when I had a bird up there.'

'Did you ever go to his house?'

'I don't even know where he lived. '

'And you haven't seen him lately?'

'Not since he got sacked from Ransom's. I thought I might see him at the club, but he's not been in there either, not when I've been in.'

'Why *was* he sacked? You said he was good at it.'

'Yeah.' For the first time, Tommy looked puzzled. 'I dunno. He *was* good. And Ewan liked him – he's the director – because he knew the ropes. He said he'd done film extra work, so he didn't have to be told all the basic stuff. He knew a lot of technical stuff, an' all. Him and Ewan got on great, chatting away about cameras and lighting and angles and frames and all that bollocks.'

'So it wasn't Ewan who wanted rid of him?'

'No, that was down to the big boss, Mr Barrow. I see Mike trying to get friendly with *him*, and I thought, good luck with that, because he don't do friendly, the boss. Mike was kind of hanging round him, trying to get him talking,

108

and I s'pose it musta got on his nerves or something, because suddenly one day when I go in
Mike's not there, and when I ask Ewan about it,
he says "Paul's let him go." That's Mr Barrow.
And he like gives me a look as if to say, "Don't
ask." So I don't. It was awkward, though, 'cos
we were halfway through a film, so it must have
took a lot of editing with one of the main actors
suddenly missing.'

'Yeah,' said Connolly thoughtfully. 'I can see
it would.'

Tommy wiped his nose on his fingers, looked
about vaguely, and then wiped them on his
trouser leg. For the first time, curiosity dawned.
'Why you asking all this about Mike, anyway?
What's he done?'

'Nothing, as far as I know. Well, thanks for
your help, Tommy. I'll leave you be now.'

'No, no wait! You must be asking for some
reason. Why d'you want to get hold of him?'

'Never mind,' she said firmly. 'You're not in
trouble, that's all you need to know. But if you
think of anything he said about his family or
background or past life, the names of anyone he
knew or any firm he worked for, you'll let me
know, won't you?'

She gave him a card, and for a moment the old
Tommy reappeared on the last fizzing of the fine
Bolivian in his brain stem.

'Woah! This your private line? Bay-bee, you
can bet yo' sweet ass I will be looking you up!
And any time you want a bit of fi–i–ine lovin'
you just call for the Flynnmeister, babe! Light
blue touch paper and retire, know what I'm
109

sayin'?'

'You'd want to listen to yourself,' she said wonderingly. 'Love a God, y' sound like a total gobshite. On second thoughts, give me me card back.' She whipped it out from his nerveless fingers. 'I don't want you usin' it if for choppin' out lines. If you think of anything, ring Shepherd's Bush nick and talk to anyone, they'll pass it on.'

She left him standing there, and as she turned out of the door towards the stairs she heard his forlorn little voice behind her still trying to be the big man. 'Yeah,' he called. 'You an' me, babe. We're happening!'

I may be happening, she retorted silently, *but you're just a big owl messy accident.*

'So you see, boss,' she concluded her report to Slider, 'there must have been a good reason for getting rid of him, to chuck him out in the middle of a film.'

'Hm,' said Slider. 'But what reason? Flynn didn't give any hint?'

'No, boss. But I get the impression he spends most of his life jacked out of his gourd, so he probably wouldn't notice if it was written on the wall in red paint. But wouldn't you say it looks as though there's something to investigate there? With Horden getting chucked out for nothing.'

'The big boss, Paul Barrow, says he couldn't act,' Slider said.

'Tommy Flynn says he could.'

'Tommy Flynn doesn't sound like the best judge of anything,' Slider said. 'But anyway, what are you suggesting?'

'I don't know,' she said in frustration.

'Don't know what?' Atherton asked, coming in.

'What there is to know about Ransom Publications,' Connolly answered.

'Another known unknown,' he said.

'But we've learned a few things about Hordenstroke-Williams,' Slider said. 'He claimed to have done film extra work, he knew a lot about music, he sought out Tommy Flynn, who didn't previously know him, to get the introduction to Ransom's, he smoked dope and may or may not have taken cocaine, and he was thrown out in the middle of a film, which suggests some urgency on the part of the thrower.'

'Interesting,' said Atherton. 'On that very topic, I've been looking into Paul Barrow.'

'And?' said Slider.

'He's not lily white, that's for sure. His most recent bust is for speeding on the M40 near High Wycombe – doing a hundred and twenty in a Maserati at two in the morning. Those Buckinghamshire cops don't take prisoners.' He looked at Slider. 'You know where the M40 leads?'

Slider got it. 'Birmingham. Ransom's works in Solihull?'

'It's an even bet. That was back in April this year. Before that, two years ago, he had a bust for possession of and driving under the influence of a class A substance, to whit cocaine. On the M25 near Staines. Going further back, there was an arrest for affray outside a club, Vanya's, in Soho. That was ten years ago. He plastered two

111

blokes all over the pavement – claimed they had picked his pocket. They were low life, but the magistrate decided the beating was out of proportion and gave him a six month suspended. The most serious bust was for sexual assault of a young woman at her flat. That was fifteen years ago. He ripped her clothes off, blacked her eye and broke her arm. A neighbour called the cops and they arrested him but the girl wouldn't make a charge and in the end it was dropped.'

'Nice class of feller,' Connolly said.

'A prince among men,' said Atherton. 'I spoke to a bloke at Central and apparently and un-officially it seems the girl was working for him and he accused her of stealing. He tore her clothes off to search her, not as a precursor to rape, hit her to stop her screaming, and broke her arm accidentally because he didn't know his own strength.'

'Stealing what?'

'It didn't emerge. Anyway, once she'd calmed down she refused to cooperate with any kind of charge, and before they could work on her she discharged herself from hospital and disappear-ed.'

'Wouldn't you?' Connolly remarked.

'Was he working for Ransom Publications all this time?' Slider asked.

'No, he was manager of Vanya's when the affray incident happened. Lost his job, appar-ently, on account of it, but shortly was known to be managing another club, the Hot Box, also in Soho – Greek Street. He went to Ransom Publi-cations ten years ago. Going way back it seems he did a course in film and photography in Holloway, so that's how he had the qualification for it. Although I expect other qualities would also be needed for that particular job. Further back still he studied accountancy at Brunel University. That's where he started. Moved on a long way.'

'How was the girl he assaulted connected to him?'

'According to my Central contact, they've long suspected him of running a string of girls on the side, but they haven't been able to prove anything. They think she was one of them, and he suspected her of holding money back, but as she disappeared they couldn't investigate any further.'

'Private life?' Slider queried.

'Nothing much. He's fifty-six, born in Bermondsey – south of the river and beyond the pale – father was a print worker. Lives in a luxury penthouse, Flat Twelve, Chiltern Mansions, Chiltern Street – just opposite Baker Street station. Was married in 1989 to a Mary Lynnette Scott, but according to the electoral register he lives alone, so presumably they're separated or divorced. Has a red Maserati – as we have noted – and Chiltern Mansions has its own underground garage to keep it safe,' he added, 'so we needn't be anxious on its behalf. It would be a crime if it got scratched.'

'Well, what's all this got to do with our body?' Connolly asked in some frustration.

Atherton looked at her blankly. 'Search me. It does make him very, very tasty, however –

113

especially the living alone. Creepy! The more I learn about him the more I fancy him for the job.'

'Ye–es,' said Slider thoughtfully. 'As against which, we still don't actually know who our body is. Michael Horden had no criminal record, the address he gave was false, and though we know he worked briefly as a porn movie actor, that's all we do know.'

'And he wasn't even still doing it when he was killed, so why should your man Barrow have anything to do with it?' Connolly finished for him.

'I don't know,' Atherton said, 'but I just bet he has.'

Late in the day, Bob Bailey appeared in Slider's room, smelling of soap and the washing-powder halitus of a clean shirt. He was freshly shaved and his hair was in damp spikes at the front.

'I've got something for you,' he said.

Slider, feeling grubby and armpit-marshy from a hot day in the office, looked at him resentfully. 'You look as though you've just come out of a car wash.'

'I popped in to see you, give you the news, and had a go of your showers while I was at it,' Bailey burbled shamelessly.

'You never used to pop in. A phone call was the best I could hope for. Now suddenly this personal service?'

Bailey grinned. 'You didn't use to have that cute new detective.'

'Jerry Fathom? Well, he's new, I grant you, but

cute?'

'Don't be a git. You know I'm talking about the lovely Rita, the green-eyed goddess from Oiled Oiland.'

'In the first place Detective Constable Connolly is from Dublin and they don't talk like that,' Slider said sternly. 'In the second place if you upset any of my firm I'll personally remove your intestines, dry them in the sun, and string you up by them.'

Bailey lifted his hands in wide-eyed innocence, though still grinning, which spoiled the sincerity of the gesture. 'Who said anything about upsetting? Window shopping, that's all. My Mastercard won't run to that sort of luxury.'

'Not with two expensive divorces behind you,' Slider said brutally.

'Two divorces only means I've got a vacancy to fill. It can't hurt to ask her out, can it? She can always say no. She's a big girl.'

'That's what worries me. Anyway, you can wait outside and ask her on your own time.'

'You're a miserable bastard. Case getting you down?'

'A little help from you would go a long way,' Slider said. 'What's this "thing" you had for me – or was it just an excuse?'

'No, no, it's a real "thing" all right. There was a bottle of vodka in the fridge, about three quarters empty, and in the fullness of process we've just got round to dusting it. Very nice palm and fingers gripping the bottle, a lot of fingers on the screw cap – a bit muddled, those, not sure if we'll be able to unscramble 'em. But

115

you see–' he demonstrated with an imaginary bottle – 'she holds the bottle in her left hand while she unscrews the cap, then switches it to her right hand while she pours the drinks. Something you do so often you never even think about it, completely automatic, then you slam the bottle back in the fridge, also automatic – which is why, when you've gone round the room wiping every surface you've touched, it's easy to forget old Mr Stolly sitting in the fridge door.'

'She?' Slider queried.

'It's a woman's prints,' Bailey said, pleased with himself.

'It couldn't be the shop assistant who sold it to Williams?'

'They aren't the only marks – there are a lot of old smudges, and we've picked out a couple of dabs from Williams, but these are over the top, the last lot of marks made. "You hop in the bath, darlin', I'll knock us out a couple of drinks," he offered in a ludicrous falsetto. Slider winced. 'Now,' Bailey continued, 'it may well be that this Mata Hari doesn't have a record, but with two full hands, plus you'd expect a certain degree of nervousness in the circs, it's just about possible they can get enough DNA off the bottle to work up a profile. I've sent it off to Tufty, anyway.' He looked at Slider hopefully. 'So now am I back on your cake list?'

'I like it,' Slider said. 'Some solid DNA evidence would be wonderful. Good boy. Have a biscuit.'

'Can I go and talk to Rita, then?'

Slider gave him a look so hard you could have

116

knocked nails in with it. 'No. Wait till after work. Sexual thoughts ruin the concentration.'

'I'll sit outside your door and whimper,' said Bailey, completely unabashed.

That was the trouble with civilian experts, Slider thought when he had gone. You had no authority over them.

Of course, Williams might have had a woman up there some other time, and it might have nothing to do with the murder. And if the prints did not match anything on record, they'd have to hope Tufty at the forensic lab could get enough for a profile, and then they'd have to have a suspect to match it against ... but even so, it was evidence, and there was precious little of that so far.

SIX

Unlimited Company

A bunch of them ended up going for a curry after work. Swilley had gone home to her husband and child, and McLaren had gone off, wistful but still doggedly in love, to his beloved, presumably to have a salad and perhaps a workout at the gym followed by a nice drink of water. Slider just hoped the sex was amazing afterwards, or poor old McLaren was suffering for nothing.

The respite of earlier in the day had ended, and the evening outside was stifling, the air warm, damp and faintly unpleasant like dog's lick. The leaves hung limp from the trees as if thinking they might as well get it over with and fall now. The traffic ground homewards along Uxbridge Road towards a swollen pink west, and there was a fin-de-siècle feeling of the dog days of school summer break.

At the suggestion of curry, Fathom groaned, fanned himself ostentatiously, and said, 'In this heat? You must be mad!'

But Connolly said, sweetly, 'It's not fearsome cold in India, y' know, Jerry.'

And Atherton said, 'Indians eat hot curries to cool themselves down. It's a well-known physiological fact that—'

Connolly interrupted him with an abrasive look that said *I'll do me own arguments, thank you*, and said, 'It's a well-known physiological fact that if I don't get a murgh makhani and a gobhi aloo down me neck in the next half hour, I won't answer for the consequences.'

Slider went with them because Joanna was out that evening, playing at the Festival Hall, and it was already too late to see George before he went to bed. He rang his father, who said serenely that he shouldn't worry, he'd hold the fort, and it was only cold lamb and salad anyway so nothing was spoiling – which settled it for Slider, who hated cold lamb and salad. Atherton went because Emily was away again, in Paris this time covering the EU budget emergency talks. 'If I didn't have a photo of her on my bedside table I'd start to think I imagined her,' he'd complained to Slider earlier.

What luck Bailey had had with Connolly Slider didn't know, but it certainly hadn't resulted in a date for this evening; and Bailey hadn't still been hanging around when they all walked out, so perhaps she had sent him off with his tail between his legs.

They strolled down to the provocatively named Anglabangla, their haunt of old. It had changed hands recently, and the new owner had brought in a chef who could actually cook, so the food was now dangerously tasty. Previously it had been rumoured that in the back they kept three vats of sauce labelled hot, medium and mild and three buckets of lumps labelled meat, chicken

119

and prawns, so a mere two scoops could assemble anything on the menu. Now, the smell of the fresh spices as you came in the door had your jaws watering helplessly.

But policemen being conservative creatures, they were all secretly hoping the new broom would not sweep away the 1970's décor – swirly orange carpet, flock wallpaper, faded plastic flowers and all. It was not retro and witty, it was original, naff and therefore priceless.

They settled down among the dim, red-shaded lamps and twangy music and, salivating, read the menus.

Mackay leaned forward. 'Here, I was in this Indian restaurant the other day. The waiter comes over and says, "Curry OK?" I says to him, "Go on then, just the one song."'

Several people groaned, and Fathom said, 'Heard it!'

'Just for that, you can get 'em in, Andy,' said Hollis. 'Pints all round.'

'Janey Mack, I'm starvin'!' said Connolly. 'I could eat a nun's arse through the convent gates.'

'In the old days, you might have had to,' Atherton said. 'Now at least it's cuisine, if not exactly haute. But there's still a touch of nostalgia somewhere deep in my heart for the old ptomaine regime.'

Connolly looked at him with bright, analytical interest. 'Jayz, I never knew anyone the cut of you at all. There's a word describes you, could I think of it.'

'I can think of several,' Atherton said. 'Hip,

stylish, dangerously cool – a little bit post-modern-ironic. Sort of Emin-meets-Eminem, but in a good way. Wouldn't you say, guv?'

'Absolutely,' Slider nodded wisely. 'You do realize I haven't the faintest idea what you're talking about?'

'That's all right, neither have I,' said Atherton.

'Oh good. I was afraid one of us had lost the plot there for a minute.'

Two smiling waiters arrived with trays of pints. Being an Indian restaurant it was only basic lager, but traditions have to be upheld. Drinking anything but cheap lager with a curry would be as unthinkable as drinking a cocktail with a ploughman's, or a pint of Boddie's with a Devon cream tea.

Conversation was fragmented and wide-ranging at first, but as the curry settled the day-long cravings and calm spread over the table, they came at last, inevitably, to discussing the case.

'The basic problem is that we still don't know who Williams or Horden really was, and without that we don't know why anyone'd want to kill him,' said Hollis.

'Way to go, Colin,' said Connolly. 'Always start by stating the obvious.'

He gave her a stern look over the top of the spectacles he wasn't wearing. 'All we know is he worked as a porn actor for a bit, and some people have said he seemed too posh for it. But there's loads of posh people, both sexes, do it, for the money. Strippers, models – prostitutes.' He appealed to Slider, who nodded. 'We've all come across high-class call girls.'

Mackay agreed. 'There was that MP last year, real posh-snob bloke with a hoity-toity accent, turned out he'd been in skin flicks before he got elected. It was in all the papers.'

'All true,' said Slider. 'So there's nothing essentially odd about Horden being a porn actor. But there is about him spreading false names and addresses behind him, and getting himself murdered by someone who tried to make it look like a suicide.'

'What did he do between leaving Ransom's and getting killed, that's what exercises me,' said Atherton. 'It seems to me he went to some trouble to get *into* Ransom's. He got the tattoos, got himself waxed, sought out Tommy Flynn for an introduction—'

'Now, that's something, guv,' Mackay interrupted. 'Given Flynn saw him around the club, and he knew enough to know Flynn was his man, it looks like he was into the club scene. Maybe that's where we ought to be asking questions.'

'Good point,' Slider said. 'We'd better get someone in there.'

'As I was saying,' Atherton went on loudly, 'he took trouble to get himself into Ransom's, and Barrow threw him out on the spurious grounds that he couldn't act, which was obviously a cover.'

'What's spurious?' Fathom asked.

'Cover for what?' Hollis asked.

'He means Tommy Flynn said he could act,' Connolly translated.

'Tommy Flynn has more holes in his head than a fine Emmenthaler,' Atherton said, 'but it doesn't mean he wasn't right about that.'

'What's an Emmenthaler?' Fathom pleaded, trying to keep up.

'It's a bunch a holes, ya divvy, held together wit cheese,' Connolly said impatiently. And to Atherton, 'What's your point?'

'Why did he want to be a porn actor, that's my point,' Atherton said.

'For the money,' Mackay answered. 'Why not?'

'That's too simple. He appears from nowhere, false name – two false names – everyone who sees him thinks he's out of his place. Barrow turns out to be a nasty sort with more form than a benefits application – and connections to the club scene, by the way. And our man ends up dead.'

'Two months later,' Slider said. 'No reason it should have anything to do with Barrow.'

'Which is why I said right at the beginning, what did he do in between?' Atherton concluded triumphantly. 'That's got to be the crux of the matter.'

Fathom opened his mouth to ask what a crux was, and Slider said hastily, 'I'd just as soon know where he came from *before* the tattoos and Conningham Road.'

'Wouldn't we all,' said Atherton. 'An ending without a beginning is no fun.'

'It could still have been suicide,' Hollis said, and everyone groaned. 'If it's just the keys you're going on—'

'Let's assume, for the sake of argument, it was murder,' Atherton said kindly. 'We know there was a woman involved in it. The whole thing looks like a night of seduction – pizza, a few drinks, then she says, how about a lovely bath together, followed by nookie?'

'And she slips him a micky, kills him, shoves his worldlies into a sack and does a legger,' Connolly concluded. 'Gets my vote.'

'But the person who came out with the sack was dressed in trousers and a beanie,' Slider said. 'Not exactly seduction clothes.'

'Women don't get all dressed up for a date these days, boss,' Connolly said. 'Little girly dress and high heels kind o' caper? That class o' sexist malarkey doesn't go down at all with your modern, free-thinkin' female.'

'It needn't a been someone he'd only just met,' Mackay pointed out. 'He could've been doinking her for weeks, and they got past the dating stage. That'd make it easier for her to persuade him to have a bath. It was hot, Sunday. She could even have said, "You niff a bit, darlin', go and have a bath an' I'll bring you a drink in."'

'Even if there were a woman up there with him,' said Hollis, who was having marriage problems and never wanted to go home, so had an interest in prolonging the discussion, 'it needn't have been a woman 'at killed him. A woman could have done the seduction and bath, and then when he was asleep, opened the door for the murderer.'

They did him the courtesy of thinking about it. Then Atherton said, 'Nah! That was a woman's

124

murder. Too elaborate. Too clever-clever.'

'Yeah, you're right,' Mackay said. 'A man would've been more direct. Bashed him on the head or stabbed him or whatever.'

'I suppose it could have been planned by a woman, and still carried out by a man,' Slider said.

'Botev had a key,' Hollis said 'He could a slipped in and done it once Williams was asleep.'

'But the one thing we know is that Botev wasn't black-sack man,' said Slider.

'If Horden did have a date up there,' Connolly said, 'it could just as easy've been a feller. You'd still get the artistic flourishes with a gay lover. In fact, everything I've learnt about Horden, or Williams, or whatever his name was, is a bit gay.'

'You're forgetting the fingermarks on the vodka bottle,' Atherton reminded her. They had been put through the system, too, and come up blank. Bottle lady had no previous.

'Which is all very nice but doesn't get us any further forward,' said Slider.

'So what a we do next, Boss?' Connolly asked, wiping the sauce from her plate with the last bit of the big greasy naan she'd shared with Hollis.

'Is that a royal "we"?' Atherton asked, watching her in pained fascination.

Slider wasn't having any divisions in his firm. '"We" is fine. Like a Berlusconi jacuzzi, we're all in this together. And what we do is keep on with what we're doing. Look for the pizza. Follow up Paul Barrow. Look into the clubs. We don't know that Horden didn't try porn acting elsewhere – we should try his photo round some other studios.' He knew how thin it sounded. 'If we can't get some kind of a lead on it tomorrow, we'll have to think about going public, in the hope that a relative or girlfriend will come forward. Mr Porson won't want this getting away from us, and it's been two days now.'

There was a silence. Going public with the photo of a corpse would have the Hammersmith PR team throwing a fit. It just didn't look good to flash pictures of dead people at the general public, whose sensitivity to 'offence' was renowned – and litigious.

'Trouble wi' going public,' Hollis said, 'is we'll get the press round our necks. It's been like a Bank Holiday, not having them around.'

'Well, never mind,' Slider said after a silence. 'Let's keep positive. When you touch the bottom of the swimming pool, the only way is up.'

'And in a public pool, you're only going through the motions anyway,' Atherton concluded.

Connolly shoved her chair back. 'Jayz, that's it! I'm outta here, before the rest of yez start chippin' in with the shit jokes.'

'Time I was going, too,' Slider agreed. 'Early night, start fresh in the morning.'

'Tomorrow to fresh woods and ghastly poo,' said Atherton. 'How are we splitting the bill?'

Slider was in bright and early the next morning, but not as bright or early as Mr Porson, who hadn't a comfortable wife to drag himself away from. Slider was summoned, before his bottom had hit his seat, to present an update on progress.

Porson tipped a sachet of sugar into his milky coffee and stirred it vigorously with a biro. Slider guessed he had not yet opened his mail or received a phone call, because he was cheerful and not even a bit angry. He listened in silence to Slider's exposition, and then said, 'Well, don't worry about it. It's not as if it's a high-profile case, no connections with anyone important. We haven't got anyone breathing down our backs to get a result. Better do it right than do it quick, that's my maximum.'

Slider almost fell over, having spent most of his life being yelled at to get it done yesterday, no matter what 'it' was. But you don't look a gift doughnut in the raspberry jam. 'Thanks, sir,' he said. 'I've got a feeling there's more to this case than meets the eye.'

'Well, feelings are in the eye of the beholder,' Porson said wisely, 'so run with it. What lines are you following up?'

Slider told him. 'And I'd like to get someone into the club he used to frequent, possibly some others that may be linked, as well. Find some people who knew him.'

'Right,' said Porson. 'There's a uniform lad you might be able to use, keen to get into the Department – bright lad – couldn't hurt to try him out. Phil Gascoyne – come across him?'

'I've seen him about,' Slider said. 'I used to know his dad, Bob – he was a lecturer at Hendon.'

'Oh yes, I know who you mean. Is that his dad, then?' Porson frowned. 'I never knew why he was called Bob, when his name was Harry. Bob's not an abbreciation for Harry, is it?'

'No, but back when *he* was a lad, the coin you put in a gas meter was a shilling – a bob.'

'Right! Gas coin. Got it,' Porson said, and looked pleased with the enlightenment as he mouthed the words to himself a couple of times. Then his phone rang. He focused sharply on Slider and his brows snapped down like an atomic-powered Tower Bridge. 'Well? What are you standing there for? Two days in and nothing to show for it – you've got no time to waste, laddie.' Slider headed for the door. 'And if you don't find out who he is by the end of today, we'll have to go public, so get a breeze on!'

It didn't last long, Slider thought. But it had been a nice change.

Gascoyne joined them for the morning meeting, looking self-conscious in his 'civvies', into which he had changed downstairs with much joshing from his fellow woodentops, and solemn warnings from Organ that they were all nuts up there. 'Watch your step.'

'And don't forget who your real mates are,' said Gostyn sternly. 'You can take the uniform out of the man, but you can't – no, hang on, I got that wrong.'

'Piss off, Gostyn, you dip,' Gascoyne said affectionately, and straightened his face to a seemly gravity and earnestness as he trod up the stairs to CID heaven.

Slider welcomed him, finding a tall young man with a broad, pleasant face that missed being handsome by such mere millimetres it was hard

128

to pin down why, close-shaved fair hair, and candid blue eyes. From the open honesty of his face to his large well-planted feet, he looked so quintessentially a copper that Slider cancelled at once the half-formed thought he'd had in Porson's office of putting him into the clubs. He'd be clocked in an instant. McLaren would have been the obvious choice before, but McLaren's edge had been blunted by salad and callisthenics. He had an undeniably clean-living look about him these days, as he drooped in the background, perched on his desk with the hunched-shouldered look of an unhappy budgie. Atherton had brought in a box of doughnuts and McLaren didn't take one, that's how bad it was – though he did sigh, which Slider took as grounds for hope that there was something left alive inside that might one day be revived. No, he'd have to put Mackay into the clubs, and use Gascoyne on Mackay's jobs.

Fathom had been working on alibis. 'Botev claims he was home all Sunday night, guv, with his wife and kids. Trouble is, his wife doesn't speak English – or he claims she doesn't – so he has to translate for us. And o'course he says *she* says he was there.'

'What about the children?'

'Four little kids, eldest one is eight,' said Fathom. 'So unless you want me to put pressure on him – get the kids aside, bring the wife in, get a Bulgarian interpreter...'

Slider saw the point. They had nothing on Botev, except that he had a key. His fingermarks had been found on the door, the radio, and the bathroom door-frame, but so far nowhere else. And they knew he was not black-sack man. 'No,' he said. 'Can't do that, unless we get something else on him. Any more witnesses among the neighbours?'

'No, guv,' said Hollis. 'So far nobody else has seen the victim go in or black-sack man come out. Two in the morning on a Sunday to Monday night ... now if it had been Sat'day to Sunday it might've been different.'

And it was an inner-London problem, Slider thought, that other people just became wallpaper and you didn't tend to notice them. It might have been different in the suburbs, but in Shepherd's Bush you expected there to be people about late at night, so why should you bother to remark it? 'What about the Pakistani boys?'

'It seems there *was* a party, guv,' said Fathom. 'House in Cobbold Road. Talked to a couple of the guys living there. It's hard getting anything out of 'em – too monged and too scared – but it seems our two *was* there, and it didn't break up finally until about four. And they said they'd never heard of Williams. I had another go at our two, threatened to search their gaff if they didn't tell me everything they knew about Williams, but they stuck to it they'd never seen him or heard of him and I believed 'em.'

Slider nodded. 'We'll keep an eye on them, but I don't think they're involved. The job was too controlled to be carried out by substance abusers. Anything on the car?' he asked McLaren.

'No, guv,' McLaren said, and defended himself. 'It's not easy when we haven't got the reg

130

number or make. Even two of a Monday morning there's a lot of motors about in the Bush. And there's no camera showing either end of Conningham Road, so any cars caught on Goldhawk or Uxbridge needn't've come out from there.' He shrugged to show it was what Mr Porson would have called looking for a needle in a woodpile. 'I'm working my way through everything from ten minutes before to ten minutes after, but so far they're all legit.'

Slider nodded. 'Well, keep at it. Anyone with connections to anyone in the house, or Botev, or Ransom House. Or anyone dodgy to any degree. When you run out of options, extend the time another five minutes either side. We've only Mish's word for the time, and she only said "about" two o'clock.'

'Wouldn't've been much later,' Hollis observed. 'I've never known a pross willingly go over time.'

'Norma – anything?'

Swilley glanced at her notes. 'I've been looking into the Marylebone Group and Ransom and all that set-up. It's not easy, as you know – it's been set up not to be easy. We can't get information out of Cyprus without prima facie evidence, and Ransom being a branch, they don't have to register with Companies House. All they have to do is provide a set of accounts to the Revenue for tax purposes. That's done by a firm of accountants – Adamou and Magnitis in Clerkenwell. And they don't have directors, just a legal representative, which is a firm of solicitors, Regal Forsdyke. The top man there is

131

David Regal. The beauty of the system as far as they're concerned is provided they pay a decent amount of tax to HMRC, no one bothers to ask any questions. And any legal liability for anything at all falls on the parent company in Cyprus—'

'Which you can't get any information out of,' Atherton concluded. 'Brilliant! Colossal dead end.'

'I didn't say I hadn't found out *anything*,' Swilley said, giving him a look that could have deboned a leg of lamb. 'I had a look into the Forty-Niners club, because that's one place we know Williams hung out. It turns out it's part of the Apsis Leisure Group. Also in the Apsis group is the Hot Box – where we know Barrow worked – and a couple of others. And Apsis is part of the Marylebone Group – who also own the buildings, and a lot of other property in Soho.'

'And Marylebone also own Ransom Productions,' Slider said. 'That's very good.'

'So now we've got a line through Ransom Productions, Tommy Flynn, the Forty-Niners, Williams and Barrow,' said Swilley.

'But I still don't see that it helps,' Atherton persisted. 'Williams uses the club – why not? Lots of people do. He asks Tommy Flynn, who also uses it, about a job. Flynn has a job with a company that's affiliated with the club – which is probably how he got it in the first place. So what?'

'The "so what" is that Williams ends up dead,' Swilley said.

'Well, excuse me if I don't see a grand conspiracy there,' Atherton retorted coolly.

'I didn't say there was a grand conspiracy. I just said there was a connection,' said Swilley.

'And what is there about this connection that gives a reason for his murder?'

'Well, why don't *you* tell us why he was killed, Jim?' Swilley asked sweetly.

'Jesus, Mary and Joseph,' Connolly interrupted impatiently, 'would yez listen to the two of you. We don't even know who the fecker was, yet.'

The telephone rang at that moment and Hollis answered it. He held out the receiver to Atherton. 'Someone asking for you.'

'Detective Sergeant Atherton,' he said, sitting on the edge of the desk and turning his back to cut out the sound of the continuing talk.

'This is John Johnson here. You know, Honest John? Blues 'n' Tattoos Parlour?'

'Yes, Mr Johnson. What can I do for you?'

'Well, you did say if I remembered anything else about that poor young man – however trivial, you said. This is really trivial, but I thought p'raps I'd better mention it. I hope I'm not wasting your time,' he concluded doubtfully.

'The smallest thing can turn out to be important,' Atherton said reassuringly. 'What have you remembered?'

'Well, when he came in, he was carrying a bag from Vinyl Heaven. That's a shop just down the road from here, deals in old LPs, vintage CDs, obscure bands and so on. Bit of a niche market. It was a CD-sized bag the chap was carrying, and it looked new. Well, you wouldn't

133

keep a bag of that size to carry anything else in, would you?'

'No, I take your point.'

'So it occurred to me that if he'd been in the shop that day, they might remember him. I mean, I don't suppose they're stuffed with customers at the best of times. And with a niche market, you do tend to know your customers – they come back. It's a small world and a bit nerdy. So they might possibly be able to tell you his name, or something about him. I mean, I know it's a long shot, but...' He trailed off as if expecting to be shouted at.

'That's a very good idea,' Atherton said. 'You were quite right to mention it, and we'll certainly look into it. Thanks a lot.'

'Just trying to help,' Johnson said, pleased. Or was it relieved?

SEVEN

Porter Coeli

'Tattoos were not my thing. Vinyl is,' Atherton said, arguing to be the one to go. 'I've looked up the address, and it's on the corner of Brook Green – the road, I mean.' Brook Green was not only the name of an area and a green space but of the road which ran along the side of the green and debouched into Shepherd's Bush Road. 'Just round the corner from Ransom Productions, in fact – another connection.'

'I thought you didn't believe in connections,' Swilley sniped.

'If you two can't behave I'll send you to your rooms,' Slider said. 'Atherton, go. He's right, it is a long shot, but we haven't got any short ones. Good luck. May the force be with you.'

'You're not allowed to call it the Force any more,' Atherton said, turning away. 'It's the Police *Service*.'

Vinyl Heaven was so niche it had a hand-painted fascia instead of the usual glossy plastic or glass job: a pale blue background with the name in black capitals in the middle and two overlapping LPs painted on either side of it, black, of course, with red labels.

Inside there were records and CDs in wall racks on either side and in a rather home-made-looking double-sided wooden stand down the middle. There was a counter across the far end, and on the walls were a number of posters, pin-ups of bands and artists and vintage bills advertising gigs, some framed, and evidently also for sale. The carpet was worn threadbare down either side from the fidgeting feet of aficionados rifling through the goodies – though Atherton guessed it had never been very good carpet, perhaps not even new when the shop was established. The place had that air about it of hanging on by its fingernails.

However, even on a weekday morning it already had two customers – or at least, there were two people in there when Atherton walked in. The air was bouncing with the relentless dub-beat and shuffling high-hats of a garage CD being played over the loudspeakers – had Atherton known it, it was DJ Luck & MC Neat – and two young men were idling about in front of the racks, twitching to the music and pretending to look at the stock.

Atherton drew his eyes firmly away from the vintage classical LPs and eased past the twitchers to the counter, where a skinny young man with wild hair, a tattooed neck and a stud through his lip was standing watching him hopefully.

Atherton showed his brief and the hope faded rapidly, to be replaced by an unfocused apprehension. 'Are you the owner?' Atherton asked.

'Yeah, I'm Steve.' Into Atherton's insistent

silence he added, 'Steve Chilcott. This is my place. Is something wrong?'

'Not as far as I'm aware,' Atherton said. 'I wanted your help with something, if you would not mind.'

He relaxed a little, and said, 'Yeah, OK. If I can.'

The music came to an end, a split second before Atherton was going to ask him to turn it off. 'I wonder if you can remember this man coming in,' he said into the ringing silence, handing over the mugshot. 'It was a while ago.'

Chilcott was looking puzzled and already shaking his head, and Atherton went on, 'We think he came into your shop on the Tuesday after Easter. It would probably have been a quiet day, so we hoped you might remember him. He was wearing cords and a sports jacket, slightly posh-looking bloke. He bought a CD from you.'

'Oh, yeah, I remember *him*,' Chilcott said. 'I wouldn't have known him from this picture though. What is he, asleep?'

Atherton sidestepped that one. 'You do remember him?' he insisted.

'Yeah. Actually, now I know who you mean, I can see it's him. But it's a funny picture. He was a walk-in. I saw him going by, as if he wasn't going to stop, but as he passes the open door he sort of stops. Must have heard the music. It was a Blur single I was playing – I think it was *Beetlebum*. So he comes in. He looks like a Blur, Oasis kind of guy – you know, a bit older, dressed like a grown-up.'

'Had you seen him before?'

'Not that I know of. Anyway he gives me a sort of nod, and starts looking through the racks but I could tell it was the CD he was listening to. It happens all the time,' he said with a faint sigh and a glance towards the two lingerers, who were evidently waiting for him to put something else on, pretending to be occupied while watching him out of the corner of their eyes, like dogs hanging about near the biscuit tin. 'They just come in for the music and don't buy anything. But you gotta get 'em in first, so when the Blur single finishes I put something else on, and suddenly he's not looking any more, he's listening like someone's put a couple of thousand volts through him.'

'The music meant something to him?' Atherton hazarded.

'Yeah – I'll tell you. When the music stopped he came straight up to the counter, all smiles, and I was just about to tell him what I'd been playing when *he* tells *me*. "That was Breaking Wave," he says. *"I Didn't Mean It*, 2005. I didn't think that was still on sale anywhere." So I said, "Breaking Wave's a bit of a cult." That's what we do here – vintage and cult bands.'

'Breaking Wave,' Atherton said. 'I don't think I've heard of them.'

'They were never very big,' Chilcott said. 'They did a couple of singles that got in the charts, and the one album, and then they disappeared. Happens all the time. But their video for *I Didn't Mean It* went viral on YouTube and they became a cult overnight. Minor cult,' he added fairly.

'But this man did buy the CD?' Atherton insisted.

'Yes, the album.'

'How did he pay?'

Chilcott looked puzzled. 'What d'you mean, how?'

'Cash, cheque, plastic?' Atherton said, mental fingers crossed.

'Well, I don't remember,' Chilcott said reasonably. 'Not this long after. Probably plastic though, given he was a smart-looking bloke.'

'Is there any way you can find out? Do you have records you can check?'

Chilcott frowned at him. The two idlers had got bored and wandered out. 'Look,' he said, 'd'you mind my asking what all this is about? What's the CD got to do with it? Has this bloke done something?'

Atherton decided to come clean. 'He's been found dead and we don't know who he is. We thought you might know him, or have a record of his name, OK?'

Chilcott had stalled at the beginning of the speech. 'Dead? What d'you mean, dead?'

'It looks as though he committed suicide.'

'Fuck,' Chilcott said reverently. 'Poor guy. What a bummer.' A beat. 'What, right after he bought the Breaking Wave CD? I didn't think it was that bad.'

People do sometimes find themselves resorting to humour when they are put off balance. Atherton thought it kindest to ignore it. 'So, can you help us? Do you have records of the sales?'

Chilcott pulled himself together. 'Yeah, I keep

139

a record of everything I sell. 'Course, I don't write down everyone's name, but as it happens,' he added with a gleam of intelligence, 'I've still got a card-swipe machine – haven't been able to afford a new chip-and-pin job – so I have the flimsies. And the flimsies show the name.'

'Brilliant!' said Atherton

He looked pleased. 'I'll have to look it up.'

'Of course.'

'Now?'

'If you would.'

'You're sure it was the Tuesday after Easter?'

'Fairly sure. Start there, anyway, and see how you get on.'

Chilcott nodded and became businesslike. 'I only had the one copy of *I Didn't Mean It*. I'll look in the sales book first.' He went through the doorway behind him to the back office and came back in a moment with a sales ledger which he slapped down in front of Atherton. He opened it, riffled through the pages, then started running his finger down the columns. 'Here it is. You're right, it was Tuesday twenty-sixth. Paid by Visa.' He looked up. 'I'll have to go through the flimsies. It'll take a minute. Can you watch the shop for me? Give a yell if anyone wants anything?'

It took ten minutes. Someone did come and put their head round the door – Atherton couldn't have sworn it wasn't one of the previous idlers – but went away again, presumably because there was no music. And then Chilcott was back, flushed with accomplishment. 'Got it!' he said. 'It was a NatWest Visa. Here's the number. And

140

the name was B.J. Corley.'

There was an odd thrill for Atherton in hearing the right name for the first time. 'You're absolutely sure?'

'That's the name on the credit card he used. I don't know if that was his real name, do I? I mean, he might have stolen it. Except he didn't look the type. And the payment went through OK. Like I said, I only had the one copy of that CD, so there's no doubt about that.'

'Right. Well, thank you very much,' Atherton said. 'You've been a great help.'

He was turning away when Chilcott said, 'I can't get over he killed himself. He seemed such a nice bloke.' He frowned thoughtfully. 'I had the feeling I'd seen him somewhere before, when he came in.'

'But you said you didn't know him?'

'No, he just looked a bit familiar, I can't say why.' He shrugged. 'But maybe he just had that kind of face.'

The credit-card company was able immediately to supply an address for B.J. Corley, and promised to email a list of all recent transactions on the card.

'Wynnstay Gardens,' Swilley said, looking over Atherton's shoulder. 'Where's that?'

'It's just off Allen Street,' said Slider. 'Kensington High Street. And the cabbie said he picked him up by Allen Street, so that fits.' It was a strange relief at last to know the victim's name.

'If that is him,' Swilley said, echoing the proprietor of Vinyl Heaven. 'He might have stolen the card.'

141

They looked up the telephone number but there was no reply, not even an answering machine.

'We'd better get round there and see what we can find,' Slider said. 'Atherton – with me. Swilley, see what there is on record for the name or the address. The rest of you, carry on with what you were doing.'

Wynnstay Gardens was a shallow crescent with both ends on Allen Street. It was lined with handsome five-storey red-brick Victorian mansion blocks, which had always been luxurious, each with a lift and porter. With their proximity to Kensington High Street, they were going for the better part of two million quid these days.

Atherton gave a soundless whistle. 'How could our victim afford to live there? And if he could, why did he work in porn flicks and pretend to live in Conningham Road? I'm beginning to think he must have stolen that card.'

'Don't say that. If we don't find answers here, we'll be right up a close.'

There was no reply to the doorbell, down at street level, so the first thing was to winkle out the porter, who to begin with was unwilling to be winkled, until Slider suggested he could stay put and they'd break the door down. Then he emerged like a hermit crab, slightly sidelong because of a spectacular limp, rumbling and grumbling and clutching a bunch of keys. He was probably in his sixties, Slider guessed, and despite the limp he moved briskly enough, leading the way to the lift, with its elaborate wrought-iron gates and mahogany-panelled interior.

'We don't have any trouble here,' he offered gratis. 'People don't pay this sort of money for a place to cause trouble. And my building's a quiet building. No rentals, all owner-occupied. There's one down the road that's nearly all rented, crying shame I call it, tore out the insides and tarted 'em up all modern, renting 'em out to dear knows who, rich foreigners and film stars. All right, they got money but it lets the tone of the place down. When I was a lad, renting wasn't known, not at all. My dad was porter here before me and he knew all the families, not just this building but the 'ole street. People don't stay put any more, that's the problem with the world today. If everyone stayed put, we'd all be better off.'

'I'm sure you know all the tenants here, don't you?' Slider said flatteringly. It was close quarters in the lift, which moved with elegant Victorian slowness, and the old man smelled of hair and paregoric sweets.

'The ones that've been here a while, I do. There's a couple of newcomers. *Seem* all right,' he added grudgingly. 'We'll have to see.'

'What about Mr Corley?' Slider asked. 'Has he lived here long?'

'Prac'ly all his life,' the porter said triumphantly, as if that proved some point he had been making. The lift shuddered gently to a halt, and he clashed open the gate and sidled out. 'Fourth floor,' he said. 'These are the best flats, up here. Quieter, and the air's cleaner. Always cost the most, the ones up the top. Closer to heaven, that's what I always say to my ladies and gentle-

143

men. Just my little joke. Closer to heaven, see?'
He pointed upwards.

The air was cool and smelled of furniture
polish, and there was a feeling of great stillness.
The heavy mahogany doors of the three flats on
this floor looked massive and motionless and a
little reproachful, as though even this much
noise and disturbance was unwelcome.

The porter approached the door on the left,
bringing his keys into the operative position.
'Course it's not *his* flat, stric'ly speaking. It's his
mum and dad's. But they've been living out East
– ooh – must be nine, ten years now. They come
back for holidays, but mostly it's young Mr
Corley who uses it. And his sister visits now and
then. Little nipper of five he was, when he first
come here, and his sister was seven. That was
when Mrs Manningham died – his great-aunt –
who owned the flat before. So that's three gener-
ations have lived here. That's the way it always
used to be, in my father's day. You knew where
you were then.'

He rang the bell and knocked, paused for a
moment listening, then unlocked the deadlock,
put the Yale in and opened the door. 'Porter here.
Anyone home?' he called. And hearing no reply,
he pushed the door all the way open and stood
aside to let Slider and Atherton pass.

'So what's all this about, then, anyway?' he
asked, coming in behind them and closing the
door. 'Why you asking about Mr Corley? What's
he done?'

'I'm sorry to tell you that he seems to have
committed suicide,' Slider said, and turned back

144

to see what effect it would have.

The porter stared at him, his mouth slightly open, his brows bent in surprised disbelief. And then he said, 'No. You made a mistake. No, he wouldn't do that, not Mr Corley. Not young Ben. It'd break his parents' heart, and he'd never do that. No, you made a mistake.'

The door had opened on to a large and handsome vestibule, containing a mahogany bookcase and a Regency side table with a massive mirror over it. On the walls were several watercolour paintings, and two portraits in oils of a young man of about eighteen and a young woman perhaps a little older, taken sitting with the same background, of a tall window and a crimson velvet curtain. The young man, Slider noticed sadly, was unmistakably their corpse, although in the portrait his hair was very dark.

'Is this him?' he asked the porter.

'Yes, that's Ben. And his sister, the next one. That's Jennifer.'

'Then I'm afraid there's no mistake. That's the same man. I'm very sorry.'

The porter's jaw was stuck out in stubborn disbelief. 'He'd never do a thing like that,' he said again.

Reluctantly, Slider produced the mug shot. The porter stared, and slowly subsided on to a chair beside the door. 'Excuse me,' he said more faintly. 'I gotter sit down.'

'That is him, isn't it?

He nodded. 'But whatever's happened to his hair? Lovely black hair he had. And last time I saw him he had a beard. Didn't like it much, made him look like a pirate, but he said it was the fashion. What's happened? I don't understand.'

Slider took a quick look round while Atherton kept an eye on the porter, who had asked for a glass of water.

The flat was enormous, big rooms with high ceilings, elaborate marble fireplaces, moulded cornices, heavy mahogany doors. There were servants' bells in every room, and behind the huge kitchen was a servant's bedroom and service door. He could see why they were worth so much, and also why it would be a crying shame to rip out all the original detail and modernize it.

It wasn't furnished like a young man's home, and it was easy to work out that the furnishings had been passed down along with the flat. There were old Turkish and Chinese carpets on the floors, large pieces of antique furniture, lamps from a dozen different periods, paintings on every wall, old clocks and fine-china ornaments, vases, figurines, framed photographs galore. A grand piano. And books everywhere: the alcoves were filled with shelves and there were besides several tall mahogany bookcases like the one in the vestibule. A flat for sitting down and being comfortable in, which probably hadn't looked much different at any time in its life.

It was also evidence of a wealthy, cultured family, which threw the mystery of 'Robin Williams' into sharp relief. Even if all this stuff belonged to his parents rather than him, surely if he had needed money he could have gone to

146

them rather than to Ransom House?

There were four bedrooms, plus one fitted out as a study. It had a desk with a computer on it, and shelving in the fireplace alcoves containing modern TV and sound equipment, and a huge collection of DVDs and CDs. On the other side of the room, along a modern built-in unit, was what even Slider could recognize as a home recording studio or audio workstation. Though he wouldn't have known the names for all the bits of kit, they included some kind of multi-track recorder, what he thought was called a mixing board, a couple of decks, loudspeakers and microphones.

He went back to the entrance hall. There was so much stuff in the flat it would take a lot of sifting through, and they would need to call in a larger team to do it. What he needed first was information about the next of kin and Corley's recent movements. The porter seemed to have recovered from his momentary weakness and was on his feet again, but he was jingling his keys uneasily and his eyes kept shifting from Atherton's face to the portrait on the wall, as if he really didn't know what to believe.

'So tell me,' Slider said as chummily as he could manage, 'when you last saw Ben Corley.'

'Well – sir – I don't see much of him at the best of times. Not of any of the tenants, really, unless they've got a complaint. Some of them are complaining all the time, but the others – well, weeks might go past without me happening to see 'em. So with Mr Corley...' He shook his head. 'I couldn't rightly say. It'd be a good few weeks.'

'So you wouldn't know whether he'd been around more or less often?'

'No, I can't say as I would. He's got his own keys. Doesn't need me to let him in or out.'

'Do you know what Mr Corley did for a living?'

'I know he was something to do with the music business. I think he worked for a magazine or a recording company, something like that. Wasn't a musician himself, though he played the piano. I heard him playing once when I was up here changing a washer on the kitchen tap – played beautiful, he did. Just like a concert hall. But he never did that for his living, far as I know.'

'His parents, Mr and Mrs Corley—'

'Sir Richard and Lady Corley,' he corrected with a faint air of affront.

'Sorry, I didn't know.'

'Knighted by Mrs Thatcher for services to government. He's a lawyer by profession, Sir Richard, but on the financial side. He's a consultant with the Hong Kong and Shanghai Bank now. They live in Hong Kong, but they've been all over – China, Australia, Canada, California. Lady Corley sends me postcards,' he said with a self-conscious smile. 'It's a little joke between us – always sends me a card when she goes anywhere new. But they come back from time to time, like I said, and they've always said they'd retire here. Still proper UK citizens. Lady Corley likes to use the British Museum for her research. She writes historical books. Not fiction,' he added sternly, as if her probity had been impugned, 'but the proper stuff. There's some of her books

148

in the bookcase there.'

Slider looked. There was a row of pristine books, obviously a series, on Tudor monarchs. 'These ones here?' he asked. 'Christine Buller-Jackson?'

'That's right. Her maiden name, that is,' said the porter. ''Cause she was already writing before she married Sir Richard.'

And Atherton said, *The* Christine Buller-Jackson? She's famous – you must have heard of her, guv.'

'It does ring a slight bell,' said Slider, who rarely had time to read for pleasure, and when he did would not choose non-fiction for relaxation purposes. 'So Sir Richard and Lady Corley are in Hong Kong now?'

'That's right. They were back for a couple of weeks in Feb'ry, but they haven't been back this summer like they usually do. I got a card from Lady Corley from Seattle, so I'm guessing they're taking their summer holiday in America this year.'

So they wouldn't be any help in the case, Slider thought. But they'd have to be informed, as next of kin. Unless... 'Was Ben married?'

'No, sir, not as far as I know. I'm sure Lady Corley would have told me if there was anything of that coming up. It'd've been a big occasion, if their son and heir got married.'

'Heir, you say? They're a wealthy family, I imagine?'

'Oh yes,' the porter said proudly. 'And a proper, old wealthy family, too. And just the two children to share it all when the time comes.'

'You mentioned the sister – Jennifer, was it?'

'That's right. Lovely young lady. Married, now – she's Mrs Shepstone. Don't see much of her, except when Sir Richard and Lady Corley are home and she comes to visit, but she comes over now and then. Her husband's in property and she's got one of them spas, The Haven, it's called, out Watford way. Lot of actresses and film stars go there. When I do see her, she likes to tell me what famous people have been in. "I had that Kate Winslet in the other day, Perkins," she says to me. I loved her in that *Titanic*,' he added in parenthesis. 'Now she's my idea of a proper film star, not like some of these scrawny wimmin that look like the chicken *after* Sunday lunch.'

'Were they close, the brother and sister?'

'Oh yes, very fond of each other, they are. Always have been. She's that little bit older than him, so she always looked after him when they were kids. She used to take him down the museums, both of 'em in their little coats and woolly hats, and she'd say to him, "Now hold my hand when we cross the road," and I'd hold the door open for 'em and she'd give me a lovely smile, and she'd say, "I'm looking after Ben because Mummy's busy." Like a little grown-up, she was.'

A pager in his pocket began to buzz and he started back to the present. 'That's for me. I gotter go.' He looked at them with the bewildered look of someone just waking up. 'He's not dead, Mr Corley? You made a mistake.'

'I'm sorry,' Slider said, gently.

150

He shook his head. 'No,' he said finally. 'I don't believe it. Even if it's true he's dead, he'd never commit suicide. That'd break his parents' hearts, and he wouldn't do that, not Ben. It'll break their hearts anyway, him being dead – apple of their eye he was. But he wouldn't kill himself.'

He turned away, but turned back to say, 'You'll be wanting their address, to let them know? You'll see to all that, I dare say. If you call in on me before you go I can give you the address in Hong Kong, though whether they're there at the moment...' He shook his head, slightly dazed by the turn of events. 'I'll leave the key with you, seeing you're police,' he said. 'I s'pose I can trust you. Make sure you double-lock the door when you go, and bring the key back to me.'

'I'm afraid we'll have to keep it for the time being,' said Slider.

He stared a moment longer, shook his head again, said, 'As you please,' and left.

EIGHT

Girls Allowed

Atherton looked at Slider. 'What have we here? Father a knight and a lawyer, obviously wealthy, mother a top historian, lives in this multimillion pound flat – I can't believe he went into porn movies for the money.'

'The flat's his parents', and by the look of it the contents are too. Doesn't mean to say *he* had any money,' Slider said. 'Though I agree with your general premise. This doesn't give the impression of a man short of a bob. Unless he'd got himself into some trouble he didn't want to tell his parents about, and needed quick money to get out of it.'

'I suppose that's possible. Although why would he bother with a rental place when he could live here?'

'Beats me,' Slider said. 'If it was me, you'd need implements to winkle me out.'

'We'll have to find his bank statements and so on. At least there seems to be plenty of stuff in this flat, not like Conningham Road. This was obviously his real home.'

Yes,' said Slider. 'Too much stuff, really. It's going to take some sorting through. I'll get on to

Hollis, have him send some reinforcements. There's a bedroom set out as an office back there – we may find a diary or something that will tell us what he'd been doing recently. And we'll have to have a word with the sister.'

'Presumably the parents are the next of kin,' Atherton said.

'But she's a lot closer. I wonder what happened about his mail?'

'I asked the porter about that while you were looking round. I noticed there was nothing behind the door when we came in. But he said he sorts it into locked boxes in the hall downstairs and they each collect their own. He's going to open the box for us when we go down.'

'All right. Oh, and let's get a lift off something in his bedroom, just to be absolutely sure the corpse is Corley. This case is confusing enough as it is without any more doubt over identities.'

Slider had just rung off from the conversation with Hollis when his phone rang again. It was the low rumble of Paxman, duty sergeant back at the station, that reached his ear.

'I've got a call for you from a Ewan Delamitri, about your murder case. Asking for you personally – won't talk to anyone else. Says it's important. He sounds nervous as hell. D'you want me to put it through to you?'

'I suppose I'd better speak to him,' Slider said. In a moment Delamitri's voice was in his ear. He did sound nervous – and furtive.

'I've got to talk to you,' he said, with an air of cupping the phone close and glancing over his shoulder. 'I can't come in to the station – some-

153

one might see me. Can I meet you somewhere?'

Slider sighed inwardly at the cloak-and-dagger stuff. 'Is it really necessary?'

'I've got some important information for you,' Delamitri muttered. 'Look, I can't talk. Someone might come any minute. Do you know The Dove, by the river?'

Probably it would turn out to be nothing, Slider reflected, but given that genius is the infinite capacity for taking pains... 'Yes, I know it.'

'That'll be OK. No one I know'll go in there.'

'All right, I'll meet you there. What time?'

'I can be there in an hour.'

'OK.'

Slider rang off, and Atherton said, 'What was all that about?'

'Ewan Delamitri, from Ransom House, fancies he has something important to tell me. And that someone might want to stop him telling.'

'Juicy,' Atherton remarked. 'D'you want me to come?'

'No, I need you to stay here and wait for the troops, get the search properly organized. I'll see you back at the factory later.'

The Dove was an ancient pub on the river bank at Hammersmith, all beams and crooked ceilings. Charles II was supposed to have met one of his mistresses there, in the days when Hammersmith was a holiday spot a good distance from London, with the same slightly louche reputation as Brighton in the fifties. The Dove's entrance was from a narrow stone-flagged alley, which was the only surviving remnant of the original riverside village, comprehensively demolished by the London County Council in the thirties in its pursuit of universal happiness. Ernest Hemingway and Graham Greene were said to have frequented the tiny hostelry, though possibly not at the same time.

In the summer now it was usually crammed with tourists, and Slider thought it was a good bet that no one Ewan Delamitri knew would be there on an August lunchtime.

In addition to its other many charms, The Dove was a Fullers pub, so Slider hastened to secure a pint of Pride before oozing carefully through the crowds to look for his date. He found him lurking in a corner just inside the busy door from the inside to the riverside terrace, popular on this hot summer day. The tide was out, and the exposed shores on either side of the river were colonized by rowdy gangs of black-headed gulls, looking sinister in their summer disguise, and busy lone pigeons, homely and nonchalant in the face of raucous screams and razor sharp bills. Faint airs were moving, bringing the flat smell of clean river mud into the hot, crowded room.

Delamitri was clutching an untouched lager in one of those glasses shaped like a flower vase. There was sweat on his upper lip, but it was pretty stifling in there, which could account for it. There was no more room out on the terrace, and Slider thought Delamitri would feel more secure indoors anyway. Pressed together, and with the cheerful bedlam of conversation all around them, they would be as safe here, he reflected, as anywhere.

'I've got to talk to you about Mike,' Delamitri said, his eyes roving nervously for approaching assassins. 'Mike Horden. You see, that's not his real name.'

'Yes, we guessed that.'

Delamitri looked momentarily thrown, but rallied. 'But you see, I know who he really is. Was,' he corrected himself awkwardly. 'When I first saw him, I thought there was something familiar about him, but it wasn't until he started talking to me about film techniques, and he obviously knew what he was talking about, that it suddenly clicked. You see, he was really Ben Jackson.' He looked at Slider for bouquets.

'Ben Jackson? I'm afraid you're not quite right. We've recently – just today, in fact – discovered that his name was B.J. Corley. His first name *was* Ben, but—' He stopped. The mother's name was Buller-Jackson. What did the 'J' stand for?

Delamitri shook his head emphatically. 'No, I'm telling you. He was Ben Jackson. I *know* he was. He'd disguised himself – dyed his hair, for one thing. It used to be dead black. And he'd cut it differently and he'd shaved off his beard. He used to have this plaited beard, like Johnny Depp in *Pirates* – you know?' Slider nodded. 'But I know I'm not mistaken.'

'Did you say anything to him, about recognizing him?'

'Well, no. I was going to, but it occurred to me that he'd gone to a lot of trouble to disguise himself, and changed his name, so I thought, he

156

doesn't want people to know who he is, so why should I give him away?'

'But if you'd seen through his disguise, it couldn't have been a very good one,' Slider pointed out. 'Did you know him very well?'

Delamitri stared. 'You don't know who Ben Jackson is?'

'I take it he's someone famous?' Slider hazarded.

'Well,' Delamitri said kindly, 'I suppose you can't know everything, and given you're, like, not young ... Ben Jackson, lead singer of Breaking Wave?'

'I *have* heard of Breaking Wave,' Slider said. No need to reveal how recent the knowledge was. So Corley had bought a copy of his own CD, had he? Perhaps he hadn't liked the idea of it languishing like an unwanted puppy in the pound of the second-hand shop. He could understand that.

Delamitri looked sceptical. 'They weren't very big. Only made a few records. *Not Even You,* their first single, never got higher than forty; their second, *You're Killing Me,* went in at thirty-five and got up to eighteen. But *I Didn't Mean It* climbed to number four when its video went viral on YouTube.' He looked at Slider to see if he was following this.

'I know what YouTube is,' he reassured him.

'It'd just been launched then, but Jackson was one of the first to see the potential. *I Didn't Mean It* only succeeded because of the video. It became cult viewing overnight. It even won a Brit award and an MTV award – not the *song,* you understand, but the video. Well, he'd practically produced and directed the video himself, and I suppose he decided the rest of it was a mug's game. He left the band and started making music videos for other artists. He was one of the great cult music video directors.'

'So how did you know him?' Slider asked.

Delamitri stared. 'I didn't know him *personally*. But, see, I'm a bit of a music vid fanatic. I mean, it's my passion, and I was just *totally* into Jackson's work. I've watched MTV and YouTube for years, I follow the directors and swap clips with other fans. He's been one of my heroes since the beginning. I've spent hours looking at him and listening to him on screen. Like, I'm a bit of an obsessive. That's why I recognized him, even with the disguise. I don't suppose anyone else would have spotted him. And even then, it was only when he started talking about the techie stuff that I made the connection anyway.'

'So, what was this famous music video director doing—?' Slider began.

'He wasn't still directing,' Delamitri interrupted earnestly. 'He was brilliant at it, but I suppose after a few successes he got bored and wanted to do something else. About three years ago he gave it up – that was a tragedy! He went to work for *Musical World* – you know, the music magazine? – and as far as I know, he was still working there. I've read articles and stuff he's done for them.'

'You seem to know a lot about him.'

'None of that's a secret,' Delamitri said. 'If

that's what you're interested in, it's all out there, on the Internet. And I told you, he was, like, a hero of mine.'

'So what do you think he was doing at Ransom House?' Slider reverted to his interrupted question. 'Did he talk to you about it?'

'No, he never said, and I didn't like to ask him. Like I said, if he wanted to be in disguise, I wasn't going to blow it for him. But it seems to me he couldn't just have been doing it for the money. He must have been getting residuals from his CDs and videos. And I mean, with his skills and contacts he could have got any job he liked in the music business. In any case, as far as I knew he was still working for *Musical World*. So I reckoned he must be after something.'

'Any idea what that might be?'

Delamitri chewed his lip, frowning and still looking round nervously, and he lowered his voice even more so that Slider had to lean in to him to be able to hear. 'I don't know,' he said – disappointingly – 'but I wouldn't be surprised if he wasn't trying to find something out about Ransom House.'

'And what is there to find out about Ransom House?'

Now Delamitri was surprised. '*I* don't know! I'm only saying maybe that's what Ben Jackson was doing.'

Slider remained patient. 'But what makes you think there might be anything *to* find out?'

He gave a curious little shudder. 'There's something about the boss – Paul Barrow ... I don't know what, but I wouldn't be surprised if he was up to something. He never lets anyone go in his office – it's always locked, even if he's just going to the bog. And he's always having phone conversations no one's allowed to hear. If you come up to him when he's on the phone he goes mad and yells at you. And he can't stand anyone asking questions. That's why he chucked Mike – Ben out.'

'He said it was because he couldn't act.'

'But he could! He was brilliant. Paul thought he was a real find until he started asking questions about the company.'

'Do you think Barrow found out who he was?'

'No,' Delamitri said judiciously. 'I don't think it was that. He'd have been angrier if he had. He just sacked Ben and forgot about him. But there's *something* going on. I don't know what, and I don't want to know, but that company isn't all legit. It's not what it seems.'

This was getting Slider nowhere. Maybe there was something shady below the surface of Ransom House – shadier than porn films, anyway – but on the other hand it might simply be Delamitri paranoia.

'If you're worried about the firm, why do you stay?' he asked.

'I like the job and the pay's good. And Paul – he's a scary bastard, but he leaves me alone artistically. I can pretty well do what I like on the floor. I just run through the basic idea with him and he says go ahead. And with the editing, he usually agrees with my ideas. It's not always like that, believe you me – producers are bastards. That's why directors have to be so pushy and

160

arrogant, to keep their end up against the producers. I am going to leave eventually, when the time's right. I want to get into mainstream movies. But it's not easy, and I'm not going to leave until I've got something lined up to go to.' He looked suddenly alarmed. 'You won't let on you've seen me? You won't tell them what I've said? '

'No, of course not,' Slider said. 'I won't give you away. But why did you risk it, if you're worried about losing your job?'

'For Ben,' he said simply. 'If someone's killed Ben Jackson, I want them caught and punished. He was my hero. He was a genius.'

'Who said anyone killed him?' Slider said.

'He didn't commit suicide. You don't fool me. Someone wanted him out of the way.' He looked suddenly bleak. 'If it was Paul, or any of *his* bosses, getting sacked will be the least of my worries.'

'I told you, I won't give you away.'

He nodded, fixing Slider with a dark, urgent gaze. 'Look into Ransom House. There's something fishy going on, I swear it. Look into Paul Barrow and Ransom House.'

'This gets nuttier by the minute,' said Atherton. 'Robin Williams stroke Mike Horden who is really B.J. Corley is actually Ben Jackson the pop singer?'

'You've heard of him?'

'No, you just told me that's who he was. And Delamitri thinks he was an investigative journalist?'

161

'Well, a journalist, anyway. And that part's true. I rang *Musical World*, and they said he used to work for them, but he handed in his notice at the end of April. They were very upset, begged him to stay, and he said he might do freelance work for them at some time in the future, but they haven't heard from him since. Oh, and his middle name *is* Jackson.'

'End of April,' Atherton said. 'When all this began. Tattoos, Conningham Road, Ransom House. But if he resigned, it couldn't be that he needed money.'

'Unless he needed a lot.'

'You're thinking he was being blackmailed?'

'No, blackmailers don't kill their victims. Just a general need for more money than he could get as a journalist.'

'But then he could have kept his job and done night work.' He shrugged the problem away. 'What are you going to do now?'

'Go and see the sister. Have you found anything interesting yet?'

'No, but there's a stack of stuff to work through. At least we now know what all this sound equipment was for. Oh, I had a look in his mail box.'

'And?'

'Nada. Some junk mail, couple of bills. People don't write to each other any more now there's email. But it struck me there's not very much of it, even the junk mail, for three months, which suggests he's been coming back and picking it up.'

162

'You'll have to check his email, then.'

'Yes. But with everything else it's going to take a while.'

'Well, keep at it,' Slider said, and rang off.

The Haven was a large, plain-faced mid-Victorian house, very square and set squarely in the middle of extensive grounds on the outskirts of Watford. Expanses of lush green, waving trees, the liquid sound of wood pigeons – all very soothing to the urban soul. The entrance was flanked with impressive gateposts topped with stone balls, and the long drive led to a gravel turning area in front of what looked a rather grave edifice, symmetrical and proper. The beauty, however, was only skin deep. Slider stepped through the portico and massive front door into a bathos of modern 'luxury' – acres of over-bright marble, fake columns, gilding, massive mirrors, chandeliers, black glass surfaces, trapped-looking single orchids in heavy angular glass vases. It was a Middle Eastern dictator's wet dream – Gadaffi's private bathroom. An expense of money in a waste of shame.

Behind the huge obsidian desk a very thin, glamorous young woman with a severe suit and an even more severe hair cut – she reminded him of *Frasier*'s Lilith – was looking at him with enquiry but little sympathy. Her enamelled face was not set up for expression, but she was managing to convey that he was not their type, in his worn suit and comfortable shoes. If you have to ask how much, you can't afford it.

She looked even more sceptical when he asked

to see Jennifer Shepstone, almost shuddered with distaste when Slider showed his brief, but consented to 'ring through', never taking her eyes from him as she did it, in case he did something to befoul the place.

Jennifer Shepstone's room, when he was finally conducted to it, was another tragedy. What had once been a handsome morning-room had been stripped back and brutalized, the mouldings and fireplace removed, the walls painted in a matt darkish grey, the floor covered in grey woodstrip, the furniture minimalist and uncomfortable-looking, metal pipe legs, grey fabric, matt black wood, and the sort of 'futuristic' shapes that brought to mind the design revolution of the 1950s. From Gadaffi's bathroom to a Soviet bureaucrat's ante-room.

Mrs Shepstone, however, seemed quite normal – a handsome woman in a beige summer suit, a little alert and wary about Slider's presence, but not frigidly hostile. Slider could see the resemblance to Ben Corley: they really were surprisingly alike, an illusion aided by her height and the firm symmetry of her perfectly made-up face. There had been nothing effeminate about Ben Corley's appearance, but extreme beauty could give that impression of being asexual. Her hair was lightly curly, and black, as his had been in the portrait in the vestibule; her eyes bright blue. It was an attractive combination.

'What can I do for you, Inspector Slider?' she asked.

'Mrs Shepstone, you have a brother whose name is B.J. Corley? Ben Corley?'

164

'Yes.' Her impassive gaze sharpened. Was that simple apprehension at the sudden presence of a police officer in your life, or was there a sensitive spot to be touched?

He braced himself for the bit they all hated. 'Then I'm very sorry to say I have some bad news for you. I'm afraid your brother has been found dead.'

There was the usual shock, pain and denial to be got through. The denial was particularly hard to break down in this case, because there was the problem of the false name and address to get past. She tried to insist for a while that Robin Williams was someone else, the tenant of the flat who just happened to look like her brother. When he told her they had taken a fingerprint from the hairbrush in his bedroom and checked it against that of deceased, she tried to hope that two people could have the same fingerprints. He was reluctant to show her the mugshot of the corpse, but was obliged in the end to do so, and she was convinced at last, and the sorrow and distress arrived like great black birds fluttering down to perch on her.

But she was too strong a woman to give way to it. Her hands clamped themselves together and her jaw was rigid with the effort, but she was in control, and she asked, 'You'd better tell me everything. I shall have to tell my parents, and they will ask questions. You say he was found dead? How?'

'It looked like suicide.' He told her how the body had been found. 'He had also taken some kind of narcotic. It wouldn't have been a painful

165

death,' he added.

'And this was on Sunday night?'

It seemed like a criticism. 'We had the greatest difficulty in identifying him, because there was nothing in the flat to tell us his name, and, as I said, he had given a false name to the landlord.'

'He went away,' she said absently. 'He wouldn't do it at home and upset everyone. He'd know Mummy and Daddy would never be able to forget if he did. They'd never be able to live there again. Did he leave a note?'

'None was found,' Slider said. He would have to tell her it was not suicide, but for the moment he was interested in her reaction. 'Forgive me – you're not surprised at the idea of him killing himself?'

'I *am* surprised,' she said. 'I didn't expect it. Of course he was upset when Annie died, and he seemed a bit strange for a while. But I thought he'd get over it. I never for a moment thought he was so upset he would...' She stared, thinking. 'I suppose he was always one for self-dramatisation. Perhaps underneath he felt things more intensely than we gave him credit for.' She took a moment to control her mouth again. 'He left without saying goodbye to me. That's very hard.'

He ought to tell her now. But there was another question. 'Who's Annie?'

She looked thoughtful. 'It's complicated. I'd better tell you the whole story.'

'If you would. From the beginning.'

'How far back do you want me to go?'

'As far back as you like. I always find the more

166

I know, the better I can understand.'

The Corley children had always been close. Though both their parents had been to public schools, they valued their happy family life and did not want to send their children away, so they had not been separated as they might otherwise have expected to be.

'When we were little we lived in a big house in Sussex, but when Mummy's aunt died she left her the flat in Kensington, so they decided we'd all move to London. It suited Daddy to be nearer his office, and it meant Ben and I could go to day schools.'

Jennifer had gone to Godolphin and Latymer, and Ben had gone to Sussex House and then Westminster.

'They're strong on music and art at Sussex House, and Ben was very musical. Mummy thought at one time he might be a concert pianist, and he had the ability, but not the application. Music is hard work. He wouldn't practice enough. He was always more interested in having fun. No ambition. Unlike both our parents, who are quite simply *driven*. But Ben says you only have one life, so what's the point of wasting it doing things you don't enjoy. I'm afraid he often got bored. Everything came too easily to him. He was so brilliant, he could grasp new things in an instant, but as soon as he'd mastered them, he got bored with them and moved on.'

She made the criticism ruefully, but with affection. Slider noticed the softening of her eyes and mouth when talking about her younger brother: there had been great love there, though she

167

evidently felt he had squandered his birthright.

His brilliance had got him to Cambridge, where he read history. 'Because of Mummy, I think – she's Christine Buller-Jackson, the historian.'

She sounded proud of that. Slider said, 'Yes, I saw the books in the hall.'

'I was forgetting you'd been to the flat,' she said, with what was almost a hostile glance – she didn't like their private space being invaded. But she went on, 'Ben was always her pet. Grandpa's too – he was named for him. Benedict Jackson Corley.'

At Cambridge Ben had got in with the artistic crowd and, always eager for anything that was not like work, he joined the Footlights. 'He was quite a star among them, partly because he was so good looking; but he was a natural actor.' She smiled at some memory. 'He was always acting parts when we were children. He'd put on funny voices or a different walk and suddenly he'd *be* the pirate or the Roman centurion. You never knew who you'd be with next. Excess of imagination, I suppose. He had so much of everything inside him it just spilled out. I'm not like that. I'm a striver. I could only get on through sheer hard work.'

Slider got the picture – the golden boy, good at everything, flamboyant and attention-grabbing; the quiet sister who shared the parents' values but somehow never got the praise. She might resent the situation, but not the beguiling brother.

With his musical background he was also in

with the musical crowd, and after a couple of false starts he formed the band called Breaking Wave. They were popular among the students, and did various gigs on an amateur basis, but in a crowded field they didn't stand out. But after graduation – 'He never got better than a third in any part of the tripos, because he wouldn't work, which is so typical of him!' – his parents offered him a gap year, and instead of travelling, which is want they expected and wanted, he used it to work on his band.

He found a new bass guitarist-songwriter, and they collaborated on writing their own material, changing their style to something more funky. For a couple of years he did odd jobs – waiting, bar work – to earn money while the band did the club circuit ('Paying your dues, it was called') and sent demos to record companies. Their distinctive style took time to find its niche, and it wasn't until 2004 they had a demo accepted, and *Not Even You* got into the charts at number forty-nine.

'He used the name Ben Jackson,' Jennifer Shepstone said, 'because Mummy and Daddy didn't quite approve of the band as a way of life, and would have been upset if "Benedict Corley" had become famous as a pop star.'

She told Slider the same story he had had from Delamitri, about Ben's change to video directing. 'He'd succeeded as a pop singer, so he had to do something else,' she said. 'I was pleased if anything – it seemed a better outlet for his talents. And he was very good at it. Some of his videos became very famous. He did *A Million*

Boys for Asset Strippers and *Here Goes Nothing* for Okay Gurlz – he won awards for both of those.'

Slider smiled. 'I don't know much about pop music. My daughter likes Girls Aloud and The Saturdays.

'*I* didn't know anything until Ben got into that scene. Now I know more than I want to,' she said with a downturned mouth. 'I was glad he was successful, of course, but I couldn't like what he was doing. I was glad when he got bored again and changed to music journalism. I thought his videos were hateful – very clever, I could see that, but all that sexual miming and the suppressed violence was – well, it's just trash, isn't it? Pernicious trash. When he could have been a concert pianist. But you can't live other people's lives for them.'

'No,' said Slider.

'All I wanted was for him to be successful. And I've no regrets for myself. I've done well out of my chosen profession, though my parents rather pooh-poohed it, as if I'd said I wanted to be a hairdresser. But there's a lot to learn in the beauty industry before you can get to where I have. Chemistry, biology, a certain amount of anatomy and medicine, dietetics, nutrition, all sorts of physical therapies. I started with a small high-street salon, opened the first women-only spa in central London, and now with Hugh's backing – my husband – I have all this.' She waved a hand round the grim grey bus shelter décor, which was probably the apogee of fashion, for all Slider knew. 'Not bad for a mere girl,' she concluded.

'You think your parents favoured Ben because he was a boy?' Slider put in, really just to keep her talking.

But it threw a switch and she stopped with a blank, arrested look in her eyes. 'He's dead. Talking like this, I'd forgotten why you're here. How could I?'

'It happens all the time,' Slider said soothingly.

'I can't believe it. And how will I ever tell Mummy and Daddy?'

The time was fast approaching when he would have to tell her it wasn't suicide, but before that there was the topic she hadn't reached yet. 'You were going to tell me about Annie,' Slider said.

NINE

Pop Tart

'I hated Ben's time in the pop world,' said Jennifer Shepstone. An assistant had brought in coffee, and she sipped slowly as she talked, holding the cup in two hands for comfort like someone drinking hot chocolate after a cold winter walk. 'It wasn't so bad at the beginning, when the band was doing the circuit and not very well known. He was having fun, and it all seemed very innocent. They would drink a lot of beer after the shows, and I suspect they sometimes smoked a joint. Well,' she added reluctantly, 'I know they did, because Ben told me. He insisted it wasn't harmful, no different from Daddy's after-dinner brandy. But at least he had the sense to keep it from Mummy and Daddy, because they would have had a fit if they knew.

'But once the band became successful it didn't stop there. It wasn't just beer it was vodka, lots of it, and it wasn't just pot–' she used the old-fashioned word without embarrassment – 'it was cocaine, and sometimes ecstasy as well. At first he was self-conscious about it – it was almost like a little boy showing off. But once he got into the video side, and he was mixing with the big name bands, it was just part of the scene. Everyone was doing it, and he didn't see anything wrong with it. That was what worried me most – that it would escalate, because he wasn't thinking about it any more. I was terrified he'd get on to something even worse.'

She poured more coffee, her hand shaking just a little, and offered him another cup.

'No thanks,' he said. 'It's excellent, but one cup's enough for me.' Each man to the drug of his choice. 'So, did he? Get on to something worse?'

'No, thank God,' she resumed. 'It was bad enough as it was, but we were spared that. And then he met Annie. Annabella Casari. English, despite the name, though the family was Italian by blood. Her parents owned a restaurant in the East End – ordinary people, comfortably off but not educated. Annie was a backing singer in Asset Strippers when Ben met her – he was doing the video for their new single. Oddly enough,' she said, looking up at him, 'it was because of seeing her in the video that he'd fallen for her in the first place. I never understood why. She was a skinny little thing, nothing to look at, and I could never see anything in her. Anyway, it seemed Ben didn't like seeing her doing that half-naked sadomasochistic act in his video, even though he'd written it himself. He got all stern and protective – quite illogical.' She gave a quavery smile. 'He thought she was better than that, that she could make it as a solo artist, and introduced her to his agent Danny – Danny Ballantine. He saw the potential and took her on.

Changed her look and her name, found her a writing team, launched her, and with Ben doing the videos she made a hit. I expect you've heard of her – her stage name was Kara.'

'Oh,' said Slider. When a pop singer was known by one name only, it was hard not to at least have *heard* of them; though searching memory, he could not accuse himself of knowingly having listened to anything she sang. The connection in his mind was from an incident – or was it two incidents? – of drink-and-drugs-fuelled public disorder leading to arrest and photographs in the paper the next day. And if two of them had made the papers, it was likely there had been more than two, on a rising scale of seriousness.

'I can see you've heard of her,' Mrs Shepstone said with some bitterness.

'I think I've seen her picture in the papers,' he said politely.

'Yes, for all the wrong things. That was when I really started to learn about the way those people live. A few drinks after a show to wind down escalates into heavy drinking sessions and late-night parties. Beer becomes vodka – or any other spirit that comes to hand, but for some reason they seem to prefer vodka. And drink isn't enough, so out comes the cocaine. But as the cocaine wears off they start feeling the down, so they drink more to compensate, and then they feel better so they take more cocaine.'

'I know,' said Slider.

But she wanted to talk. 'And so it goes on. Waking up feeling terrible, breakfasting on vodka and orange juice, taking a line or two before rehearsal just to give them an edge, more drink before the show, more drugs, more and more of everything after the show. Staying up all night partying, not eating properly. Tremors, nausea, sweating, anxiety, paranoia, fits of temper, loss of boundaries, promiscuity, dangerous, stupid behaviour. Annie turned out to be as weak-minded as the worst of them. Got herself into such a mess, Ben and Danny persuaded her to go into a rehabilitation centre – The Denes. Not far from here, as it happens.'

'I know it,' said Slider.

'When she came out, she promised Ben she wouldn't take any more drugs. The one thing she did for him was to put him completely off it himself. After her first crash he stopped, and as far as I know he never touched another thing. He even moderated his drinking.'

'And were they...' He wasn't sure what the right word was in this circumstance. 'A couple? Were they together?'

'Oh, he was mad about her. I could never understand why – unless it was a Svengali thing. And she loved him – well, why wouldn't she? They weren't living together officially, but they were together so much they might as well have been. She had her own place by then, a flat in St John's Wood. He was still living at home, and the parents were around a lot more at that point, so he didn't bring her there. They stayed at her place, when they weren't on the road.'

'So, what happened? After she came out of The Denes.'

'It all went wrong again very quickly. I think she only stayed straight about a week. Weakminded, as I said. She was back on the cocaine, and it just escalated until after a few months she was as bad as before. If not worse. I think I read somewhere she started smoking heroin as well. Can you smoke heroin? Anyway, eventually she got into some kind of trouble with the police outside a nightclub, got arrested, and it was all over the papers the next day. Her record company insisted she go back into The Denes. When she came out, Ben told her it was over between them.'

'He'd fallen out of love?'

She hesitated. 'I don't think it was that. I think he still loved her – though he was angry and hurt that she'd let him down – but he couldn't cope with what went with it. Now *he* was straight, the stupidity of the drugs scene bored him, and the one thing he could never cope with was boredom. They still met from time to time and they were still friends, but not lovers. He said she could have cocaine or him but not both.'

'And she chose cocaine.'

'I'm not sure there was much choice in it by then. You probably know better than me how these things go.' She shrugged. 'Ben had left the pop scene by then and gone into music journalism, though of course his contacts were what made him valuable and he still visited backstage to get interviews and gossip. So he watched Annie's deterioration from a not very great distance. She spiralled downwards, lost her recording contract, lost everything, had to give up her flat and go home to her parents. Apparently with their help she got off the cocaine again, but it was too late. She died on the twenty-fourth of February from what they said was a heart attack. At the age of twenty-six.'

Slider knew the pathology: it was all too common. Cocaine increased the heart rate and the blood pressure, but in large doses it also reduced the heart's ability to contract. So a decreasing myocardial oxygen supply met the increasing demand of the faster heart rate, leading to convulsions, respiratory failure, myocardial ischaemia or infarction. Not only that, but cocaine and alcohol taken together created a chemical called cocaethylene in the body which was extremely toxic and directly affected the heart. Parts of the heart tissue could die – he had seen extensive necrosis at post-mortems. Even someone who was now completely straight could have so damaged their heart that the slightest extra strain – getting up out of a chair – could be too much.

'How did Ben take it?' he asked.

'Shocked, of course – she was so young – and, as I said, I think he still loved her. Angry about the whole drugs scene and how everybody just pretended it was all right, that cocaine was no different from a gin-and-tonic. In retrospect he hated the lifestyle he used to be part of – the stupidity of "living it large" as they say.' She gave a tired smile. 'It's the zeal of the convert, isn't it?'

'There's nothing worse than being stone-cold sober when everyone around you is giggling drunk,' Slider said.

177

'Hm,' she said, as if doubting he was taking it seriously enough.

He went on quickly. 'You said earlier that he became a bit strange. What did you mean by that?'

'Well, for a while he went on about drugs and drug pushers and saying that Annie could have stayed straight if people hadn't egged her on. Though personally, I doubt it. She was rather a whiny, defeatist sort of person, from the little I knew of her. Self-indulgent and self-pitying – she did what she wanted to, but the consequences were always someone else's fault. But then it stopped and he went very quiet. All you could get out of him was a "Hmm", and a "Sorry?", as if he wasn't really listening. The next thing I heard was that he had left his job with *Musical World*. He rang me one day and told me, and I asked him how he was going to earn his living. Mummy and Daddy let him live at the flat, but they've always insisted that he pays his way. Although they're pretty well off, as I imagine you must have guessed, they've never allowed either of us to count on that. They wanted Ben in particular to stand on his own two feet.'

'And what did he say he was going to do?'

'That's what I meant by strange. He was being secretive about it, which was not like him. He said, "Don't worry about me. I'm going to be very busy for a while." And when I asked him, busy doing what, he wouldn't tell me.'

'How did he sound when he said it? Happy, sad, excited – what?'

'Nothing in particular. He just said it; as if it

178

was quite ordinary, just something he had to do. That's why I thought he was over Annie, and getting on with his life. I was pleased – only wondering why he wouldn't tell me what it was.'

'What did you *think* it was?'

'I suppose I suspected it was something Mummy and Daddy might not approve of. Or some mad scheme he knew I would tell him was impractical. But he wouldn't say any more, so I had to leave it. Oh, and he said he might be away from home quite a bit, so not to phone him – he would phone me.'

'And did he?'

She frowned. 'Well, now you mention it, he didn't. But that wasn't unusual. We were always very fond of each other, but we had our separate lives. It wouldn't surprise me not to hear from him for a couple of months – and vice versa. We tended to catch up when the parents came home, but this year they haven't been home since February – Daddy had work to do in Canada, so he said they'd holiday on the west coast of America this summer.'

'So you last heard from him – when?'

'It would be – about the beginning of April, I suppose. About six weeks after Annie died.'

'And you've no idea what he might have been doing since then?'

'Not the slightest.' She looked haunted now. 'I should have tried to find out, shouldn't I? I shouldn't have just left him to his own devices. But I thought he was all right. And you know how it is. The days go by so quickly when you're busy and you don't notice how long it's been. I never really have time to stop and think – there's always something coming up. When you run your own business, it's twenty-four-seven and three-six-five. I didn't know he was so unhappy he would do something like that.'

He had felt sympathy with her until she said 'twenty-four-seven and three-six-five'. But he squashed his linguistic sensibilities and said, 'You don't need to feel guilty. Everybody's busy these days. And in fact, although I said it looked like suicide, I don't think he did kill himself.'

She stared. 'What? What do you mean?'

'It looks,' he said carefully, 'rather as though someone killed him and then staged it to look like suicide.'

She was almost speechless. 'But you ... Why did you say—?' She reddened. 'You let me think—'

'I wanted to give you time to get over the first shock. Now I have to ask you if you can think of anyone who might have had reason to harm your brother.'

'No,' she said, sounding bewildered. 'I told you, I don't know what he's been doing these past few months. Before that – well, I don't know who he knew. I never mixed in that circle. What are you saying – someone *murdered* him?'

'I'm afraid it looks that way. Your brother was left-handed, wasn't he?'

'Yes, from babyhood. They say left-handed-ness often goes with artistic talent. Mummy's left-handed too. Daddy and I are both right-handed.'

'The fatal wound seems to have been adminis-

180

tered by a right-handed person. And there are other factors I can't go into that suggest it was murder.'

'I can't believe it,' she said flatly, staring at him as if to force him to recant. 'People don't get murdered. Not ordinary people.'

'I'm not sure everyone would think of your brother as being an ordinary person,' Slider said. 'And he doesn't seem to have led a humdrum life.'

'No,' she said. 'Not humdrum. Not Ben.' And then she made a strange sound and put her hands over her face.

There was a little knot of people around Atherton's desk – Hollis, Swilley and Atherton himself – looking over the shoulder of someone clattering away at the keyboard. As Slider moved across the room he saw it was Emily. She was in a business suit, and there was a flight bag on the floor beside her, from which he deduced – being the ace detective he was – that she had just got back from Paris and had called in to see Atherton on the way home.

No one looked up at him, so he said, 'I know all about Ben Jackson now. *And*, he had a relationship with Kara.'

Swilley answered at him. 'We know. That's what we're looking at.'

'Emily knew,' Atherton said. 'As soon as we said Ben Jackson, she was off and running.'

Emily peered apologetically round the screen. 'I remembered the various fusses. Well, it's my job to keep up with the news. She died of heart failure from excessive use of cocaine.'

'I know,' said Slider sturdily.

'We've looked at one of her pop videos,' Atherton said with a mild shudder. 'It's important to try to remember that Kara comes from the Greek, meaning sweet melody.'

'She's a sexy dancer, though,' Hollis said.

'Violent hip thrusts, suggestive of someone with their skirt caught in a lift door, is not sexy.'

Hollis ignored him. 'Guv, is it possible there was someone connected with Kara who blamed Ben Jackson for her death?'

'Why should they?' Slider asked.

'Well, because he got her started as a soloist. She were just a backing singer before.'

'I'm sure everyone in the business comes into contact with drugs,' Slider said. 'She'd have been backstage with the stars and the roadies and the hangers on long before she and Jackson – Corley – whatever – were an item. We'll have to decide what to call this man,' he added peevishly, 'before he drives us all nuts. I think we should go with Corley from now on.'

'What did you find out from the sister?' Atherton asked.

'Nothing much. Except that he *was* left-handed. He apparently rang her in early April to say he was going to be busy, wouldn't say busy doing what, and said he might be away from home quite a bit, and not to ring him. And that's the last she heard.'

'April,' said Swilley. 'Just about when all this starts. So he deliberately cut himself off, took the flat under a false name, got the job as a porn

182

star – what the hell is it all about?'

'Porn star?' said Emily, startled.

'She did say the parents, though rich, did not pony up at the slightest demand,' Slider said. 'Wanted both children to stand on their own two feet. He was allowed to live at the family flat but had to earn his own living.'

'So maybe he did the porn thing just for the money after all,' said Hollis.

'What porn thing?' Emily pleaded.

'But then why would he take on the rented flat?' Swilley said, while Atherton answered Emily's question in a murmur.

'And it was the beginning of May when he got the job at Ransom's,' Slider pointed out. 'What was he doing for the month before?'

'Research,' Swilley suggested.

'More's the point, what's he been doing since?' Hollis added. 'He was out o' Ransom's by the end o' May.'

'Well, we all identify the questions very readily,' Slider said. 'What I'd like is someone to find some answers. Where's everyone else?'

'McLaren, Connolly, and Fathom are at the flat. Gascoyne was still out hunting pizza last we heard, and Mackay will have gone off to the clubs by now,' said Atherton.

'All right, well you can finish up and get off. Nothing more to do here tonight.'

'What'll you do?' Atherton asked. 'Emily and I are going for something to eat.' He saw Slider was not really listening, and added provocatively, 'We're going to try that new Jewish-Italian place, Kosher Nostra.'

'Thanks,' Slider said vaguely, 'but I want to talk to Jackson's agent.'

'Corley's agent, boss,' Swilley corrected. 'Though that sounds wrong given he was Jackson when he needed an agent.'

'Oh, blast the man,' Slider said. 'Too many names spoil the broth.'

'As Mr Porson would say,' came a composite murmur from the troops.

He reached for his telephone but it rang before he could touch it.

'Bill, my old fruit bat!' someone bellowed in his ear.

Tufnell Arcenaux from the forensic lab usually referred to himself as the bodily fluids man, and given his huge appetites in all fields of human enjoyment it was an apt sobriquet. With the reorganization of the service he was also now in charge of toxicology, which was fortunate for Slider. Tox results had always taken weeks in the pre-Tufty days, but now Tufty put a rocket under anything that was wanted for his old chum Bill.

Tufty was a huge man – six foot five and muscled to match – and he had a huge voice, a sonic boom that could have unclogged drains from thirty feet away. Slider always had to hold the receiver some distance from his ear or risk having his fillings shaken loose.

'Tufty,' he said mildly. 'Is that you, or has Krakatoa erupted again?'

'Sorry!' Tufty howled at a slightly decreased volume. 'People tell me I tend to shout a bit. I'll try and lower the jezebels. How are you, anyway, my old banana? Getting any?'

'Getting so much I'm thinking of opening a branch,' Slider said. 'How about you?'

'You know me, old horse. Life affirmation is my creed. How's the lovely lady?'

'A bit thoughtful at the moment. Wondering whether to go for a more stressful job or give up on ambition.'

'Bugger the way it always comes down to that,' Tufty roared sympathetically. 'Shinning up the ziggurat's all very well, but like the gorilla and the waistcoat, you have to have the stomach for it. Any idea which way she'll jump?'

'None. I wish I had, then I could say the right things.'

'You could give her an honest opinion.'

'Haven't got one. I can see arguments on both sides.'

'Ah, yes, the curse of Libra. Well, chum, to take part you have to send off the entry form. Who dares wins. You can't be in two minds without having two faces. And it's the rolling stone that escapes getting cemented into the foundations of a dinky bungalow on the Chelmsford Bypass.'

'Thank you, Old Moore.'

Tufty's voice became a sympathetic bellow. 'Chin up, old bean. You know what I'd do if I were in your shoes?'

'You'd limp. Your feet are twice the size of mine. Have you rung up for a reason, or just to swap aphorisms?'

'A for isms and L for leather. And T for tox work rushed through the system.'

'You've got a result for me already?'

185

'Miracles we do while you wait. The impossible probably not until tomorrow. The drug your corpse ingested was an old-fashioned barbiturate. Not enough to kill, just enough to put him to sleep – in the human, not the veterinary sense.'

'Barbiturate?'

'Phenobarbital, if you want to be picky. In injectable form it's used to control seizure. As a sleeping pill it's pretty much been superseded, but some doctors still prescribe it for people who are intolerant of the benzodiazepines, or find they don't work for them. Trouble with insomnia, it's largely self-diagnosed. Someone says old Morpheus is on permanent secondment, you can't prove otherwise. You have to take their word for it, or—'

'Or not.'

'Quite.'

'So easy enough to get hold of?'

'Easy and peasy. You get it from your own GP if you know the right words, and if not, you can get it on the Internet these days. And the beauty of barbiturate is it comes in a white powder which dissolves readily in alcohol without leaving a taste. So you can slip it in your sipper and Bob's your uncle.'

'I see. Well, thanks, Tufty. That's cleared up one thing. There were no capsule cases in the stomach.'

'So I understand. Phenobarbital goes well with suicide or murder, but white powder's a pain to carry about in your pocket, so if you didn't find the handy container—'

'Which we didn't – it's another pennyweight

186

on murder's side.'

'And how's the case going?' Tufty asked kindly.

'As smoothly as a Jerusalem artichoke through a pasta press.'

'That smoothly? Ah well, keep buggering on, old gumshoe. You'll get there. Eventually.'

The name Danny Ballantine had led Slider to expect another skinny young Scot like Ewan Delamitri, an expectation stubbornly not dispelled by the voice over the phone, which was older, richer and more undeniably English than it had any right to be.

Ballantine had said he would wait on at his office in Archer Street to speak to Slider, though it was past home-time. The office was above a vegan restaurant called SeEds, the extraneous capital in the middle giving Slider something to wonder about as he climbed the stairs. The large outer office, supplied with plenty of hard chairs for the hopeful or desperate, was empty and dark, but the door to the warmly-lighted inner office was open, and as Slider arrived a figure appeared in the doorway with a decanter full of amber liquid hospitably in hand.

'Drink?' he said. 'Sun's over the yardarm.'

'Thanks,' said Slider.

The man before him was as little like *his* Danny Ballantine as it was possible to be. In fact, he was nothing like any Danny Slider could have imagined, though he could have been a Dan or a Daniel. He was tall, well over six foot, and massive, with the figure of an Edwardian clubman straining against the waistcoat of his expensive and beautiful three-piece suit – which was finished off with a spotted bow-tie and a watch-chain across the embonpoint. He had thick, kinky dark hair, ferociously slicked back and down. Enormous glasses rested on a small, sharp nose like a little hard triangle in the middle of his wide, fat face, and he had so many spare tyres round his neck he looked as though his chin was resting on a stack of crumpets. But he moved briskly on exquisitely-shod feet, and his pudgy hands knew their business, as they arranged two cut-glass tumblers, poured generously, and injected a short stream from the siphon into one.

'Soda?' he offered. ''Ice?'

'Just as it comes, thanks,' said Slider.

'Ah, a purist, eh? Well done.'

Slider had followed him back into the inner office, which was just as it ought to be, dim, mellow, book-lined and panelled, so much mahogany you could have reverse-engineered a rainforest. There was a vast antique desk, leather chairs, comforting lighting, and even a leather globe of the world in a mahogany stand which opened up to reveal the drinks cabinet inside. It was a superb piece of theatre. Yet when Slider managed to get a proper look at his face – hard to do with the fat and the chins and the big spectacles and the whole distracting air of anachronism – he was not that old, probably not above forty-two or so.

'Well,' he said, easing himself into the chair behind the desk and waving Slider to another.

188

'Ben Jackson, eh? Have that chair, it's the most comfortable. Cigar? Mind if I do? I don't smoke during office hours, but I do like one when the day's toil is over. I find it relaxing. Not that it all ends with office hours in this business, as I expect you can imagine. So what's happened to Ben?'

'When did you last see or speak to him?' Slider countered.

Ballantine was lighting his cigar, but the eyes watching Slider through the initial puffs were thoughtful. 'Like that, is it?' he said, when he removed it from his mouth. 'What's he done? No, I understand, you won't tell me until I've told you. Well, I won't disguise he was one of my favourite clients. So much talent it was hard to know where to start with him. I was devastated when he went into journalism – terrible waste. But I never thought it would be permanent. He'd do it for a few months and get bored and come back to me. That boy's capacity for boredom is terrifying, you know. And then there was that Kara business – you know about that?'

'I know they had been going out together, and she died.'

'That's it. Terrible when they burn out so young. But some people have that seed of self-destruction in them, and she was one. There's nothing you can do for them when it's like that. I tried to warn Ben not to get involved, but he'd been smitten with Saint George-itis when she was an unknown. She had that waif-like look – and she *was* a nice girl underneath, should have been a suburban housewife, really, except that she was cursed with the ability to sing and a longing to be in "showbiz".'

Slider could hear the deprecatory inverted commas he put round the phrase. It was obvious that getting Danny Ballantine to talk was not going to be the problem, but he had a rich mellifluous voice and listening to him was no hardship at all; though Slider got the impression he had learned to do the talking-schtick at some point as a form of self-defence. Had he been a tall, fat teenager who was made fun of? Had girls laughed at him instead of going out with him? Had boys called him jelly belly and nancy-boy because he was no good at sports? The bow tie, the suit, the office, the cut glass, the cigar – they could all be smoke and mirrors, so that no one would ever get a glimpse of the real Danny Ballantine, cowering inside the fat dude, not wanting to be looked at.

'So he was really upset about Kara's death?' Slider prompted.

'Of course he was. Although, to be frank, I think he'd fallen out of love with her almost completely by the end. It's hard to remain in love with someone who vomits on your shoes as a means of communication. And who has sex with roadies and assistant stage managers in the dressing room.'

'She was unfaithful to him?'

'Oh, I wouldn't call it that. She wasn't responsible for her actions when she was wired. That's rather the point, isn't it? Anyway, they weren't still together by then so it's moot whether you can call it unfaithfulness. But he was still fond of

190

her, and he felt responsible for her. He'd tried so hard – we both had – to get her straight, but it was not to be. As a matter of fact, dying was the best thing she could have done for her career – her sales took a tremendous upturn. But you couldn't expect Ben to see it that way. So I understood that he had to go away and get over it. He was entitled to a period of mourning. Interestingly, I'd say his reaction to her death was more anger than sorrow.'

'Anger?'

'Absolute bloody fury that Charlie had got her in the end, despite all his efforts. Now is that love or pique at being bested? No, let's be generous and say both. He was furious at the whole drugs culture and the people who pushed it and the people who profited by it. I said, "Ben, my pet, pick a war you can win. It's only in the Bible David beats Goliath". And of course he knew that. After the anger, the languor. He rang me to say he'd given up the journalism job and he was going away for a bit to get his head together.'

'Are those the words he used?' Slider asked.

'I can't remember – does it matter? He said he was going away and would be out of touch for a bit. I was rather heartened that he told me, because obviously there was nothing for me to do for him while he was working for *Musical World*, but it didn't mean there was nothing I *wanted* to do for him, and if a little break like this could get it out of his system and put him back on my books I'd be delighted. I'd told him all along he had to come back. We could have reformed the band – comebacks are all the rage now, and the record companies love them: the fans are that much older, with more money and a lot of nostalgia, jobs and mortgages, want to recapture their carefree youth. And they're the ones who *buy* music, rather than illegally downloading it, so the labels know they can actually make some money. And on the tours, of course. That's where the real money is now, in the music business, the live tours. Or he could have gone solo. Voice like an angel, very musical, and a nice bod. I've got a very sweet boy, new on my books, songwriter looking for an artist, Ben would be just right for him. But it's hard work unless you're dedicated, and I was never entirely sure he was, so I know exactly what he *really* ought to be looking at – TV presenting!' A real enthusiasm, as opposed to the theatrical one, now lit his eyes behind the safety glass. 'He'd be absolutely bloody brilliant as a youth presenter – the looks, the voice, the charisma, the acting ability, the pop credentials! And I happen to know that Five is commissioning a new early-evening pop- and gossip-based teen programme – *Large on Saturday*, or *Saturday Large* or something like that. They're looking for the right presenter, or they will be as soon as everyone comes back from the summer break, and I *know* I can get it for him. He'd be perfect – *beyond* perfect. So if the foolish boy will only contact me, we can get our word in before the usual tired old names muddy the pool. I'm not the only one who'll have heard about the new show, sadly. And I happen to know that Phil Silverstein, the old ghoul, wants to get something for his kid Ash

Dooley, to get him off cable and into the mainstream.'

'When did you last speak to Ben?' Slider got the question in before another stream could carry him away.

'When he told me he was going away,' Ballantine answered, straight for once. 'That was – let me think – three months? My God, no, must be nearly four. April, it must have been.'

'And nothing since then? Not a phone message, postcard – anything?'

'No,' said Ballantine, looking at him seriously now. 'So what's he done? If he's in trouble, I want to help. He's impulsive, like all these artists, but he's a good boy underneath, I promise you. Whatever he's done, he's not malicious. What is it? Tell me the worst.'

So Slider did. 'I'm afraid he's dead.'

A long and desperate stillness came over Ballantine. He had spoken regretfully of Kara, but there was real feeling here.

'No,' he said at last.

'I'm sorry,' said Slider.

'No,' he said again. 'No. Not Ben.'

And Slider saw with consternation that the eyes, the colour of coffee beans, behind the big glasses had filled with tears.

TEN

A Little Night Music

'But who would kill a lovely boy like Ben?' he mourned.

'That's what I'm hoping you can help me with,' said Slider. 'Did he have any enemies?'

'No, no, everybody liked him. They all thought he was a great guy. He was friendly to everybody – not just the artists but the crews as well. Remembered their birthdays, asked after their mums, that sort of thing.'

'Well, did anyone have a grudge against him? Someone jealous of his success? Maybe a rival for Kara's affections?'

'Not that I can think of.'

'Someone who blamed him for Kara's death?' Slider thought he might as well try Hollis's suggestion.

'No, nothing like that. If anything, it was the other way round.'

He stopped himself abruptly at the end of that sentence, and Slider said, 'What is it? You've thought of something.'

He looked uneasy. 'No, not really. It's nothing. Look, I don't want you to read too much into this.'

'I promise I won't,' Slider said with a sort of grim whimsy. 'What is it?'

'Well, he did have a bit of a dust-up with a chap, Jesse Guthrie. I'm absolutely not saying he has anything to do with it, you understand? Because it was nothing, just a bit of flying fisticuffs, that's all. Apparently Ben bumped into Jesse at a night club and had a row with him. This would have been about March-time, in his angry period. He accused Jesse of selling cocaine to Kara. I've *no* idea if there was anything in the accusation. But he started shouting, threw a punch, the two of them got into an undignified scuffle, and the door attendants threw them both out. That was all. Really.'

'Who is Jesse Guthrie?'

'Oh, sorry – he's one of Asset Strippers' crew. That's the name of a band.'

'I know.'

Ballantine gave him a 'Really?' eyebrow. 'He's a gofer, I believe. Nobody important. The only reason I knew about it is that Murray Mann, the Strippers' manager, rang up to complain to me the next day. He said my boy's attack was unprovoked, and Jesse was peeved that he'd been thrown out of the club as well, when it wasn't his fault. I told Murray that Ben wasn't my boy any more and it was nothing to do with me, and I also told him, gratis and free of charge, to tell Jesse Guthrie to grow up or go home to his mother. End of story.' He looked anxiously at Slider. 'You see why I said it wasn't important?'

'It probably *is* nothing, but you never know what will turn out to be important in the end, so

195

you were right to tell me,' Slider said. 'What night club was it?'

'Oh, blessed if I can remember. They're all the same, these places, loud music and sloppy kids, whether it's Annabel's or – *Vanya's*.' He short circuited himself. 'That was it. Didn't think I'd remember. Vanya's. It's a club just round the corner in Wardour Street.'

'I know,' said Slider for the second time. The things he knew nowadays! And Vanya's had also been one of the places that Paul Barrow worked. Oh, he did like it when things linked up. 'One last thing,' he went on, to take Ballantine's mind off his treachery, 'money. Was Ben earning anything from royalties, if that's what they're called?'

'Well, not a great deal. Breaking Waves' CDs aren't still being sold, except second hand. But the songs are still sometimes performed as covers, so as the writer Ben gets a royalty each time. He gets performance royalties when they're played on radio or TV – they're quite strong in the States; there's a little cult thing going on there. And he gets something from the videos he did for the big-name bands. I suppose all in all it amounts to about twenty thousand a year.'

Slider hadn't expected it to be so much. 'So he's not broke.'

'Given that he lives rent free in his parents' flat, he probably manages,' said Ballantine. 'But we can all do with a little more, am I right? Why did you want to know?'

'I just wondered how badly he needed a job.'

'A job? That's not at all Ben's style.' And suddenly there were tears again, and he drew out a pristine handkerchief, the sort it would be a crime to blow on, and snuffled into it. 'Look at me,' he apologized. 'I can't get used to the idea. Who would *do* such a thing?' He removed his glasses carefully and dried his eyes. 'I'm going to have to have another whisky. How about you?'

'Thanks, but I have to get back,' Slider said. He felt a bit guilty about leaving him, though – large and fleshy and hurting, like a melancholy manatee.

It would be silly not to go to Vanya's while he was so close, so he rang home to check that Dad was all right. Joanna had also been out all day, with three recording sessions – ten to one, two to five and six to nine. Precious income, but it made a long day for his father.

But Mr Slider said calmly, 'All's well here, son. My boy's in bed and asleep, and I'm having my bit o' supper and watching the cricket, so you do what you have to do.'

He wished Dad hadn't mentioned supper. He was starving, but he couldn't face any of the fast food on offer, having smelt it. Subs, KFC, Big Macs – it was a shabby outpost of the Great American Dream. Even the one fish and chip shop he passed was reeking with doner kebab, and Phil Rabin's had closed down years ago. His stomach would just have to get on with it and growl.

The evening was stifling, with a wet, oppressive weight to the air that kept all the smells contained. It didn't seem to bother the crowds – mostly tourists at this time of year, milling with an aimless sort of movement, gaping about them, stopping in the middle of the pavement to consult maps. Natives identified themselves by their brisker pace, Londoners threading their way through the knots at breakneck speed like slalom skiers; groups of youngsters from out of town clattering and guffawing and shrieking on their way to a night out that would not be nearly as 'mental' as they hoped, though they would do their best to make enough noise to disguise the fact.

At Vanya's there was a queue of young people waiting to get in, the girls with micro-skirts and white legs, balancing on heels so high they'd need the fire brigade to get them down; boys lounging, hands in pockets, trying to look cool and scornful, a little army of spotty James Deans. Slider walked past them and up to the bouncer – though you weren't supposed to call them that any more. Even door attendant was not flattering enough; these days it was probably Personnel Admittance Executive; or Vice President of A&Cs.

This one was a collector's specimen: a huge and immovable bald man in dark glasses, with the sort of body never meant to fit in a suit. A menhir in Man at M&S. His upper arms were like thighs, his wrists like ankles, his fingers thick as pork sausages. His chest was so broad his nipples were in different time zones. He looked as if he could lift weights with his tongue. He inspected Slider's ID carefully but without comment, and unhooked the velvet rope to let him past with massive indifference. He had one of those curly plastic wires behind his ear and seemed to be less interested in Slider than in what was coming through it, though whether that was terse orders from Pennsylvania Avenue or something humalong from Take That there was no way of knowing.

Inside they were still setting up, though the music was already on, at brain-bouncing volume, and the pink and blue lights were throbbing as the staff hurried about their tasks. They were all wearing black trousers, white shirts and sparkly red waistcoats with striped backs and matching bow ties. Slider went up to the bar and managed to attract the attention of a young man who was stacking bottles of champagne into a glass-fronted chiller. Presumably the clientele who were going to be ordering them would not be queuing with the polloi outside.

It was hard to make himself understood against the volume of the dance music, but the flash of his ID got the man to stand still at least and listen. Inevitably, he said he didn't know anything about the fracas. 'But I only been here two month,' he said in an all-purpose mid-European accent. 'You want talk to François. He long time – many, many month.'

François was tall, brisk, and introduced himself as line manager, and though impatient to the point of exasperation at being interrupted in his duties when the barman called him, he quickly resigned himself when he saw the ID and led Slider into a stockroom behind the bar where the music was at least muted. Here, standing among the stacks of boxes and the clean smell of cardboard, Slider put his question about the incident.

'Yes, I remember it,' François said. His English was good, his accent mellifluous. 'The Asset Strippers' crew come here often. We have many people from that scene. Many artists, also. My little sister loves the Asset Strippers, this is how I remember. And the other man in the fight, he was also an artist.'

'Ben Jackson,' Slider offered.

François shrugged. 'Him I didn't know, but he was the boyfriend of Kara, who also my little sister loved. Very sad that she died. This man was still very upset, I think. He try to hit other man—'

'Do you know his name?' Slider asked. 'The man from Asset Strippers' crew?'

François looked at him carefully. 'It was not his fault. He did not start the fight.'

'You know his name,' Slider concluded.

'I see him in here a lot. He is very friendly to the staff.'

'Jesse Guthrie,' Slider said, and François bowed his head slightly in bare acknowledgement. 'Look,' he said, 'it's very important that you tell me the truth about this. Did Jesse Guthrie sell cocaine?'

A stubborn look came over François' face. 'There are no drugs in this club. It is clean place.'

Slider smiled. 'Come on. You can't stop clubbers taking drugs unless you have one-on-one policing the whole time. I know it and you know

200

it, and your managers know it. I'm actually not interested in that. I'm not in the Drugs Squad and that's not what I'm investigating. I swear to you this will not come back on you, and no one will ever know what you've told me. But I do need to know the truth. Ben Jackson attacked Jesse Guthrie because he said he was selling drugs. I just need to know if that was true.'

There was another hesitation, while François' dark eyes searched Slider's face for bona fides. Then he shrugged and gave in. 'He sold cocaine and E. I have seen people go up to him. You know what it looks like.'

'Yes,' said Slider, and he saw it in his mind's eye. The casual approach, the murmur in the ear, the avoided eye contact, the hands low down making the quick exchange, the immediate disengage. Once you knew, you could spot it across a room or across a street as easily as if it was attended by party blowers, horns and helium balloons. 'So he was well known for it?'

'I have heard it from other people. You want stuff, you go to him. Not just here, but backstage. So maybe this – Ben Jackson? – was right.'

'Have you seen him recently?'

'No,' said François, and there was nothing evasive about it. 'Not for a long time. Maybe he goes to different club now. The management here don't like to have fights. Maybe they bar him.'

Still, he could find him easily enough through the band, Slider thought. No need to trouble this man further. 'Well, thank you,' he said. 'You've been very helpful.'

François' manly jaw grew square and gritty. 'I have told you nothing,' he said forcefully.

Slider smiled. 'That's right. You've told me nothing. I'm going away disappointed.'

François relaxed slightly, but he did not smile. 'There are no drugs in this club. It is clean place.'

'No drugs,' Slider said. 'I get it.'

Joanna had not long been home when Slider arrived – the bonnet of her car was still hot. As he walked up to the front door he saw the lights go on in his father's annexe, so she must have just relieved him of responsibility, and he had gone home.

He opened the front door, and she came out from the drawing room into the passage. 'You're late,' she said.

'I've been clubbing,' he answered.

'Seals or discos?'

'Just following up a clue in Soho. You look tired.'

'I'm absolutely knackered,' she said. 'Nine hours, and hardly any retakes, so we were playing for most of that. I'm getting too old for this kind of thing.'

'Fancy a drink?'

'Boy, howdy!'

'Whisky? G and T?'

'Whisky makes me thirsty. I was just making myself a G and T,' she said. 'Fetch yourself a glass and some ice. I've got the tonic.'

When he returned from the kitchen, she was

202

forcing open the French windows (warped with age and damp – needed replacing – couldn't afford it yet). 'There's not a breath of air,' she said.

'There's going to be a storm,' he offered.

She gave him a crooked smile. 'There speaks the countryman. What was it, spider webs lying down? Cows flying north?'

'Weather forecast on the car radio.'

'Well, we need it. Maybe it'll cool the air. The heat today! I don't know why recording studios are always like the black hole of Calcutta. You'd think record companies could spring for a bit of air conditioning.'

She sounded disconsolate, and he opened his mouth to ask her what was wrong, but she got in first. 'So how's the case going?'

He sighed. 'It's all very complicated. Nothing tangible to go on, just a lot of hints and suggestions of things that ought to connect up and don't quite.'

'So, are you all right with this one?'

'All right?'

'Well, it's not a woman, and it's usually the women that bother you.'

He looked at her. 'Is that what you think of me?'

'I don't mean it in a bad way,' she said. 'You just seem to mind more about women.'

'I always mind,' he said. 'Whoever it is. Someone destroys a piece of work that's taken years to create, something they couldn't come near to making themselves.'

'What a piece of work is man,' Joanna said.

'How noble in reason, how infinite in faculties, in form and moving how express and admirable. Ragni and Rado knew a thing or two.'

'Who?'

'The blokes who wrote *Hair*.'

'Oh, is that who said that? Well, they were quite right. I hate waste and destruction.'

'I bet when you were a boy you never kicked down another kid's sandcastle.'

'What about you?'

'I was never a boy.'

'I mean, how's by you?'

She looked at him – he thought, a touch warily. 'Specifically?'

'You've been down the last couple of days.'

'Sorry. I didn't mean to be a grouch.'

'You're never a grouch. I know when there's something on your mind, that's all.' He hesitated. 'Is it the LSO job?' She hadn't mentioned it for ages, but if she'd given up on the idea she'd have told him. 'The applications close this week, don't they?' he asked.

'How d'you know that?'

'I'm a detective, remember?'

She didn't smile, just drew a troubled sigh. 'Can we not talk about it? Please? I just— I don't want to think about it now. I'm worn out with it.'

'Whatever you like.'

Somewhere quite near, probably in the next garden, two young foxes started squabbling with their piercing yips and squeals, and further off a dog barked in response. The new urban soundscape, he thought wryly. Perhaps on hot Baltimore nights it would be gunshots and sirens. We all have our wildlife.

Silence fell again. Slider drank from his glass, relishing the fragrance of gin, the tang of lemon, the cold bubbles on his tongue. When he put the glass down, the ice cubes rang daintily like wind chimes. As if conjured by the sound, there was a sudden, cool breath of air. He lifted his head and snuffed, smelling the ozone on it. 'Here it comes,' he said.

A moment later there was a tremendous flash of lightning that made Joanna jump. A few fat drops of rain smacked the concrete, making dark marks the size of pennies. Another lightning flash, so intense it almost fizzled; and this time, close behind it, a positive bark of thunder.

'I'd better see if Boy's all right,' Joanna said nervously.

'Wait a second,' Slider said, catching her hand.

A few more scattered drops, then a faster rattle, and then it came down like Hollywood rain, in a hosepipe torrent. The temperature dropped ten degrees. The trees rustled and bent. The water pelted the dry garden and soaked the grass. The gutters and downpipes gurgled. It was as satisfying as watching an elephant drink.

'Wonderful!' Slider shouted against the drumming.

'The bedroom windows are open!' Joanna cried. But she was laughing as she pulled her hand free and hurried away.

It was like a different world the next day, cool and fresh, with a sky of high grey clouds, the

205

pavements washed clean, the smell of water everywhere.

At work it began with negatives. Ben Corley had not made any calls on his mobile phone since April. 'He could've had a new one, o' course,' said Hollis. 'Bought a pay as you go, and black-sack man took it away wi' everything else. We'll never know.'

There was disappointment, too, from the credit card statement, which showed that had not been used, either. And there had been no activity from his cheque book; nothing on his bank statement but a couple of regular standing orders.

'But he did take out a large sum of money in cash just before Easter,' Atherton reported. 'Had to order it from the bank specially – from a very healthy savings account, by the way, so he wasn't hard up. Fifteen thousand pounds, he took out. I suppose that's what he's been living on for the past three and a half months.'

'But *why*?' Swilley said.

'It's obvious,' Connolly said. 'Your man's doing the vanisher. Dyes his hair, shaves off the beard, takes a rented room under a false name. Living on cash so's no one can check up on him.'

'What was he gonna do when the cash run out?' McLaren said.

'Get some more, ya divvy,' said Connolly. 'Sure, didn't you just hear he had plenty? Anyway, we know he was earning for part of the time at least, so he probably didn't get through it all.'

'So where was the rest, then?' McLaren asked.

'We didn't find any cash in Conningham Road.'

There was a brief pause and then several people said at once, 'Black-sack man.'

'Or maybe it's hidden at the Wynnstay Gardens flat,' Atherton said. 'We haven't gone through every drawer yet. And we think he went back there from time to time, so maybe he collected some more dosh at the same time.'

'But you still haven't answered the question,' said Swilley. *Why*?'

'Maybe he was hiding from someone,' Fathom said. 'He'd got into some shit with someone and they were after him, and he decided to hole up until the heat was off.'

'I suppose it's a possibility,' Slider said. 'There seem to have been a lot of drugs in the background story.'

'Yeah, and he tried to punch out this Jesse Guthrie bloke,' McLaren said, taking it up. 'Maybe Guthrie got some of his pals together and went after him.'

'Or maybe Guthrie wasn't the only one he pissed off,' Fathom added excitedly. 'If he got in shtuck with some drugs ring...'

Slider took a pull on the reins. 'He doesn't seem to have been acting like a man afraid for his life. For a start, he didn't move very far away. And to go on with, he didn't exactly "hole up". Getting yourself a job in porn films is not the action of a retiring personality.'

'So, what then?' Swilley asked. 'What *was* he up to?'

Into the silence, Atherton said, 'There was another thing he stopped doing, as well as using his credit card and mobile phone. He stopped tweeting.'

They all looked at him.

'Emily and I were looking at it last night. He used to be a regular on Facebook and Twitter. Of course, there was a lot of activity after Kara died – people condoling with him and saying what a great artist she was and what a tragedy, etcetera etcetera. Then he started tweeting about the evil of drugs, especially the culture of acceptance that had grown up around the pop scene and youth culture in general. And that turned into ranting – and I do mean ranting – about the people who supplied the drugs, and how they had effectively murdered Kara. But then suddenly, in the middle of March, it stops. Cut off, just like that. Tweetless as a strangled budgie. Since then, not a dickie bird.'

'So that's before he goes to Conningham Road?' Swilley said.

'That was about the time he got into the brawl with Jesse Guthrie,' Slider said slowly. 'Maybe that incident does have something to do with it. We'll have to see if we can't have a word with him.'

'How'll we find him?' Fathom demanded.

'Easiest thing to do is to ask Asset Strippers' agent,' said Slider.

'And who,' Atherton asked rhetorically, 'is that?'

'Murray Mann,' Slider said without thinking.

Atherton gave him an admiring look. 'The things you know, guv! You'll be humming the tunes next.'

'Don't be cheeky. Just for that, you can ring Mr Mann. I'm going to see Mr Porson.'

Porson listened intelligently, and said, 'It certainly sounds as though drugs come into it somewhere. These clubs are all riddled with it. But from what you say, the frackarse doesn't sound that serious.' He pronounced it the Shepherd's Bush nick way. 'Not enough to put him in fear of his life. These players down the end of the food chain aren't supposed to draw attention to themselves.' He stuck his biro between his teeth and chewed absently while he thought. 'No, there's something else going on as well. It's more like he's gone under cover. You said he was a journalist?'

'A music journalist. But he'd given in his notice,' Slider said. 'I did wonder myself about an undercover investigation, especially given that Vanya's is where Paul Barrow used to work. But that was years ago. And if Corley had already identified Guthrie as the man who supplied charlie to Kara, what was there to investigate?'

'No use asking me the questions,' Porson barked. 'What are you doing about it?'

'We're going to have a word with Guthrie. And we're still going through the Wynnstay Gardens flat. There's a lot to look through. The longer we can keep the media away from that the better.' He said it on a hopeful note, looking at his boss appealingly.

'*We're* not going to break it,' Porson said. 'We're still putting it out as Robin Williams, unknown nobody. But sooner or later someone's

209

going to blab. The sister knows, and now the bloke's agent or manager, or whatever he is, knows. They'll mention it to someone, and – boom! – media feeding frenzy. Too much good stuff for the press to ignore. So it's no use giving me the spaniel look. I'll do what I can to keep the address out of it but ... ' He shrugged.

Slider agreed it was hopeless. 'I'm surprised it hasn't leaked out before this. Apart from anything else, the porter knows who he really was. But maybe he'll keep quiet out of loyalty to the family.'

Porson snorted. 'Hope springs internal!' he mocked.

ELEVEN

Hansel and Regrettal

Mackay hadn't been there first thing, and as Slider returned to his office from Mr Porson's, he met the delinquent DC on the stairs, looking ragged.

'Sorry, guv,' he got in first. 'Very late night, doing the clubs, didn't hear the alarm.'

'I hope it was a productive late night. You look like a piece of cheese. I'm not signing an expenses sheet for a debauch, you know.'

'It wasn't the drinks, guv, it was the noise,' Mackay said. 'Trying to ask questions *and* hear the answers. But I did get something.' He managed a smile, the sort a dog gives you when your sandwich has gone missing. 'Something good.'

'All right, let's all hear it,' Slider said, leading the way. He cast a sideways glance at Mackay as he tramped beside him. The strip lighting was not doing him any favours. 'You're not going to throw up, are you?'

'I hardly had anything,' Mackay protested. 'I just need a cuppa and an aspirin the size of Middlesex.'

Mackay had gone first to the Forty-Niners. He had a new photo to show round, not the corpse

211

mugshot but a good one taken from the Wynn-stay Gardens flat and photo-shopped to remove the beard and change the hair. He had not seen Tommy Flynn, and when he asked after him casually, no one seemed to have seen him for a couple of days.

'It was a smart crowd,' he said. 'Notting Hill types. Loads a dosh, and a lot of people kept nipping off to the bogs, if you know what I mean.'

'We know what you mean,' Atherton said.

'Yeah,' said McLaren. 'The day someone goes in the gents and actually takes a dump it'll be like a breath of fresh air.'

'There was a lot of monged kids around, I can tell you. I didn't have any trouble getting 'em to talk, but when they weren't talking rubbish they didn't seem to know anything about Corley. One bloke looked like he might be gonna recognize him, but then he just said he looked familiar.' He looked at Slider. 'Maybe it was Ben Jackson he was recognizing.'

'That's always a danger,' said Slider.

Mackay gave up in the end and went on to Vanya's, where the crowd was so thick it wasn't far off achieving critical mass and collapsing into a black hole. The noise was so loud he was afraid he'd spontaneously combust. 'I couldn't get anything out of anyone, they were all just jiggling about looking stupid, right out of their trees. I asked all the staff I could find, but they just shrugged. Most of 'em seemed to be East Europeans, so I'm not even sure they understood the question. In the end I gave it up and went to the Hot Box.'

It was quieter in the Hot Box, not because the music wasn't loud but because there were fewer people. Fewer and richer seemed to be the Hot Box's philosophy. 'I've never seen so many bottles o' champagne outside of a wedding,' Mackay said. Seduction seemed to be the dominant theme. There were older men trysting young people of both genders; businessmen fêting other businessmen, both sides desperately pretending this was what they really enjoyed; well-heeled couples in their thirties and forties; twenty-something singles on dates, and gangs of both sexes on the hunt. The décor was Las Vegas Lite, featuring a lot of chandeliers, multiple shades of pink, and shiny and sparkly surfaces. There were strobing lights, the barmen were in pink waistcoats over bare chests, and the table staff were all female, in pink hot-pants, high heels and sequinned bras.

The Hot Boxes themselves were small round raised platforms, each with a pole going up through the middle, on which girls danced wearing only a thong. There was a raised rim about six inches high round each table, either to stop the dancers falling off or, more likely Mackay thought, to stop punters absent-mindedly putting their glasses down on them, since they strongly resembled the 'stand-up' tables in pubs – except for the gyrating flesh above.

Fathom listened to the description with his jaw dropping like the ramp of a horsebox. 'Gor, you lucky bastard,' he said, when Mackay got to the naked dancers.

Mackay shrugged. 'When you've seen one

pair o' tits, you've seen 'em all,' he said, with massive sangfroid and even more massive untruth.

'Never mind the ornithology,' Slider said sternly.

'Orni – what?' Fathom queried.

'Birdwatchin',' Connolly helped him. 'Only these tits weren't blue. Love a' God, Jerry, could you not knock off the dribbling? You're soaking me arm.'

'You said you'd found something out,' Slider prompted.

'Yeah, boss,' Mackay said, lurching back on track. 'This barman I spoke to, middle-aged bloke, been at the Hot Box years, name of Terry Villiers, he took a good long look at the photo and said he knew him.'

'Only he had face fungus then.'

'You mean a beard?' Mackay offered.

Villiers shook his head, still staring at the picture. 'No, just pooftah stubble,' he said, gesturing with his free hand. He had a residual Australian accent, but had obviously been away from God's Own Country a long time. 'And his hair was different. Shorter. And he had an earring, ya get me? But it's the same bloke all right. Reddish hair, brown eyes, right?'

'Right,' said Mackay. Coloured contacts – you could buy them on the Internet, right alongside the joke ones, vampires and devils and cats. And hair could be dyed.

'So what's he done, this joker?' asked Villiers.

'How d'you know him?' Mackay countered.

214

'Used to work here,' said Villiers. 'Temporary barman. He was here about six weeks, then he left. Well, they never stay long. Pity though – he was OK. I reckon he'd done it before. And it makes a change to get one 'at speaks English. The guys we get work hard, all right, but it's a strain tryna talk to 'em.'

'How long ago did he leave?' Mackay asked.

'Must a' been – what – about the middle of July? He started the sixth o' June, I remember that, 'cause I'd just got back from me holidays and he was starting the same day. He was here six weeks. Good little worker – keen. Asked a lot o' questions. Cos o' that, I thought he wanted to work his way up – thought he was a stayer. But no, he comes in one day and gives his notice. Says he's got an opening somewhere else, more money. Can't argue with the moolah, can you? So off he goes, and I haven't seen him since.'

'Did he say what sort of opening?'

'He said something about dancing,' Villiers said. 'He'd never said anything to me before about being a dancer, but I s'pose he could've been.' He shrugged. 'Maybe he was just resting between parts, like a bloody actor, eh? There's a lot o' musicals on in the West End these days, he could be a show dancer, chorus line, that sort o' thing.'

'You didn't ask?'

'Not interested enough. And too busy. He was like wallpaper, ya get me? He came, he went, like they all do. What's he done, anyway? I can't stand here talking all night.'

'He's dead,' Mackay said, trying a bit of shock

215

tactic.

Villiers stared at him a moment, and then said, 'That's different. Poor bastard. Well, I don't know what else I can tell you.'

'Did you see him talking to anyone in particular while he was here?'

'Not really. He was a friendly geezer, chatted to everyone. Like I said, asked a lot of questions, seemed interested in everyone. The big boss took quite a shine to him. Another reason I thought he was gonna stay and work his way up.'

'Big boss?'

Villiers threw a conspiratorial glance sideways and leaned forward a bit more. 'We're not supposed to know about it. He's supposed to come here incognito – I dunno if he's checking up on us, or he just likes a night out. But I've been here so long now I know all about this place. The managers come and go – not as often as the staff, but they get moved on eventually – but the bloke they report to never changes. He's a good-looking geezer, got a tan and silver hair like Richard Gere, you know? Well, he quite took a fancy to this bloke, like I said, always waited to be served by him, they'd chat away for hours. The big boss looks like the kind of bloke who might back West End shows, you know? Nice suits and bags of money. So maybe he got this feller a part.'

He paused, looked at the photo again, and remembered why they were talking about him. 'Poor bastard,' he said again. 'He's young to croak like that. Funny thing, I always felt I'd seen him somewhere before, but I couldn't put

216

me finger on it. Seeing him without the face fungus, he looks even more familiar, but I can't think why.'

'Names, give us names,' Atherton demanded. 'Or didn't you think to ask?'

''Course I asked. What d'you take me for?' said Mackay indignantly. 'He said our man gave the name of Colin Redgrave.'

'Colin? With an "L"?' Atherton said. 'He did like his little joke, didn't he? For a man with a broken heart.'

'Maybe he was leavin' a trail o' breadcrumbs, case anyone had to try and find him,' Connolly suggested.

'Well, it does give us an indication that it really was Corley,' Slider agreed. 'Any other names?'

'The manager's called Eugene Kumis,' Mackay said. 'I managed to get a quick chat with one of the kitchen staff, who'd gone outside for a smoke, and he said Kumis is from Kazakhstan, wherever that may be. I asked him to describe him, and he says he's a big, burly dark bloke with a five o'clock shadow, which doesn't match Villiers's description of the big boss. So this Richard Gere type is obviously higher up. But he didn't know his name.'

'If he *was* the big boss, why would it be a secret? More likely he's a pal getting free drinks and the manager doesn't want it known,' Atherton said.

'Well, whatever it is, it'd be nice if we knew,' Slider said. 'Swilley, find out what you can about this Kumis and whether there are any connections with anything else in the case. Gascoyne, you're still on pizzas and Italian restaurants in general.'

'Yes, sir.'

'McLaren, cars?'

'Yes, guv. Nothing so far.'

'And the rest of you, back to the flat. Atherton, you were checking on Guthrie?'

'I'm just going to.'

'I wonder if Tommy Flynn would be worth another pass, now we know a bit more.'

'D'ye want me to go round there?' Connolly asked, pausing on her way back to her desk.

'No, I think we'll bring him in. Might concentrate his mind. I'll get uniform to go round and give him a tug.'

It was not long before Atherton was back at Slider's door, with a face that foretold difficulties. 'I rang the Murray Mann agency, spoke to the Mann himself. We're not going to get to talk to Guthrie. He's dead. Overdosed on cocaine, apparently.'

'Apparently?'

'He didn't turn up to work, so one of the other members of the crew went round to his flat after work. Couldn't get an answer, got worried in case he was ill, rang his sister, who had a key, to come round, found him dead in bed.'

Slider considered. 'If Corley was right and Guthrie was a supplier, he'd surely be too savvy to take an overdose. On the other hand...'

'On the other hand, there's no getting past the stupidity of people who take drugs,' said Atherton. 'The interesting thing from our point of view is the timing. It was just less than a week after his little bust-up with Corley at Vanya's.'

'You're not suggesting—?' Slider began.

'Certainly not, guv. Not suggesting anything. Just said it was interesting.'

'Interesting. Yes,' Slider said. 'Someone from the local police must have investigated it. I'd better have a word with them. Did you get Guthrie's address?'

'Yes, guv. Ex-council flat off the Holloway Road.'

'That's Islington,' Slider said, reaching for the telephone.

Islington Police Station was a rather agreeable-looking building in Tolpuddle Street, of yellow London stock bricks, square and three storeys high, with arched windows on the ground floor, edged with red brick, and a three-arched entrance porch. Nice for some, Slider thought. The DI in charge of the Guthrie case was John Care, though as Slider saw from various bits of paper around his office he called himself Jonny Care and spelled it without an 'H'. He was a lot younger than Slider, and taller, with light brown hair cut very short, and a pleasant-looking, non-descript sort of face – the sort of face you would have difficulty remembering as soon as you had left him. He would also, Slider thought, be almost impossible to photofit: bit of a waste he wasn't a criminal, really. Or a spy. You could feel yourself forgetting him even as he spoke.

'So, the Guthrie case,' he said, giving Slider a very sharp once over that proved him a copper.

A young woman in a black skirt suit and green blouse brought in a tray of coffee and biscuits. 'Thanks, Sara,' he said. She also clocked Slider good and proper as she put the tray down on the desk, gave him a smile and went away. One of Care's DCs, he supposed. He must have them well trained – no order for refreshments had been given in his presence. He rather wished it had been. It was instant coffee – he could smell it – and he hated instant. But in the interests of good relations he would have to make himself drink it.

'Not that it was much of a case,' Care went on. 'It went down as accidental death in the end.'

'But you always had suspicions,' Slider said, as though he was finishing Care's sentence.

'Well,' Care said doubtfully. He pushed a cup towards Slider. 'Sugar?'

'No, thanks. Would you tell me what happened, from the beginning?'

'What's your interest in it?' Care countered. He had a very slight accent Slider was trying to pin down – Hertfordshire? Something country, anyway.

'We were hoping he would be a witness in a case we have on at the moment. A murder case.'

'You think he was involved?'

'We really haven't got that far yet. He was just someone we were going to interview for background information, and finding out he was dead was a bit startling, that's all. How did it happen?'

Care sipped his coffee and gave in. 'He hadn't showed up for work, and wasn't answering his mobile, which was worrying – these people live by their mobiles. So a colleague went to look him up. I suppose you know what line he was in?'

'One of the support crew for a pop band. The Asset Strippers.'

'That's correct. He was one of the gofers. The friend who looked him up was one of the sound technicians – chap called James Harnett. He could hear music inside, playing quite loudly. He rang the bell, banged on the door, tried the phone, all to no avail. So he rang Guthrie's sister, who lived in Barnsbury. She said she hadn't heard from him, and once Harnett had convinced her he was worried, she came round with the key. She was only five minutes away. She let them in, and found Guthrie in his bedroom. The bedside lamp was on, and he was lying naked on top of the bedclothes. There was a mirror and glass tube on the bedside table, and traces of white powder round his nostrils.'

'So who called you in?'

'Harnett did. Apparently the sister wanted to call a doctor, but Guthrie was dead and cold, and Harnett was worried he would get into trouble for having been the one to find him. So he insisted on calling the police. But there was never any reason to suspect him. There were no marks on the body, no sign of any break-in or struggle. And the post-mortem established that death was due to an overdose of cocaine, causing electrical malfunction of the heart and syncope.' He looked at Slider to see if he understood the medical terms.

Slider nodded. 'So what were your particular

221

concerns?' he asked. 'I can see there was something about it that bothered you.'

Care put down his cup and drummed his fingers a moment on the desk, as though considering whether to entrust Slider with the valuable contents of his mind.

'You're right,' he said at last. 'There were a couple of things. The lethal dose of cocaine was less than a gram, but it was pure. You understand what that means?'

Slider nodded again. Before it was sold to users, pure cocaine was cut with other materials – corn starch, vitamin C powder, icing sugar, even talcum powder. Cocaine seized on the street was typically little more than 20% pure – sometimes as low as 15%. Even at that strength, too much of it could disrupt the heart's action; so suddenly to ingest pure cocaine would be very dangerous.

'The traces of cocaine on the mirror and in the tube were also pure. But we found a large quantity of other cocaine in the flat – a whole kilogram bag and several wraps – all of which was already cut down to around eighteen per cent. There was no other pure on the premises.'

'So Guthrie was a dealer?'

'We weren't able to establish that, but he wouldn't have had such a large quantity in his possession for his own use. He must have been providing it at least for friends and acquaintances.'

'Did you find any money?'

'No, and there was no indication of any great wealth. It was a fairly tatty flat. He had an

222

expensive television and sound system, but no large sums in the bank.'

'Any indication where he might have got the stuff from?'

'If we knew that, we'd have pursued it,' Care said. 'If he was a dealer, he wasn't one of the organizers, but he must have been fairly high up the food chain. But we had nothing to go on. And he was dead. We passed what we had over to the drugs squad and left it at that. It's their baby now.'

There was always so much to do, Slider thought, and this was a self-cauterised canker. No point in flogging a dead duck, as Mr Porson might say. He didn't know that he wouldn't have done the same. And you had to be careful about treading on the toes of special squads. They tended to know people...

'What else worried you?' he asked. Care looked enquiring. 'You said there were a couple of things.'

'Oh.' He frowned. 'Well, it probably isn't significant. But the post-mortem showed that the testes were empty. Which suggested he had ejaculated very shortly before death.'

Slider's scalp prickled. 'So you think there might have been someone else there?'

'Even if there was,' he said defensively, 'it doesn't follow they had anything to do with it. He could just have easily have taken the pure after they'd left. Something he'd got for himself only, as a treat – that sort of idea. Or the person might have witnessed the death and made themselves scarce out of panic.'

'When did the death take place?'

'Some time during the previous evening or night. He was accounted for at a recording session, with a meeting afterwards, until ten o'clock. After that, he went off, and no one seems to have seen him or spoken to him again. No one that *we* know about, anyway.'

Slider suspected Care and his team hadn't tried very hard, but that wasn't a thought he could possibly voice.

'Do you think I might possibly have the name and address of Guthrie's sister?' he asked with the maximum injection of politeness.

Guthrie's sister, Joyce Finnucane, lived in a council flat in the Barnsbury district of Islington, but Slider caught up with her at a primary school just up the road, where she was working as a dinner lady. He found her in a wonderland of stainless steel, multiple burners, steam cabinets, gay nylon overalls and deep fat fryers, part of the dedicated team crafting that days' culinary high-light, cottage pie and chips. He almost felt guilty about taking her away from so much delight, but she followed him willingly into a yard full of dustbins behind the kitchen where she lit a cigarette with the desperate urgency of a smoker just getting off a long-haul flight.

She was in her thirties, pale and rather pudgy, but with a hard mouth and eyes and a voice you could scour pans with. She had the look of some-one who 'knew her rights' and would take offence with almost professional promptness at anything she thought infringed them.

'What you dragging all that up again for?' she

demanded. 'He's dead. Can't you lot leave him in peace?'

'I'm sorry, I wouldn't bother you if it wasn't really important. Do you know who Jesse's friends were?'

'Didn't have any,' she said, on an exhalation. Slider managed not to flinch as it hit him full in the face. 'He was always a loner, even from a kid. Left home as soon as he could and never went back. You wouldn't think he lived just round the corner, number of times I see him of a year. Always remembered the kids' birthdays, I'll give him that – I got two. Bought 'em both bikes for Christmas. And he was talking about an Xbox next time. But sending a present's not the same as being around for 'em. And they love their Uncle Jesse, my two – worship him. But he's always too busy. I could count on the fingers o' one hand the times he's took 'em to a football match or the park or whatever.'

'But you had the key to his flat?'

'Yeah, he give me that, case of emergencies.'

'Did you go there often?'

'Never. When I see him, it was out. Pub, usually, or a restaurant. He'd get us tickets to his shows, sometimes. Tell you the truth, him and my Dean – my husband – didn't see eye to eye. So it didn't make for happy families, you know?'

'Why didn't Dean like him?'

She shrugged, dragging on the fag with a power that could have sucked the ink out of a biro. 'Dean thought he was a bit slick, too full of himself. Reckoned Jess thought he was better than us.'

'And did he?'

'Jess? Nah. He was just a loner, like I said. Never had time for no one. But he was still my brother, all right? He loved me and I loved him, and that's it and all about it.'

Slider could imagine the rows on the subject between husband and wife.

'Did he have a girl friend?'

'Nah. Never had time for that sort of thing.'

'Boyfriend, then?'

'Piss off! He wasn't one o' them. Nothing wrong with my Jesse. He had women when he wanted – just didn't want a relationship with it.'

'So he never talked about any particular woman? Never brought one with him when you met?'

'Married to his job,' she answered elliptically. 'That's all he ever cared about – his bloody job, running back and forth for them bloody Asset Strippers. It wasn't just a day job, you know. He had to hang around them all the time, not just at work but when they went out and everything, case one of 'em wanted her fag lit or her arse scratched. Couldn't do nothing for themselves. I said to him, you're just a skivvy, that's all. But he loved it. Sucker.'

Slider had come to the conclusion that Jessie Guthrie had not allowed his sister inside his life much. But there was one more question to ask, and he put it bluntly, to see what her reaction would be. 'Did you know he was dealing drugs?'

'Piss off!' she said scornfully and at once, but her eyes gave her away, the alarm followed by

226

the steely caution. 'He never done nothing like that.'

'It's all right,' Slider said soothingly, 'I'm not trying to get you into trouble. It won't come back on you if you tell me the truth, I promise. We know he was dealing. We found the stuff in his flat.'

'Planted it, more like,' she said, but it was a routine objection. Behind the automatic hostility she was worried.

'Did he ever mention anything about where he got the stuff? Mention any names or places? Anything at all that you can remember. It's very important,' he added beguilingly.

She remained unbeguiled. 'He never,' she said emphatically, 'dealt no drugs.' She threw down the fag end and ground it out with a vehemence that suggested it should be Slider's head down there. 'I gotter go.'

'What did he do before he started working for the Asset Strippers?' Slider asked, a last bid to catch her attention. 'Did he have a trade, or training in anything?'

She paused, considering why he was asking. But she said, 'Yeah, he went to stage school.' Her sisterly feelings had overcome her reluctance to cooperate. She spoke with pride. 'He wanted to be a dancer. Not bally, I don't mean – in shows and that. He was good, an' all. He got parts. He did *Starlight Express* in Glasgow and *Guys and Dolls* in Bournemouth, and then he was in *Les Miserables* for two years.' She pronounced it the English way. 'He was brilliant. It was a bloody rotten shame he give it all up for that stupid job. He was nothing but a skivvy to that lot, but he could have been up on the stage himself. I told him he'd regret it. And now look where it's got him.' Tears jumped into her eyes, surprising her as much as Slider. She dashed them away impatiently, wiped her nose with the back of her hand, tugged her nylon hat down more tightly, and said, 'Now if you've *quite* finished.'

'Thank you for your help,' Slider said.

'Been a pleasure talking to you, I *don't* think,' she said, and stalked away, honour satisfied.

What a crushing retort, Slider thought humbly, and took his leave. Trying to fit these pieces together in his mind was like doing a jigsaw puzzle from the back, with the picture face-down. Things were obviously connected, but you couldn't see what they meant.

But 'hear a new word, and you'll hear it again within the day', as his mother used to say. Corley had left the Hot Box saying he was going to be a dancer. Guthrie had been a dancer who had left to become a gofer. What the heck was that all about?

TWELVE

The Swiller's Feeling for Snow

'Well, Corley never trained as a dancer,' Atherton said, finishing his prawn and avocado sandwich in Slider's room, 'though he was an actor, in Footlights. I suppose he might have done some dancing, but as far as we know not professionally. And why on earth would he say that to Villiers, when he didn't need to say anything? He could have just said he'd got a better job and left it at that.'

'It is a bit odd,' Slider said, throwing the wrapper from his cheese 'n' pickle into the bin and wiping his hands on his handkerchief.

'More fishy than a sushi restaurant. Unless Connolly's right and he was laying a trail of breadcrumbs. But what was he up to?'

'The similarities between Guthrie's death and Corley's are suggestive,' Slider said. 'In both cases they were found alone and it was meant not to look like murder – Corley's suicide and Guthrie's accidental overdose. Both had their clothes off and in Guthrie's case sex had certainly been had, while in Corley's we know someone else was there. Given there was no struggle, it looks as though a tryst of some sort was involved.'

'Right, the killer—'

'If there was a killer.'

'Let's cast caution to the winds for a minute and assume it was murder – the killer sets up some kind of romantic encounter, does away with the victim when they're in a vulnerable condition, and has it away on their toes, in Corley's case with just about everything, including the remains of his fifteen thousand pounds, and in Guthrie's—'

'Possibly with his secret store of cash,' Slider concluded, 'given that if he was a dealer and it wasn't in his bank account, it must have been somewhere.'

They looked at each other in silence. 'So what does it all mean?' Atherton asked at last.

'Badgered if I know,' Slider admitted. 'I'm beginning to think maybe Mr Porson was right, and he—'

One of the uniforms, Willans, appeared in his open doorway, tentatively tapping on the architrave in apology. 'Sorry, sir – got some bad news.'

'Is there another sort?' Slider sighed.

'D'Arblay's called in – he was the one went round to Tommy Flynn's house to bring him in. Apparently, he'd dead. Flynn, sir. And it's not an accident.'

Despite the address of Palliser Road being West Kensington, it was in fact still in the borough of Hammersmith, which was a great relief all round, especially as the Kensington lot were known to be very fussy about rival Vogons on their ground. By the time Slider and Atherton got there, two more uniforms had taken up position, one on the door and one on the gate, keeping the interested neighbours back, while D'Arblay was at the top of the stairs guarding the door to the flat, and little Jilly Lawrence, one of the female PCs, had corralled Mrs Panda from downstairs, who was hysterical and enjoying it.

'A neighbour's taken her two kids,' she whispered to Slider. 'I don't think she knows anything but she's the sort to make trouble.'

'Hang in there,' Slider said. 'I'll come and speak to her in a minute, but I want to take a quick look upstairs first.'

On the upper landing, handsome, blue-eyed D'Arblay was looking a little pale, but resolute. From inside the flat the music was playing, loudly but not at offensive level, unless you were trying to get to sleep.

'I could hear it as soon as I got out of the car, sir,' he said, 'and I could see the window was partly up. But when I rang the doorbell there was no answer. I rang the other bell and got her downstairs.' He made a graphic face. 'She said she was fed up with the noise, she'd been banging on the ceiling but it made no difference. She said she heard him come home in the early hours, he'd put the music on then and it hadn't been off since. I went upstairs and she insisted on following me up, but there was no answer when I banged on the door. She said she would not be surprised if he hadn't overdosed and what kind of policeman was I?' He gave a rueful

231

smile. 'Well, sir, she didn't have a key and the lock looked pretty frail so I thought I'd better shoulder the door. It was easy – that old Yale was half off anyway. Unfortunately, she got a look inside before I could stop her, and she was off, screaming like a banshee, so I had to deal with her before I could radio in. I haven't been inside but you can see from here he's dead. With all the blood in there, I thought it better not to step in it.'

'Good thinking,' Slider said. 'We'll wait for the forensic boys. I'll just take a look from here.'

'Funny, with all that blood, there's no footprints on the stairs,' D'Arblay said over Slider's shoulder as he looked in. 'You'd think the murderer could hardly help...'

Tommy Flynn was naked, lying on his side half way between the bed and the window, in a positive welter of gore. The reason was easy to see – his throat had been cut right across and to the bone, so that his head lolled back, only held on by the cervical spine. Even for a policeman, it was as nasty a sight as you'd want to bargain for in a lifetime. Near his outflung hand, Slider could see a bloody knife with a decorative ivory-inlaid handle and double-sided blade about a foot long – the sort of thing years ago people brought back from Africa as a souvenir. There wasn't much else to see without going closer. The music was coming from a sound system in the chimney alcove near the window. The bed was up against the wall, the covers rumpled and thrown back, and there was an open door on the back wall through which could be seen a corner of the kitchen, which was at the back of the house overlooking the garden and the railway line. Presumably the bathroom was through there too. It was a tiny place, the original two bed-rooms of a two-bedroom terraced house – but presumably it had been cheap. Nothing in the furnishing or accoutrements suggested Tommy Flynn had ever had more money than it took to keep him going from week to week.

'Right,' said Slider. He looked at D'Arblay. 'Are you OK?'

'Yes, guv,' he said sturdily. 'I've seen worse road accidents.'

'Good lad. Hang in there.'

Lawrence had done a good job of calming Panda Woman, whose name turned out to be Kelly Watson, so that she had stopped shrieking and was now bravely cradling a cup of tea and demanding her kids back. 'They'll be going mental wivout me,' she asserted. Slider asked her a few questions while they were being fetch-ed, but it was obvious she didn't know anything. She had heard 'him upstairs' come in in the early hours, banging the door and going up the stairs. She didn't know what time, but she had been watching a movie on TV until 12.30 and then gone to bed, and she'd been asleep so it must have been after one. Then she'd heard the music go on, but she'd fallen asleep. The next thing she'd woken with her baby crying, and it was seven o'clock. Once she'd got the kids up and fed she'd noticed the music was still going. After a bit she got fed up with it and banged on the ceiling with the broom handle, but to no effect.

Then that policeman had arrived.

No, she didn't know if he'd come home alone. No, she hadn't seen him, only heard him – she was in bed. No, she hadn't heard any sounds of rumpus from upstairs, nor anyone leave. He had friends back a lot but she didn't know any of them. She didn't know if he had a girlfriend.

The children arrived and interrupted this litany of negatives. They were as stolid a couple of little nose-miners as Slider had ever seen, and plodded in with nothing more than mild enquiry on their faces as to what was going on. But their mother flung herself at them with shrieks of anguish and clutched them to her bosom, which soon had them bawling in sheer fright in one-and-a-half-part harmony. Slider was glad of the excuse to leave.

Outside, Connolly was just arriving, despatched by Hollis as reinforcement on the grounds that she knew more about Flynn than anyone else. She brought the news that the doctor and forensic were on the way, and that Mr Porson was asking Hammersmith central nick for manpower to cover the basics, since they were already stretched.

'Jeez, the poor bastard,' she commented on Flynn, having had the permitted look through the door to get her up to speed. 'He was a mouthy skanger, but he didn't deserve that. What does your wan downstairs say?'

'She knows nothing, except that he came in in the early hours. Heard, not seen.'

'Is it to do with our case, boss? Sure it must be? Corley and Guthrie and now your man, all

234

killed in the early hours with music on in the background.'

'If you so much as think the words serial killer you're going straight home,' Slider said.

'I wasn't going to, honest. But doesn't it look like they're popping anyone who might be able to lead us to them?'

'And who is "them" in your script?'

'Them that's doing the popping,' she said unhelpfully. Something occurred to her. 'Boss, d'you need me here? Only it might be worth seeing if Tommy Flynn's pal is up the pool room again. It was their usual hang-out.'

'Good thinking,' Slider said. 'Go.'

The local doctor on call pronounced life extinct – these little rituals had to be performed – and left with his eyes on stalks and his mouth distinctly wry. The inside of the human neck had not been designed to be seen. By the time Freddie Cameron arrived, forensic was in, and he clothed up and oozed up the stairs to insert himself into a distinctly crowded room.

He came down to make a first report to Slider before going back to secure the body for removal. 'Well, the weapon looks right for the weapon,' he said. 'It's hellishly sharp. Cut was made from behind and from left to right, which gives us a right-handed murderer.'

'No chance it was self-inflicted?'

'None. Angle's all wrong.'

'Would it have taken a lot of strength?'

'Strong hands, perhaps, but determination rather than mighty muscles, provided he didn't struggle – and there's no sign of struggle. It's more a knack than brute force. Judging by his pupils he had ingested a large dose of something, which probably rendered him docile. The murderer would only have to manoeuvre themselves up behind him and be quick – tug the head back by the hair and make one quick, hard movement. The droplet pattern suggests he was killed where he fell; and of course the murderer would have been shielded by his body from most of the blood.' He regarded Slider a moment. 'No attempt to make this look like suicide. If it's the same killer as in the Corley case, it looks as though he's getting more impatient.'

'Thanks for reminding me I'm getting nowhere fast,' said Slider.

'No charge,' said Cameron elegantly, and went back upstairs.

Connolly had a distinct Groundhog moment when she entered the pub. The scene was unchanged. It could have been the same men sitting there staring at the television screen – it could even have been the same sporting event for all she knew. As she slipped discreetly upstairs, she toyed with the idea that the broadcast companies had been showing old tapes for years without anyone noticing.

In the pool room she struck lucky. In a lazily-moving curtain of illegal smoke, there was a group of young men standing around the table, two playing and the other three watching, and one of the onlookers was the lad she had seen with Tommy Flynn. As soon as he spotted her he started to sidle, but she had positioned herself between the exit and the only other door – to the gents – so she could reach either before he could.

'I just want a chat with you,' she said, holding eye contact. 'It's not trouble for you, I swear on me mammy's grave.' His eyes were flitting about, looking for escape, and the others had now had their attention caught and were looking at her with their mouths open. 'Ah, c'mon, what harm? I'll buy yez a pint,' she said, giving him a friendly smile and gesturing to the door.

''Kin'ell, Baz, if you don't I will,' said one of the others. 'You don't get offers like that every day.'

'Yeah, get it on,' said another.

Her quarry gave a foolish smirk and came towards her, trying to put on a swagger. Through the door on to the landing outside, with Connolly close behind him; and just at the point when she felt him think about bolting, she caught his wrist and snatched his arm up behind his back. 'Don't even think about it,' she said grimly. 'Ever heard an arm break? It'd put y'off your lunch.'

'Lemme go, y' lousy bitch!' he squealed.

'Now, now, none o' that. Don't show yourself up in front of your mates. I just want a talk. No harm to you. Walk downstairs nicely now, because if you trip and fall y'arm might come right off in me hand.'

At the bottom of the stairs was the room she had noted before, where special matches were screened, but there was nothing on today and the room was empty. She marched him in and sat him down behind a table, and sat herself on the

237

other side as he rubbed his arm and looked sulky.

'That bloody hurt,' he complained. 'Whadda you want, anyway?'

'You're Tommy Flynn's mate,' she said. 'I just want t'ask you about Tommy.' He seemed to find that consoling. 'What's your name?' she asked.

She had though it would be Barry, because they had called him Baz, but it turned out to be Derren Basilides. He was a skinny creature in his early twenties, with a spotty, underdeveloped face and greasy no-coloured hair, and he was wearing what seemed to be the uniform of baggy khaki pants, trainers and a grubby top: a Staxx T-shirt with the annoying words DON' NO NO BETTA printed under the name, which in his case was probably true as well as making it an antique.

'When did you last see Tommy?' she asked.

A look of low cunning crossed his face. 'Get us a pint an' I'll tell ya.'

'No, Derren, you tell me and then I'll get yez a pint. Love a God, d'ya think I fell off the Christmas tree?'

'Baz,' he said sulkily. 'Me name's Baz.'

'OK, Baz, here's how it'll be. I ask you questions, you answer them, you get a pint and no trouble from me. Got it?' He nodded, resigned. He had caved in so easily, Connolly wondered whether he had a tough Greek mother who kept him in line. 'So when did you last see Tommy?'

'Las' night. He was here. We played a bit o' pool, then he went off.'

'Off where?'

'I dunno. He was meetin' someone. A bird.'

'What bird?'

'I dunno. He didn't say.' To Connolly's insistent look, he amplified. 'He had this phone call. Then he says, "I gotta go, I'm meetin' this bird." And he like makes kind of yum-yum faces.' He demonstrated, ludicrously, rubbing his stomach with one hand. 'Showin' off she was tasty. He's always like that.' he grumbled. 'Yeah, we get it, Tom, you have a lot o' sex. Don't haveta rub it in.'

'What time was this?'

'Be about, I dunno, half eleven, quart' to twelve. It was near on closing, anyway.' He seemed to suffer a spurt of backbone and asserted himself. 'What's this about? What's Tommy done?'

'Tommy's dead, Baz,' Connolly said. 'Someone killed him last night.'

Baz blenched; all his blemishes stood out against the sudden pallor. 'Killed him?' he bleated. 'Who killed him? What – is he, like, dead?'

The boy was quick, you had to hand it to him. 'Dead as a fish, Baz me boy, so now you see why it's very important that you help me out here. This woman he was meetin' – have y'any idea who it might be?'

'No, he never said.'

'Is he seeing anyone regularly?'

'Nah, you know what the Flynn's like – different bird every night.'

In his dreams, Connolly thought. Not on cocaine. 'Did he say where he was meeting her?'

'Nah, that's all he said – gotta go, I'm meetin'

239

this bird. I'd tell you if I knew. Honest.' He tried to give her a reassuring look, but it was smeared with alarm, and his knee was jiggling under the table. 'He's dead? Tommy's dead?'

'Yeah, they got him, all right,' she said, hoping to spark a reaction.

'What, the drugs people?' he said, his eyes widening.

'It's possible,' she said, concealing her satisfaction. 'Tommy dealt drugs, didn't he?'

'Nah, not *dealt*. He'd get it for you, but he only like sold it to his mates and that. He didn't go out like on the street or anything. And it was just a few wraps. I mean, if he was like *dealing*, he'd have been rich, right?'

'But he would supply charlie if you asked him?'

'Yeah, and E, and Viagra. Bit o' speed sometimes. But that's all.'

Viagra to counteract the effects of the cocaine, Connolly thought. So that's how he kept the women happy. 'And where did he get the stuff from?' she asked.

Now he looked really alarmed. Beads of sweat appeared on his upper lip and his leg was doing a fandango. He stuffed a dirty and bitten fingernail into his mouth and tore at it. 'I dunno! I swear I dunno!'

'Don't bite your nails, it's a dirty owl habit,' she said sternly. He dropped his hand as if he'd been slapped. 'Sure, you must have asked him?'

'No! Tommy never said and I never asked. I never wanted to get into all that. Them people – you don't wanna get mixed up wiv 'em. I told

240

him that. But he liked the money. And it was the only way he could pay for the stuff. He took a shed-load o' charlie, Tommy did. He was mental.'

'C'mon, Baz, you've known your man, how many years?'

'Since school. We was at school together.'

'Right, all those years, you're his best friend–' she was punting here, but he didn't deny it – 'and he's never told you where he got the stuff? Not a hint?'

'All I know is, he picked it up at the club.'

'The Forty-Niners?'

'Yeah. But I don't know how, or who sold it him. I swear. He would never have told me. He was careful, Tommy. He'd've knew it was dangerous.' He licked his lips. 'How – how'd they do it?'

'You don't wanta know,' she said, and he blenched a little more. 'Come on, now, Baz, there must be something you can tell me, to help me catch 'em. Poor old Tommy!' she urged, and when this did not do the trick, she added, 'And what if they come after you next?'

He almost whinnied in fear. 'They wouldn't! I ain't done nothing! I don't know nothing!'

'Well, they might just think, bein' Tommy's pal, he'd have told you a little bit. Drugs dealers shouldn't have friends. Most of 'em don't. But Tommy had you, didn't he?'

'The motor!' he cried in desperation. 'I saw the motor!'

'What motor's that?'

'What he was picked up in. When he went, I

241

was a bit pissed off, because he hadn't said nothing about meetin' no one. I thought we was gonna go back to his place and play some sounds and do some blow. But he gets this phone call and just buggers off. Typical Tommy. So I was standin' by the window finishing me pint and I looks down and I see him come out and get into this motor across the road, and it drives off.'

'Did you see who was in it?'

'Nah.'

'C'mon, Baz, the driver's your side, you musta seen something. Was it a man or woman?'

'I didn't see, honest. They musta been leaning back or summink. But it musta been a woman, musnit?'

Not if the telephone call was just an excuse to get him out of there. But she didn't say that. 'What sort o' car was it, then?'

'Astra.' He was pleased to have a detail pat. 'Coupé I think.'

'Colour?'

He frowned, thinking. 'I dunno for sure. Maybe black. Dark colour, anyway.'

She smiled encouragingly. 'Now, I don't suppose you happened to see the reg number, did you, Baz me darlin'? Even a little bit of it would help.'

He shook his head miserably. 'I never looked. Tommy just got in and it went off, fast. It just beat the lights on to Talgarth Road.'

'Left or right?'

'Right. Towards Earl's Court.' He thought a bit, and then added, hopefully, 'It looked like a new car.' He looked at her as she frowned in

242

thought. 'Do I get that pint now?'

'Sure you do. Just a couple more questions and I'll get it for you. Are y'll right?' she asked, noticing that he was very pale and sweaty.

'It's Tommy,' he said. 'I was only playin' pool with him last night and now he's—' He put a hand to his mouth, and from behind it said, 'Oh Christ,' in a choked sort of voice.

Connolly scowled at him. 'If you throw up on me, y'can kiss that pint goodbye, ya ganky eejit.'

He gave her a look full of woe. 'Not sure I want it now,' he said, and it was the saddest thing she'd heard that day.

She was back at Palliser Road before Slider left, and told him what she had learned. 'Oh, and the knife was Tommy's, boss,' she added. 'It seems he kept it just under his bed in case of trouble from punters or suppliers. Bought it years ago from a geezer in a pub. Liked to boast about it and flash it about to visitors, so it's likely whoever he took home last night knew about it or got shown it.'

Baz had also told her that Tommy's father had died in an industrial accident when he was six, and his mother, his next of kin, had quickly taken up with other men. After giving Tommy a succession of 'uncles', she had remarried when he was sixteen and moved to Oldham where she was now living with his two little half sisters. Tommy had been living on his own since then. Baz, with two still-married parents on the scene, seemed to have been the only stable influence in his life – Tommy had spent as much time round his house when they were boys as in his own, and when his mother and stepfather departed he had colonized the Basilides' sofa until he got on his feet enough to find a rented room. But despite their different backgrounds, Baz had always accepted Tommy's own assessment of himself, that he was Captain Cool and a love god, livin' it large on the fast track, while boring Baz was lucky to be allowed to be his humble lieutenant.

'And now he's dead,' Slider said to Atherton when he got back.

'Gone out in a blaze of glory,' Atherton said. 'Some might say he would have wanted it that way. But listen, why did the murderer use his own knife? If the murder was intentional, and part of our series, surely they must have taken their own with them. A Stanley knife and a small cut would have been easier, assuming Tommy had taken enough of something to slow him down.'

'Could it have been a last-minute attempt to make it look like a suicide?' Slider mused. 'Using his own knife.'

'But I've never heard of a suicide managing to cut his own head off,' Atherton mentioned.

'No, obviously not, but perhaps the murderer mistook his own strength or the force needed.'

'Or was overtaken by rage and exasperation and went too far,' Atherton offered. 'From what I've read in Connolly's reports, Tommy Flynn was an annoying kind of bloke.'

'It's got to be connected, hasn't it?' Slider said.

'And hasn't it got to be the drugs?' Atherton added. 'Corley's killed, then Flynn's killed when we ask him questions about it. Flynn presumably was in a position to reveal something about the process by which he was supplied with drugs. And Corley was hanging around all the same people.'

'As was Guthrie.'

'And we know he was dealing drugs. And visiting the same clubs.'

'But Corley wasn't dealing,' Slider said. 'Or using.' There was a silence, then Slider said, 'I'll tell you one thing – it looks as if they're getting panicky. We didn't really have much of a connection between Guthrie and Corley – just that dust-up they had outside the club. But killing Tommy Flynn is trying to stop a leak before it happens. And it was clumsily done. If he'd simply disappeared, we might never have heard about it. And if he'd overdosed, we could never have proved anything. Now they've just drawn attention to themselves.'

Atherton gave a small smile. 'If only we knew who themselves were.'

Slider sighed, staring out of the window at the mute, grey day – summer grey, warm and windless. 'Well, we've got the car details, such as they are. No reg number, but a make, at least, to give to McLaren to narrow it down.'

'That's not much to be grateful for.'

If Porson had had hair to rumple, he'd have rumpled it. In the days when he wore a wig, he had been known to push it noticeably askew in moments of agitation; now all he could do was make unquiet passes of his hand over his bumpy baldness. He was a phrenologist's dream.

'Bloody Nora, what next? It doesn't look good when people get topped for talking to us. Mr Wetherspoon's not happy, not happy at all.'

'I don't like it either, sir,' Slider said.

Porson paused and met his eye. They both knew that Wetherspoon, the borough commander and their boss, didn't like Slider for historical reasons and would use any excuse to disapprove of him. And he didn't like Porson because Porson stood up for Slider. And he didn't much like anybody because he had been passed over for promotion and was always looking for someone to blame. So Mr Wetherspoon's condition of unhappiness was chronic rather than acute, and did not necessarily signify you were doing anything wrong. On the other hand, like the weather, it still affected you.

'I know, laddie, I know,' Porson said in a gentler tone. 'But we need to put something together, something that makes it look as if we know where we're going.'

'If I had anything, I'd give it to you, sir,' Slider said in frustration.

'If we had the sniff of a reason,' Porson urged with a certain pathos. 'Never mind who, if we knew why.'

Slider tried for him. 'I don't think it was personal, or financial. I think he trod on someone's toes. A motif that keeps coming up is that he asked a lot of questions.'

'I asked for a motive, not a motif,' Porson snapped in frustration.

'It was you who suggested it sounded like

246

undercover work, sir,' Slider said. 'All the false names and disguises – what if he was investigating something, and the people he was investigating have finally found out?'

'If that was it, he must have written something down somewhere.'

'He had a laptop when he moved in to Conningham Road, which wasn't there when we went in. It must have been taken away along with everything else. Presumably that's where he kept his notes – if he didn't just carry everything in his head, which would have been safer.'

'Safer until you get your head cut off – then where are you?' Porson demanded unanswerably. 'I'm betting he put his jottings on that laptop. And if he did, he must have backed it up somewhere, in case of a crash.'

'Most likely the memory stick, or whatever it was, was taken along with the laptop.'

'Rubbish,' Porson snapped. 'He'll have put a copy somewhere else, in case of fire. Find that, you've got your story.'

Slider thought of the flat at Wynnstay Gardens. Most likely that was where he'd keep a copy – if there was a copy – if he had kept notes – if Porson was right about the investigative journalism idea. But the flat was enormous and full of stuff, and he didn't have enough people, so without a stroke of luck it might be weeks before they found it, if they found it, if it existed. And Mr Wetherspoon wanted things done yesterday. He was the original hard case that made it bad for the law, in the person of a lowly DI on the job.

THIRTEEN

The Land of Lost Content

The canvass around Flynn's house was yielding nothing – not that Slider had expected anything. The early hours of the morning were a prime time for everyone to be in bed and asleep, and people who lived with a railway at the bottom of their garden tended to have a high tolerance of ambient noise. It gave McLaren another few sets of traffic cameras to trawl through. If it was the murderer who picked Tommy up outside the pub, they did not take him straight home – they would have turned left, not right, at the end of the road to do that; and in any case would have been home much earlier, as it was only a couple of minutes away by car. Kelly Watson might not be the world's most reliable witness, but they had checked, and the film she said she had been watching did not finish until 12.35, so even if she had gone straight to bed and fallen asleep at once, Tommy Flynn must have been somewhere else before going home.

McLaren, the Shane Warne of Shepherd's Bush nick, had a new patience along with his new look – probably the result of much-lowered blood pressure – and simply took on the fresh work with a nod. Slider couldn't help feeling that under the Jackie regime he wasn't enjoying life as much as he used to, but there was no doubt it made him a useful employee.

The papers on Friday went to town on Tommy Flynn, with the fancy knife, buckets of blood and known cocaine-habit aspects of the case. Mrs Panda had not been slow in putting herself forward, and must have been gratified to see herself on the newsreels, leaning against the door jamb, a vision in Lycra, with her saggy-bottomed children lurking behind her legs while her words were immortalized on the news screens. Porson and Slider were happy enough with the distraction. So far, they had managed to keep a lid on the Corley murder. The death of the unknown Robin Williams in the rented flat had not rated more than a paragraph and no one so far had made any connection: Mrs Shepstone was not one to go to the press, and the porter, Perkins, had evidently remained on his dignity. It could not last for ever but it was good for them while it did.

Slider went to Hammersmith straight from home on Friday morning, summoned to a meeting, aka bollocking-and-frightening at the hands of Mr Wetherspoon, at which it was decided to keep the Corley aspect secret for as long as possible. If there was a drugs or gang side to it, it was best not to alert the denizens of that world that they were going to be investigated. But, if it turned out to be personal after all ... Mr Wetherspoon said, and left it hanging in his most menacing way.

And what had Corley been doing after he quit the Hot Box job, he demanded.

'That's what we're looking into right now, sir,' Slider said, and got a look so icy it could have sunk large liners.

'Well, get on with it, then! I want some results, pronto. Do I have to put a rocket under you?'

When Slider got in to his office at last, Atherton had gone over to Wynnstay to supervise the search, but Hollis was there with a piece of paper and a hopeful expression.

'They found this, guv, in Corley's room,' he said. 'Atherton scanned it and emailed it over – thought it might be something.'

It was a printout of a Google map showing a part of rural Hertfordshire. On the white border at the top of the page was handwritten 'New Farm, Gubblecote' and a postcode; the Google arrow was pointing to a group of buildings with NEW FARM printed beside them in tiny writing. And in the border at the side of the page was scribbled '2.30 Tues 19th'.

'It were in a mess of papers on the desk by the computer in the bedroom that's been made into an office,' Hollis elaborated. 'Atherton says the thing in the pile straight underneath's a gas bill for the Wynnstay flat with the due date twenty-first of July, so it looks as though it might be from around the time we're interested in – after he left the Hot Box, which Villiers said was mid-July. And the nineteenth of July was a Tuesday.'

'It certainly looks like an appointment. Of course, he might just have scribbled it down on the nearest piece of paper. It might have nothing

250

to do with New Farm,' Slider said.

'Aye, guv, but Atherton says it does look like the same ink, both scribbles,' said Hollis. Of course, Atherton would have thought of the same thing.

'I wonder how he'd get out there,' Slider mused. 'He didn't have a car, as far as we know.'

'Train to Tring, most like,' said Hollis, 'and then a taxi. You see from the map it's only about three or four miles from the station. Unless he hired a car.'

Slider shook his head. 'Train's more likely, I think. He'd have had to show a driving licence to hire a car, which would have revealed his identity, which he seems to have been at pains to conceal all along.' He thought a bit while Hollis looked at him hopefully. 'I think I'll go and have a look,' he said at last. 'See what's there.'

'Not on your own, guv,' Hollis said. 'If it's something to do with the case—'

'If it's not, I'll have had a wasted journey.'

'Take someone with you,' Hollis urged.

'Everyone's busy,' Slider said. 'I won't take any risks, don't worry. If there's anything interesting there, I'll call for backup.'

It was good to get out into the country again, and especially on a lovely summer day. The muggy oppressiveness had been dispelled by the storm and the greyness of yesterday had given way to a deep blue sky with big white cauliflower clouds. The best sort of day, and this part of Hertfordshire was the best sort of English countryside, soft, green and rolling, the pastoral idyll at its wholemeal and buttery best. You

251

expected a film crew round every corner shooting food commercials.

He parked the car on the road by the farm lane entrance, deciding to walk the last bit. As he stopped the engine and got out, the profound silence of countryside settled round him like a mantle. There was nothing but bird sounds: a flock of jackdaws, rollicking from tree to tree deleting expletives; greenfinches canarying away in the hawthorns; unseen robins threading silver beads on invisible strands. A testosterone-rich cockerel was ushering some of his wives along the field edge, pausing every few steps to crow, arching his body spasmodically as though it were being pumped out of him. But under that, you could feel the silence like a great benign pressure on the skin.

Slider stretched and stared, his tensions releasing themselves, country boy that he was. All around, the green patchwork of field and hedge, corner-pinned with tree clumps and occasional snugged-down farm buildings, rolled to the horizon and the long curve of the Chilterns. The downs were tree-clad – Ashridge Forest, Tring Forest – and impossibly blue with the distance, as though they were exhaling a soft cobalt smoke.

He walked down a grass and baked-earth path between fields – wheat on one side, late this year after the bitterly cold spring and still only half ripe, the olive-yellow colour of oak flower. On the other side, the cockerel's field was a hay meadow, long cut but still fringed with blue scabious and yellow goldenrod, kex and mallow

252

and purple knapweed, the hedge tangled with bramble and bee-heavy old man's beard.

The smell of summer-warm grass came up to him, and suddenly he stopped, riven with such a piercing sense of place that for a moment his breath caught. It was the smell of his boyhood, the freedom and innocence and endless goodness of being nine years old, growing up in the country, in the summer. He stood paralysed with an agony of loss and longing for the fields he had roamed in summer days that seemed to go on for ever; when his mother was still alive. You could go back to a particular point on the earth's surface, but it would not be the same *where*, and it would not be the same *when*. Adulthood is the unending exile, from which there is no return.

He was brought back to the present by the familiar sound of hooves on packed earth, and of warm breath blown out from soft, velvet-edged nostrils. He turned the corner and came upon the next field, post-and-rail fenced, and a handsome, fine-boned bay horse was suddenly right before him. His quick eye had taken in the woman on the far side of the paddock, bucket and rope in hand. He assessed the situation before he was aware of it, and as the horse, which had been prancing light-heartedly, stopped in surprise at his sudden appearance, it was an action without conscious thought that put out his hand and caught hold of the head-collar.

The bay jerked back in reaction, but it knew it was caught and submitted good-naturedly, lowering its head, and mumbled at Slider's buttons. He scratched gently at its forehead, and it regarded him with large, lovely, calm eyes.

The woman was coming towards him – middle-aged, and slender with the natural leanness of constant activity; dressed in jodhs and jodhpur boots and a dark green polo shirt, face and arms nut brown, short curly brown hair. There was another horse in the field, a thickset, cobby chestnut with a heavy blonde mane and tail, which he recollected had been frolicking and bucking in the other direction at the moment he appeared, and was now still, watching developments.

'Thanks,' the woman called as she grew near. 'He likes to play up a bit before he's caught, but I'm in a rush this morning. They always know.'

'He's a fine fellow,' Slider said. 'Bred?'

'Three quarters,' she said. 'His name's Mansur.' She looked over her shoulder. 'Clover will come now he's caught. Afraid of missing anything.'

Slider looked, and, yes, the stout chestnut was hurrying towards them as fast as she could waddle without actually breaking into a trot.

The woman regarded Slider consideringly. Her face was smooth and all-weather brown, lightly fretted around the eyes with sun-frown lines. She seemed late forties but could have been older – hers was not the sort of face to show age – and you would not have called her beautiful, but she had fine eyes. Slider had to stop himself staring.

'You know about horses,' she said, and it was not a question, more a laying down of a marker for ways in which they could relate to each other.

'I grew up on a farm.'

'Not many people can say that now,' she remarked. The chestnut reached them, blowing, fussing; laid her ears back to establish precedence and shoved her head forcefully into the bribe-bucket. But the bay paid no attention, only breathed out contentedly into Slider's jacket and settled itself more comfortably into his caressing hand.

'Did you know he's lost a shoe on the near hind?' Slider said.

'Yes, I found it by the gate last night. God knows how he managed to get it off. He's always casting them. Luckily the smith's coming this morning anyway to do removes. But I got behind, and they always know when you're in a hurry.'

'I'll lead one back with you,' Slider said.

'There's no need,' she began, and then considered him again. 'Did you come to see me? You're not a farmer now, are you.' It was not a question. The suit was a dead giveaway.

'I'm a police officer,' he said, and saw her register an *Ah, that's what it is about you* conclusion. 'You're in a hurry. I'll lead one, and we can talk on the way.'

'You can take Mansur, then, since he seems to like you,' she said. She had to pull the chestnut's head out of the bucket to clip on the lead rope. The bucket was empty now, but the greedy blonde muzzle was still hoovering about in there looking for stray oats. Slider climbed over the fence, and they started off towards the gate on the far side. Beyond it there was a nice, square

Victorian farmhouse, tile-hung and with tall chimneys, Hertfordshire style, and a collection of farm buildings, some old, wood with red-tiled roofs, some all corrugated iron, and some hybrid, wood with corrugated roofs.

'What sort of farm were you brought up on?' she asked, and the topic lasted them, along with discussion of how farming had changed, until they reached the yard, where there was a range of well-kept looseboxes, and two more heads looking over doors. The newcomers whickered and were answered, and Slider wondered, not for the first time, what it was horses said to each other.

'Are they all yours?' he asked.

'Oh no. I do liveries,' she replied. 'My husband and son farm, but every little helps, you know, these days. Can you put him in that end box? Leave the head collar on.'

When he came out again, bolting the door behind him, she was waiting for him, hands on slim hips, enquiry on her face. 'I'm Angela Kennedy,' she said. 'What can I do for you?'

'Bill Slider,' he replied, holding out his hand. Hers was grubby, but he never minded clean horse dirt. 'I should show you my identification.'

'I believe you,' she said, but he showed it anyway. He didn't want this nice woman ever to be taken in. 'Detective Inspector?' she said. 'Does that make it something serious?'

'Serious for us, not for you,' he said. 'I wonder if you'd mind looking at this photograph and telling me if you know this man.'

'Oh yes,' she said at once, studying the picture carefully. 'I recognize him, though he looks a bit different – the hair, I think. It's Colin.'

So he was being Colin Redgrave when he came here, Slider thought. 'When was that?'

'When I last saw him? It would be, let me see, the middle of last week. Wednesday? Why do you ask? Is he in some kind of trouble?'

He read honesty from every line of this woman, just as he knew the gelding was a good horse. 'I'm sorry to have to tell you that he's dead. He appears to have committed suicide.' Her face registered shock and distress. 'He had no form of identity about him, and we've been trying to find out who he is. We did find a Google map of your farm among his things, so we thought he might have come here.'

'Well he did, you're right – but what a terrible thing! He seemed so nice, and not at all de-pressed. Why did he do it, do you know? Did he leave a note?'

'No, nothing at all. It's a mystery to us, too. You say he came here – would you like to elaborate?'

She frowned for a moment, assembling her thoughts. 'I'll tell you everything I know about him, which isn't much, but you're applying to the wrong person. You need to be speaking to David. Come in the tack room and I'll get you his phone number. I'll put the kettle on, too – I think I need a cup of tea, now, before the smith comes.'

In the tack room she lit the gas ring under a large, battered kettle, and as she dropped tea

257

bags into mugs she began to explain. 'I told you I take in liveries. A lot of them are local children's' ponies, and I have hunters in the winter – they're out at grass at the moment – but Mansur and two others in the boxes belong to a long-term client of mine, David Regal.'

Slider's mind twitched under the sting of the familiar name, but his face betrayed nothing.

'He's a wealthy businessman – very wealthy, I gather,' she went on, 'and he's very keen on horses. I think he owns a couple of racehorses as well, but he's been keeping riding horses with me for, oh, it must be five or six years, now. He can't get down to ride them as often as he'd like, so I have to keep them exercised and schooled. But when he can get away, it's usually at short notice, so I have to keep them up. He telephones me to get them ready and he drives down from London with a friend or two, and goes out for a long hack. We have good riding country round here.'

'I can see that you do. So he brought this young man Colin with him, did he?'

She looked uncomfortable, and played with a teaspoon. The sunlight, struggling in through the small and filthy window, played with her unkempt curls. 'David's a good client of mine,' she said.

'I promise I won't tell him that you told me anything, but I wish you would be perfectly frank with me. It may be very important.'

She sighed and looked up. 'All right. I suppose it might have something to do with ... Anyway, David comes down to ride, and he always brings a friend with him. Usually just one. Always a good-looking young man. Sometimes he'll come with an older man as well, and it's clear he's a business client, but the other is always a beautiful young man.'

'I see,' said Slider.

She nodded slightly. 'They don't last long. After a few weeks or sometimes months, it'll be a new one, and you never see the previous one again.'

'You think he—' Slider began.

'I don't think anything,' she said hastily. 'He's a valued client and pays me very well for keeping his horses. The rest is his business. But you asked, so I'm telling you.'

'I understand. What did you make of Colin?'

'I hoped he'd last a good, long time, because I liked him. He was a cut above the rest – a very bright young man, I thought, friendly and polite to me. Some of them seemed to think they had to treat me like a servant. And he could ride. It was embarrassing sometimes when the ones he brought couldn't. Colin said he'd ridden a lot as a child and I could see he'd been well taught – he had a very good seat and good hands. And he loved horses. I was happy to send them out with him. I know they're not mine, but I care about them, and I can't bear to see them hauled about by the mouth, or have some sack of potatoes banging about on their backs.'

'Do you remember when David first started bringing Colin here?'

'It's not very long,' she said. 'Probably only three or four weeks ago, something like that. But

David seemed quite keen on him, because he's been bringing him more often than usual – twice a week, three times one week. Funny thing—'

She stopped, and at the same moment the kettle boiled, which gave her the excuse to turn away. She filled the mugs and began stirring the tea bags, frowning down at them.

'You were saying,' Slider prompted. He was aware time was short. If they were interrupted she would probably clam up. 'It was a funny thing?'

'I wouldn't have thought Colin was – well, gay,' she said, not looking at him. 'You get a sort of feeling about men, the way they react to you, you know? I'd have thought he was – not exactly interested in me, but noticing me.'

'I understand what you mean.'

She looked up. 'Perhaps that's why he didn't last with David?' she said, making it a query. 'Perhaps he was bi, or undecided. Could that be why he killed himself? He seemed happy when he was here. Maybe that was the horses. If you love them it's hard to be completely unhappy around them. But he chattered to me quite naturally, as if he hadn't a care in the world.'

'Did he ask a lot of questions?'

She smiled. 'Odd you should say that. Yes, he did. I teased him about it, called him a question-box, just like my own son was – though that was when he was much younger.'

'What did he ask about?'

'Anything and everything. I can't remember, specifically. About me and the farm and David and the village and everyone in it. He was inter-

260

ested in everything. It was rather charming, really. Young people can be so shut away these days, only interested in themselves.'

'Do you know what he did for a living?' Slider asked.

'He never said anything about a job,' she replied. 'I can't say I got the impression he was a toiler – I mean, he came here on weekdays with David. Maybe he had money, or his own business. He was well dressed, and he had that look about him, of money.'

'And what about David? What's his line of business?'

She shook her head. 'I really don't know. It's silly, but after all this time I really know very little about him. I know he has his own company in London, and I think he lives in London too, but that's about all. The cheques arrive on time, he pays me in advance, and any extras that are needed he never makes any bones about, so he's a good client, and good clients you don't alienate by asking questions if they don't want to answer them.'

'What about the other businessmen he brought here? What can you tell me about them?'

'Oh, a mixed sort of bunch. Some of them didn't really look like my idea of a businessman. A lot of them were foreigners, and I suppose he was showing them a good time to grease the wheels.'

'What sort of foreigners?'

'I can't be sure – I was never introduced to them. A lot of them I'd say were probably East Europeans or Middle Easterns. At least they knew how to ride, even if they were a bit too dashing in the saddle for my liking.'

Slider got the image: Kazakhs galloping across the Steppes, Arabs galloping across the deserts, Bulgarians – what did they gallop across? David Regal greasing the wheels of business – but what business? And what else did he share, besides his horses?

'So you last saw Colin on Wednesday last week,' he resumed. 'And have you heard from David since? Has he brought anyone else here?'

'No to both questions. I didn't think anything about it, because David doesn't come on a regular basis, and sometimes there'll be a gap of a few weeks. But if poor Colin has – well, that would explain it. I thought he'd come this week-end just past, since he'd seemed so keen on Colin, but he didn't. Was that...? When did it happen?'

'Last Sunday night,' Slider said.

'Oh dear. Oh, it's so dreadful. I hope they hadn't had a row or something like that. And what about his family? They'll be devastated. He was so nice. Well, I expect David will be able to tell you who to get in contact with. How odd that he didn't have any identification with him. Did you say—?'

At this slightly perilous moment they were interrupted by the sound of wheels and a diesel engine, and they both looked out of the window, sealed shut with genuinely antique dust and cob-web, to see a van with a trailer bouncing slowly over the imperfections of the yard. 'Oh damn, it's the smith,' she said. 'I'll have to go. You finish your tea – you won't be in the way here.'

'I'll have to go too,' he said. 'By the way, if David should ring you before I've seen him, don't tell him anything, will you? Don't even say I've been here.'

'Not if you don't want me to.' She gave him an odd look, and he could read the question hovering on her lips: *do you suspect him of something*? But either pressure of time or natural discretion suppressed it. 'Oh, I was going to give you his phone number,' she said instead. She went to the door to wave to the smith, then came back to open a large and mud-smeared ledger, from which she copied down a telephone number on to a Post-it. 'You'll think it foolish, but I don't even have his address. But if I leave a message on his answerphone, he always rings back, so it hasn't been a problem.'

Slider glanced at the number. It was a land line.

'Don't worry, we can get the address from the number.'

'Yes, I suppose *you* can,' she said.

FOURTEEN

Dancing in the Dark

'This case just gets nuttier all the time,' said Atherton, back from the Wynnstay flat. 'What's Corley doing going horse-riding with David Regal?'

'David Regal?' Swilley said. 'Of Regal Forsdyke? The solicitors that're the legal representatives of Ransom – which belongs to the same group as Apsis, which owns the Hot Box. Boss, couldn't David Regal be the big boss that Villiers said was getting very friendly with Corley?'

'It's a bit of a leap, but it's certainly possible,' said Slider.

'So was Corley gay all the time?' McLaren asked in wounded tones. 'No one's ever said that before.'

'He had an affair with Kara,' Hollis said. 'That's definite. 'So he wasn't gay then – or not exclusively.'

'But if he *was* gay, maybe the murderer's a man after all,' said McLaren. 'Black-sack man.'

'What about the woman's print on the vodka bottle?' Swilley objected.

'That could've got there any time,' McLaren answered.

'If he weren't gay but pretending to David Regal he were, he'd get found out,' Hollis said. 'Maybe that'd be enough to make Regal murder him.'

Slider said, 'If it turns out to have been personal after all, Mr Wetherspoon will murder *me*. Obviously we've got to get after this Regal type, but we've got to tread carefully.'

'Sir,' said Gascoyne, 'I don't think it was Regal that was with Corley on the night he was murdered.'

They all looked at him. 'Have you got something?' Slider asked.

'You tracked down the pizza? Good lad,' said Hollis.

Gascoyne looked pleased. 'It wasn't a pizza restaurant, it was an Italian restaurant. Called Giardino, in Elgin Crescent. I was just working my way through them one by one – there's a hell of a lot of Italian restaurants in Notting Hill, you know. It's like looking for a curry house in Brick Lane.'

'Thick as leaves in Vallombrosa,' Slider murmured.

Gascoyne cocked him a look, and seeing no more was forthcoming, went on. 'Well, at first it was all, no, no, just like the other places. But I made everyone look at the photo, and there was this one waiter that kind of clocked it. He said no, like the others, but he gave me a look, and sort of flicked his eyes towards the back, so I went round and waited, and after a bit he comes out the kitchen door.'

He wasn't Italian, though he looked the part –

slim and olive-skinned with dark curly hair. In fact he was Portuguese, but he'd been in the catering trade since he left school, and coming to London for the better money, he'd learned enough of most languages to be anything the punters wanted.

'I see this man,' he said eagerly, having another look at the photo. 'He was in here Sunday night, with a lady. But the manager, Pietro, he says to say nothing, because he was in disguise, this man. We get a lot of famous people in here,' he added proudly. 'Film stars, politicos, all sorts. They don't come in if we talk about them, so Pietro says always, never show you know who they are.'

'And did you know who he was?' Gascoyne asked.

'Me? No, I not know him, but Pietro say he was pop singer in old days.'

'Ben Jackson?' Gascoyne suggested.

'Yes, that was name Pietro say, but I no heard of him. Anyway, he was with lady, came in late, ten o'clock, have meal, then he pay cash, leave good tip, and they go.'

'What time did they leave?'

'Maybe midnight, little bit before? I hold the door for them when they leave. They were nearly the last, we got the last ones out about quarter past twelve.'

'Can you describe the lady to me?'

'Is hard to say,' he said. 'Whenever I come to table, she looking down, or search for something in her bag. I not really see her face much, not close up, just from passing by. I think she good

266

looking, maybe a bit older than him. Had red hair, short like—' He made a curved gesture with both hands from the top of his head to his chin. 'Tight black top, black trousers, very sexy lady. They having good talks and getting romantic, I think. They holding hands across the table at the end.'

'You said you held the door for them. Did you see where they went when they left the restaurant?'

'No, they cross the road, maybe going to car, I don't know. But,' he added eagerly, 'as he go past me, I hear him say to her, "Which club we going to?" But I no hear her answer. She gone in front, not turn her head, I don't know if she hear him, anyway.'

'So you see, sir,' Gascoyne finished his story, 'he was having a romantic meeting with a woman at around midnight, so it's likely it was her he took back to his flat, isn't it?'

'I always thought that bath thing was more like a woman's seduction,' Atherton said.

'It was too early to let him take her home,' Slider mused. 'People might still be around at that time of night. Hence the club. But which one?'

'This is like the Flynn murder,' Atherton said. 'Repeating her effects. Maybe she took Flynn to a club as well.'

'The Forty-Niners is near the Giardino restaurant,' Hollis said. 'Maybe she took him there.'

'And that was Tommy Flynn's club,' McLaren added.

'But we've already canvassed the Forty-

Niners,' Mackay said. 'Couldn't get anyone to recognize Corley.'

'Better ask them again,' Slider said. 'Any other clubs in the area as well. Meanwhile, we've got to think what to do about David Regal.'

'Boss,' said Swilley, 'the phone number you got for him from the horse woman goes to the same address as his office, but when I tried it, there's an answering machine on. And the number listed for the office is different. Doesn't that seem a bit suspicious?'

'You didn't leave a message, did you?' Slider asked.

'No, boss,' Swilley said, managing to convey in two short words that that question should never have been asked.

'Good. The Regal side needs thinking about before we move. Leaving it aside for the moment, I'd like to know why Corley said he'd got a dancing job, and whether there was any connection with Guthrie. Talk to Guthrie's sister, try and find out more about his dancing career: where he trained, was it genuine, did he really dance in those shows, how did he get the jobs – anything that might connect him to anything to do with Corley, the clubs, Apsis, and so on.'

'I get the idea, boss,' Swilley said, still a little wounded. 'You can leave it to me.'

'And I think I had better have a chat with an old friend of mine, who knows more about the clubs and drugs scene than I do.'

The phone had rung and Hollis had answered it. Now he said, 'Guv, there's a lady to see you.'

Slider looked up, and Hollis made a sympathetic face. 'It's Corley's mum.'

She was so obviously and extremely posh that someone from the shop had conducted her straight upstairs to the small interview room, rather than leave her in the cloisters of sin downstairs, where anyone might come in – and frequently did – and where the background smell of disinfectant only served to remind you of the smell of sick it was deployed to cover.

She stood as Slider came in, looked at him seriously and offered her hand. She was tall and slim, beautiful in a well-preserved way, exuding a faint waft of subtle perfume as she moved; her clothes simple but so expensive they put her way outside Slider's realms of experience. Her shoes were a poem, her hands beautifully kept, her thick, sandy-fair hair exquisitely cut, her pearls at neck and ear so good he wanted to bite them. Apart from her tallness, it did not look as though either of her children much resembled her – certainly not in colouring, with her fair hair and fine hazel eyes. He supposed they took after her husband. He remembered Mrs Shepstone saying that Ben had been her pet, and he felt a quickening of sympathy.

He shook her cool hand briefly, introducing himself, and said, 'I'm so sorry for your loss. Won't you sit down? Can I offer you tea or coffee?'

'Nothing, thank you,' she said, sitting. 'You are the officer in charge of – I suppose I must call it the case?'

Her voice was as exquisite and upper class as

the rest of her. One did not meet many people like this any more – there were, to begin with, few of them, and they tended to lead a life so much apart that the circles never intersected. What had she made of Ben's strange career? But he reminded himself that she was a writer, and must therefore have experienced, at least in mind, many different kinds of life.

'My daughter says you do not believe it was suicide. I'm not sure if that makes it worse or not.'

'Neither option can be easy for you,' Slider said. 'You must be devastated.'

'It's hard to take it in,' she said. 'I still expect-ed Ben to be there at the gate when I came through at Heathrow. He always made a point of meeting us when we came home.' She gave a faint smile. 'I think he just liked airports. My husband will be coming back tomorrow – he had business he could not abandon. But I suppose there's nothing we can do anyway. It makes one feel so helpless. Still, I had to come. Perhaps you could tell me what one does about funeral arrangements. I have no experience of what happens in a case of – murder.'

She hesitated slightly on the word. She was afraid of making it real by saying it out loud. But it was already too late for that. He spoke to her calmly and quietly about the procedures, and saw her brace herself on the practicality. At the end of it she said, 'If there is any way in which I can help – any questions I can answer for you ... But I expect Jennifer has already told you every-thing.'

'It's never possible to know everything,' he said. 'That's the problem. But there is something I wanted to ask, and it would save bothering Mrs Shepstone again.'

'Please,' she said, almost eagerly. 'Anything.'

'Did Ben have any training in dance? I know he studied music, and he was a member of Footlights which showed he had acting ability, but was there ever any formal stage training?'

'No,' she said. 'He studied piano, clarinet and classical guitar at school. He never went to stage school, or a dance school. Why do you ask?'

'When he left the last job we know about – as a barman in the Hot Box club – he told them that he had a better job, as a dancer.'

'A dancer? Where?' she asked with surprise.

'That's what we're wondering.'

She shook her head. 'He learned a few dance moves when he was in Breaking Wave, for their videos, but that was all. He must have been joking.'

Or laying a trail, Slider thought.

'But I don't understand – what do you mean, the last job, as a barman? Ben was a journalist, for *Musical World*.'

Slider looked at her carefully. 'I think I had better tell you what we know so far.'

'I wish you would,' she said.

She listened in silence to his exposition, but her face became more bewildered by the sentence. When he had finished she said, 'False names? Dyed hair? Night clubs and pornographic films? I can hardly believe all this. It's – it's farcical! Are you quite sure it's Ben you're talking about?' Before he could answer she waved the question away with a hand, and closed her eyes in a pained way. 'I'm sorry. I can't believe I said that. Of course you're sure. But what on *earth* was he doing?'

'I rather hoped you might have an idea about that.'

She shook her head, but lapsed into a silence so obviously intensely thoughtful that he waited it out, and when at last she looked up, he said quietly, 'What is it? Please tell me.'

She drew a breath, gathering her thoughts. 'I don't *know*, of course – it's the purest guesswork – but what it *looks* like is–' another pause, perhaps searching for the right word – 'knight-errantry.'

'Knight-errantry?'

'It would have been very like him. He was a very gallant person, underneath the careless exterior, and very protective of those he loved.'

'You are thinking of Annie Casari?' She nodded. 'What did you think of her?'

'I thought her a sad, weak, lost soul – out of her place and out of her depth. I was unhappy about Ben's relationship with her, because it was very bad for him, without, as far as I could see, offering any real hope for her. Horrible as it is, I have to admit a small part of me was relieved when she died – though desperately sad for her and her family, of course – because it set Ben free.'

'But I thought he was no longer going out with her?'

'He wasn't, officially. But that didn't mean he

didn't still care for her.'

'Your daughter said he was over her.'

She gave a small nod. 'Yes, I can understand Jennifer saying that. She probably convinced herself that it was so. She was always inclined to underestimate the strength of Ben's feelings for Annie, because she didn't want it to be true.' She sighed. 'Poor Jennifer. She has always believed I favoured Ben.'

Slider said, 'She told me he was your favourite.'

'It's very hard, when one of your children is brilliant and the other is not, to make them both feel you are treating them alike. Ben didn't think I favoured him, and I made every effort not to, even sometimes being harsher with him that I would otherwise have been, so that Jennifer would not feel hard done by. But some things seem to be beyond reaching. Jennifer felt herself inferior to Ben and so assumed everyone would treat her as second-class. The miracle is that it didn't make her hate her brother. She loved him and tried to protect him, always, from childhood upwards. And one of the things she wanted to protect him against was Annie, because she could see, as we all could, that Annie was not good for Ben. Of course, she would never have thought anyone was good enough for Ben. But Ben loved Annie, and there was nothing to be done about that.'

'So at the time of Annie's death, you think he was still in love with her?'

'I know he was. He wrote to me, several impassioned letters. They were very hard for me

273

to read.'

'You were not at home – in England, I mean – when Annie died?'

'No. We had come for our spring holiday early, but we left England a week before it happened.' She looked at him carefully. 'You are thinking that I ought to have come back to comfort Ben. But he specifically asked me not to, in his letters. He said there was nothing I could do, and that it would only fret him to have me change my plans on his account. And he was quite right, on both counts. But what occurs to me now is that he may have had another reason.'

'The knight-errantry?' Slider said.

'Yes. If he was embarking on some kind of campaign to – I don't know – save other young women in Annie's situation – going undercover, perhaps, to get close to them and the men who exploited them – it would have hindered him to have concerned relatives enquiring tenderly where he was going every minute.'

'I can see that,' Slider said. 'So you think perhaps he was involved in – shall we call it – investigative journalism? Concerning the drugs scene?'

It had been Porson's idea quite early on – one had to give the old boy credit. He was an oddity, but not a fool.

'It seems to me to make sense of what you've told me. And it would be in keeping with his character. His grandfather used to say he was born asking questions; and he was always careful of those weaker than him. At least,' she said, with a quick frown, 'I hope it was that, and not

274

just revenge. Though perhaps the two are not unconnected.'

'Revenge against whom?'

'The suppliers of drugs. Those who make fortunes out of it, out of the weakness of people like Annie. He did–' she looked uncomfortable – 'write to me in that vein, immediately after Annie's death. But his later letters were more full of love than hatred, so I didn't take it seriously. What do *you* think he was doing?'

The question was sudden and abrupt and took him unprepared.

'I don't know. I think he may have been trying to bring something to light, but what his state of mind was, I can't judge. And I'm no closer to knowing who killed him.'

She winced at the word, but said, 'It must surely be someone from that world, the drugs supplier he was trying to uncover.'

'So one would assume. But unfortunately he hasn't left us anything to go on. If he made any notes about what he had discovered or what he suspected, we haven't found them. There's a missing laptop – stolen, we believe, by the killer – and if there was a backup – a disc or a memory stick or something of that sort – we haven't discovered it yet.'

She frowned. 'If he was taking all these measures to disguise himself, he must have thought what he was doing was dangerous. So if he took a copy of his notes, he would have hidden it – don't you think? Deposited it in a safe place?'

'Yes,' he said, and waited for her to complete

the sequence, as he knew she would, being an intelligent woman.

'But he would have told someone he trusted where it was. "If anything happens to me, open this letter" – that sort of thing?'

'Yes,' he said again. 'So who would he trust?'

'Me. His father. Jennifer. I'd have thought, any of the three of us. Danny, his agent, perhaps. Some old friends. I don't know who his new friends were. But whoever it was, they haven't come forward?' She reached the end of the reasoning.

'No,' Slider said. 'Which leaves us trying to follow in his footsteps.'

'And always a step behind,' she added quietly. Slider's only comfort was that she didn't say it as an accusation.

Hollis was waiting for him when he got back to his office. 'Guv, we've had a call about Flynn on Wensdy night. This bloke saw all the guff and the picture in the paper, and rang in to say Tommy Flynn was in Missie's in Earl's Court Road with a female.'

'Missie's?'

'It's newish, guv – cocktails, cult films, pool, live music, DJs an' dancing – got a good reputation so far, no trouble, and very popular wi' the kids. Opens five in the afternoon till two a.m., Wensdy to Sat'dy. Bloke who phoned in's a bouncer, name o' Derek Ademola, saw Tommy come in the club around midnight with a woman, saw 'em leave again maybe about half one.'

276

'He's sure it's the same man?' Slider asked.

'Yes, guv. Soon as he saw the picture in the paper and realized it was the same guy, he asked one of the barmen that's a friend of his, and this barman says he remembers him too. Had a lot of double vodkas, and danced with the woman very smoochy.'

'What about the woman? Do they know her? Can they describe her?'

'Barman says he never got a look at her close up. It was Flynn 'at come up to the bar and bought the drinks. Says when they were dancing he noticed she had a nice body, wearin' a tight black dress, but that's all. Ademola says she had black hair, kind of square cut like a Chinese girl's, but he never really saw her face because as they went past him she was fishing in her handbag for something, and coming out he only saw their backs. I'm getting 'em both in, just in case, see if they can put anything together between 'em, but it don't look hopeful.'

'How was Flynn, did they say? What was his mood?'

'Ademola says he was in a right happy mood, grinning like a monkey, dead pleased with himself. Had his arm round the woman, and coming out he looks back and gives Ademola a big wink, like, "I'm gonna get it tonight". That's why he remembers him so well.'

'Well, he got it all right, poor fish,' Slider said.

'At least he died happy, guv,' said Hollis. His marriage was on the rocks, so perhaps he could be forgiven.

Swilley appeared at his door. 'Boss?'

'Come in. Sit down – you look tired.'

'No, I'm all right, thanks. Been sitting all day.' She was wearing high-waisted camel-coloured slacks that made her look even taller and slimmer than she was, and a cream blouse, and with her thick blonde hair she was a symphony in coordination. If it wasn't for her rather blank, doll-like features, she'd have been distractingly good-looking. In fact, most of her male colleagues had been distracted at one time or another – to no purpose: she was unattainable, and had a range of searing looks in her armoury that could have taken paint off ships. Slider she had always treated like a father, and he had often wondered whether to take that as a compliment or not.

'I've had a chat with Joyce Finnucane – Guthrie's sister?'

'Yes, I remember.'

'Well, the whole dancing thing is genuine all right. He went to the Arkady Stage School in Tottenham Court Road. Took a lot of stick for it – you know, Billy Elliot style – but there was one teacher there that thought he had talent and took him under her wing. And it was apparently her that got Guthrie his first break, with a touring company doing *Starlight Express*. He was with the same company for quite a while, but then apparently this same teacher got him into *Les Miserables*. I've rung the theatre company and checked, and they say he was in the chorus for just over two years, but he left of his own accord, and quite suddenly. Guthrie's sister says he left *Les Mis* for the Asset Strippers job, but

I've rung the Asset Stripper's management team, and the date he started with them means there was a gap of about six months between the two jobs. And when I asked them how he came to get the job, because there's always a lot of stage-struck kids hanging around who'd love to be a gofer for their favourite band, they said it was someone at UniDigital – that's the Asset Strippers' record company – who asked them to take him on.'

'Who, at the record company?'

'His name's Ed Wilson, and he's Product Manager, which doesn't sound like much, but apparently he's responsible for marketing and promotion strategies for a number of acts. He has to coordinate all the press and promo around record releases and live events, and run the acts' media campaigns, so he's quite important enough to get them to take on a new gofer if he wants it. But why he'd want it I don't know. Why Guthrie'd want it, come to that. It doesn't pay very well, but I suppose it's a lot less work than hoofing for your living.' She looked at Slider, eyebrows raised. 'Want me to find this Wilson and ask him?'

'Yes,' said Slider, after a moment's thought. 'It's an odd sort of intervention, and it doesn't sound as though Wilson and Guthrie were cut from the same cloth, so how did they know each other?'

'Might have been childhood buddies,' Swilley said. 'Life can change a lot from when you're eleven. I know mine did.'

It was a tantalizing opening, but sadly Slider

279

simply didn't have time. There was too much to do. He waved her gently away, and got his head down, trying to complete various bits of paperwork before he had to leave to keep the appointment he'd made to see his old friend from Central days, John Lillicrap.

FIFTEEN

The Get In

The Asset Strippers were on the road and Swilley learnt that Ed Wilson was with them, but fortunately they hadn't gone very far. Saturday would see them in the NEC arena in Birmingham in a line-up of top names, but they were doing a Friday night gig at a stadium on the way, where they would top the bill and give the good burghers of Luton a sniff of the high life, and incidentally conjure an income of half a million quid or so out of their vocal cords and pelvises.

Swilley arrived in the middle of the 'get in', to an organized chaos that brought to mind a kicked ants' nest. Vast artics were being unloaded of lights and staging, and tough-looking road crew were sweating it amid the clanging of spanners, the whining of fork-lifts, thumps and crashes and spine-tingling curses. There was so much writhing black cable underfoot it looked like a scene from an Indiana Jones movie. There were vans unloading crates of beer and Australian champagne, pies and Pepsi, flowers and fruit, racks of costumes, sound boxes and drum kits. Catering caravans pumped out the smell of chips and sausages to add to the fizz of oil and diesel and sweat on the air – shut your eyes and add sawdust and you could be smelling a fairground. Smart PAs and fixers, technicians, publicists, caterers, cleaners, management legs, make-up girls, wardrobe mistresses and gofers darted everywhere like mayflies; arena staff and health 'n' safety officers clutching clipboards wandered among them looking worried. Nearly everyone had either a radio or a mobile to his ear.

And then there was the security contingent: huge, bald men with gold chains and rings on their knuckles like pile drivers, and tattooed, shaven-headed women in big boots. Swilley was tough, and she had the law on her side, but still she reckoned the only reason she got past them was that the limos containing the Asset Strippers and the other acts had not yet arrived. And also she only wanted to see Ed Wilson, the git from the record company – nobody important. She was passed into the care of a small, thin gofer who had been surgically grafted to his radio, and hurried behind him through the ferment to an indoor Portakabin where a sharp-suited, over-cologned middle-aged man, with a permatan and thinning hair carefully eked out to hide the fact, was talking to someone who was so obviously a reporter from the local paper that Swilley felt sorry for her.

Wilson, learning who Swilley was in a breath-less gush from the gofer, smiled very whitely and said, 'I'll be with you in just one second,' and finished rather abruptly with the reporter, who looked almost relieved to be let go – and probably not just because of the aftershave. If she could blend in with the frenetic activity outside she might get a glimpse of the Asset Strippers themselves before security spotted and ejected her.

'Sorry about that,' Wilson said, giving Swilley another flash of the teeth. They were so white he'd have been useful to have around on a rocky shore in the fog. 'How can I help you? I've got a lot more press coming, and I have to be there when the girls arrive, so it'll have to be quick.'

Swilley detached her mind from the problem of whether he was wearing make-up and took his mind back to the distant time two years ago when he had persuaded the AS's management to take on Jesse Guthrie as a gofer.

His frown of thought was so exaggerated he might have been demonstrating it to an acting class. 'Jesse Guthrie?' he pondered.

Swilley didn't want her allotted time to run out into the sands of prevarication. 'Died a few months back of an overdose. Surely you haven't forgotten him already?' she said nastily.

He snapped out of it. 'Oh, I remember him all right,' he said hastily. 'I just wondered why you were asking about him. It's not about the overdose business, surely, because you can't think that has anything to do with me. We at Modern—'

'Modern?'

'That's our record label. We're a subsidiary of UniDigital,' he informed her kindly. 'And all of us at Modern *and* Digital are very anti drugs. Digital contributes extremely handsomely every year to various programmes, and we are zero tolerant of any employees who—'

'But Guthrie wasn't your employee,' Swilley interrupted, in the interests of not falling unconscious from the boredom of the corporate homily. 'So no one could hold you accountable for his death, could they? What I want to know is, why did you get him the job?'

'It was a favour for an old friend,' he said warily.

'What old friend?'

He licked his lips. 'Look,' he said, 'I didn't do anything wrong. I didn't know the kid was going to overdose, did I? It's the last thing I'd want, bad publicity like that.'

'Just tell me everything,' Swilley invited, almost motherly.

A smartphone with a girl stuck to it came through the door, and he said sharply, 'Not now, Tiffany. In fact, I can't see *anyone* for ten minutes. Make sure I'm not disturbed.'

When they were alone, he perched himself on the edge of a table, folded his arms defensively across his chest, and said, 'All right. I got Jesse put on as a favour to an old friend. Well, I say friend – he and I were at school together, and I never much liked him then, but I bumped into him again by chance years later in Canary Wharf and, you know how it is, we went for a drink, got chatting, and he said there was this young friend of his needed a job, and could I get him something. So I did. End of.'

'That's not half a story,' Swilley said. 'Who was this old friend, for a start?'

'His name's David Regal.'

'The solicitor?' Swilley said calmly.

'You know him?'

'I know of him,' she said, as if indifferently.

'And what was his interest in Guthrie?'

'I don't know. He didn't say.' She stared him down. 'All right, look, I *don't* know, but I gathered that David butters his bread the other side, all right? And I suppose Jesse was his – *friend.* Jesse was over age, it was his business – *their* business – nothing to do with me. It's not illegal, is it?'

Swilley kept up the stare. 'What is it you're not telling me? Come on, it's better to get it off your chest, otherwise I'll keep asking and you'll never get rid of me. Why did you do a favour for this bloke you hadn't seen for years and didn't like anyway?'

Wilson hugged his arms closer, his feet fidgeted on the floor, his face looked drawn. 'It's ... I don't want...' He dithered. 'If it got out...'

'It's not you I'm interested in, if that helps,' Swilley said. 'Just tell me everything and I'll go away and you'll never see me again. C'mon, what did you do? It can't be that bad.'

'It would be if it got out. Look, the fact is, I *had* to do David a favour.'

'He blackmailed you?'

'Sort of.'

'How did he manage that if you hadn't seen him since schooldays?'

He blushed. 'Well, that wasn't quite true. I'd met him a few times. He had an office not far from mine. I was just out of my first divorce, I was at a loose end. David seemed to have a pass

285

to all the clubs. It was better than sitting at home being miserable. Then one night after work he invited me to this party at a private flat, one of those converted warehouses. It was hot stuff. Shedloads of booze and charlie. Everyone got pretty spaced. There were girls – and boys.'

'Are you into boys as well?'

'*No*! I told you, I was married. Twice. But I had a thing that night with a couple of the girls. And then there was a raid.' He looked at Swilley resentfully. 'I don't know why you lot can't leave people alone. We weren't doing anyone any harm.'

She ignored the bait. 'Go on. What happened?'

'David got me out. There was a fire escape at the back. The police were down the bottom, in the back yard, but he took me up the stairs, and we hid at the top until they'd gone. Damn near froze to death, but it was better than getting arrested. In my business, that would have been curtains for me. It was in the papers the next day, and a couple of businessmen got photographed coming out still in bondage gear. UniDigital would have had my guts for garters if it'd been me.'

'So you were grateful to him?'

'Yeah, kind of. But I'd learnt my lesson. I stopped meeting him, made excuses when he rang, and after a bit he stopped asking. I didn't see him for about a year. Then I bumped into him, like I said. Except, looking back, it may not have been accidental. Anyway, he said come for a drink, so I did, reluctantly, and then he said he wanted to ask me a favour. Get a job for this young man.

286

When I hesitated – because I didn't want to get involved – he said I owed him, and it would have been easy to get out himself that night and let me take the rap. And he said he could still tell the story if he wanted to. I said he had no proof, but he said on the contrary, he had photographs, and my employers might be interested.'

He looked at her in a drawn way.

'So it was blackmail,' she said.

'He didn't put it like that. When I got angry with him, he said it was just a favour for a favour, and I'd never hear from him again if I did this one thing. He said he wanted the boy in the Asset Strippers team, but it could be something lowly, like a gofer. He wanted him to have plenty of spare time, he said. Well, you can never have enough gofers, but when you've got plenty of them, they can take time off. Not that any of them usually want to – they do it for the bands, not the money. Anyway, I did it – got him the job. I can tell you, I felt sick about it – it's horrible being manipulated – and I kept thinking, what's coming next? Because I couldn't believe that was all he'd ask. But in fact I haven't heard from him since.' He shuddered. 'But it hangs over you, you know. Like a shadow. Waiting for the blow to fall. And every time I saw Jesse, it was like it was David watching me, like a death's-head saying, *I'll be coming for you – today, tomorrow, sometime.*'

Too much imagination, Swilley thought dispassionately. It made him easy to work on. And even yet she was sure she hadn't heard the all of what he had done that was blackmailable. But it

287

didn't matter. 'What do you know about Jesse?' she asked.

'Nothing. Never met him before, don't remember ever speaking to him afterwards. Saw him around, that was all. I'd got him the job, that was all I wanted to know. Then I heard he was dead. End of.'

Swilley hated that expression. 'And what do you know about David Regal?'

'More than I want to.'

'What sort of solicitor is he?'

'I don't know. He never really talked about it. But I imagine its commercial or corporate law, not your high-street wills and conveyancing because he makes a shedload of money. Fabulous suits. Big house in Highgate, Bentley convertible. He backs shows, owns a couple of racehorses. I know where it goes, all right, but not where it comes from.' He laughed, and then heard how inappropriate it sounded, and stopped. 'Look, is that all? Because the girls will be here any second and if I'm not on hand it could be my job.'

Swilley nodded. 'All right. That will do for now. I might have to come back, so don't go anywhere.'

'Where would I go? Unless you get me sacked.'

'I don't mean to do that. I'd like you where you are.'

She had reached the door when he said, 'Bit late, asking about Jesse now, aren't you? It was months ago he died. What gives?'

'Just clearing up a few details,' she said.

288

She was half way out of the door when he added, 'He's married, you know. David. Lovely woman. I've seen her in the glossies at premieres and so on. So the boy thing can't be exclusive.'

'Regal's office is in Leadenhall Street,' Swilley said.

'So, not notably close to Canary Wharf,' Slider said.

'Which sounds as if the meeting was engineered,' said Atherton.

'Or he was in Canary Wharf for some other reason,' Slider concluded.

'Yes, boss,' Swilley said. 'I did a bit of digging, and it looks most likely the party that Wilson was at, that got raided, was the one in Royal Victoria Docks a bit over three years ago. The flat was one of those luxury warehouse conversions, done out regardless, but no one lived there. It was a corporate hospitality flat, owned by the Marylebone Group. And that *is* just round the corner from Wilson's office. So maybe that's what Regal was doing in the area – using it for his own purposes.'

'Sounds likely,' Slider said. 'How did you find out about the raid?'

'Oh, worked out the rough date, looked through the newspapers online, then I rang the Newham police. Spoke to a sergeant who was on the raid – it was a bit of a highlight for them so they still remember it. Copped a few celebrities, and quite a lot of high-up businessmen doing naughty things. They had porn films, S and M, rent boys and girls, booze and drugs. Funny thing is, he said they had an anonymous tip-off about it, and he's convinced in his own mind it came from inside.'

'Inside what?'

'Inside the corporation.' She looked at him levelly. 'So what if it was a put-up job?'

Slider followed her drift. 'You mean what if all those people were invited there to compromise them? What for?'

'Blackmail.'

'But that's blown out of the water if it's all over the papers,' Atherton objected. 'You can't blackmail people over stuff that's already in the public domain.'

'Yes, but Ed Wilson wasn't the only one who was saved that night. My sergeant said when they went in, the inspector in charge told them which people to arrest and which to leave alone. There were about half a dozen players, he says, who were sent into another room while the rest were taken out. He thought at the time they were maybe foreign diplomats, or high-ups they'd been told to leave out of it, because prosecuting 'em would embarrass the government. But what if they weren't? You could get a nice double-whammy that way, ruin people who were in your way, and make some others grateful, or black-mailable in the future.'

'Put them on ice, for when you needed them,' Atherton said. 'Clever.'

Slider frowned. 'But something like that would have required a degree of cooperation from the police. Who was the officer in charge?'

'It was an Inspector Stuart Mellon, boss. And I asked: he left the Job soon afterwards. Voluntarily. Went to live in Florida. Apparently he inherited a lot of money from an old auntie. Brought in champagne and a cake and everything to celebrate his good fortune.'

'That's so lame,' Atherton said. 'Inheritance from an old aunt? Couldn't he have thought of something a bit more original?'

'It could have been true,' Slider said, putting on the brakes. 'But it is suggestive.'

'Marylebone don't still own the flat, by the way,' Swilley added. 'They sold it soon after the raid. Made a big profit, so maybe that was just good business.'

There was a silence. Then Slider said, 'I wonder if Corley had any idea before he died what he was getting himself into?'

'What're we going to do, boss?' Swilley asked.

'All this about the party being rigged is speculation,' Slider said.

'Though very nice speculation,' Atherton urged.

'But it seems to bear out Wilson's story, and that means Regal had some very good reason for wanting to get Jesse Guthrie that job.'

'It could just be that Guthrie was one of his young men, like Corley – or like he thought Corley was – and he was setting him up for himself,' Atherton said in fairness. 'It might well be difficult to carry on an affair with someone who's doing seven shows a week singing and dancing. Limited spare time and even more limited energy.'

'Yeah, and Regal did ask Wilson to get him something that wasn't too much work,' Swilley said.

'Whatever the reason, I think it's time to pay a little visit to Regal.' He looked at his watch. 'There's just about time to get down to his office before closing. I can't go – I've got a meeting set up. It'll have to be you,' he said to Atherton.

'Shouldn't I ring first?' Atherton said. 'He might not be there.'

'No, I don't want him alerted. Even if he isn't there, you can get a good look at the office itself before they're prepared – see who else works there, maybe get a squint at some papers that tell you what they do. And try to find out about that answering machine Regal's number went to. Where is it, who monitors it, who else uses the number.'

'Anything else you want to know?' Atherton asked in a pained manner. 'The postman's shoe size? No use in making it too easy.'

'That's why I'm sending you,' Slider said, with the nearest he could manage to an insincere smile.

Atherton drew himself up. 'In that case, I shall sift the evidence down to the last atom and quark.'

'You don't know what a quark is,' Slider challenged.

'I do. It's the sound made by a posh duck,' said Atherton.

Slider felt a reprehensible little quiver of Schadenfreude to discover that John Lillicrap, who was the same age as him, looked a lot older and was bald right over the top of his head, with the bit left round the sides and the back quite grey. It made up for the fact that Lillicrap, starting from the same place, had made superintendent in an SO squad – until ill health brought on by the strain had forced him to step down and sideways to an administrative post in a quieter backwater.

They hadn't seen each other in quite a while, but despite the new slap-top, Slider recognized him at once when they met outside Leicester Square station, and it only took one look into his pleasant, nondescript face and honest brown eyes to remember the liking they had had for each other back in Central days.

They walked together, talking about old times, families and careers, through streets that smelled sweet and sour – sour with garbage and sweet with Chinese five-spice – over pavements that were pocked with chewing gum, but these days, thank heaven, free of dog-doo. 'Remember how you used to have to skip about like a flea to avoid it?' Lillicrap said when Slider mentioned this.

'I used to think Soho must be hosting the World Incontinent Dogs Conference,' Slider said. 'Where are we going?'

'Little place I've discovered. Bit of a haven in this gastro-tourist-trap, especially in August.' They turned into Frith Street, past Ronnie Scott's, where they had spent many pleasant hours after coming off duty in the old days, and a few doors down Lillicrap stopped.

'Here it is. Doesn't look like much – that's why the tourists stay away. I've booked us a table. Not too early to eat is it?'

It was called the Bon Bourgeois, and featured a window and door both net-curtained and impenetrable and a rather shabby fascia board above. Slider could see how tourists would pass right by unless they'd been recommended to it. Inside, the door led on to a short passage with stairs straight ahead, and another door to the right led into the restaurant, which was comfortably lit, low-ceilinged and cosy, with square tables covered in fine white tablecloths, plain wooden chairs, and nothing on the walls but the light sconces. This was a restaurant where the clients looked at each other and not the décor.

A young waiter in black with the traditional long white apron came at once to greet them and seemed to know Lillicrap, for he began leading them to a table without anything being said. As they sat, a female version, smiling, gave them menus and enquired about drinks.

The food was regional French, and the smells wandering about the room were certainly agreeable, and were worming their insidious way into Slider's saliva glands. 'Let's get the order in, then we can talk,' Lillicrap said. 'I'm going to have the onion soup – not very summery, but it's a favourite of mine. And then the roast lamb.'

The roast lamb was billed as *pre salé avec persil et salicorne*, but there was no way John Ernest Lillicrap was going to show himself up trying to order anything in French. Slider chose the *millefeuilles de saumon fumé*, which

294

sounded intriguing, and then staked his evening on the *boeuf bourguignon*, a dish that could be wonderful or terrible, but which Lillicrap said was wonderful here.

'So, Bill,' said Lillicrap when they were finally left alone, 'what was it you wanted to talk to me about?'

'It's a bit of a complicated case, seems to be spreading in all directions, but it keeps coming back to the clubs. And cocaine. So I wanted to get your reaction and pick your brains. Maybe I'd better tell you about it from the beginning.'

'I've got all evening,' he said comfortably. 'And I like a good story.'

'There's not much good about it,' Slider said. 'But here goes.'

The exposition lasted them right through the starters – which were excellent – and Lillicrap had to order a second bottle of Beaujolais with the main course. Slider's *boeuf bourguignon* proved a triumph – made properly with fat bacon and sweet garlic and lots of tomato paste, long-cooked until the beef was as soft as butter and the sauce was velvety and dark as love.

'Secret ingredient,' Lillicrap said. 'They grate a bit of dark chocolate into it.'

It was so good it took Slider some self-discipline to get back to the sordid story. He finished at last, and there was a silence as Lillicrap digested it and Slider digested beef stewed in burgundy wine.

'It does sound as if you're on to something,' he said. 'It has all the hallmarks of a nasty little operation – except not so little.'

295

'Jesse Guthrie – has he come on to your radar?'

'Not that I recall – but there's more than one ring working in London, Bill. I know of the Hot Box but it wasn't one of the places we were watching. You can only do so much at a time. You follow one line and shut it down. But there's always others working alongside all the time, and as soon as you create a vacuum something else fills it up.'

'Tell me about the clubs,' Slider said.

'Oh, the clubs!' Lillicrap drained his glass, reached for the bottle and poured for them both. He looked a little worn. 'Of course the clubs are one of the main markets – clubs and pop concerts and some of the pubs – wherever the young and stupid hang out, begging to be parted from their money. We know that's where the final sales are taking place – and most of the consumption too. But there's fifty clubs in Soho alone; take the radius out another mile and there's a hundred more. And then there's the older set, the thirty-somethings, bankers, MPs, media types, various high-flyers, who have their own exclusive clubs, plus private and semi-private parties – a whole different ring. We know where the stuff is being sold to the punters, all right, and sometimes we know who's selling, but that's not the level we were interested in. What we wanted was the level above, who could lead us to the distributors. It's no good tugging 'em too low down – the trail just blows away like breadcrumbs.'

Interesting he had used that analogy, Slider

thought. Hansel and Gretel again.

'Your Jesse Guthrie sounds like one of the intermediate level. The middle men. He'll pick up his stuff from his distributor, probably a kilo at a time. That makes a package about the size of a bag of sugar, so it's easy to conceal – stick it in a plastic carrier or in your backpack, all looks as natural as can be. Then he'll divide it up into wraps of a gram apiece – he may cut it further at that point, depends on his distributor and his market – and pass it on to the bottom-feeders, ten, twenty, fifty wraps each, whatever they can shift. Your Tommy Flynn was probably one of those. And they sell it to the punters at fifty quid a time and upwards. So his little bag of sugar's worth anything between fifty and a hundred thousand pounds. Let's be conservative and call it fifty. Your distributor's only got to have ten middlemen taking two packages a week, and there's an income of a million a week, fifty million a year. Plus extra for big events, high days and holidays. If they're working that from more than one base, you're starting to talk serious money.'

'Worth killing a few people for,' Slider said, 'if they look like getting in your way.'

'And they do,' Lillicrap said. 'Bodies everywhere, and most of 'em never get into the papers. To tell you the truth,' he added, leaning forward a little more, 'I wish to God they'd legalize the bloody stuff. All this time and effort trying to stop people snorting their disposable cash – who cares if their heads cave in and their hearts explode? That's their business. And it's not the nose-bleeders who give us the trouble, it's the criminals who import and distribute the bloody stuff. Make it legit, there goes their profit, they're out of business overnight. But you can't say that in public, or the media will string you up. And I didn't just say it to you, either.'

'Of course not.'

'Your Guthrie overdosing on pure – you think that was murder?'

'Yes.'

'So do I. What we call summary justice. He must have done something wrong. A quiet execution.' He shrugged. 'He's not important. If you want to break a set-up, you need to find out two things – where the charlie comes from, and where the money goes to – because it's got to be cleaned up somehow to be enjoyed. And those are the two things they'll go to any lengths to conceal.' He looked at Slider levelly. 'But you don't want to go there.'

'Why?'

'Because A, it's dangerous, and B, you might get in the way of an SO operation that's on the same tracks. And that's also dangerous – to you, at any rate. Don't tread on toes, Bill.'

'I have to,' Slider said. 'You know what'll happen if I turn this over to the drugs squad – they'll say Corley's murder's not important in the grand scheme of things. He'll get forgotten. And I don't want him to be forgotten. I like him.'

Lillicrap gave a faint smile. 'You're a daft bugger, Bill Slider. You always were – thinking you can fight for right and justice.'

'Why not?' Slider said, though he knew the

answer to that.

'Because there's only partial right and comparative justice, and there are a lot of vested interests who don't even want that if they have to rock the boat for it. I won't say you're a legend in your own lifetime, but there are places around the Yard – and the corridors of power – where I could mention I was a friend of yours and expect a few chilly looks.'

Slider smiled. 'Feel free to deny me.'

'Oh, I would, mate, don't worry, and I wouldn't wait for cock-crow. I didn't make superintendent by making myself unpopular. And I've got Linda to think of, to say nothing of the kids. Universities don't come cheap these days. You might start thinking along those lines yourself, you know. How much would this Corley have risked for you?'

Knight-errantry, Slider thought. And his mother had called him gallant. 'That isn't the point,' he said.

SIXTEEN

Warm Precincts, Cheerful Day

The office of Regal Forsdyke in Leadenhall Street was in one of the old buildings, tall and severely handsome in glazed red brick to halfway up, with high windows and a massive and forbidding wooden door under a classical broken pediment. It put Atherton in mind of his council primary school. Inside the heavy door was the same smell of industrial polish and the same pitted dark green lino on the floor. A legend on the wall showed the building was divided into a warren of chambers, occupied by various small concerns. The office he wanted was on the second floor. As the lift was some-where up above, and he could hear it rattling and wheezing like an emphysemic chest, he took the stairs.

The door to the office, like all the others he passed, was of heavy dark wood with a frosted-glass panel in the top half, on which REGAL FORSDYKE was painted in neat black capitals, without any other information. He listened a moment and could hear nothing from within, so without knocking he turned the brass doorknob and pushed. For some reason he had become convinced since arriving in the building that the door would be locked, so he almost fell inside and had to make a rapid adjustment of balance to save his dignity.

Inside was an office that could have come straight out of the 1950s, or BBC Broadcasting House, which was much the same thing. Moss green carpet, dark wooden furniture, including hatstand, cream walls, industrial olive filing cabinets, and a middle-aged, grey-haired, comfortably-figured woman in a twinset sitting behind a desk. The only difference was that instead of a typewriter she had the ubiquitous keyboard and monitor in front of her. It was a small office, and wouldn't have held much more than it did without some very un-fifties-like hugger-muggering. The window on to the street, roman-blinded, was in the wall to Atherton's right, and in the wall to his left was another door, standing half open. The room beyond evidently had no window and as the light was off it was dark inside, but Atherton could just see the back of a desk with a handsome leather chair behind it. There seemed to be nothing on the desk but an old-fashioned leather-bound blotter.

The woman had looked up at Atherton's entrance, and now said, 'Can I help you?' in the sort of voice that wished to do anything but. Her hair was short and done in an old-fashioned style that suggested rollers and a hair-drying hood, and her glasses had a pearl chain disappearing round the back of her neck. Atherton felt uncomfortably as though he had fallen through a wormhole into Enidblytonland.

Still, he had a job to do. He smiled his most innocent and engaging smile and said, 'I do hope so. I'd like to see Mr Regal, please.'

She didn't smile in response. It was hard to see her eyes behind the glass of her spectacles, but Atherton got the impression he was being given a very thorough and professional once-over. 'I'm afraid Mr Regal is not here. It is not his day for the office.'

Her accent went with the 1950s BBC motif as well. He wondered if she was a retired civil servant augmenting her pension, and toyed with the notion that she had been in MI6. She'd have made a chilling M.

'Perhaps Mr Forsdyke, then?' Atherton said.

'There is no Mr Forsdyke. Mr Regal bought him out fifteen years ago. May I ask what it is concerning? Perhaps I can help you.'

Atherton let himself appear to consider. 'You're very kind, but I really think I had better speak to Mr Regal in person.'

She gave him another long, considering look, and then reached into a drawer and brought out a large desk-diary. 'Perhaps I can make you an appointment. May I ask your name and company?' she said, opening it and leafing through. Atherton raised himself a little on the balls of his feet, but she tilted it towards her in such a way that he could not get a good look at the pages. Still, in the instant before she did that, he got the impression there was nothing, or next to nothing written there.

'Detective Sergeant Atherton, Shepherd's Bush Police,' he said, watching her face for reaction.

There was nothing, so much of nothing that it

was suspicious in itself. Not a twitch. Not a flicker. She looked up and said smoothly, 'Mr Regal will be in the office on Monday and I can squeeze you in in the afternoon, if that would suit. But if it's urgent, if you would care to tell me what it's about, perhaps he could meet you somewhere else before then.'

To stir or not to stir? Only instinct to go on. 'It's concerning the death of Robin Williams,' he said. 'But I won't put you to any trouble. I can just as easily contact Mr Regal at home myself.'

He thought she would argue about that, but after another look that felt as long as the Pleistocene era and about as warm, she said, 'As you please.' And she poised her hands over the keyboard in a form of dismissal.

Atherton gave her a final, 'Thank you so much,' and left. Outside he stepped to one side, so that his shadow wouldn't be on the glass, and listened. There was no sound of typing, though he had heard it through other doors he had pass-ed, so it couldn't be a question of soundproofing. What had she been doing before he arrived? There was nothing on her desk. Had she seen his shadow pause and concealed whatever she was working on? Or, more suspiciously, had she not been working, but perhaps reading a novel or knitting to pass the time? Was she, in fact, just a caretaker of the address? Because it came to him that the telephone had not rung once while he was within earshot, and while his visit had been short, in his experience solicitors' phones rang all the time.

* * *

303

As it was Saturday, Slider had stopped on his way in and bought doughnuts for everyone. He put the box on the table in the CID room, and a crowd formed and dispersed rather magically, like one of those starling displays. Atherton, last up, peered in and said, 'There's one left. Who hasn't had one?' Mumbled sugary denials left only McLaren, sitting forlornly behind his desk with something red and watery in his mug – it looked like fruit tea, Slider concluded in wonder.

'Maurice?' Atherton said. McLaren shook his head. 'Go on! It's one of those with custard in the middle – your favourite.'

'No thanks,' McLaren said, as joyfully as a man refusing the blindfold.

'Right, let's get on with it!' Mr Porson arrived at that moment, carrying his cup with the saucer balanced on top as usual. 'Are these for anyone?' he asked, and took the last doughnut after a pause for denial so brief Planck would have had trouble measuring it. Did Slider hear a little broken sigh in the background, or was it just the idle wind?

He described his meeting with Lillicrap, and then Atherton recounted his visit to the office of Regal Forsdyke.

'Looks like an accommodation address,' Porson grunted, licking sugar off his lips. 'Set up to repel boarders – anyone making casual enquiries, looking for someone to write his will or sell his house, gets a polite put-off from the madam.'

'There'd be a certain amount of official business connected with Random – and Apsis, if he's

304

their representative,' said Slider.

'I checked, boss, and Regal Forsdyke is named for Apsis as well,' said Swilley.

'And since there's no Mr Forsdyke...' Atherton added.

'Someone would have to deal with the paper-work,' Slider went on. 'And if the landline number Mrs Kennedy gave us goes to that address, I'd imagine the answer machine was in that other office.'

'That was my thought,' said Atherton. 'If it rings and Regal's not in the office, the secretary bird listens to the message and passes it on to Regal, who phones them back – or not, as the case may be.'

'So you're getting round to thinking David Regal is the big boss of your suppostitious drugs ring?' Porson said to Slider. 'The capo di monte, or whatever it's called. What do we know about him?'

'Not much, sir,' Hollis answered. 'He's got a big house in Highgate – we had a look on Google Earth, and it's right grand, got big gates and a high wall right round it. Regal bought it fourteen years ago for five million and change. Islington police say there's never been any trouble there. They didn't like me asking about him. Not keen to have their rich ratepayers upset. They said he gives generously to charity.'

And probably, Slider thought, police charities were numbered among them. He didn't say it aloud, but he didn't need to. They all knew how it worked.

'He's married,' Hollis went on. 'The wife's a

Sylvia Scott, apparently well known in the field of theatrical costume design.' He shrugged in a way that said, *but I've never heard of her*. 'They've been married twenty-three years, could not find mention of any kids anywhere,' Hollis went on. 'He drives a Bentley convertible. Wife's got a Mercedes S class.'

'And that's it?' Porson said when he paused. 'You don't know much, and that's a fact. All right, our boy's a careful boy. Wouldn't last long in this business if he wasn't. We'll assume, for the sake of argument, that it's drugs and he's the big boss. So who did the murders?'

'The two we know about follow a pattern,' Slider said. 'Corley and Flynn each had an encounter with a woman, involving a visit to a nightclub – certainly, in Flynn's case, and probably, in Corley's – before going back to his house in the early hours, when there are few people about so the chances of being seen going in or out are small. With Guthrie we don't know if he met anyone, but of course it's possible. In all three cases, music was put on – presumably to hide any incriminating noise – and left on. Drugs were ingested in all three cases, throat-cutting was employed in two of the three, and there was no struggle by any of them.'

'Presumably the purpose of the drugs,' Atherton put in.

'In Guthrie's case,' Slider resumed, 'it could have been accidental death, or just possibly suicide, but other evidence suggests murder. The other two were certainly murder.'

'So he's got two different women doing the

killing for him?' Fathom said.

'Why not the same woman?' Atherton said. 'From what we've learned she was reluctant to let anyone get a good look at her face.'

'But one was a redhead and one had black hair,' Fathom objected.

Atherton gave him a sidelong gawd-'elp-us look. 'Ever heard of a wig?'

There was an instant of electric silence. In the days when Porson had earned his nickname of The Syrup because of his hideously obvious hair piece, no one had ever dared mention the word 'wig' anywhere within a radius of thirty miles of him. Now everyone desperately tried to think of something to say to take away attention from the blunder, and came up dry.

It was Porson himself who spoke, with no apparent consciousness of his subordinates' brief agony. 'All right, maybe this woman is an accomplish, but she may not be the killer. She might just be bait. That Flynn throat-cutting was a bit drastic for a woman.'

'Doc Cameron said it took determination rather than great strength,' Slider said.

'But in Corley's case it could've been black-sack man who did the murder,' Mackay offered.

'Black-sack man could've been a woman,' Hollis added helpfully. 'The woman Corley was with that evening was dressed in black trousers, the same.'

'But black-sack man was wearing a beanie,' Mackay objected. 'Where'd she hide that while she was wining and dining the victim? And the black sack?'

'Them big handbags women carry these days, she could've easy had the hat stuffed in there. And if Corley didn't have a black sack under his sink, which he probably did, she could've had one of those in there as well. A whole roll of 'em, if she wanted.'

'But who *was* the woman, or women, and how does she relate to Regal?' Porson asked. 'Regal looks like an iffy character, I grant you, but where's the evidence of this drugs ring?'

'We've got him linked to Guthrie,' Hollis said, 'and Flynn worked for one of his companies. Guthrie was a known pusher and Flynn was a big user and sold stuff to his friends. And he's obviously rich, sir, without doing anything for it.'

Spoken out loud, Slider thought, it didn't sound like very much. There was just the gut feeling to go on, that accretion of odd and wrong things about a certain figure.

'If Regal is the head of a drugs ring,' he said, 'then according to DCI Lillicrap, we have to find out where the drugs are being distributed from, and where the money goes to. The only two businesses we know Regal is involved with are the clubs, under Apsis Leisure, and the porn films under Ransom House.'

'Boss, about Ransom House,' Swilley said. 'You know I've been looking at their finances, and there's something weird about it. As they're a branch of a foreign company, they only have to provide simplified accounts to the Revenue and pay their tax, and as long as the Revenue's getting its cut it won't bother them. Well, they're posting a turnover of about fifty million. I mean, what does an adult DVD cost? A legal one. Call it twenty quid, to give us a round figure. That means they're selling two and a half million of 'em. That's not a lot for a Hollywood DVD, but it is for a niche movie. And where are they all? I rang round every place I could find in the Yellow Pages, and nobody had a copy of any of the *Office Orgy* series. A couple of guys I spoke to said they hadn't seen them in years, and they'd never seen any of the later ones – nothing after *Office Orgy Five*. Same with the other series. I know it's not exactly a scientific experiment, but still. A lot of people have heard of them – they seem to be an urban legend – but when you press them, nobody's actually watched one.'

Slider turned to Mackay. 'You were enthusiastic about the series when it was first mentioned. You said they were witty.'

'That's what everyone says,' Swilley objected.

Mackay looked sheepish. 'Yeah, well,' he said, 'I haven't actually watched one for years. Not to say, the real thing. I think number three or four was the last I've seen. But everybody's heard of 'em. And there's any number of knock-off versions around. It's like a genre in its own right, *Office Orgy*. And I've met loads of people who said they've seen one.'

'Like you did,' Swilley said witheringly. She turned to Slider. 'Boss, could that be where the money goes – how it gets laundered? Because if they're admitting to fifty million, it could be ten times that sum that's really going through.'

'There has to be a point to Ransom House,'

Slider said cautiously. 'Paul Barrow's early training was as an accountant. But maybe the DVDs all go for export. They've got that warehouse near Heathrow.'

'We ought to have a look at that,' said Atherton.

Slider looked at Porson. 'DCI Cliff Lampard at Hayes is a friend of mine – he used to be at Uxbridge. I could ask him to have a little look, find out what's going on down there.'

'All right,' Porson nodded. 'But softly softly,' he added. 'Don't want 'em to go tramping in with their size twelves and frightening the horses. But I wish we had something to go on, apart from vague suspicions. You can't make bricks without fire. What else have you got to follow up?'

'Boss, there's one thing I got yesterday,' Connolly said to Slider. She had spent the day with the borrowed bodies from uniform still going through the Wynnstay flat.

'Tell me you found a memory stick,' Atherton begged.

'No, but it's interesting,' she said. 'It was in one of your man's jacket pockets – a little bit of paper.'

She showed it – a piece four inches square of the sort that you tore off a desk note block, which had been folded in half. She unfolded it, and on it was written in hasty script, *Arkady Dance School Tott Ct Rd*, and a phone number.

'The writing matches various bits of Corley's we've found around the place, and there's a pad on the desk that matches this, so it's likely he wrote it down while he was in his office, maybe on a phone call or surfing the net,' she said. 'And the Arkady school—'

'Is the one Guthrie went to,' Atherton concluded for her. 'So at the very least he could have been checking up on Guthrie. I wonder if that was before or after Guthrie got topped?'

'And how long before Corley got topped?' Connolly added. 'No way of knowing. But it's got to be worth a look? I had a squinny on the Internet. Arkady School of Dance and Dramatic Art – that's full handle. Principal, Miss Mary Lynn and a bunch of letters – sure your wan's a genius if all that lot mean anything. Ages twelve to eighteen. Private tuition and adult classes by arrangement. If Corley took a notion to dance, maybe he tried to arrange lessons.'

'What about this Mary Lynn?' Slider asked. 'Anything on her?'

'Practically nothing, boss. She's a shrinking violet all right. No criminal record. There's fourteen million entries for the name Mary Lynn, and a stack o' pictures, but it's not an unusual name and most of 'em aren't for the same woman. The only photo I could find that's reliably her we're looking for is not a very good one. She's in a line-up with the cast of some show she must have been involved with.'

'May I see?' Slider said, holding out his hand.

'Work away,' said Connolly, passing over the printout.

It was one of those 'Back row, left to right,' efforts, and she was on the far left, but the resolution was poor, and all you could see was

311

an impression of attractiveness and the short, curly fair hair.

'Well, we haven't got so very much to go on,' Slider said with a sigh. 'Might as well follow it up. Atherton, do you want to head over there now. Saturday morning's a good time to look at a dance school, isn't it?'

As everybody dispersed, Mr Porson beckoned Slider aside with a look, and turned to him to say, 'You know, if this *is* a drugs ring and Regal turns out to be the big cheese, we've got to tread carefully. Ought really to hand it over to the drugs squad.'

'Yes, sir,' Slider said unhappily. 'But if we do that—'

'Corley gets mothballed,' Porson finished for him. 'I know, laddie. I'm not saying hand it over now, but tread a bit careful, that's all. There's a lot of toes to be put out of joint. If you can get something good and strong linking Corley's death with any of these people, I can swing it, but if it's just vague superstitions – well, there's a limit. A couple more days, and unless you get something it'll have to go. Savvy?'

'Yes, sir.'

Porson nodded and went away. Slider sat down, picked up the phone, and dialled Cliff Lampard's number.

Where the bad end of Oxford Street makes a junction with Tottenham Court Road there's a strange little area, a little seedy and shabby-looking, but filled with interesting small enter-prises. Print shops and kebab shops, sandwich bars and adult books 'n' mags, bureaux-de-change and language schools; electronics and camera shops where the staff and customers converse almost entirely in numbers; surgical appliances, stamps and coins and airfix model kits and all sorts of specialist goodies in shoplets with dedicated if nerdy staff.

On one corner of the crossroads the glass and concrete office tower, Centre Point, rears its thirty-four stories like a sore finger, the Cenotaph of folly and greed. Otherwise the area is all low-rise, a shop floor at street level with three or four storeys above, joined in seamless terraces on either side along Tottenham Court Road and New Oxford Street; and up from Tottenham Court Road tube station boils such a mix of humanity it is probably the best place on earth to go unnoticed.

The dance school was near the corner, and must have had the phallic Centre Point tower visible from the windows of the studios where little girls learnt that frappés did not always come in Starbucks cups. It was an old, brick-built edifice, and probably would have been handsome if it weren't for the decades of rain-streaked soot that disfigured its facade. It took the space of perhaps three or four shops, long enough anyway to have ARKADY SCHOOL OF DANCE AND DRAMATIC ART spelled out just under the first-floor windows in large screwed-on metal capitals. There was an alley down one side of the building that seemed to lead into a rear yard. The main door was in the centre: double, half-glazed, imposing, set back with two shallow steps up to a black-and-white tiled landing. Atherton saw that there was a second, single door at the end of the facade, and as he approached it opened and a lithe-looking young man with a drawstring bag over his shoulder trotted out and strode off and across the road to disappear into the crowd. The door that had closed behind him had a sign on it that said NO ENTRANCE – SENIORS ONLY.

Atherton went to the main door and pushed in to a hall with the same black-and-white tiles, though they looked a little worse for wear and were chipped here and there, and the walls were scuffed and marked by hands and bodies and swung bags. It smelled like a school, he thought, a dusty, worn sort of smell with an undertone of sweat and liniment. On one side the wall was taken up with an enormous and well-used notice board, set into a varnished wooden frame with a sort of curly carved pediment on top, with the words painted in gold ARKADY SCHOOL OF DANCE AND DRAMATIC ART – PRINCIPAL MISS M LYNN.

Occupying the same space on the other side of the hall was a shallow glass display case with a hand-printed notice in the top saying SCHOOL SHOP and showing a variety of different kinds of shoes, leotards, tights, practice dresses, hair bands, and other necessities including the same kind of drawstring bag he had seen the young man carrying – made of thick, glazed black cotton and labelled SHOE BAG – all neatly arranged and priced. Judging by some of the prices, he thought they must make a nice little side earner from all this stuff.

Beyond these a corridor ran off to left and right, and straight ahead of him was a pair of part-glazed swing doors, from behind which came the grating thud of a piano being played with grim determination for rhythm rather than musicality. Atherton suppressed a smile and went in. A dozen skinny little girls in leotards, each with an exiguous frill round the middle, were lined up like so many frenched lamb cutlets, while the teacher in front of them put them through their paces, her back to the barre and mirror that covered the entire wall. The pianist was just inside the door on the left, and on the right was a bench all along the wall with coat hooks above, and a jumble of outdoor clothes, shoe bags, and a few mothers with nothing to do between chauffeuring duties.

Atherton's appearance brought all this worthy activity to a halt. The pianist, her attention on the music, whacked out a few more bars before she realized the little girls had sprawled to a halt, and eighteen pairs of eyes swivelled round to regard Atherton with enquiry not unmixed with horror. The teacher was the first to move. She hurried to place herself between her pupils and the invader, and said, 'Can I help you?' in the sort of tone that really said, *I believe you to be the sort of pervert who likes looking at little girls and I'm on the brink of calling the police.*

'Are you Miss Lynn?' he asked, reaching into his pocket for his brief. Her eyes followed the movement with alarm that was only slightly abated by the sight of what he brought out. 'I'm a police officer. Detective Sergeant Atherton.'

'No, I'm not her,' she said. 'Did you want to see her? What's it about?'

'Is she here today?' Atherton asked instead of answering.

'She's taking a class,' she said defensively. 'It's her day for private pupils.'

'Would you take me to her? It is rather urgent,' Atherton said, and tried a reassuring smile.

She stared a moment longer, then shook herself into action. Turning back to her class, whose eyes were out on stalks, she clapped her hands briskly, and said, 'Girls, to the barre. Twenty-four *ronds de jambe* with the left leg, turn and repeat with the right. And if I'm not back, continue with twenty-four *demi-pliés*.'

She ushered Atherton out into the hall. Just round the left-hand corner was a door with a sign saying WAITING ROOM on it, and she almost shoved him in. 'Stay here. I'll fetch her,' she said, and was gone, closing the door hard behind her as if to emphasize that he must not stir. It was a municipally dismal room, about ten by twelve, painted in pale green gloss to half way up and matt cream above, with a row of hard wooden chairs down either side and a low table at the far end with some desperately geriatric magazines on it. Miss M Lynn with an alphabet soup of letters after her name needed to work on her PR skills, he thought. Or perhaps it was intended to deter visitors. *Repelling boarders*, the phrase wandered through his mind and out again. The only window was high up and had frosted glass in it. The reading matter, he discovered, was old copies of the National Trust magazine and the supplements from various Sunday papers. *Nice touch*, he thought.

Fortunately, the threat of his unfettered presence about the hallowed precincts of this temple to Terpsichore evidently got them motivated, for in quite a short time the door opened, and a woman came in. She was wearing a black practice tunic with a grey crossover cardigan on top, footless grey tights and ballet slippers. Her hair was short and fair, and formed natural feathery curls in a halo round her head. 'I'm Miss Lynn,' she said.

So far so good; but what had come in the door with her was such a powerful aura of physical attractiveness it made Atherton's scalp tingle. It was something a few, rare women had – he had met perhaps two before – and it was nothing they did or said and not even really to do with the way they looked. They just had it, a magnetism that made every man's eye turn to them when they came into a room or walked down the street. She was tall, about five foot eight, and slim of course, in the muscular, dancer's way, and she was probably in her early forties, though it was hard to tell; likewise it was hard to tell anything about her features, except that she had fine eyes and a sensationally beautiful mouth, because what she had was not looks but this – this *thing* that threatened to turn his knees to water and his brain to mush.

He heard himself introducing himself, and without meaning to he extended his hand. Hers was smooth and warm and strong, and the handshake was brief. He was glad she disengaged herself because he wasn't sure he could have, or not in time to avoid embarrassing himself.

'You wanted to see me?' she said, to help him along. 'You said it was urgent?'

Her voice was warm, too, and full of suppressed amusement, and made you think that uniquely among womankind, she would really *understand* you. He shook himself mentally.

'I wanted to ask you about Jesse Guthrie,' he said. 'He was a pupil here – a star pupil, I believe.'

She looked sad. 'Yes, he was. Poor Jesse. It was a dreadful thing, his dying so young. Drugs take a terrible toll on our young people, and tragically it's so often the really talented ones that are the most vulnerable. I don't know why. Perhaps the strain of brilliance – we are meant to be ordinary, don't you think?' she said with a small smile that was anything but. 'And when we're not ... Humankind cannot bear very much reality.'

'Eliot,' he said, out of his dream. So she was educated, too.

'But, forgive me, poor Jesse's death was some time ago,' she went on, 'and you said the matter was urgent?'

'Some aspects of the case relate to another murder we're investigating,' he said.

A small start of surprise. 'But Jesse's death was an accident, surely?'

'It may have been. Things have come up recently – I'm not at liberty to tell you all the details, I'm afraid. But please tell me about Jesse. How and when did he first come here?'

318

She had been thinking; now the slight frown smoothed out and she said, 'Perhaps we'd better sit down.' He took a chair, and she sat opposite in that disjointed, dancer's manner, perching well forward on the seat, her knees fallen apart, her hands linked together between them. The room was so narrow – and they were both on the tall side – that his knees were almost touching hers. He felt her closeness almost like the heat from a fire.

'Jesse came to us when he was twelve for two classes a week, and full-time from the age of sixteen. He came from a disadvantaged background – his father had walked out on the family and his mother was not much of a coper. By all the rules Jesse should have gone to the bad, but the dance saved him. He came for an audition for a bursary, and I saw straight away he had something I could work with. We took him on, and – all credit to him – he worked hard, though it can't have been easy for him at home, and facing up to the teasing of other boys. There were times when he wanted to give up, but we wouldn't let him. When he came full-time, I taught him myself, and I was glad afterwards to be able to get him started with a professional company.'

'I suppose you have lots of contacts in that world,' Atherton offered. 'Producers and directors and so on.' She assented with a slight nod. 'And the backers of shows – what do they call them – angels?'

'It's a rather old-fashioned term – mostly they're just called backers these days.'

'But they must be important people to know.

Nothing can happen without the money.'

'That's true,' she said, as if she wondered where this was going.

'David Regal – do you know him? He's quite a keen backer, I believe.'

Was there the tiniest hesitation? 'I've heard of him. I don't remember if I've actually met him. There are quite a number of them, you know,' she added with a smile.

'Of course,' he said. 'Go on about Jesse. You got him several jobs, I believe.'

'I was glad to put him in the way of work. He was very good.'

'But then he gave it up – why was that?'

She sighed and looked down at her hands, which were clasped tightly. They looked very knuckly that way – not very feminine. 'I don't know. It was a great disappointment to me. I suspect it was the drugs. I think he must have started using by then. He got a very menial job with a pop band, and I didn't see him again. The next thing I heard, the poor boy was dead. I understood it was an accidental overdose.'

Now she looked up, and he had to withstand the full force of meeting her eyes. Hazel, they were hazel, he discovered; and they almost glowed.

He had to ask something to distract her. 'Have you had the school long?' he managed to make it sound conversational.

'It will be twenty years this autumn,' she said. She didn't seem to mind the change of direction. 'We're planning a Gala Day for parents and ex-pupils, and a special entertainment – a performance of *Alice In Wonderland*. Lots of animal parts for the younger ones. Parents do like to see their offspring on stage before they write a cheque.' She made a comical moue. 'Roof repairs, and the plumbing is not what it ought to be,' she explained. 'Sadly, as school principal one has to attend to the practical side as well as the artistic.'

'Will you be taking a part?'

'In *Alice*? Good heavens, no. It's for the pupils.'

'But I can see you were a dancer.'

'I *was* ballet trained,' she said. 'I was a ballet-mad little girl, and my sole ambition was to dance professionally, but in my teens I grew too tall. When I realized I could never go as far as I wanted – and my ambition in those days was limitless – I had to swallow the pill. So I started to teach. Vicarious fame, you see,' she said with another smile to show she wasn't bitter. 'Then I met a generous backer who enabled me to buy this school, and – here we are. It isn't dancing on stage, but I find there are compensations to running a school like this.'

'You take the older pupils, I suppose?'

'A few special ones, but my time is mostly taken up with administration now. Though I do find time for some of my ex-pupils, those who are out in the world, dancing professionally. They come to me for private coaching. As a dancer you never stop taking class, you know. It's the bedrock of all dance – class every day.'

'The school takes boys as well as girls?' he asked.

321

'Yes,' she said. 'We're lucky to be popular with boys. Statistically there are always fewer of them so we have to cherish every one we get. They're so much more fragile and easily put off.' She glanced at her watch. 'Forgive me, I've enjoyed talking to you but I do have a pupil waiting for me. What was it in particular you wanted to ask me?'

He brought out the mugshot of Corley and handed it to her. 'I believe you were approached for lessons recently by this young man.'

She looked at the photo for a long time – or perhaps it only seemed like a long time in this quiet room with his intense awareness of the woman in front of him. 'No, I don't think so,' she said. 'I don't know this face. What's his name?'

'Robin Williams,' he said.

'No, I don't know him,' she said, and tried to hand it back.

He didn't take it. 'He knew Jesse Guthrie, and we have a very strong suggestion that he came here to ask for lessons.'

'I don't know him,' she said again, still holding out the picture.

'Perhaps he might have approached another member of your staff?'

She met his eyes, and they were so bright he had to look at her mouth, which was a mistake. 'It's possible he approached someone else. Leave this with me, and I'll ask the others, and let you know. Do you have a card?'

He gave her one, and they both stood up. She examined the card, and ran a finger over his name. 'Atherton,' she said. Her voice felt like velvet. 'What an interesting name. Is it Danish in origin?'

'I don't think so,' he said.

She smiled at him. 'With your colouring, I can see you marauding in a long-ship. I'm sorry I have to dash away. But I'll ask about your – what was his name again?'

'Robin Williams.'

'That's right. I'll ask everyone, and let you know what they say, either way.'

She escorted him to the front hall and shook his hand again, looking up into his face with a warm and quizzical expression. 'I've so enjoyed talking to you,' she said, with a little hesitation. 'You're not at all what I would have expected in a policeman.'

'I was just thinking the same about you,' Atherton said, and the moment extended itself perilously until again she broke contact and he was able to extricate himself. She stood where she was, with a dancer's poised stillness, until he was out of the door, and he felt her eyes like heat on the back of his neck until he finally turned out of sight. It was like leaving a warm fireside for a cold world. He crossed the road and leaned against a wall for a while to get his strength back. After a bit another young man with a shoe bag slung casually over his shoulder came out of the seniors' door and sloped off towards the tube station. He imagined her teaching this highly-hormoned and fit young athlete one-to-one. *Lucky bugger*, he thought, though he was not entirely clear whether he meant her or him.

SEVENTEEN

Care in the Community

'You missed all the excitement,' McLaren said as Atherton came in through the door. He was hunched over his desk still labouring through the task of collecting and cross-referencing hundreds of car registration numbers. It was thankless work, but the new model McLaren didn't seem to think he deserved any better, which was rather sad.

'What excitement?' Atherton said. 'Where's the guv?'

'Gone,' said McLaren cryptically, before Atherton could find a blunt instrument with which to swat him, Hollis came in through the other door.

'So much for Regal being the big boss,' he said perkily, seeing Atherton.

'What? Why?'

'He's dead. The guv's gone to 'ave a look.'

It was DI John – or Jonny – Care who had come through from Islington asking to speak to Slider.

'Your Sergeant Hollis put in an enquiry about David Regal yesterday,' he opened.

'That's right,' Slider said. 'It's part of that enquiry I came to you about before.'

324

'What, the Guthrie case?'

'Yes. We found a connection between Guthrie and Regal.'

'I see,' said Care, suddenly sounding interested. 'But as I remember, you only wanted to know about Guthrie because he was connected to another case of yours.'

'The murder of a young man called Ben Corley. Corley had a connection to both Guthrie and Regal.'

'Have you interviewed Regal?'

'Not yet. We're still getting our ducks in a row. Your super wasn't keen on our upsetting Mr Regal unless we were sure of our ground.'

'Yes, that sounds like our super,' he said, with a hint of sympathy. 'Well, I'm sorry to say you've missed your chance. David Regal was found dead this morning.'

'Found dead? Where? Who by?'

'At home. His wife was away for the night. She got back this morning and found him dead on the floor in the downstairs loo. It looks as though he committed suicide.'

Slider left Mr Porson to apply to the Islington Super, one Bob Keyes, for retrospective planning permission for him to attend the scene of the crime. Jonny Care, as behoved the copper at the coalface, was amenable and friendly to his opposite number from Shepherd's Bush, especially when it turned out the forensic surgeon in attendance was Freddie Cameron, who claimed Slider with warmth and eagerness as an old friend.

The house was a 1930s cod-Georgian villa of

the sort that abounded around Hampstead and Highgate, of red brick, with eight-paned windows complete with fake green shutters and unnecessarily tall chimneys. It had a gravelled yard in front and a manicured garden behind, the whole surrounded by a high wall, and the yard was shut off by nine-foot wrought-iron security gates with a keypad, camera and intercom with the house. The gates were open now, though guarded by blue-and-white tape and two policemen, and inside the yard, among the official vehicles, Slider could see a silver Mercedes S class. The constable allowed him under the tape, while the press pressed forward out of sheer instinct, like greyhounds in the slips, and asked each other who he was.

Care met him in front of the door. 'Just to get you up to speed,' he said as they walked in, 'Mrs Regal went to an opening night of a play she did the costumes for. Did you know she's a theatre costume designer?'

'Yes, under the name of Sylvia Scott.'

'That's right. You have done your homework.'

Slider was afraid he thought his toes were being trodden on. 'I can't say I've ever heard of her,' he confessed chummily.

Care shrugged and smiled. 'Me neither. But I gather it's a bit of an arcane world. Anyway, she went to this opening night in York – it's a pre-season try-out, I think that's what they call it, of an *Antony and Cleopatra* production that's coming to London in the autumn. And there was a party afterwards so she stayed the night at the Royal York Hotel, and drove down this morning.'

'A pretty good alibi, then?'

He looked at him oddly. 'She apparently went up on stage with the producer to take a bow at the end of the show. And she was interviewed at the party afterwards by the *Yorkshire Post*.'

'I'm not trying to be smart,' Slider said humbly. 'It's just that on my last case we had a man who claimed to have been at a wedding, and we almost didn't check it out.'

Care nodded. 'You can't be too careful. But the *Yorkshire Post* online's already got a photo of her up on the stage with the producer and cast, and the hotel confirms they brought her car up from the garage this morning, so barring the supernatural I think she's covered.'

'You have done your homework,' Slider offered him his words back.

He quirked his lips by way of a smile in response. 'With this sort of resident it's important to make sure you've covered the bases. Regal's a golfer: he's in very big with the commander. Was, I mean. Anyway, she got here about eleven and found him dead and cold. Do you want to come in and see?'

'Yes, please, if I may.' They clothed up in the hall, and Care led him through towards the back. The house was just as Slider would have expected from the outside, spacious and well-proportioned, furnished and decorated with the sort of neutral 'good taste' you pay an interior decorator to have for you. The 'antique' furniture was too new and too well kept to be anything other than reproduction, though from the

327

top end, and expensive. There were large formal arrangements of flowers here and there that Slider guessed were also brought in by a firm. It felt more like an exclusive hotel than a home – he couldn't imagine anyone kicking off their shoes or laughing in a place like this. He almost felt sorry for David Regal.

The kitchen was huge, and so modern it hurt – every gadget known to man, lighting so concealed you'd need a map to find it, glassy black marble tops, and enough stainless steel to keep Sheffield going for a year. It was spotless, and looked as though no one had ever cooked in it. Judging by modern trends that could well be true: Slider had noted that, as a rule, the posher the kitchen, the less it was used.

The downstairs loo was off to one side of it, past a small lobby with a door to the utility room. 'Loo', in any case, was far too humble a term to apply to the spacious marble palace that contained WC, bidet, basin, vanity unit, mirrors, sofa, orchids, matching towels and a haunting fragrance of frangipani.

It was a place you would hesitate to sully even by washing your hands, so it was an outrage to all senses that it also contained a dead man, sprawled on his back on the floor. He was dressed in fine woollen slacks and a silk shirt with the top button undone, no tie, leather loafers with tassels. Slider guessed him to be about five foot nine or ten, no more, and probably in his late fifties; well preserved, and with a good figure. He had the sort of tan you had to go abroad for, silver hair beautifully cut, and his features were small and neat, almost boyish. The likeness to Richard Gere lay only in the colouring and general impression of handsomeness.

His eyes and mouth were a little open; his outflung left wrist had been deeply cut, and there was a pool of blood on the floor under it and his arm, staining the beautiful shirt under the shoulder and armpit where it had spread back. Near his right hand was a bloody kitchen knife, very sharp-looking.

Cameron, another Tyvek-clad ghost, looked up and said, 'There you are! Jonny said you were coming. You know Jonny Care, do you? Your Islington counterpart and much beloved in his community.' Care smirked shyly at this accolade. 'I must say, as downstairs loos go this is a pleasure to work in. I was expecting to have to do gymnastics to work around the body. So, Bill, what do you think of this? Another bug for your collection, maybe?'

'How can you be so cheerful on a Saturday?' Slider countered.

'All days are as one to the pure of heart. He's been dead about twelve hours.'

'Which makes it some time yesterday evening,' said Slider. The wife was well covered, then.

'First reaction?' Freddie asked facetiously.

Slider stared, taking in the scene and the corpse. 'You said it looked like suicide,' he said to Care.

Care met his eyes. 'Perhaps I should have said it looks as though it's *meant* to look like suicide.'

Slider returned the look. 'There's not enough

blood.'

'Bingo,' said Freddie. 'He didn't bleed out. To judge from his pupils, he's taken rather a large dose of some narcotic or other. I wouldn't be at all surprised if we were to find it was the drug that killed him. The cutting isn't post-mortem of course, or there'd be no blood to speak of. But I'd guess his heart gave out under the strain of the overdose before he'd managed to exsanguinate. And of course once the heart stopped, the bleeding would stop.'

Slider said, 'In Corley's case, it was phenobarbital.'

'Could be the same. We won't be able to tell until we've had a tox screen,' said Freddie.

Slider looked at Care. 'Phenobarbital administered in alcohol most probably. It dissolves readily and leaves no taste.'

'There's an empty glass in the sitting room,' said Care. 'Smells like vodka.'

'What else?' Freddie asked almost jovially. He was enjoying himself, like a prof egging on two bright pupils.

Slider looked carefully around and then worked his way backwards from the bathroom across the kitchen, with Care following. Beyond the kitchen was the sitting room, an informal area with a sofa, armchairs and coffee table, a built-in wall unit containing books, sound equipment and television, and a wood-burning stove screened, at this time of year, with another large flower arrangement. One side of the sofa bore a man-sized indentation in the cushions. On the table in front of it was a cut-glass tumbler with dregs of clear liquid in it, an untidily-folded newspaper, and the TV remote. The glow of a red light on the television itself showed it was on standby.

'No note?' Slider asked.

'We haven't found one yet,' said Care. He almost seemed to be enjoying himself, too.

'He sat here, drinking his vodka and tonic. Do you know what was on television?'

'It's on BBC One. There was the news at ten. After that, an action film. Before it, a programme about soldiers in Afghanistan,' said Care. 'I looked it up.'

Slider smiled inwardly. Good for you, he thought. 'So he might have been half-watching while he read the paper. He finishes his drink, throws the paper down, walks into the bathroom, and cuts his wrist with the knife he's collected from the kitchen on his way.'

'There *is* one missing from the knife rack. Matching handles,' said Care.

'Not forgetting to turn off the TV first,' Cameron called. 'Is it me, or is that deeply unconvincing?'

Slider went back over the ground. 'He was dragged. You can see the marks of his heels, here on the carpet, where the pile lies differently. And in the kitchen, here, and here where they had to swing round for the doorway.' They were faint, the scuffs, just dullnesses in the polish of the kitchen floor's surface. Slider straightened up and tilted his head. 'The light would have been different – artificial, not daylight – and at a different angle. They probably couldn't have seen the marks then.'

'That's what I thought,' said Care.

'They gave him the drugged vodka, and when he fell unconscious, dragged him into the bathroom, tidied up his clothes, and cut his wrist to make it look like suicide.'

'Then washed up the glass and poured another vodka and tonic into it for the show,' said Care.

'But the glass would then have had no fingermarks on it,' said Slider.

'They emptied it again and took it into the bathroom, wrapping his right hand round it for verisimilitude before replacing it on the table.'

Slider agreed with all that.

'But what I don't understand is, why bother?' Care went on. 'Why not cut his wrist right here where he sat on the sofa?'

'Instinct, perhaps. Or maybe they thought it looked more natural in the loo. Perhaps Regal was a clean and tidy sort of person who wouldn't have liked to stain the carpets and upholstery, even in death,' Slider said.

'In your Corley murder, deceased was actually *in* the bath, wasn't he?' Care commented.

'Yes,' said Slider. 'But presumably the murderer was not on intimate enough terms with Regal to persuade him to take a bath.' He pondered a little, pursuing a fugitive thought.

Care interrupted his brown study. 'I'm going to have another word with the wife. My super will probably kill me for offering, but would you like to come? '

Slider came back with a start. 'Yes,' he said. 'Yes, very much. Thank you.'

Sylvia Scott, or Sylvia Regal, was in a different sitting room, which had French windows on to a terrace. There were chandeliers, brocade upholstery and Chinese carpets, an Adam fireplace, repro Georgian side tables with bronzes of horses and dogs on them, oil paintings in heavy gold frames on the walls. This was the formal drawing room and it felt chilly and unused, though it was still hot outside.

Mrs Regal was in her late thirties or early forties, but looked younger, her face remarkably line-free, as though she had never had a care in her life. There seemed something faintly familiar about her that Slider could not put his finger on. She had bronze-gold hair in a jaw-length bob, so well cut that it moved all-of-a-piece, like an elastic bell, and if she was not beautiful she was so well presented and made up you would never notice. She was wearing grey slacks and a white blouse, patent shoes, a heavy gold choker and gold earrings, all very smart and restrained apart from a massive diamond engagement ring against her wedding ring. Despite her long drive and the subsequent horrors, she seemed both fresh and composed, her make-up unsmudged, no hair out of place.

She was sitting on a slippery-looking brocade sofa and there was a brandy glass on the onyx coffee table in front of her. A woman detective stood stolidly behind and to one side of her. It was the one who had brought Slider coffee in Care's office – what had he called her? Sara, that was it. She smiled a deferential greeting at Slider as he came in.

The woman looked up at Slider too, with a

quick frown, quickly smoothed away. You didn't stay line-free by engaging facial expressions willy-nilly. It was to Care she addressed herself. 'How long is this going to go on?'

'Is what, ma'am?'

'How long must I sit here? I've had a long journey. I would like to go to my room, change out of these clothes, have a shower. In any case, I have a meeting this afternoon at the RSC and a fitting this evening that I must attend, or my whole schedule will be thrown out.'

'I'm sorry, ma'am,' Care said, 'but there are always procedures attendant upon a death which have to be observed.'

She stared at him as if trying to read his thoughts. 'Look, you might as well know right away, David's and my marriage was a matter of form only. It suited us both better to stay married than to divorce, but he went his way and I went mine, and it's more years than I can remember since either of us cared what the other did. We were as good as strangers. So I don't see any point in playing the hypocrite and pretending to feel deep grief, when I don't. I'm sorry he's dead, and I'm sorry he felt so badly about something he wanted to take his own life. But that's all.'

'Why do you think he might have wanted to kill himself?' Care slipped the question in.

She looked exasperated. 'I don't *know*. Haven't I just told you, we went our own ways? I've no idea what he was getting up to recently.'

Was she telling the literal truth, Slider wondered, or was she trying to distance herself from anything they had found out about Regal?

'When you came home this morning, you would naturally go straight to your bedroom, wouldn't you?' Care asked neutrally.

'Yes, as I should like to do now,' she said with irritation.

'Then how did you come to find him before showering and changing?'

That made her pause an instant. But she recovered quickly. 'I knew he was at home because his car was there, so I just popped along to say, "Hello, I'm back." I didn't say we weren't friends. I saw the glass and the newspaper, went into the kitchen, and saw him through the open door.'

Slider could feel Care not saying something at that point. There was something about that statement that was wrong.

'Was he in money trouble?' Care continued.

'Good heavens, no! David's very well off.'

'Romantic entanglements?'

She paused, considering, and sighed. 'I suppose you'll probe and probe until you find out. David liked boys. Not little boys,' she added hastily. 'I mean young men. And his affaires, as I suppose one must call them, have always tended to be rather emotional. I believe that's usually the case with that sort of liaison. But I don't know if he was seeing anyone lately.'

'How long had he been – interested in young men?'

'Always. He was always like that.'

'Then why did you marry him?'

She drew a short, exasperated sort of breath, as

335

if she didn't like being questioned about her private life. But she continued very fluidly, almost as if she had thought it out, or had had to explain the same thing before. 'I didn't know to begin with, of course. I met him when I was stage managing a play he was backing. I was very young, he was very handsome, and charming, very much a grown-up. All the other men I knew were so callow beside David. He took me out to restaurants and clubs. It was all so sophisticated. I fell for him, and when he asked me to marry him, I couldn't believe my luck. But the other thing was always there. Looking back, I could see the hints, but at the time I was too young and innocent to realize. But he was good to me, very generous. He set me up in business. Gradually the other thing – the boy thing – took over more and more, and the feelings I'd had for him died. One day I came home and he had a young man with him – in our bed. There was a terrific row. I said I was leaving him. He begged me not to. In the end, we worked it out to suit us both. We bought this house where we could have separate suites. He promised to be more discreet, and in return he helped and supported my career. It's been a happy arrangement, and I have no regrets. I'm only sorry he was so disturbed underneath that he had to take his own life. If only he'd spoken to me about it, perhaps I could have talked him out of it. I shall always blame myself for not realizing.' She sighed.

Slider glanced at Care, aware that he had a good rapport with him, for someone he'd only just met. Care met his eye for a fraction of a second, and they almost exchanged thoughts.

Certainly Care said just what Slider would have. 'There's no need to feel guilty,' he said to Mrs Regal. 'You see, he didn't take his own life.'

She jerked her head up, like a deer in the forest hearing a rifle being cocked. 'What do you mean?'

'I mean that we don't believe your husband killed himself. He was murdered.'

For a moment she could not speak. Perhaps it was the normal reaction of any normal person faced with the 'm' word. Or perhaps it wasn't. Perhaps there was something else there. Slider saw now that under her appearance of calm there was a strained blankness, an air of listening to sounds beyond human reach. One of her hands was trembling very faintly, and she placed the other over it. It could have been the effect of natural shock at the death of her husband. Or – was her alibi really as perfect as it sounded?

She recovered herself. 'Nonsense! What are you saying? You've no reason to think that, none at all. I don't believe it for a minute. Who on earth would want to kill David?'

'That's what we hope you can help us with,' Care said smoothly. 'I believe you know more about it than you are letting on.'

'But I tell you I don't know anything about his life,' she cried. 'How many more times? And I wasn't even here. I was hundreds of miles away in York. *I wasn't here*!'

'Then Detective Superintendent Keyes turned

up and threw me out,' Slider said, at the end of his exposition. 'Poor old Care's in for a wigging. Mr Porson said he couldn't talk Keyes round, no matter how hard he flirted. Showed his legs and everything. Keyes said he'd liaise with us over anything they discover that's pertinent to our investigation, but he won't let us actually be there.'

'That's a bummer,' Atherton said.

'Well, yes and no. It's not our case, and that's as long as it's broad. We've got enough on our hands as it is.'

'Yes, but it's got to be part of the same sequence, don't you think?'

'I do think,' said Slider. 'For a start, there was no sign of a break-in. Either Regal let the murderer in, or they knew the keypad code and had a door key. Either way, I think we can assume it was someone he knew, because again, there was no sign of a struggle.'

'And he knew whoever it was well enough to accept a drink from them.'

'And there's another thing,' Slider said. 'Care walked me to the door on my ignominious exit, specifically to tell me that all the security cameras – the gate, front door and inside the house – had been turned off, and the tapes in the recorders were new and unused.'

'Why not just wipe them?' Atherton wondered.

'Wiping takes time. Quicker just to replace them and take the old ones away,' said Slider.

'But that doesn't fit so well with trying to pretend it was suicide,' Atherton said.

'Not if you're suspicious to start with. But

there's no way of knowing how long the cameras had been off, and you can't prove Regal didn't do it himself – realized the tapes were full at some point and replaced them, and forgot to turn the cameras on again. There was one thing Mrs Regal said, though, that might trip her up. She said she knew when she got home that Regal was in, because his car was there. But his car was in the garage, and she parked hers outside, so how would she know? She couldn't have seen it without opening the garage door, and why would she do that and then not put her car in as well?'

'But from what you say, the wife was the one person who couldn't have done it.'

'True. But it doesn't mean she didn't know about it,' said Slider, rubbing his hand backwards through his hair.

'A paid assassin?' Atherton said, with a pained air.

'Or just someone she's in league with.' He stood up. 'We'd better get the rest of them up to speed. And give McLaren another set of security cameras to add into the mix. If there are any near to the Regal house.'

Atherton snorted. 'Any security cameras in Highgate? Are there any legs in the Folies Bergère?'

'I really wouldn't know,' said Slider with dignity.

'So if David Regal isn't the big cheese, who is?' Mackay asked in resentful tones.

'Whoever it is,' Atherton said, 'the murders are getting more panicky. Guthrie was good – could have been an accident, can't prove otherwise. Corley was good – they'd have got away with it if they'd realized he was left-handed. But then Flynn was just a slash-and-grab.'

'Regal wasn't bad,' Fathom said. 'Could've been all right.'

'Except for the drag marks,' Mackay added. 'They should have checked for those.'

'But *why* were they all killed?' Gascoyne asked. He hadn't had to come in, but he'd turned up anyway, keen to keep up with events – or to show his suitability for joining the firm, Atherton thought.

'Anyone who's a threat to the organization has to be eliminated,' he answered.

'Guthrie because he drew attention to himself in that fight with Corley,' Swilley suggested.

'We don't know that there wasn't another reason,' Slider said. 'He was mixed up with David Regal somehow, and perhaps that was becoming a problem.'

'Then Corley because he'd been asking too many questions,' Atherton went on.

'Yes, but what actually triggered it with Corley? He'd been asking questions for a while,' Gascoyne objected.

Atherton shrugged. 'I don't know the answer to that one. Then Flynn because we'd been talking to him.'

'Ah, sure, God, don't say that,' said Connolly. 'I've a bad conscience anyway about the little twerp. Maybe he'd still be alive...'

'You did your duty,' Slider told her firmly. 'It's the murderer who's guilty, not you.'

340

'And then David Regal because we'd started asking questions about him,' Atherton concluded.

'But how did they find that out?' asked Gascoyne. 'We asked the Islington police – you can't think they're in on it.'

'I went to his office,' said Atherton. 'But surely his own secretary, or whoever she was, wouldn't rat him out? Then there was Ed Wilson. And Mrs Kennedy.'

'I'd be willing to bet Ed Wilson wasn't in on anything,' Swilley said.

'And I feel the same about Mrs Kennedy,' Slider said. 'But you never know who they might have dropped an innocent word to. At all events, someone at the top got to know we were interested in David Regal. I wonder if he hadn't been identified before as a weak link, though. This young-man thing might have been getting out of hand. As long as we thought he was the man at the top, we assumed he had the power to do as he liked. But what if he was only a figurehead?'

'The legal representative of the branch companies,' Swilley said. 'He doesn't necessarily have to do anything or have any skills, but I should think the one thing the Marylebone Group would ask of him is *not* to draw attention to himself.'

'And one way or another, attention has been drawn,' said Slider.

'But it doesn't leave us any nearer to answering my question,' Mackay complained. 'Who *is* the big cheese?'

Mr Porson summoned Slider to his room. 'I've got some news. The Birmingham police had a little looksy at Ransom's production works for us.'

'That was very quick, sir,' Slider said in surprise.

'Very obliging of 'em,' Porson agreed. 'Sent a unit straight round. But it's quiet at the moment, everyone on holiday, including the villains. Anyway, this industrial estate's a bit of a flagstaff development for Solihull – award-winning design, prestigious urban-regeneration scheme, bags o' civic pride – so they want to make sure no one casts any nasturtiums. Everything's above board and bony fido about the estate – you couldn't have a more kosher address – and Ransom's place looks all right from the outside. No reason anyone would ever have asked any questions.' He paused for effect, and Slider obliged with the prompt.

'But when they *did* ask questions, sir?'

'Different story,' he said triumphantly. 'Inside there's a small DVD processing unit and printer, two blokes reading magazines and smoking, and a storeroom with half a dozen copies each of fifty or so films. All with the Ransom House name on the spine. File copies. Chummy and his pal look shifty as hell when plod bursts in, try to pretend it's a slack period. Reckon they're run off their feet normally, thousands of copies packed up and sent off every week. But our friends in blue say the dust was thick, and the neighbours have never seen a van of any size leaving the place. No activity at all, they say, bar Mutt and

Jeff turning up for work with their round o' cheese-and-pickle and the *Daily Mail* under their arm. And *that's* not every day.'

'But Ransom claim to be selling fifteen million quid's worth a year,' said Slider.

'So someone's telling porkies,' Porson said. 'Our counterpoints in Birmingham are not best pleased with finding out everything is not hunkey-dokey, I can tell you. The Prince of Wales opened the industrial park, they get delegates from Europe coming on jollies to admire it. Moist eyes all round just talking about it. So now they're upset. Want to know what we want them to do about it. I told 'em, nothing at the moment. But we'll have to move fast before the fat hits the shin.'

He paused, puzzled for a moment as to what had gone wrong in that sentence, and cocked an eye at Slider, who was thinking hard. 'So they process the film and print a few copies, in case of enquiries. The director would want one, and the actors might order some for their friends. But otherwise—'

'Otherwise there's about as much action as a quiet day in the morgue,' Porson finished for him.

'If they're not actually producing any copies, what's in the warehouse in Staines?' Slider asked.

'We'll have to find out. But if it's drugs, and that close to Heathrow, we'll have to start thinking about involving some other people. The drugs boys for a start. Customs. Anti-terrorist – you never know who's going to want to shove an oar in.' He looked uncomfortable. 'It's going to start going pear-shaped, I can feel it in my water. They're going to ask what the ruddy hell we've been doing faddling about on our own all this time. Are you any closer to working out what's going on?'

'Yes, sir. A lot closer. But not there yet,' Slider said with a worried frown. 'If I could have just a bit longer...'

'You don't ask for much!' Porson said explosively. 'You were sure it was this David Regal who was the head huncho. Now they've topped him, who's your next target? Some completely new bastard we've not looked at yet?'

Barrow? Slider thought. Atherton had always wanted it to be Barrow. They'd had nothing on him, not even any connection to Regal, bar the fact that Regal was representative of Ransom – and did Barrow even know that? But if Barrow wasn't producing thousands of films for the Marylebone Group, what was he doing to deserve his salary? Laundering the proceeds looked more likely than ever. But it still didn't mean he was involved in the murders, and drugs ring or no drugs ring, it was the murders Slider wanted to get to the bottom of.

'I'm nearly there, sir,' he said pleadingly. 'If we can work out who did the killings, I think we can give the Drugs Squad the whole thing on a plate. But if they go in—'

'The murders'll go by the wall,' Porson finished for him. 'I know. All right, you've got the rest of today anyway. And I don't suppose our brothers in advertisy will want to bust any chops on a Sunday. See what you can do before Monday. But if anyone comes asking, I'm going to have to tell.'

'Yes, sir,' Slider said. He couldn't expect better than that.

EIGHTEEN

Fresh Hoods and Bastards New

Slider sent some of the troops home – there was nothing really for them to do until something new came in. Hollis was office-managing, Atherton was going through reports, Connolly was on the computer, and McLaren was still beavering away on his car reg numbers. In the comparative quiet, Slider tried to put in some heavy-duty thinking, re-reading everything in the hope that it would present itself differently to his brain and give him a new idea. Outside the day was mute, the sky pale grey, the sunlight diffused, the air still. It was neither hot nor cold, neither rainy nor sunny, there was no wind. It was as if all weather had been cancelled in deference to Slider's preoccupation.

He was beginning to think he needed a cup of tea when McLaren came to his door, sadly not with a cup, but with an armful of paper. 'Guv?' he said. Slider looked up. With the way the light was striking his face, McLaren looked almost gaunt. And sad, like an unloved dog – a good dog, who did as he was told, but was never petted. How Slider longed to give him a biscuit. Or a doughnut. Or a cheesy-nacho-tikka-marinara-sweet'n'sour meatball sub. With chips.

'How's it going?' he asked.

McLaren dumped his papers on the edge of Slider's desk. 'Well, guv,' he said, 'there was a lot of traffic on the Talgarth Road and round Elgin Crescent at the time we were looking – I mean, a *lot*.'

'So I imagine,' said Slider encouragingly.

'Not so much along Goldhawk and Uxbridge Road early Mundy morning. I had over fifty matches for Talgarth and Elgin. And the Astra's a popular make. But it narrowed down to half a dozen for all three times and places. I looked into those, and came up with nothing – no crim-inal record, no iffy connections, they all looked legit. I was gonna start going interviewing 'em, but then you wanted Highgate added in. There's a lot o' cameras in Highgate,' he said.

'I know. I'm sorry,' said Slider.

'S'all right, guv. Turned out I got a ping from an ANPR camera on Highgate High Street, at the junction with West Hill. One of my six went past it last night at ha'pass ten.'

'Terrific!' Slider said. 'Good man.'

'Trouble is, guv, I've already looked into this person and can't find anything. But it's gotta be something, hasn't it? I mean, to be at all four places at the right time – and the only one that is. And Highgate's a long way out from the other places.'

'It has to be our suspect,' Slider said. 'Who's the car's registered keeper?'

'It's a Miss M Lynn, address Flat Twelve, Chiltern Mansions, Chiltern Street – that's by

Baker Street station, so gawd knows what she was doing all the way out—'

'Mary Lynn?' Slider exclaimed. 'That's the owner of the ballet school Atherton went to see this morning. The school whose address was in Corley's pocket. Haven't you been listening?'

'I've been doing these numbers,' McLaren said in aggrieved tones. 'It's a lot of work. Takes a lot o' concentration. I haven't been able to think about anything else all week. Anyway, I only got the last connection a few minutes ago. I came straight to you.'

But Slider had moved on. He frowned in thought. 'Wait a minute, what was that address? Chiltern Mansions? That rings a bell.' He burrowed through his notes and his mind simultaneously. 'Somebody lives in Chiltern Mansions.'

'Yeah, guv, this female with the Astra,' McLaren began patiently.

'Barrow!' Slider exclaimed – and satisfyingly, just the instant before he came across it on paper. 'Here it is. Paul Barrow, Flat Twelve Chiltern Mansions – the luxury penthouse. Mary Lynn lives at the same address as Paul Barrow.'

'Maybe she just uses the address,' McLaren said with Sliderian caution.

But Slider was pursuing his finger down the notes. 'Paul Barrow married a Mary Lynnette Scott in 1989. Mary Lynn must be her stage name. Electoral register says he lives alone so she hasn't put herself on.'

There was something else. Yes, he had it now. 'Regal's wife is Sylvia Scott. Now I know why

348

she looked faintly familiar. They're sisters! Mary Lynn and Sylvia Scott are sisters, and they're married to David Regal and Paul Barrow, so the whole thing is connected.'

'Yeah, guv, you must be right,' McLaren said, with a glow of animation in his eyes that had been missing recently. 'We got 'em!'

'We have indeed.' Mary Lynn had told Atherton she didn't know David Regal. She had made a proper mistake. 'All your painstaking work has really paid off,' Slider said to McLaren – credit where credit was due.

'But which one's the boss?' McLaren said, smirking under the praise. 'It's gotter be Barrow, ennit? If it's not Regal.'

'I really don't care,' Slider said, 'as long as I nail the murderer. The drugs squad can do the rest.'

Out in the CID room, Slider told the rest of the assembled firm the news. Conversation broke out.

'Barrow must be the big man, then, and Regal was just a figurehead,' Hollis said. 'Question is, did Mrs Regal know her husband was being offed, or did they just wait for her to be out o' the way?'

'Sure God, if you think that's the only question,' Connolly objected.

'We oughta get him in and grill him, guv,' McLaren suggested. 'Barrow.'

'I always fancied him for First Murderer,' said Atherton.

'We still don't know who did the murders.' Connolly.

'We know it wasn't Mrs Regal – she had an alibi.' Hollis.

'Who ordered 'em? That's the point.' McLaren.

'An alibi for one of the murders. We don't know they were all done by the same person.' said Connolly.

'How to prove any of it is the point,' said Atherton.

'Check everybody's alibis for all the murders,' Hollis suggested.

'Maybe we ought to wait until we get some news on the Staines warehouse,' Atherton said. 'We've only got half a story as far as the drugs are concerned. In fact, we don't even really know Barrow's involved. He could just be a stooge.'

'We'll have to keep Mr Porson up to speed, whatever we do,' Slider said. 'Let's go through it point by point and try to get some kind of order into it.'

Atherton was just coming out of the men's room when his mobile rang. He was alone in the corridor, and stopped to look at the display. 'I don't know that number,' he said to himself, and took the call.

The voice that answered his made his hair stand on end – warm, low, full of humour and sex. 'I wasn't sure I'd remember what your voice sounded like,' she said with a soft laugh. 'You have a very attractive voice, you know.'

'I could say the same to you, but that would be banal,' he replied.

'I'm sure nothing you say is ever banal,' said Mary Lynn. 'I'm flattered that you recognized me so quickly, though.'

'It's not that long ago since we spoke,' Atherton said, trying not to notice the warmth creeping up under his collar. 'What can I do for you?'

'It's more what I hope I can do for you,' she purred. 'You were asking me about a young man – Robert Williams?'

'Robin,' Atherton corrected automatically.

'Yes, that's right. I said I'd ask the rest of my staff about him, but actually, I think I've come across some information that would interest you.'

'About Robin Williams?'

'Yes, but you see, I don't think that was his real name. And I think it concerns poor Jesse, as well, Jesse Guthrie.'

Was she about to tell him about the fight at the Hot Box? 'That will certainly interest me,' he said invitingly.

There was a pause. 'The thing is,' she said, 'I would far rather tell you face to face. Telephones aren't secure, you know, and – well, what I have to say is rather sensitive.'

'That's not a problem,' Atherton said. His mouth was dry, for some reason, and his pulse was too rapid. 'You could come in to the station.'

'Oh, I'd rather not do that,' she said quickly. She paused again, as if waiting for him to suggest something else, and then said, even lower, in a voice that thrilled the back of his neck and all the way down his spine, 'Do I have to spell it out? I really want to meet *you*.'

'Oh,' said Atherton inadequately.

'Did I make a mistake?' she asked. 'I felt such a strong attraction to you the moment I saw you, and I was sure you felt the same.'

'You weren't mistaken,' he said. 'I did feel it, but – well, you know. I didn't want to presume.'

'You're too modest. You are a very remarkable man, you know, and I – well, I haven't felt anything like that for a long while. So can we meet? Just you and I? Somewhere privately, where we can talk.'

'Do you really have information for me?'

'Yes, I really do.' There was humour in the response. 'Does it depend on that?'

'Not at all. It just makes it even better. Where would you like to meet?'

'It must be somewhere discreet. You see, I'm married.'

'Are you indeed, *Miss* Lynn?'

'That's my stage name. But don't worry, we've been separated for some time.'

Atherton knew she was not on the electoral register for Chiltern Mansions. It might be true.

'We're getting divorced, but if he found out I had been seeing someone else he could make things very difficult for me. The settlement and so on. He's very vindictive.'

Atherton could believe that about Paul Barrow.

'So I must ask you not to tell anyone, anyone at all, about it. Can you do that? Be utterly discreet?'

'I wouldn't last long in my job if I couldn't keep a secret' he said. 'And – I'm living with

352

someone as well.'

'Oh.' She sounded taken aback. 'I knew someone like you couldn't be single,' she added ruefully.

'But she's away at the moment. She travels a lot. She won't be back for a couple of days.'

'It must be lonely for you,' she murmured.

'It is,' he said. 'I hate going home to an empty house. And she's away such a lot, I sometimes wonder if it's worth carrying on with the relationship at all.'

'Perhaps,' she began, and then stopped. He could hear the silence thinking.

He took up the invitation of the word. 'Perhaps we could meet at my place, for a drink, and a talk? That would be as private and discreet as anywhere.'

'Yes,' she said, pleased. 'Better than a public restaurant or bar, where you never know who might see you.'

'And more comfortable,' he suggested silkily.

'Oh, much. So – when?'

'The sooner the better. Tonight?'

'Yes, tonight,' she said eagerly. 'But I'm working until quite late. I could come round afterwards. Where do you live?' He told her. 'I could probably get there by about eleven.'

'That would be perfect,' he said. He could feel himself trembling lightly all over like a tapped leaf.

'But you won't tell anyone?'

'Who would I tell? I don't particularly want to get found out either. I hate rows.'

'Well, I won't tell if you don't. Absolute discretion?'

'Absolute,' he said. 'I won't breathe a word to a soul.'

Atherton had got ready well in advance of the hour, but he sweated so much he had to shower and change again. The house seemed horribly empty without the cats, Siamese twins with loud voices and acrobatic habits. But he could not have concentrated with them around. They had complained vociferously at being bundled next door. Atherton had told his neighbours he wanted to paint the bedroom before Emily got home and said with absolute truth that it was impossible to paint with them in the house – everything ended up hairy. He said he couldn't shut them in anywhere because they had learned how to open doors, which was also true: one jumped up and swung from the door handle while the other hooked it open from the bottom. It was a ballet of cooperation. The neighbours had taken them with only a mild roll of the eyes.

Maybe she wouldn't come, he thought for the umpteenth time. Did she really have information about Guthrie she was willing to tell him? Or was it just his gorgeous body she was after? Women in plenty had wanted him in pre-Emily days.

She wouldn't come.

Perhaps she was the innocent party, trapped in a loveless marriage with a crime boss, and she wanted to expose Barrow and throw herself on Atherton's protection. Perhaps she was just an ex-dancer running a nice school for ballet-mad little girls like she had been.

She was late. It was after eleven. The waiting was stretching his nerves. He longed for a drink but didn't want to greet her with it on his breath. If she came. He couldn't stop thinking – he wished he could. The image that came to mind again and again was of those young men slipping out of the 'seniors only' door and merging anonymously with the Tottenham Court Road crowds. The young men with a strong black cotton shoe bag slung casually over their shoulders. A parcel about the size of a bag of sugar could be concealed in any carrier or backpack. Or shoe bag. Something innocent that would draw no attention to itself.

She only now taught the boys who had gone out into the world, but came back for coaching. Boys who had parts in ballets or shows. Boys like Guthrie.

A soft knocking at the door made him jump half out of his skin. She hadn't rung the doorbell – perhaps she knew that in a terrace house you could always hear next-door's bell. He opened the door and she slipped in as soon as there was a crack wide enough, and pressed it closed behind her, like a conspirator. She looked like a conspirator, dressed in black trousers, a light black jacket and a beanie hat.

His mouth was dry. 'I didn't think you'd come,' he managed to say.

'I almost didn't,' she said. 'You didn't tell anyone?'

'Not a soul.'

'Good.' She stepped past him – the door opened straight into the sitting room – looked around and said, 'This is nice.' With quick movements she pulled off the hat and jacket and dumped them with her big shoulder-bag on a chair, shook her hair free, then turned back and put herself straight into his arms. He was too surprised to avoid the embrace. Her body was pressed against his all the way up. Under his hands it felt hot and smooth; lithe and packed full of muscle. It was like holding a big cat. Her warm, full lips were on his mouth, her hands touching the back of his neck. His whole body reacted to her, and she must have felt it – you couldn't have slipped a cigarette paper between them. He couldn't help it – it was automatic – though he was half-horrified that he could spring an erection so immediately for another woman when there was Emily. But the physiology operated on a different system from the mind. Arousal could happen in the most inappropriate situations.

He was about to release himself when she disengaged, stepped back, looking into his face, and gave a smile that would have started him tingling if he weren't already.

'Sorry,' she said. 'I shouldn't have done that, but I wanted to be sure.'

'Sure of what?'

'Of what I felt was happening between us this morning. That's why I wanted to meet you somewhere other than your office. I couldn't imagine having to sit and talk to you and not be able to touch you. It would have made me crazy.' She ran her fingers along his arm, but only in passing. She walked round the room – which didn't take long, because it was tiny.

356

Bijou, he called it.

'This is a nice place,' she said,

'It's a small place,' he answered.

'Cosy. I bet it's lovely in the winter when you have a fire lit. It is a working fireplace, isn't it? Yes, I knew it was. You're the sort of person who would have real fires.'

'Why do you say that?'

'I know a lot about you just by looking at you, James Atherton. Is it James, or Jamie?'

'Jim.'

'That's nice. Unaffected. You're not a bit like my idea of a policeman, Jim.'

'You've already said that.'

'Sorry. Repeating myself. It must be nerves.'

She had done the circuit and come back to him, and they were standing in front of the fireplace.

'Talking of policemen, you said you had some information for me,' he said.

'Oh, let's leave that a little while, I'll tell you everything later, but let's just relax first.' She stepped closer and put her hands on his chest. She must have been able to feel him trembling. She looked up into his face. Her breath was sweet, like recently-cleaned teeth. 'We won't be disturbed, will we? Your partner's not likely to come back?'

'No, she's away,' he heard himself say, as from a great distance. She was going to kiss him again and he wasn't sure he could stand it. 'She won't be back until Monday.'

'Wonderful,' she breathed. 'Then we can take as much time as we want. I do hate having to hurry.'

She didn't kiss him. She stepped back and looked at him rather quizzically. 'Aren't you going to offer me a drink?'

'Of course,' he said, and managed a smile. 'Sorry. What would you like?'

'A vodka and tonic would be nice,' she said. 'And maybe some sounds?'

He walked towards the kitchen, and she followed but paused by his sound system. In the kitchen he rested his hands a moment on the counter top while he took a few deep breaths to control his shaking – undispersed hormones, that's all it was, he told himself – then got out the vodka bottle and two glasses. He had just got the tonic and a lemon out of the fridge when she came in behind him, and all the hair stood up on his neck.

'I daren't mess about with your sound system,' she said in a smiling voice. 'I'm lousy with technology, and it looks like a good one. I'd be afraid to break something. Why don't *you* put on some music, and *I'll* make the drinks. That I can do.'

'All right. What sort of music do you like?' he asked.

'Anything but ballet music,' she said with a laugh. 'Something light. Have you got any jazz?'

'Yes, lots,' he said.

'I knew you'd be a jazz lover. Me too.'

'What's your favourite?'

'You pick. I have wide tastes,' she said, and turned to the drinks.

He picked out a Miles Davis album, taking his time about it, and put it on quietly, every nerve-ending taut, listening for sounds from the kitchen. But she made none. She came back in at last with two glasses, lightly effervescing, each floating a silver-beaded lemon slice.

'That's nice, what is that?' she asked.

'Miles Davis,' he said. 'Don't you recognize it?'

'I can hardly hear it, it's on so low. Can you turn it up a bit?'

He obliged, then turned to her and the drinks. 'Which is mine?' he asked, almost playful now.

She sensed his mood and smiled too. 'This one,' she said, holding it out to him.

'Ah, thank you. That's just what I needed.' He reached out and slid his hand underneath it, gripping it with his fingertips around the bottom edge. 'Excuse me if I just put it down over here. I shouldn't like any of it to get spilled.'

She had been surprised into letting it go when he took hold of it, but as he slid it on to the table without touching the sides, her face hardened with suspicion. 'What are you doing?' she asked.

'Making sure I don't spoil your fingermarks,' he said. 'You know they're called fingermarks, not fingerprints, don't you? The prints are the copies we make for identification purposes.'

'What do you mean? What are you doing?'

'You see, you've been very good, very careful, but you made one little mistake at Robin Williams's flat. When you went round wiping off all the fingermarks, you forgot that you had already put the vodka bottle back in the fridge. Out of sight was out of mind.'

'I don't know what you're talking about,' she said, but she was alert now, like a cat whipping its tail.

'We got a lovely print, palm, five fingers and thumb – the lot,' he said. Demonstrating with his hand in the air, gripping an imaginary bottle. 'And now I've got yours to compare it with.'

'You're mad,' she said. 'I've never been to Robin Williams's flat. I don't even know who he is.'

'Then you've nothing to worry about, have you?' he said. 'But I'll still be analysing the contents of that glass you just gave me. Vodka and tonic is a nice, clean drink – very pure. But I suspect there's a little something extra in mine, isn't there?'

From nothing she moved like lightning, dashing the contents of her glass in his face and leaping for the table where his was sitting. But he was so keyed up his reactions were just as fast. He had jerked his head sideways enough not to get it in his eyes, and sprang to intercept her. 'Oh no you don't!' he said, putting himself between her and the table.

She didn't hesitate an instant, turning and crossing the room in a couple of athletic springs, grabbing for her handbag. He was after her, passing his hands round her from behind and gripping her wrists. She wrestled to get free, making no sound but her panting breaths. She was horribly strong. He shouted, 'A little help, here!' and was relieved to hear the instant response of movement, footsteps cascading down the stairs. Despite what you see on television and the movies, it is amazingly hard for one person to subdue another if they are determined.

Slider and Connolly came across the room, Slider drawn and Connolly excited. There was a moment of trampling, panting effort until they got her to the ground, and with Connolly sitting on her legs the other two managed to get her hands behind her back and cuffed.

Still she struggled. 'Stop it,' Atherton said. 'You'll hurt yourself.'

Suddenly she was still. 'You'll pay for this,' she said in a low, fierce voice. She twisted her head towards Slider. 'He attacked me. Lured me here and attacked me. He would have raped me if you hadn't come in. You've handcuffed the wrong person.'

'We'll see,' said Slider quietly. Atherton could see he hated this. 'Connolly, have a look in her bag. See what she was going for.'

Connolly, gloved, opened the bag and brought out a roll of black plastic sacks. 'What every real lady should carry,' she commented; and then, carefully, a Stanley knife with what was obviously a new blade. 'Wasn't me mammy always telling me, be prepared. You never know who you'll meet down a dark alley.'

'Evidence bags,' Slider snapped. He didn't like her taunting. 'And a container for the liquid. Is it the one on the table?' he asked Atherton.

'Yes, I managed to stop her getting to it. This is hers that's dripping from my face.'

'Bag the glass as well,' Slider told Connolly. And to Atherton, 'Let's have her on her feet, see what's in her pockets.'

'Touch me, and I'll sue you for assault,' she snarled, her face hard and bright with fury. There seemed no fear in her. Even at this disadvantage, Slider could see what Atherton had meant. She was astonishingly beautiful, in a feral way.

'No you won't,' he said quietly. 'I'm arresting you on suspicion of murder of Ben Corley, and attempted murder of Detective Sergeant Atherton. That'll do for a start. You do not have to—'

'Who the hell,' she snarled between clenched teeth, 'is Ben Corley?'

'You knew him as Colin Redgrave, or perhaps Mike Horden or Robin Williams. He had many names in his time, including Ben Jackson, the singer and video director.'

She tilted her head up to the ceiling, the cords of her neck taut. 'Christ!' she ground out in an agony of discovery.

Connolly had done the liquid and the glass and Slider called her over with a jerk of the head to go through Mary Lynn's pockets. There was not much in them, just a white envelope, folded up, which, when opened, proved to have contained a white powder, a faint dusting of which remained. Enough to analyse, anyway. 'Evidence bag,' Slider snapped again.

'What was it?' Atherton asked Lynn, easy now in his power over her. 'The same as you gave the others?'

She swung her head round to look at him, and her face changed. Her eyes were bright, but no longer with fury. She was smiling, projecting all her considerable magnetism at him. 'You don't know what you've missed. We could have had such an evening together, something you'd remember the rest of your life.'

362

He felt it, even in this situation he felt it, but he would not give her the satisfaction of knowing it. He screwed up his face and laughed. 'The rest of my life? Yes, all five minutes of it! Not much of a bargain.'

She hated to be laughed at. She began struggling furiously, and it took the three of them to get her back on the floor and quiet again

NINETEEN

Llama Sutra

Slider hadn't liked it, Mr Porson definitely hadn't liked it, and Emily had thought it was a terrible idea, as well as resenting being put out of her own house for the evening for another woman. The cats hadn't liked it, and the neighbours obviously thought Atherton was a bit bonkers, painting at night – but they had already thought he was nuts anyway.

'Who's really nuts,' Connolly said, 'is your woman. What a looper! Does she not know you're a policeman? Did she really think you'd not tell anyone?'

'She was desperate,' Atherton said. 'It was a risk she felt she had to take.'

'You obviously shook her with your questioning this morning,' Slider said.

'Hey,' Atherton objected, covering up for the fact that she had really shaken *him*. 'You're not making allowance for the fabulous attractions of my manly bod.'

'Yeah,' said Connolly derisively, 'and she knows all men think with their mickeys. Why wouldn't she trust you?'

So Slider pulled another all-nighter, going

through the processes. Mary Lynn was as furious as a cat in a carrier and refusing to say anything, but that suited him at the moment, while he waited for the result of the fingerprint comparison and the vodka and tonic analysis. Let her steep a bit and have time to think. And he needed time to think, too. If the results came back as he expected, he would have her on the murder of Ben Corley, which was the main thing, the thing he had been holding out for. But it was not intellectually satisfying. He still didn't know what had been going on. He wanted to see and understand the whole picture.

Early in the morning he went up to the canteen to get some breakfast, and was just dabbing a sausage in some tomato sauce when he was called to the telephone. *Sic transit glorious breakfast*, he thought with a sigh.

It was Jonny Care. He sounded excited. 'I've got something on Sylvia Regal,' he said.

It seemed that she had not been invited to the opening night in York after all, but had invited herself. Her booking at the Royal York was made at the last minute; she had come into the theatre after the start via the stage door, and watched from the wings. And, at the end of the play, when the curtain calls were being taken, she had simply walked on when the producer did. Everyone had been too polite to object, had allowed her to take her part of the ovation, and had invited her to the party. There she had almost mugged the *Yorkshire Post* correspondent to be interviewed. The *Yorkshire Post* correspondent being a young man – and Sylvia

Scott being tolerably famous and reasonably good looking – had not put up much of a struggle. The costumes had, in fact, been very good, and she made a good photo, so he didn't mind submitting her along with his other bits.

'So she was manufacturing an alibi?' Slider said.

'That's what it looks like,' Care agreed. 'And combined with her mistake over her husband's car, we've got enough to put pressure on her. She's already jittery as hell – I think she'll break. Obviously she didn't do the actual killing, but I bet she was in on it. Once she understands she's just as liable as the murderer, I think she'll give it up. I'm going to have a crack at her this morning. Want to come?'

'What'll your boss say?'

'I've squared it with him. He knows you've got an interest in Regal. He says as long as you're not in the room. We'll put her in the pokey and you can watch through the glass.'

'I've got some news, as well,' Slider said, and told him about Mary Lynn.

Care whistled. 'That puts a different complexion on it. What's the betting sister Mary did the actual job? What are they like!'

'A blest pair of sirens,' said Slider.

'Well, with all that, if we can't make her sing I'm a monkey's uncle. You coming?'

'Wouldn't miss it for worlds,' said Slider.

Presented with the evidence about her alibi, her mistake about her husband's car, and some pointed questions about who would inherit his fortune, Sylvia Regal had been rattled; topped off with the news of the arrest of her sister for murder, it had been enough to break her. She sang, and kept singing, urged on by a terror of prison and the golden glimmer held out to her that turning Queen's evidence might get her off more lightly.

'I never wanted David to be killed,' she cried several times. 'I know he was a weak link, like Mary said, but I was fond of him. I didn't want him to be killed, but Mary insisted.'

She was terrified, too, of Paul Barrow, and of nameless 'others' in the organization who 'never forgave mistakes'. She didn't want to be released – she wanted protective custody, because once they knew she'd spoken to the police, they'd come after her. Remembering Tommy Flynn, Slider thought she might be right. Which gave them the necessary lever against the solicitor advising her to say nothing.

While the interview was going on, a joint operation between the Uxbridge police and the drugs squad had gone into the warehouse in Staines, where they had discovered packing cases marked as containing Ransom House DVDs waiting for export. They, however, proved only to be in the nature of a false wall: behind them there were crates and crates of – ballet shoes. They were made by a Japanese company, at a factory in Portugal, and despite the proximity to Heathrow they came over by lorry. Portugal being a favourite entry-point into Europe for drugs from South America, it had not deeply surprised the squad to discover that under a top layer of pink practice pumps and pointe shoes there were neatly plastic-wrapped parcels about the size of so many packets of sugar.

'Ballet shoes!' Porson had said almost gloatingly afterwards. 'All lying there like pink baby mice. Genius! You'd feel like a brute even turning 'em over, let alone suspecting they were hiding anything!'

The news, telephoned to Slider and relayed by him to Jonny Care, had allowed Care to direct the rest of his interview like a targeted missile. They knew pretty much everything now – always the best position from which to ask questions. It was for Sylvia Regal to confirm and fill in the detail.

'Fancy using the same warehouse for both companies,' Porson snorted. 'I suppose that was Barrow, trying to save money. Once an accountant, always an accountant. But there's such a thing as false economy, you know.'

'I don't think I'll ever be able to look a vodka and tonic in the face again,' Atherton said, lounging elegantly on Slider's sofa. Outside summer rain pattered down with the relentlessness of heartbreak or a Bank Holiday; but Emily was beside him, and inside it was bright with lamps and friendship.

'Good thing too,' Joanna said. 'It's a silly drink. A drink for people who don't like drink – in which case, why drink it?'

'So many drinks in one sentence, and not one in my hand,' Atherton mourned.

'I'm coming as fast as I can,' Slider said, com-

368

ing in from the kitchen with a tray. 'Here. One gin and tonic. Wrap your gills around that.'

The tumbler was blue with gin and smelled like a forest in the high mountains. Ice clinked and jostled like the Arctic spring calving. 'Aah!' said Atherton. 'That's more like it.'

Slider handed out the other drinks, G and T for Emily and himself, a glass of wine for Joanna and a beer for his father, and raised his glass in a toast. 'To a job well done.'

'And all hazards survived,' Emily said. 'I'm not sure I shall ever get over your inviting a murderess into our house. Especially a seductive murderess.'

'Just doing my job,' Atherton said. 'Without her witnessed attempt on me, we mightn't have enough on her for the CPS.'

'Without it, we might not have got everything out of Sylvia Regal,' Slider added, 'so it was all in a good cause.'

'So it turned out to be Mary Lynn who was the big boss?' Joanna queried, making herself comfortable in the old armchair with her feet tucked under her. 'There's no glass ceiling in crime, then?'

'Not if you have determination,' Slider said. 'And she had plenty of that.'

The Scott sisters had lost both their parents when Mary was eighteen and Sylvia sixteen. Their nearest relative was their paternal grandmother, who was widowed and quite frail, not up to bringing up teenaged girls. Under her nominal guardianship, Mary had taken charge of their lives and they had more or less fended for themselves.

Both were at the Barbara Speake school, on scholarships, but Sylvia went into the acting side while Mary had always wanted to be a dancer. It turned out that Mary had all the talent as well as all the looks, and there had always been an unacknowledged undercurrent of resentment in the younger sister, which perhaps helped to push her into giving up Mary when the police had her cornered.

Sylvia, with no real future in acting, had tried stage management for a bit, which was somewhat of a dog's life. She met David Regal, who took a fancy to her. They married, and then she discovered a minor talent for costume design which he was happy to encourage. He helped her career with his contacts, and she gathered enough talented people around her to do quite well.

'And meanwhile,' Emily asked, 'Mary was becoming a professional dancer?'

'Yes,' Slider said, 'but she knew early on she could never make it to the top. She taught ballet, then met Paul Barrow, got hitched up with him, and bought the dancing school with his money. At some point was recruited by the Marylebone Group. Exactly how that happened Sylvia doesn't know and we haven't got Mary to tell us yet. I suppose she's afraid of reprisals too.'

'I wouldn't have thought that woman could be scared of anything,' Atherton said feelingly.

'Well, it's fear or loyalty, take your pick,' said Slider. 'According to Sylvia, Barrow was supposed to be quite a player, and maybe it was his air of power that attracted Mary. And maybe it was Barrow who introduced her to Marylebone. He was already working in the clubs. But he blotted his copybook – kept getting into trouble with the police, and Marylebone couldn't have that. So Mary overtook him. Marylebone had the clubs for distributing to end users, but they needed a way to get the product to the middle men. Mary set it up through her school – what could be more innocent than a ballet school, after all? And laundering the money through Ransom House was genius, because everyone would assume that a porn-film business would have to be whiter than white.'

'So how did David Regal get into it?' Joanna asked.

'He really was a solicitor, but his business was suffering because he spent more time chasing Adonises than working. So Mary got him the sinecure as legal representative for Ransom House and Apsis. He bought out his senior partner, and it gave him a nice income, social status, and lots of time left over for boy-chasing. Of course, she shouldn't have used him – he was always going to be a danger to security. But she did it for Sylvia. It was odd that she showed so much loyalty to her sister. I suppose everyone has their weak spot.'

'I hope Sylvia appreciated it,' Emily said, with a sort of grim humour.

'But then a series of little problems rolled together into a disaster,' Slider said. 'She'd been grooming Guthrie, and recruited him into the drugs trade when he came back to London to join *Les Miz*. But he got involved with David and quit the show, and then David got him the job with the girl band, where he was flashing drugs about like a card sharp in a street market. So Mary decided he had to go.'

'I suppose it was the fight with Ben Jackson that triggered it?' Emily asked.

'Oddly enough, no,' said Slider. 'She'd already decided to kill Guthrie, and Sylvia says the fight didn't bother her. These things happen in show biz. And we had thought it was probably Barrow who reported to her when Corley, as Mike Horden, started asking questions, but in fact he didn't register him either, just kicked him out and forgot about him.' He shook his head. 'Corley had two narrow escapes. If only he'd left it at that. But at the Hot Box he managed to get close to David Regal, who was extremely smitten. Mary kept a distant eye on Regal's paramours, just in case, and when Corley turned up at the ballet school as Colin Redgrave, asking questions and mentioning Regal, alarm bells rang.'

'So he had to go,' Atherton concluded.

Slider nodded. 'She'd been stringing him along to keep tabs on him. Of course, Corley was only too willing to be strung. She arranged to have dinner with him, then obviously took him on to a night club until it was late enough, and let him invite her back to his place. She hoped to find out what he knew before killing him, but according to Sylvia he was a tougher nut to crack than Mary had reckoned. So she topped him and took away everything, including his laptop.' He paused. 'It was a well-executed murder, except for her not noticing that he was left-handed.'

'And forgetting to wipe the vodka bottle,' Atherton added.

'Still, that wouldn't have helped us without her to suspect,' Slider said. 'If she'd left it at that, she'd have been safe. I don't suppose we'd have ever caught her.'

'But she went on to kill Tommy Flynn?' Emily suggested.

'Yes. That was triggered by our visit to Ransom House, of course. Barrow reported it to Lynn, naturally enough, and it was only then that they connected Mike Horden with Colin Redgrave. She never did know him as Robin Williams – until Atherton turned up at her school asking about him.'

'The Flynn murder was a clumsy business,' Atherton commented.

'It was supposed to look like suicide, but either she didn't know her own strength or she lost her temper,' Slider said. 'And finally, we get to David Regal. He'd already put himself on the to-do list over Corley; but with Corley neutralized he might have stayed on probation. According to Sylvia, it was Angela Kennedy who blew the gaff. I'd asked her not to say anything to Regal about my visit, but she obviously had second thoughts, and left a message on the answer machine that the police had been asking about him and his friend who'd killed himself. The secretary, of course, reported it to Mary – who was her real boss.'

'How much did she know?' Joanna asked. 'The secretary, I mean?'

'Almost nothing, though I imagine, being reasonably intelligent, she guessed there was something dodgy going on. According to Sylvia, she and the Ransom secretary, Alice, and Ewan Delamitri, and the two blokes from the plant in Solihull, were all legit, whatever they might have suspected. Where was I?'

'David Regal,' Joanna reminded him.

'Oh, yes. Well, that phone call moved him up the agenda. She told Sylvia that he had to go, and when Sylvia objected she pointed out that she would inherit his money.'

'Oh, that's cold,' Joanna winced.

'I dare say some threats were applied as well. And Sylvia was fond of him, but she was fonder of her comfort. He hadn't been a proper husband since the early days and he was older than her. The idea of being a rich widow and finding a new, younger husband must have appealed. But she pointed out that if she was going to inherit his money, she would have to have a cast-iron alibi. I suppose Mary thought the further Sylvia was out of it, the better, because Sylvia is not the brightest sparkler in the packet. Hence Sylvia's sudden dash to York.'

'And then,' Atherton said, 'I turned up at the school asking to speak to Mary. It must have been a terrible shock, just when she thought she'd stopped all the leaks.' He shuddered. 'I can't help remembering how natural and relaxed she seemed when I was talking to her, when she'd been murdering David Regal only hours before.'

There was a brief silence.

Slider broke it. 'She certainly is the most cold and heartless killer I've met in a long time,' he said thoughtfully. 'She doesn't seem to have any remorse or feeling at all. She was simply determined to make her little empire work for her, in her own way. Nothing was allowed to get in her way.'

'A case of absolute power corrupting,' Mr Slider commented. 'It's not a natural way for a woman to live. Neither of them sisters had any kids, you notice.'

'Not every woman wants children,' Emily said mildly. Atherton glanced at her, wondering if she was sending him a message. They hadn't talked about it yet, but he'd started thinking that it might be rather nice...

'Well,' Slider said, 'it was panicking that trapped her. If she'd kept her head after killing Corley, we probably wouldn't have been able to bring it back to her. And her attack on you–' to Atherton – 'was very ill-advised. She *knew* you were a policeman.'

'She believed in her power over men. After all, she'd proved it often enough,' Atherton said. 'And killing gets easier the more often you do it. You see it with serial killers. It's almost like greed – you want one more and one more and—'

'Don't,' said Emily.

'Oh, now here's an interesting little titbit,' Atherton added to her. 'It was Sylvia's insistence that when Mary killed David Regal, she had to do it somewhere it wouldn't make a mess.'

'You're kidding me,' Emily said suspiciously.

'Seriously. After all, it was her house and she had to go on living there. I just love the thought of Mary dragging the unconscious Regal into the downstairs loo, puffing and straining, and cursing her sister under her breath for being so house-proud.'

'That's not nice,' Emily said sternly.

'You're taking all the fun out of it.'

'Steady, children,' Slider admonished.

'Everybody's nerves'll be a bit on edge after a case like this,' Mr Slider said peaceably. 'Supper must be just about ready. I'll go and have a look, and maybe you ladies'll lay the table?'

Left alone, Slider and Atherton looked at each other and Atherton shrugged. 'We'll be talking about this one for a long time,' he said.

'Probably,' Slider said. He felt exhausted. There was almost more work in the aftermath of a case than when investigating it: everything had to be got together for the CPS file, every t crossed and i dotted, top brass briefed, explained to and placated. And there was the drugs angle in this one as well. He was glad he had Porson to stand between him and the abyss when the pip hit the spam about why they hadn't handed it over sooner.

'I wouldn't be surprised if there weren't other deaths we don't know about yet,' he said. 'I somehow can't believe that she started her killing career with Guthrie – it was too well carried out. And I have my suspicions of Barrow. We ought to start looking back through unsolved cases and sudden deaths where the same elements were involved.'

'You're a devil for work,' Atherton said, stretching himself languidly. 'Anyone would think you were on commission.'

'We should go and see if Dad needs help,' Slider said, standing up.

'He won't,' said Atherton. He had had to learn to leave people alone when they were cooking in their own house. Cooking had always been his release from the tensions of the Job, and he had never been able to stand by idly and watch someone else do it. But now he had Emily.

Oh, wait, to be truthful his release had been cooking and sex. But, again, now he had Emily.

'One thing that does intrigue me,' he said, following Slider out. 'When Corley finally got to meet Mary Lynn, which was pumping the other harder, her or him?'

'We'll never know,' said Slider.

'Wish I'd been a fly on the wall, though,' said Atherton.

Securing a large haul of cocaine and getting a definite line on the Marylebone Group put the SOs and the big brass in such good humour they were able to overlook the fact that they ought to have been brought in on it sooner. In fact, in breaking up the drugs ring in a purple cloud of publicity and self-congratulation, they managed to forget that Slider and his firm had been involved in it in any way, which suited Slider down to the ground. The CPS had decided they were going to proceed against Mary Lynette

Scott for the murders of Benedict Jackson Corley and David Edward Regal, and at some point in the proceedings, the press were bound to pick up the connection and toss it all over the papers; but sufficient unto the day, Slider thought.

So when the last file went off, all there was left was to have the firm's usual post-case drinkie-do at the Boscombe Arms. They made it a double celebration, with the news that Gascoyne had been accepted into the CID and would be joining Slider's firm. Gascoyne shuffled and blushed as they congratulated him, and then, just as Connolly was thinking *God love him altogether, the wee dote*, he proved his mettle by telling the story about the desert unit and the camel in such delicately obscene language that it was clear he had found his spiritual home.

It was a memorable celebration, and not just because of the magnitude of the case. McLaren turned up alone, although at the last couple of firm's drinks he had insisted on bringing his new woman, Jackie. No one asked him about her, because they didn't want to encourage him another time. Nobody had really liked her, and they didn't like the way she had dispirited McLaren – though Swilley, for one, said Jackie would always have her gratitude for getting rid of Maurice's nostril hair. 'You'd sometimes think he was keeping a couple of hamsters up there.'

Slider thought McLaren was looking somehow different when he arrived through the door, but he couldn't put his finger on it. Then the food was brought out, and McLaren dived straight for the pork pies. They weren't the little cocktail ones, they were the intermediate size about two inches across, and knives and plates had been provided, but McLaren cut straight to the chase and put one into his mouth whole.

Slider waited until he had finished chewing so as not to risk choking him, and then said, 'I thought Jackie didn't approve of your eating pastry.'

McLaren swallowed noisily and licked the glorious, greasy crumbs off his lips. 'We broke up,' he said.

There was a stunned silence.

'Why?' Slider asked at last, on behalf of all of them.

'Ah – I got fed up. All that dieting and grooming. I'm not a bleeding racehorse.' He looked around the staring faces, and then added, compelled by honesty, 'Anyway, she's met this new bloke. It was her broke up with me, really.' He sniffed. 'I dunno what she sees in him,' he added. 'He's a right scruff-bag.'

There was a tactful silence, until Atherton intoned, in quotation marks, 'My work here is done.'

McLaren's eyes were on the snack plate. 'Anyone want that scotch egg?'

'Work away,' Connolly said kindly. 'Your need is greater than ours.'

Just as Slider got home, George woke, crying, and Joanna, in the middle of kissing him, broke off to say, 'I think he's teething.'

'I'll go,' Slider offered, but she had already turned away.

'No, I'll do it. You make us both a drink. I want to talk to you.'

'Oh-oh,' he said. 'That sounds ominous.'

'God, why do men always say that?' she said with mock exasperation, and ran lightly up the stairs.

She was gone rather a long time, and he carried his drink through to the small sitting room they used as a study, where the computer was set up. He had been thinking about it, for some reason, all day – perhaps just because they had been putting the case to bed. When Joanna came down and came searching for him, she found him looking at a pop video on YouTube, of all things.

'What's that?' she asked, leaning on his shoulder and kissing his ear. 'He's gone off to sleep again.'

'Good. It's Kara, otherwise Annie Casari, Ben Corley's girlfriend. I wanted to see her for myself.'

They watched for a moment in silence. The girl seemed very thin, with stick-like white arms. She clutched the big black mike to her face and bucked her hips and made the other current stampy moves. She was wearing a short sequinny flared skirt of many colours, and various tops in messy-looking layers, and her thin white legs ended in what looked like hiking socks and big laced boots. Her hair was a rat's nest, but that seemed to be deliberate, and her face was made up witchy white with black smudgy eyes. She had a pleasant sort of voice, small and husky but true, and she sang about lost love: 'I waited till the break of day. I knew that you had gone away.

I don't know why, what made you go.'

She seemed rather frail and vulnerable but not otherwise remarkable. He had heard other voices as good, and many more better. She didn't, in his admittedly uninformed opinion, have anything much about her that would have propelled her to the stars. But Corley had loved her enough to go on a crusade to avenge her, and gone to his death in the process. This skinny girl, who couldn't keep off drugs, had set all this in motion; it had led to the death not only of Corley but of Tommy Flynn and David Regal too, whom she had probably never even heard of.

He thought of Corley's mother and sister, of Danny Ballantine, of the portrait in the hall of the family flat, of the young man full of promise. Was it worth it? Corley wouldn't have thought in those terms. Maybe he couldn't have done any differently. Sometimes Slider thought that people's lives were laid down for them, and they could only follow the trail, with the end implicit in the beginning. But it was a weary thought, born of his tiredness.

'Enough?' Joanna enquired.

'Enough,' he said, and clicked it off.

'She seems quite an ordinary girl,' Joanna said; and he let that be her epitaph.

They went back to the sitting room. Autumn was coming and it was almost chilly enough to want the heating on, with damp August darkness outside. *Fin de siècle*. He put on an extra lamp for comfort and sat down on the sofa. 'What did you want to talk about?'

She walked up and down a bit, like a cat not

sure where to settle, and then sat in the armchair catty-corner to him, perched rather forward, nursing her glass in both hands on her lap. She hadn't drunk much of it, he noticed.

'I've been a bit grouchy lately,' she said abrupt-ly.

'Have you? I didn't notice,' he said gallantly.

She gave a wry smile. 'You did. And I'm sorry. But I had something on my mind.'

'The LSO job,' he said. 'I know. And you decided not to go for it in the end.' She hadn't discussed it with him, but he knew she hadn't been to the audition, so she must have made up her mind.

'Are you glad?' she asked.

'No,' he said. 'I mean, neither glad nor sorry. It was your decision to make. I could see points on both sides, but as long as you feel you've made the right decision...'

'I hope I have. I'm sure I have, really,' she said. 'But it wasn't exactly – it wasn't straight-forward.'

'No, I know. Your career versus home. It would have been a lot more work. You'd have been away a lot.'

'In the end, I felt I'd have to give up too much if I took it. There's one bit of it you don't know, you see.' She was looking at him intensely, and he tried to brace himself. 'I'm pregnant again,' she said.

He had not expected that, and it left him with-out words.

'How?' he said eventually, as men do.

'Oh Bill! These things happen.' She was still

watching him for his reaction, but he couldn't think yet what it was. She said, 'I couldn't have taken the job and had another baby. And I know we're not exactly flush with cash. Thanks to your dad we don't have a mortgage, but everything's so expensive, and the house needs a lot doing to it, and George doesn't come cheap. We could have done with the extra money if I'd taken the job. But to do that I'd have had to – to get rid of the baby.' He was shocked, and he knew it showed. She gave a wry sort of smile. 'And when it came to it, I found I couldn't do it.'

He came up out of his seat and crossed to her, and had to kneel down to be on the same level. 'I should think not!' he cried. 'How could you even consider it?'

'I had to consider everything. And you said all along it was my decision.'

'Yes, but I didn't know all the facts.'

'We can't afford another baby, that's a fact. It's hard enough with two wages. What happens when I have to stop work?'

He surveyed her face carefully. 'Don't you want it?'

Tears came into her eyes. 'Of course I want it, you idiot,' she said, trying not to cry. 'And pay no attention to the waterworks. It's just hormones.'

'If you want it, that's all there is to say. We'll manage. We *will*,' he added to her uncertain look.

'Do *you* want it?' she asked.

'Oh, God, Jo, of course I do. I love you. I love George. I'd have ten children if I could, if you

383

were willing.'

She gave a watery smile. 'Not ten, I'm not up to that. But two's a nice number, don't you think?' she said hopefully.

He took her glass and put it aside, and folded her hands in his. 'Two, three, or any number, our children, yours and mine, they're precious, and they're wanted.'

'You're a nice man, Bill Slider,' she said, and kissed him.

'You should have told me,' he said. 'You should have let me help you decide.'

'You had enough on your plate,' she said. 'And I knew what you'd say, anyway.'

'Which is?'

'Exactly what you did say.'

'It's pitiful to be so easily read,' he complained. 'I always wanted to be a man of mystery.'

'No you didn't,' she said with some certainty. 'So it's all right then? Really? About the baby?'

'Better than all right,' he said. 'It's – magnificent.'

'Nappies and broken nights and no money and all?'

He stuck out his chest boastfully. 'Bring it on,' he said. 'I can take it. Bring it all on. And any dragons you want slaying. That's what men are for.' He flung out a hand in a magnificent gesture, and knocked her glass flying. 'I don't know my own strength,' he apologized.

She was laughing. 'How do you think I got pregnant in the first place?'